THE
FORMULA
FOR
MURDER

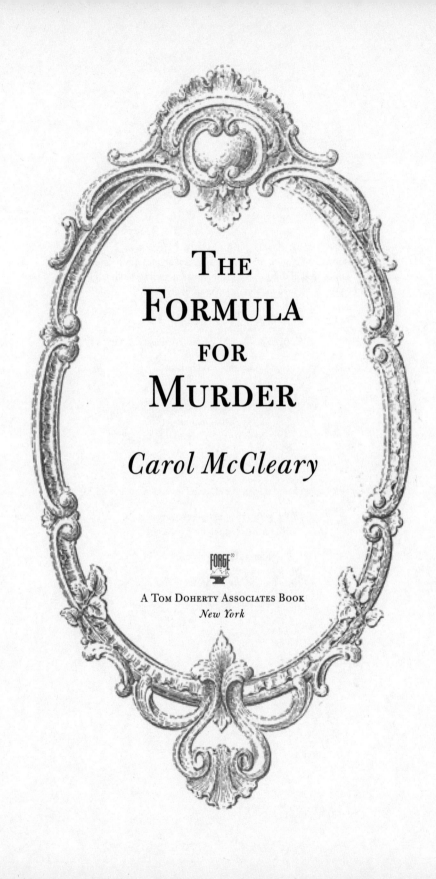

THE
FORMULA
FOR
MURDER

Carol McCleary

FORGE

A TOM DOHERTY ASSOCIATES BOOK
New York

This is a work of fiction. All of the characters, organizations, and events portrayed in this novel are either products of the author's imagination or are used fictitiously.

THE FORMULA FOR MURDER

A Forge Book
Published by Tom Doherty Associates, LLC
175 Fifth Avenue
New York, NY 10010

www.tor-forge.com

Forge® is a registered trademark of Tom Doherty Associates, LLC.

ISBN 978-0-7653-2869-4 (hardcover)
ISBN 978-1-4299-4362-8 (e-book)

First Edition: July 2012

Printed in the United States of America

0   9   8   7   6   5   4   3   2   1

GENEVIEVE J. FOXEY MCCLEARY

A strong woman who has the courage to change
and a heart of gold,
My sister . . .

ACKNOWLEDGMENTS

Sometimes we have an opportunity in life and don't see it until later down the road. I have been given a very wonderful opportunity to write about Nellie Bly, and for this I shall always be grateful to Linda Quinton, Bob Gleason, Tom Doherty, and Harvey Klinger.

I would also like to extend my thanks to Katharine Critchlow, an incredible young lady who was very helpful with *The Formula for Murder,* and Whitney Ross, who is constantly coming to everyone's rescue. *Thank you, Whitney.*

I wish I had the names of each of the people in the Production department, because each and every one of you has done an incredible job with *all* my Nellie novels and I am eternally grateful. And my copy editor, NaNá Stoelzle—thank you for doing such a great job.

Michelle Mashoke-Anderson, a young business lady here on Cape Cod, has helped me in more ways than one. *Thank you, Michelle.*

Karen Vail, an enormous *thank-you* for constantly being in my corner. What would I do without you? Again, *thank you!*

There are three newspaper reporters to whom I am very grateful for being here on Cape Cod—Melanie Lauwers, Laurie Higgins, and Kathleen Szmit. *Thank you!*

There is also the Cape Cod Writers Center that all writers here on the Cape are very lucky to have. I would personally like to thank Moira Powers, Nancy Rubin Stuart, and Kevin Summons, for all your hard work and dedication to helping authors, especially me! *Thank you!*

And I can't forget the Cape Cod Community Media Center, which is constantly promoting authors. I want to thank each and every one of you for your dedication and having me on your show. And a special thanks to Shirley Eastman—the beautiful lady who "interviewed" each Nellie book. *Thank you.* You have a fabulous gift for making a person feel relaxed in front of the camera.

And very, very important, I shall always be forever *thankful* to *all* the bookstores that have Nellie on their shelves and *all* the people who have read my Nellie books: "Thank you a million times. Nellie and I are internally grateful."

Nellie Bly

We must not allow the clock and the calendar to blind us to the fact that each moment of life is a miracle and a mystery.

—H. G. WELLS

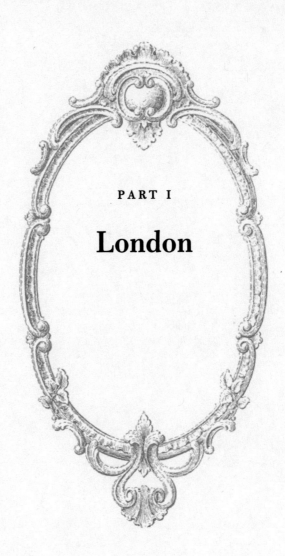

PART I

London

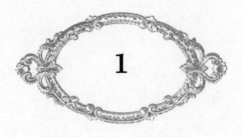

1

Journal of Nellie Bly, 1890

Before I went to England early in the year, I had heard tales of the haunted moors of Dartmoor, that bleak, windswept land where strange creatures are said to roam on moonless nights, but nothing prepared me for murder and science gone mad as men tempted the heavens by trying to create in a test tube that which only God possesses the right to do.

What I came to witness in these dark days was men of science crazed by their demented dreams of creating something no other mortal has done. It wasn't the first time murder and madness was born in scientific experiments. And like the question of the chicken and the egg, I wonder—is it the science that drives men mad? Or do the scientists taint their formulas with a bit of their own insanity?

Was Mary Shelley's Victor Frankenstein insane to have brought the dead back to life with powerful jolts of electricity—or did the monster he created drive him mad when it became murderously uncontrollable?

Victor Frankenstein warns another ambitious man of the dangers of trying to achieve what no one else has ever accomplished, calling his success a serpent that has stung him: "Do you share my madness? Have you drunk also of the intoxicating draught? Hear me; let me reveal my tale, and you will dash the cup from your lips!"

I have no doubt Victor Frankenstein would say that Mr. Stevenson's ambitious Dr. Jekyll actually was the murderous beast rather than the alter ego he created with a potion, the violent Mr. Hyde.

Be what it may, the matter that was to draw me into the dark side of science in the tors and crags of the moors began, appropriately enough, in a place of the dead.

2

London, 1890

I shiver as I leave a gloomy London day behind me and step into a dank morgue near the banks of the River Thames. This small branch of Her Majesty's Coroner's Office is on a wharf near London Bridge in that area called the Pool, the busiest part of the biggest waterfront in the world.

The breath of the dead in this examining room has a sharp edge to it, smelling like paint thinner poured over ice. Blocks of ice are scattered about the room, lowering the temperature to slow down decomposition of the bodies, with the runoff from the ice and blood slipping through slats in the wood floor.

After the first attack on my nose, another smell is apparent, hidden under the prickly acidic tang of cleaning fluid—*death,* a bouquet of decomposing flesh, blood, and body fluids.

In a curious way, the chill air accented by the scent of blood and flesh remind me of a visit I made to a meatpacking plant in Pittsburgh when I went undercover to investigate the conditions. Comparing an animal slaughterhouse with an examining room for the dead is a gruesome thought; usually I'm not this morbid, but the unstirred cold air full of strange smells has awakened the dark side of my imagination.

My name is Nellie Bly. I'm a crime reporter for *The World,* Mr. Pulitzer's newspaper in New York City. I came to London and this chamber of death not for a news story but to lay to rest a dear friend.

The room had been washed down recently, probably moments before I stepped in because the slated wood floor is still wet. The narrow openings on the floor permit whatever comes out of the bodies to flow into the river and back to the sea. The thought of human essence returning to the ocean is a comforting one since some say that life began in the sea, but as

I stand for a moment to let my eyes adjust to the gloom of the windowless room, the smell of the Thames—poisoned by the noxious wastes of man and machines—rises to become a dominant stench in the room.

"The river stinks worse than the dead," Inspector Abberline says. "Sorry. That was badly thought out, wasn't it."

The Scotland Yard inspector, who I met the previous year when I was in London following a lead on a murder case,* gives me a look of concern as he hands me a vinegar-scented nosegay meant to stun my sense of smell.

I put it in my lace hankie but don't put it up to my nose. I am here for a dear friend and I don't want my senses muted.

Butcher-block slabs are set out in two rows, a dozen on each side, like beds in a hospital ward. Wood is a cheap but an unfortunate choice for morgue tables because it stains. White sheets, many stained with blood and other body fluids, are tossed haphazardly over bodies not being worked on.

Inspector Abberline had entered before me to "prepare" the room for my visit—covering the naked dead lest they offend my fragile feminine constitution. I could have told him that I had already seen things in my life that no woman—or man—should have seen.

From the appearance of the bodies that are not covered, most of them had been pulled from the river already in an advanced state of decomposition. Like New York City's waterways, the Thames is not a gentle environment for human flesh. One wonders how the poor fish survive.

I'm grateful that most of the bodies are sheeted, hiding the cruelties of man, machine, or that done by their own hand. I have been in morgues where bodies are left uncovered, lined up like dead fish ready to be gutted.

A woman dressed in widows' black from bonnet to shoes is sitting next to a male body on the first slab in the room. Her head drifts down and then jerks back up as she fights dozing off. A bell tied to the man's wrist tells me that she's his wife or other close relative there for "the waiting." The procedure occurs when the morgue attendants are not entirely certain that the man is dead. Rather than risk burying him alive, the bell is placed on his wrist for twenty-four hours. If it rings, he will be transferred to a hospital rather than the cemetery.

* The London matter was part of the investigation related in *The Alchemy of Murder*. —The Editors

My heart goes out to the woman. She is a lonely figure, full of hope that has little promise.

Two tables down from her an attendant wearing a white cloth apron is scrubbing a male body, dipping his bloody rag into a bucket and bringing it back, bloodred water flying off the rag as it is pulled out of the pail, splashing on the floor and draining through the slats into the river.

Against the back wall are wood shelves with knives, scalpels, saws, and other medical instruments and supplies. A small cart next to it is piled high with dirty, bloody rags and clothing.

As a crime reporter I have been in morgues before, so as my eyes sweep this room I recognize that it's not a fully functional coroner's examination room, despite some of the "tools of the trade" on the shelves. Rather than doctors with saws and knives cutting into bodies or testing vials of blood for poisons in a hunt for a cause of death, I see only *Dieners,* morgue assistants, whose duties are to handle and clean the bodies.

Inspector Abberline catches my look at the *Dieners* and reads my thought. "If there's a serious issue about the cause of death, the body is taken to the central morgue for examination. Most of the poor souls in here gave up the ghost voluntarily or were hastened to their maker by a blunt instrument in a dark alley, so there's no reason for further investigation."

Kind man that he is, he avoids using the word suicide. But that is why I am in this chilly purgatory that is a temporary repose for bodies fished out of the river before finding a permanent place six feet under.

Something about the *Dieners* with their white cloth aprons stained with blood is familiar to me, but my thoughts are too crowded with keeping my feelings under control to put it together. The cloth aprons are something of a puzzle because the morgue attendants I've seen in the past had worn rubber ones.

"The remains of Hailey McGuire are at the end of the line," Inspector Abberline says.

The remains of Hailey McGuire.

A few weeks ago I knew a lovely young woman with that name, full of life and spirit. The spirit has escaped for what I hope is a better place and now her name is simply the inscription on a morgue toe tag attached to a "body" that constitutes the "remains" she left behind.

I can see at a glance that almost all of the bodies in the room are male, which is to be expected for a morgue on the docks. I imagine mostly sailors, fishermen, and dockworkers, along with an occasional prostitute, are brought here. Hailey was none of these, but people driven to end their lives not infrequently find their way to water.

Hailey. Suicide. How sad that is. How hard it is to believe.

The inspector gives me another concerned look and gently takes my arm. "We're almost there."

I give him an "I'm okay" smile as we make our way down the path of the dead.

A gruesome thought that comes to mind is unavoidable: One day the gray corpse of Nellie Bly, linked to the name by only a toe tag, will be an empty carcass in a place like this. I just hope my spirit will have moved on to what I sincerely pray is a better place and not hot as *hell*—if you know what I mean.

The inspector hadn't wanted me to view the body, not even after it is transferred to a funeral home. "These cases where the body has been in water are best laid to rest with a closed casket viewing," he'd said. But I feel that I would be cowardly if I avoided seeing my friend and holding her hand as I say good-bye. She has no one else.

We pass a man, who I take from his mackintosh and high rubber boots to be a fisherman, as he bends over a male body, perhaps that of a shipmate whose last port of call was Davy Jones's locker. The fisherman is putting coins on the eyelids of his mate.

"Paying toll to the ferryman," Inspector Abberline says.

I know the superstition. "A payment to Charon, the boatman who ferries the souls of the dead across the River Styx in the Underworld, is how my mother explained it to me when my father died. I was six and an old friend of his bent over the coffin before it was lowered into the ground to place coins on my father's eyes."

"I'm sorry."

I can only nod my head in thanks for I still miss my father dearly and the memory of his interment hits me hard as I see the fisherman placing the coins. It had been a rainy gray day with a deep-bone chill in the air, not unlike the funeral atmosphere I find today in London. Seeing the cold, stiff pallor on my father's face scarred me, making it difficult for me to deal with death.

The coarse, brutal man my poor mother married in desperation to keep us children fed after my father's untimely death had made the scar a permanent open wound when he forced me to watch a cow being slaughtered when I was a young teenager. "I'm making you tough," is what he said. But I knew he was being cruel and mean because he found pleasure in playing the bully.

I try to put aside those bitter memories as we come to a covered body on the last slab in the line.

A *Diener* wearing a fouled white apron stands by on the other side of the table waiting for us. He's overweight, with large jowls that quiver as he purses his lips. He slaps a fly off his cheek and looks to the inspector for permission to remove the sheet.

My knees start shaking and my heart jumps into my throat.

3

Just a few weeks ago I was in Manhattan covering a story about the sex trafficking of young girls from the Orient when Mr. Cockerill, the managing editor of Mr. Pulitzer's newspaper, called me into his office.

"You need to sit down," was the first thing he told me. This proclamation, coming in the tone that something was desperately wrong, alarmed me. My first thought was that something had happened to my mother, who lives with me.

"Hailey McGuire committed suicide."

He had been right. I needed to be sitting when I heard the news.

Hailey was not just a dear friend, but a young woman who, like me, had struggled hard to get a job in the male dominated world of newspaper reporting. A product of an orphanage, without even a high school diploma, Hailey had been destined for work as a household servant or worse, the terrible life of a prostitute. Having fought tooth and nail to break into reporting, and having left high school myself before completion because of a heart problem,* I empathized with Hailey's struggles.

Actually, I was the person who first directed her toward working as a reporter after watching her testify at a court trial I was covering two years ago.

The criminal case was against a man who owned a service that referred household servants. He was accused of raping a young girl who had applied for servant work. Hailey had also applied through the agency

---

*Nellie hid her lack of education with a vague reference to a "heart problem." She actually left high school after the first year because the lawyer her father had entrusted with the money for her education stole it.—The Editors

and testified in court that the man had indecently touched her and she had fought back to avoid being raped.

As I watched her on the witness stand, reading from a narration giving the precise time, date, and details of the incident, I realized her description of what had happened sounded like the newspaper articles I write—even down to the "rocky grammar" my first editor said I had.

I spoke to her after court and began giving her small assignments to help me gather information and was delighted when she came back with not just what I had asked her for, but information that showed she had a nose for the news.

Expending no less energy and determination than Hercules had done in performing his twelve labors, I managed to get Mr. Pulitzer to take Hailey on as a cub reporter running errands in the newsroom and finally getting her own beat at the criminal courts building.

Both Cockerill and Pulitzer, with their instinctively negative view of women in the workplace, had been hesitant first about hiring and then promoting Hailey, finding her too "soft-hearted" for crime reporting. I disagreed and didn't want to see her pigeonholed into reporting about weddings and funerals, the only jobs open for women in news reporting—and even then, few were filled by women.

"She gets too emotionally involved with people she's reporting about," Cockerill complained.

"That's what makes her a good reporter," I said, knowing it was only partly true. Injustices needed to be reported with an impassioned appeal for the victims, but a reporter has to remain a neutral observer while gathering the story. I admit that I don't have a talent for keeping my feelings to myself at any stage of the process, but I didn't see her getting worked up emotionally when dealing with wrongs.

"She knows how victims of crimes hurt because of her own background," I reminded Cockerill.

Hailey had not been born an orphan. She became parentless at the age of five when her stepfather bludgeoned her mother to death in front of her, hitting her mother over and over with a short club until the woman's face was a bloody pulp and Hailey had passed out on the floor after begging and screaming for him to stop.

I rejected Cockerill's accusation that my experience with my own stepfather, against whom I had testified in court about the cruel treatment he gave to my mother and us children, was affecting my judgment.

"She can do the job," I said.

I was right—and I was sadly mistaken.

Yes, like me she had a nose for the news and was instinctively drawn to battle injustice, but I was able to remain impartial while doing a story, never stepping over the boundaries and getting emotionally involved, even though I might cry into my pillow at night for what I saw and reported during the day.

Unfortunately, Hailey stepped over the line when interviewing a woman on trial for stabbing her abusive husband as he was beating her. The police commissioner approached Mr. Pulitzer with suspicion that after Hailey had interviewed the woman a number of times in jail, he believed she aided the woman by retrieving the murder weapon, a kitchen knife, from where the woman had hidden it. "She dropped it in the East River during a ferry ride," the commissioner said—but couldn't prove it.

Hailey denied the allegation, but Mr. Pulitzer wasn't 100 percent convinced of her innocence because the battered woman's situation was too close for comfort to Hailey's own trauma. I wasn't convinced, either.

If Hailey had crossed the line, she would end up in prison for her näiveté. I didn't believe she would lie to me if I asked her right out, so I didn't ask and refused to discuss the situation with her when she appeared ready to take me into her confidence.

To avoid very bad publicity if one of his reporters ended up in jail for aiding and abetting a murder, Mr. Pulitzer, whose heart beats with exactly the same rhythm as the circulations of his newspapers, decided to take no chances. He buried the problem by sending Hailey off to London to temporarily fill the shoes of the paper's London correspondent when the man returned to New York with a medical problem.

The correspondent's job was mostly to cable home stories reported by British papers rather than hoofing it to Old Bailey and Parliament to find news, so there was little opportunity for her to get personally involved in a story. There was also little chance that Hailey would find her job waiting for her when she returned to New York after the heat over the murder case had cooled.

After telling me that Hailey had killed herself, Cockerill had gotten to his feet and began pacing. He does not have an easy job. Mr. Pulitzer is a ruthless taskmaster, even going to the extreme of employing two men to do the same job to see which one would pass Mr. Darwin's test of survival of the fittest.

"He wants you to get over to London and make sure that your friend didn't leave any dirty laundry behind."

Still stunned by Hailey's death, I just stared at him. "He" of course was Mr. Pulitzer. And by calling Hailey "my friend" meant that any dirty laundry I couldn't clean up would be dumped at my door.

"I warned him not to send her to London," he continued. "Who knows what happened over there to cause her to kill herself? She wasn't quite balanced; the job was too big for her to handle, being raw in the business and all. This is your fault, you know, she was your protégé."

All but his last words had to fight their way through the haze I'd fallen into when he told me Hailey was dead. *Your fault* were hot, burning words that made me want to cry.

Adding to the emotional trauma of Hailey's death was the fact that I am still agitated by what I consider to be Mr. Pulitzer's cavalier treatment of me after I sent the paper's circulation figures soaring a few months ago as I raced around the world to beat the record of Jules Verne's character in *Around the World in Eighty Days.** I would have quit on the spot had my concern not been to protect Hailey's memory. She was a wonderful person and I was not about to let another reporter trash her name or mine as her advocate.

I left his office fighting back tears, walking through the newsroom that suddenly became quiet as I entered. Reporters looked up and then back down to avoid making eye contact, while a couple of them so jealous of my success in their "old boys' club" of reporting that they openly smirked at me. But I didn't give them any satisfaction of witnessing a female breakdown. Instead, I walked past each and every one of them with my head held high and my features showing nothing but determination until I made it to the ladies' powder room. Then I burst into tears.

I cried for Hailey, but I was racked with guilt. Did I drive the poor young woman to kill herself because I kept pushing her to jump hurdles that she was incapable of leaping?

I sat on a toilet, twisting my handkerchief around my right index finger until it was red and throbbing from pain. Mr. Cockerill didn't have to *order* me to go to London. If anything, it was vital I went. I had to make

---

* Nellie's adventure of going around the world in seventy-two days is recorded in *The Illusion of Murder.*—The Editors

sure Hailey was properly laid to rest and not thrown in a pauper's grave, sandwiched between strangers.

I also prayed to God that I would prove that they were wrong about Hailey's too gentle disposition, and that my insistence on pushing her into the line of fire as a reporter hadn't so shattered her fragile disposition that she came to believe killing herself was less painful than facing life.

"Nellie." Inspector Abberline's voice brought me back to *this* horrible reality.

I gasp as the sheet comes off and I stare into the terrible face of death.

What chance, good lady, hath bereft you thus?

—JOHN MILTON, *Comus*

4

It isn't Hailey, at least not the vibrant, happy, intelligent young woman I knew. Instead, it is *a body. Remains. Corpse. Deceased. The departed.* It is bloated, corpulent, with the bloodless pale complexion of a fish's belly.

"*Jesus—Joseph—and Mary,*" I uncontrollably exclaim. "I'm sorry," I tell Inspector Abberline, and the morgue assistant who has thrown the sheet back over the body. "It—it caught me by surprise."

The inspector takes my arm. "Come, dear, we'll talk outside."

I shake my head and pull away from the compassionate man's grip. "No, it's my duty to her to see this through." I cleared my throat. "How do we know that—she—is Hailey? For certain."

Inspector Abberline pulls a charm bracelet out of his pocket and hands it to me. "Recognize this?"

"Yes."

The bracelet has two dangling objects—a tag with her name scratched on it and a Statue of Liberty trinket.

"I found it curious a young woman of her status as a reporter would wear something this, uh, inexpensive," he says.

"Cheap is a better word for it. They're sold by street vendors at the dock where the boat to the Statue of Liberty boards. It's tourist junk, but it had great meaning to her. You see, Hailey was an orphan. When she was eleven, she was sent to work as a household servant. She worked long hours and no matter how it was figured, what they charged her for board and room always exceeded the pittance they paid her."

"Sounds like she was indentured."

"Exactly, like a slave. It happens all the time because orphanages are overcrowded. She finally broke loose and moved into a settlement house for impoverished young women, picking up work wherever she could. To her that trip to Liberty Island, which she paid for with her earnings, was confirmation of her success. She took the trip after she got her first reporting job." I choke up and can't admit that I had gotten her the job.

Inspector Abberline pretends to busy himself, looking at the bracelet to give me a chance to compose myself.

"There was a ring, too." I point at the other side of the shrouded form. "On the other hand, please let me have it."

My request is to the assistant. The ring with a fake emerald made of glass is on her right hand. It is the only other piece of jewelry I knew her to wear. I had bought it for her last birthday. "I want the ring to remember her by. It's not valuable." That is said to assure the morgue worker that I won't be taking something of value he could have poached off the body himself.

He gives the inspector a look and Abberline nods. The assistant pulls back the sheet just enough to expose the hand it's on. The fingers are bloated.

"No!" I gasp as he takes his knife to cut off the finger. "No, leave it on."

"Before we leave, snip the ring off with a cutter," Inspector Abbeline tells the *Diener*. "You can have the band repaired by a jeweler," he says to me.

"No, let it stay with her." I feel queasy and weak-kneed, but regain my equilibrium. I meet the *Diener*'s eye. "I will check to make sure it's there when she is laid to rest."

"Are you certain that it's her ring?" Inspector Abberline asks.

"Yes, I bought it for her. Why?"

"Just an added point of confirmation that confirms identity. We have the bracelet, ring, and a suicide note. The name on the bracelet led us to her rooming house where we found the note. She'd left out several days' of food for her cat and asked in the note that her landlady find a good home for the cat."

"What else did the note say?"

"It's in the file at my desk so this isn't verbatim, but she said . . . 'I am so sorry, life is no longer worth living. He's left me and I have nothing to live for. I feel so lost, alone. There is no way I can go back to America. The thought of prison . . . no, I can't go back. I have no place to go and no one to live for. Whoever finds this note please make sure my cat is given a loving home.' She also left money for cat food on her dresser by the note."

Killing herself in despair over a man. I don't know how to fit it in with my memory of Hailey. She was emotional, but I have a hard time coming to grips with her taking her own life for a romance gone sour.

"She has a birthmark." I almost forgot about it.

"Where?"

"Behind her right ear, a red mark about the size of a shilling between her ear and hairline. She always pulled her hair forward to cover the ear."

I turn away as the sheet is removed and turn back around after I hear the *Diener* say, "Don't see a mark."

"Can you show me where you remember it?"

Forcing myself, I bend down closer and look. "It's not there!"

Inspector Abberline strikes a match and uses it to take a look. "You're certain it was there?"

"Absolutely. She used to joke and call it the Mark of Cain."

"Could've been washed away by her time in the water," the morgue assistant says.

"Quite so," Inspector Abberline agrees.

"I—I've never heard of that." My thoughts are jumbled by the lack of a mark. "Birthmarks are imperfections in the skin, not a stain that can be washed away."

"Quite true, but her body has been bleached as well as it might be had it been laying in a washtub. The river's so sour it could peel the hide off a rhino."

"I don't know . . . I just don't understand it." I stare down at the bloated face, trying to find Hailey in it. "Wait." I bend down to get a closer look at her head. "What is this?"

"A wound," the *Diener* says.

"How did she get it on her head?" I look to Inspector Abberline.

"She most likely hit a rock when she threw herself into the river."

"Or," the *Diener* adds, "it could've been caused by the impact of hitting the water if she jumped from a bridge, or a passing boat could have knocked her."

The inspector nods to the *Diener* to cover the body and takes me firmly by the arm, back down the path of the dead.

"I don't understand it," I repeat. "I don't see Hailey killing herself over some man who—"

"She was pregnant."

"What?" I stop and stare at him.

"Nellie, dear, I didn't want to tell you and color your memory of the sweet girl. She didn't tell you anything about it?"

"Only that she had met a man she had fallen in love with." On my voyage to England, I had kept reading over and over the last letter I received from Hailey. She was all excited about a new beau and how much they were in love, but she had not given a clue as to who he is.

"Do you know who the father was?" I ask.

He shrugs. "Don't know and won't ever know. Most likely a married man. Not an uncommon situation." He gives me a look. "Or an uncommon choice for the woman to make."

He is right, frightfully so that it shakes me to my roots. There is nowhere for a pregnant young woman without some means of support to go except the foul conditions of a poorhouse.

I knew Hailey. She would never return to that life. She would rather die than end up back in a house for paupers or, worse, watch her baby starve.

"Requiescat"

Tread lightly, she is near
Under the snow,
Speak gently, she can hear
The daisies grow.

All her bright golden hair
Tarnished with rust,
She that was young and fair
Fallen to dust.

—From Oscar Wilde's poem written in
memory of his sister, Isola, who was
nine years old when she died

5

A cool breeze off the waters of the broad River Thames is welcome as I come up the steps from the mortuary and into fresh air. When I arrived earlier, the air had that fouled saltwater smell of waterlogged docks, fishing boats, and coal-burning steam ships even though the great Port of London is many miles from the North Sea. After experiencing a dank taste of a place of the dead, the salty air is a perfume to me.

The hansom cab I had arrived in is waiting for me, the driver chatting and smoking with the driver of a freight wagon who is adjusting his horse bindings. I shake my head, letting my cabbie know I'm not ready to leave. I want to thank Inspector Abberline for taking the time to accompany me to the remains of Hailey. He stayed behind to fill out a form releasing the body to a mortuary he assured me would treat Hailey with respect. I will contact them to make the arrangements.

The thick gray clouds give the impression of a massive dark blanket hanging over my head like a shroud—a perfect atmosphere to fit my mood.

A sudden wind comes off the water, gathering packing materials lying outside a warehouse, sending the rubbish swirling around just like the thoughts in my head: guilt, frustration, helplessness, anger, sadness.

My thoughts are a jumble and I need to clear them.

Suicide . . .

I truly hate this feeling of frustration and guilt. How do people cope with suicide?

My mind still rebels at the thought that Hailey was so desperate, so alone, that she took her own life. I experienced a sense of guilt from the moment I had heard the news, but now I am also angry at myself for pushing her when she wasn't ready to be a reporter. Infuriated, too, at the lover who stole her innocence and then cast her out.

If he had only cast her out—and hadn't murdered her to keep her quiet. I know where the thought comes from. It's that old familiar voice in my head that is always far too suspicious of the dark hearts of others. I must accept the fact my friend killed herself, but paranoia is almost on the list of my faults, though I've found most of the paranoia I've experienced as simply being heightened awareness.

The fact she was pregnant and suffered a blow to the head raised the short hairs on my paranoia. Bedeviling me also is the primal instinct in my gut telling me that suicide just doesn't fit Hailey's excited, energetic, love-of-life personality.

Still, I have to listen to the other voice in my head, the one that I sometimes try to ignore but which is calmer and more analytical than the one in my gut, and it is saying that Hailey was gullible and impressionable, and impulsive—a young woman who would often leap first and think afterward.

That she would get emotionally involved and make love out of wedlock with the threat of pregnancy is in line with how I see her. *Even with a married man?* I ask myself. As impulsive and emotional as Hailey can be, yes, even with a married man.

Shame on any man who impregnates a woman and leaves her disgraced and a burden on our society—if they don't end up in a river or a house of prostitution.

The more I think about it, the more tempted I am to track down the married scoundrel who destroyed her life and write an exposé on the abuse of impressionable young women by older, married men.

With my anger rising, I mosey away from the morgue, trying to separate my thoughts from what I saw in there and what I would do to the man who caused her death. I should return to New York rather than wreak vengeance on Hailey's seducer. There is much to occupy one's attention on the docks. Boxes of cargo are coming out of the holes of ships in great netted bundles and set down on the dock where swarms of dockworkers pack them away onto wagons and into warehouses.

Down the wharf is a forest of tall masts and smokestacks black from the coal burned in their steam engines. I see bales of tobacco from Virginia coming off a Yankee clipper ship, beef from Argentina being unloaded from a freighter whose name should be *Bucket of Rust,* blocks of ice from a Norwegian ship moving down a long slide, disappearing into an icehouse.

The slide is several stories high, leading out to a wharf where the ice blocks are coming out the hole of the ship. As the cargo net with a single large block sits down on the slide, a man on each side uses hooks on long poles to pull the block free of the thick rope netting and send it skidding down the ramp.

Convenient—an icehouse next to the mortuary.

On my way back I realize that on the other side of the mortuary is a meatpacking plant where, according to the sign in front, Argentine beef is processed. I find it distasteful that the mortuary is so close to a slaughter-house.

Putting a morgue between a meatpacking house and an icehouse on a busy dock offends my sense of order in the world and respect for the dead. The Chinese would say the morgue's position is not an auspicious setting for a place of the dead, that it's not feng shui correct because it isn't in harmony with the hustle and bustle of its surroundings.

The workers on the docks also strike me as a rather depressing lot, not unlike how they are on the docks in New York. There is a horrible exploitation of cheap labor for handling cargo, with immigrants from Ireland and other countries brought in to keep a constant force of backbreaking labor. To add insult to injury, they are housed in terrible conditions and work for long hours for starvation wages.

Seeing how truly ragged some of the dockworkers are, and having passed, en route to the docks, poor neighborhoods with shoeless children looking dirty and malnourished, adds to my sense of how unjust the world is in distributing wealth.

Some of the workers wear the tattered uniforms of workhouses, those poorhouses where paupers are taken in and sent out to work for their board and stay in dormitories where husbands, wives, and even their children are housed in separate buildings. The atmosphere is grim and intimidating, with workhouse "inmates" treated not unlike prisoners—men and women on admission are stripped, searched, washed, and have their hair cut. Work is tedious and laborious, living conditions disgusting, reminding me of the small boy in Charles Dickens's novel *Oliver Twist* who lived in a workhouse—poor, miserable, and always hungry.

Thinking about the haves and have nots and my own miserable years as a factory girl, but fortunate as a woman to even have gotten a job where

I was paid far less than the men doing the same tasks, I am lost in a brown study when I hear a shrill cry and look up to a raven on a lamppost.

"Wonderful," I tell him, "how appropriate. Did you come by to taunt me with 'nevermore'?"

"It appears he did," Inspector Abberline says behind me. A Victoria carriage bearing a door insignia of the Metropolitan Police Service, commonly called "Scotland Yard," has arrived. As the inspector approaches me, he looks up from reading a missive apparently delivered by the police-uniformed driver.

"'And my soul from out that shadow that lies floating on the floor shall be lifted nevermore,'" he continues. "My favorite poem." He waves one of the messages he's holding. "My commissioner needs to communicate with the New York City Police Department regarding Miss McGuire's passing. We received a query concerning whether she had mentioned anything about her actions in the New York matter in her suicide note. She hadn't."

"Has her, uh, letter been examined by a handwriting expert?" I couldn't bring myself to say "suicide note."

"I examined it. I've had a bit of experience looking over such things. By comparing it to her handwriting, it's quite easy to see that it was done by her own hand. She wrote with something of an excited flourish that would not be easy to duplicate. Had the note been very short, say just a sentence, I would have had an expert examine it. But it would be very difficult and time consuming for even a clever forger to get close to a person's handwriting style when dealing with that much writing."

I know he's right; he's a good policeman who wouldn't be fooled by a forgery. But before I return to New York, I'll sweet talk him into letting me see the note anyway. Still, I need to ask him about fingerprinting.

"I just wish you could check for fingerprints."

"Really . . . so you know about Dr. Henry Faulds's awkward concept for identifying criminals?"

"Yes."

"I'm impressed."

I hold my chin an inch higher. I revel in it when I surprise people, especially men, with knowledge they don't think a woman would have.

"Then you know the method of identification was dismissed by our Metropolitan Police five years ago."

"Yes and I think it's a shame. It's quite a clever idea, taking a person's fingerprints with printing ink and using them for identification. Do you know how Dr. Faulds discovered this?"

"No, do tell."

"While accompanying a friend to an archaeological dig he noticed in some ancient clay fragments that the delicate impressions left by workers could be detected with the human eye. He decided to examine his own fingertips and then compared them to those of his friends. Each pattern of ridges was uniquely different."

"Interesting," Abberline says, "however, when he presented his theory to the commissioner, his evidence didn't show that prints are always unique to a person or that they can be practically classified, and that's just naming a few holes in his notion." He eyes me gravely. "You must accept that your friend killed herself."

"It's doesn't even look like her."

"Nellie, she was in the water for at least a week. I hate to bring this up, but you saw her face. It's awful what water does to a body and then you have the fish and . . ."

"*Stop*. Please, I understand."

"I'm sorry. That was insensitive of me."

"No, you're correct."

I look down at the ground. I wish I could erase that moment when I saw Hailey's bloated face.

He takes my arm and leads me toward the carriages. "My job as a policeman would often be simpler if we were able to identify criminals and their victims with fingerprints."

He has changed the subject deliberately and I welcome it. I ask him, "Did you know that while Dr. Faulds was living in Japan his hospital was broken into and the police arrested a staff member?"

He shakes his head. "I know very little about the man's background."

"Dr. Faulds thought the man was innocent and he compared the fingerprints left behind at the crime scene to the man they arrested and they were completely different. He was released."

"Very good."

"It puzzles me that police agencies are still dismissing his fingerprinting method."

"Because we would have to have *everyone* in the world's fingerprints to make his method useable. And that is impracticable and impossible." He pauses and gives me another look of concern. "Don't think of the situation as the loss of a friend. She is gone and that is her choice, and she is no longer suffering the mental maladies that caused her sorrow. She's at peace now."

I give Inspector Abberline a peck on the cheek. "You're right."

He turns beet red and clears his throat with a guttural rumble. "Now, Nellie dear, please let me drop you off at your hotel. We have the commissioner's own fancy carriage." He indicates the Victoria, a four-wheeled carriage with a calash top, a seat for two passengers, and a perch in front for the bobby driver.

"Thanks, but I need to drop by Hailey's old office on Fleet Street to see what needs tending to."

"I'll drop you off. And on the way you can look at Hailey's suicide note."

"I thought it was at your office."

"I knew you would want to see it, so I requested it be brought here."

I do want to see it, but I know in my heart it will throw out the possibility that Hailey's death was not by her own hand. I don't know if I'm ready for that.

"Shall we go?"

"Of course."

Before we pull away, a man comes out of the slaughterhouse next to the morgue and goes inside. He has a bloody apron on and a saw in his hand.

Now I remember what the morgue attendants and their aprons reminded me of—the Pittsburgh meatpacking house I had done a story on.

"Change of shift?" I ask the inspector.

6

My hands are shaking as I hold Hailey's suicide note. Inspector Abberline is gracious enough to turn his head and look out the window.

If anyone can recognize Hailey's handwriting it's me. I've seen enough of it. I believe that Inspector Abberline has alternative motives for getting the suicide note to me. He also wants to make sure it's Hailey's because of my reluctance. Like he said to me at the morgue, "Just an added point of confirmation that confirms her identity . . ."

I take a deep breath and look down. *"Oh no."*

"It's not Hailey's handwriting?"

"No . . . it's hers."

He nods his head and looks back out the window.

Tears roll down my cheek as I read her letter. *I am so sorry for what I am about to do, but my life is no longer worth living. He's left me and I have nothing to live for. I feel so lost, alone, I don't know what to do. There is no way I can go back to America. I can't bear the thought of prison. No, I can't and I won't go back. I have no place to go and no one to live for. There is only one thing I can do. Whoever finds this note please make sure my cat is given a loving home. Hailey McGuire.*

7

Archer stands near the corner of Fleet Street and Hood Court as he watches the entrance to the International News Building halfway down the street. He is waiting for a woman he has never seen in person before.

A cautious man, he occasionally opens up a newspaper to look at a sketch of the woman he is on the lookout for. The story about the woman in the paper is not current news, but a report months earlier on the progress American reporter Nellie Bly was making in her race around the world.

Archer stamps his feet, trying to keep the blood flowing. It is a cool, damp day with the overcast acting as a ceiling to trap the cold, wet air.

He would not have noticed the chill in the air if he had been walking instead of standing around, waiting and watching. He can feel middle age creeping up on him, with arthritic pain starting at the bottom of his often aching feet now that he went everywhere by shank's mare, no longer able to afford cabs thanks to his dear ex-wife who not only put him in this situation, but once the money stopped coming in, she upped and left. Some gratitude.

For years he lavished her with expensive clothing, even those silly fancy hats she wore like she was going to a garden party or something; a big apartment; dinners out in better restaurants than either of them had ever been in before; even going to plays like they were real gentry . . . then when he's ratted out by his fellow policemen at the Metropolitan Police Service for having his hand out too often, she leaves.

Women . . . trouble, that's what they are, nothing but trouble.

A street vendor is selling roasted chestnuts on the corner. The chestnuts are roasting on a rack over a bed of hot coals in a half-metal barrow set atop a rollaway cart.

The warm smell of the chestnuts breezes over to Archer and he steps to the vendor and holds out his hand with a piece of newspaper on it.

The peddler gives a look at Archer's worn suit that needs sponging off and a hot iron, at his soiled collar; the slightly turned rim on his bowler hat, and his scuffed shoes. He puts two chestnuts on it.

"Four," Archer says.

The man puts two more on. "Four pence."

"Police," Archer says, stepping away.

"You're not a copper anymore. I know who you are." The vendor grabs the poker he uses to stir the coals with and takes a step toward Archer.

"Back off," Archer hisses, pulling back his coat, exposing a knife in a sheath hanging from his belt, the only good thing he acquired as a dock-worker after he was ousted from being a cop. "A pity job" is what his wife called it just before she left him. And she was right. His cousin, a lead man on the docks, got it for him. Archer hated it, but handling cargo gave him eating money.

The vendor returns to his chestnuts, muttering curses. "Your kind spits in the soup to spoil it for everyone else."

Archer ignores the man as his attention is drawn to a woman getting out of a carriage in front of the building. He glances back at the newspaper sketch of Nellie Bly and then at the woman as she disappears through the entrance.

Certain it is her and that she will be in the building for a time, he mo-seys away, toward a tea shop where he will muscle a cup of tea and bis-cuits much like he did the chestnuts.

Old habits are hard to stop; besides, he enjoys exerting the privileges he had when he carried a detective's badge. It had made up for the lousy pay.

He's elated that he's been hired to do something easier and better paying than carrying cargo like a mule. Following the American woman since she got off the boat from America has gotten him enough for a good bit of beef and gin and his instincts are telling him that there is a lot more to be made.

He'll be back watching the entrance when she comes out. His work with her is just beginning. If he plays it right, he will be back on top again.

8

As the carriage pulls away, I stand on Fleet Street, the hub of London's newspaper world.

In New York, the major papers have similarly gathered along Park Row, which is nicknamed "Newspaper Row." Mr. Pulitzer and other publishers claim they put their papers there to be close to City Hall, but it also proves convenient for their reporters to spy on what the other papers are drumming up. As with thieves, there is no honor among reporters when it comes to gathering news.

Even before I enter, I know that behind the good-natured bonhomie newspeople maintain publicly toward each other, the true atmosphere of the place will be cutthroat and secretive—whoever has a door, locks it when they leave, those only with a desk lock that, too.

The International News Building houses correspondents from just about everywhere that can be reached by the world's undersea cables and overland telegraph networks. It even has its own cable office, humming with messages sent off across the Channel to Paris, Berlin, and Rome, to New York on the other side of the Atlantic, and as far away as Bombay, Hong Kong, and Tokyo.

It is truly a miracle of modern science that a reporter can send a story that will travel several thousand miles under the sea by cable and then race more thousands of miles on telegraph lines strung on poles across the continent to a newspaper in San Francisco.

Sadly my presence at this building is not to send exciting reports of wars and the rise and fall of empires, but to dispose of any confidential information on the news stories Hailey might have left behind.

The *World*'s regular correspondent will be back in a few days to keep the news moving. In the meantime, Mr. Pulitzer has arranged for a correspondent from another of his newspapers, the *St. Louis Post-Dispatch*, to also cover for *The World*.

I hesitate, hating to go in and rummage through Hailey's office. I feel like a child who's been dropped off at school and doesn't want to enter. A little rain has begun to fall, more of a mist than drops. I wish it would pour so no one would know I've been crying.

First I had to see Hailey's body and say "good-bye" to her, then I read her suicide note, and now I have to leaf through her work. Sometimes I hate life.

"Let's get this over with," I mumble to myself as I reluctantly enter the building.

The newsroom before me is a familiar one, not unlike the large bay where reporters hug desks at *The World*—there is also the same cloud of pipe and cigar smoke hovering and the sharp reek of tobacco smoke, along with spittoons that need a good cleaning. Like most males of the species, reporters—almost all of whom are men—believe they have a God-given right to foul the air and spit disgusting juices at brass spittoons, missing often.

A few cubicles along the wall offer some privacy and for the biggest newspapers, a category in which *The World* falls, a stairway to the right leads up to a balcony lined with doors to small offices. I already know that Hailey's office will be on the second floor.

Another common feature of the newsroom is a railing keeping people out and a person I call the "gatekeeper" posted next to the swinging gate to bar entry to all but the privileged.

To get my first reporting job, I had to make a mad dash past the newsroom's guardian and through *The World*'s gate rushing into the office where I confronted Mr. Pulitzer and Mr. Cockerill with my plan to prove I could be a reporter by spending ten days in the madhouse for women on Blackwell's Island.

I will never forget that day in New York.

I was penniless and desperate for work. For four months, since arriving from Pittsburgh, Pennsylvania, I went to every newspaper on Park Row and was rejected by them all. And to make matters worse, the night before seeing Mr. Pulitzer, my purse was stolen in Central Park while walking home, leaving me without a cent. That morning, I not only borrowed a coat from my landlady, but cab fare.

Determined to get an audience with Mr. Pulitzer, who had just returned to New York from abroad, filled with pride and persistence I hurried through the newsroom. I was not about to go back home defeated. Instead, I plowed through like a steadfast ship, its bow breaking water, keeping my chin high and carefully lifting my skirt off the floor at least an inch to keep the bottom from being fouled by tobacco juice that didn't reach the spittoons.

My heart had been pounding and I was thrilled to have stepped into a realm where stories of life and death, the stock market running amuck, fame and disgrace came to life as reporters yelled back and forth at their editors and a boy ran up and down the aisle grabbing copies from the reporters so they could rush them to the copy editors.

Nothing has changed.

Now, over three years later and having earned my salt with stories written down the street and around the world, I still must face the stares of several dozen men as I, a woman, dare to invade their territory.

Once again I put my chin up an extra inch, but I can't help wonder how Hailey took the animosity and joking here in London. I had already broken in the newsmen in New York to a feminine presence, so she didn't face as much prejudice as she would have had to experience here.

Their stares and jabs would probably make someone as sensitive as Hailey feel like she was walking onto the battlefield with bullets flying all around her—a reflection that hits me again with my editor's assertion that she hadn't been ready for a newspaper reporting job, especially in London, the hub of the newspaper world for all of Europe.

Having to walk past these men every day without having proven herself capable of doing the job, as I did with a sensational story, would chip away at any person's soul no matter how strong they are, and Hailey was innocent in a beautiful, soft way.

"May I help you, madam?" a young man sitting behind the desk asks.

"Yes, I'm from *The World* in New York. I'm going to our office here."

"You must be Nellie Bly."

"Yes, I am. How did you—"

"Recognize you? From a newspaper clipping Hailey—Miss McGuire had. She spoke of you often. I'm very sorry about—about what happened." The young man stammers and blushes, then gets up to hold open the gate for me. "It's a pleasure meeting you."

"Thank you."

"If I can assist you in any way, please let me know."

A thought hangs with me as I go up the stairs. Hailey was a bright and attractive young woman and pregnant. Knowing Hailey, the young man doesn't appear to be a candidate for her lover . . . but, he might have gotten close to her or even simply went out of his way to observe her. I must stop and chat some more with him on my way out because he might be a wealth of information.

With a key I brought from New York, I unlock the door and enter.

The room is a cubbyhole, big enough for a rolltop desk against the wall to my right, three wooden filing cabinets against the wall to the left, and a dirty window allowing a bit of dull gray light in between.

Beside the office door is a metal umbrella stand that has one large black umbrella in it; above it is an empty wooden coatrack with a man's hat and a rain slicker.

A chair on rollers is in front of the desk. A bookcase and stacks and stacks of faded newspapers and newspaper clippings occupy every space something else isn't taking up. Even the filing cabinets are piled high with newspapers. Cobwebs make up the rest of the furnishings. I just pray no spider rears his ugly head while I'm here. I hate spiders.

On top of the desk is a soft blue vase filled with pink roses, Hailey's way to add cheer and femininity to this cluttered, messy, male office that is laden with the heavy smell of tobacco smoke imbedded in the wood.

The roses are wilted. I wish I had new ones to replace them. I hate looking at the dead roses—they speak of Hailey's death. But, they were Hailey's and I am not prepared to trash them.

I roll up the top of the desk. Shoved into the back right corner is a pipe rack holding four pipes; next to it is a closed, round-metal tin that contains tobacco. The desk has coffee mug marks, cigarette burns, and ink stains, all the signature of the correspondent who regularly occupies the office.

The desktop is cleared of most paperwork, which surprises me because there's only a small space to lay items and Hailey wasn't better than any other newspaper person, myself included, in keeping manageable the notes, pictures, and other items we gather for stories.

Either Hailey wasn't working on any stories for sometime leading up to her death or she came to the office and cleaned up her desk before killing herself.

She was an orderly person and it isn't beyond the realm of reasonableness to conclude that she would straighten up her desk before ending her life. I've heard of people who washed their laundry before killing themselves.

Going through the desk drawers, I find her "hot news" folder—a slim red leather envelope purse. Hailey had admired the one I have that I keep my current work in. As a surprise going away gift, I gave her one.

There's very little in it, some notes about a society wedding, a minor incident at sea between a British freighter and German warship, the failure of a medium-size London bank. Not the sort of news interesting to Americans that she was expected to dig up. I recognized the articles as "fillers" that reporters on deadlines keep to fill in on those days when all the good stories are hiding from you.

She must have been so depressed she wasn't working on anything of importance in the days before her death.

As I pick up a pencil to tap the eraser against my teeth, an old habit of mine, I notice the eraser is blackened. It's been burnt.

Why would an eraser head be burnt?

I look under the desk for a wastepaper basket. *Voilà!* Someone had burned paper in the metal basket and stirred the ashes with the pencil.

Another "why?" pops into my head. Why would Hailey do this? Reporting isn't *that* competitive. What was so important to Hailey that she not only had to burn it, but destroy it completely?

Or . . . did the man who ruined Hailey's life pay a visit to the office to destroy evidence of their relationship? Or her murder?

Here I go again. Am I barking up the wrong tree or have I discovered something? My problem is I don't want to face what I have been told. I want to find another truth.

It's time to speak to the gatekeeper.

9

My instinct about the young man at the gate is that he is or was in-fatuated with Hailey. The pale, thin young man with gold-rimmed glasses strikes me as rather shy and perhaps even a little timid. Hailey had a more outgoing personality. I can't see them as a match.

Exuberant, excited by life, and even rather adventurous, Hailey was more likely to fall into a swoon over a knight in shining armor than a mild-mannered clerk. But that doesn't mean they hadn't become friends or that he didn't quietly observe Hailey and know more about her than she even suspected.

"Did you find everything satisfactory?" he asks as I come out the gate and he rises to speak to me.

"Somewhat. Mr. . . . ?"

"James Anderson. Please, call me James."

"James, do you know what trolley I can take to Hailey's boarding-house from here? With the rain, if it's much the same as in New York, there is little possibility of me catching a taxi." I didn't give him the ad-dress because I am curious as to whether he knows where she lived.

"You're so right." He chuckles and his face brightens up, "Hailey and I used to laugh about how the cabs mysteriously disappeared off the streets the minute it just starts to sprinkle."

"You shared taxis?"

"No, neither of us could afford getting to and from in a hansom. We rode the same trolley, number eighty-seven. Her boardinghouse is just a couple of blocks from mine and the trolley stopped in between. Go to your left when you leave the building; the trolley stop is three blocks up the street. I see you are already outfitted with an umbrella. A must in London."

I hold up the black umbrella that was in the basket. "I requisitioned the one from our office. James, I need to know the stories Hailey was working on, but I found very little in her office. Did she by chance mention anything to you?"

"No, she wouldn't have spoken openly, not with them being able to hear." A jerk of his head tells me that "them" are the reporters in the newsroom.

"She never mentioned anything at all?"

"No, I'm sorry."

"Do you know who she might have been dating?"

He shook his head. "No idea. I suspected she was seeing someone because she was so happy and excited."

"She spoke about the person?"

"No, not really. It wasn't anything she said, but how she acted. And there were the flowers."

"Flowers? She received flowers from a man?"

"Yes. I don't know who sent them, but I can tell you the man was wealthy."

"How do you know this?"

"The flowers were exotic. Not your normal roses or daises."

"Any chance you remember the name of the florist?"

"That won't do you any good."

"Excuse me? Why would you say that?"

Instead of responding, he instantly blushes and looks down at his shoes.

I gently touch his arm. "You were fond of Hailey, weren't you?"

"Ya—yes," he stammers.

"You wanted to make sure no one would take advantage of her, so you asked the deliveryman who had sent the flowers?"

He nods. "Yes, but he didn't know. A messenger always came with instructions and payment."

I bit my lip as I think about that. It sounds very much like the actions of a married man.

"Miss Bly, did—did Hailey ever mention me in her letters to you?"

"Yes, she did," I lie. "She was very fond of you."

"I was very fond of her, too."

"I appreciate your help, James. If you remember anything, please contact me. I will be at the Langham Hotel for the next few days."

I turn to leave and stop as he says, "I don't believe it."

"Believe what?"

"That she killed herself."

I take a sharp intake of breath, trying not to expose my feelings. "Why don't you believe it? People kill themselves every day."

"Aren't people supposed to get depressed over a period of time, slowly getting worse, and then finally ending it?"

I almost blurt out, "Not if they're pregnant!" but hold my tongue because I don't want to damage his memory of Hailey. Instead I ask, "What do you mean?"

"She wasn't depressed. She was excited . . . even secretive."

"About what?"

"Don't know. But she acted like any of these reporters act when they think they have a big scoop. They go around like they're holding their breath. They're dying to tell someone, but don't dare even give a hint."

"When did you last see Hailey?"

"Two days before the police say she killed herself."

"Two days. Were there other times when she didn't come to the office for days at a time?"

"Not that I recall."

"And she didn't appear depressed?"

"No. I'm telling you she was secretive."

"As if she was onto a big story?"

"Yes. I'd swear by it. It was like she wanted to blurt something out but couldn't." He gave me a long hard look. "What do you think, Miss Bly? Why did she do it? Why did she throw herself into the river and—"

"Everyone is different," is all I can manage before I flee out the door.

10

Never have my feet moved so fast to remove myself from a building and I keep walking fast once I hit the street—very fast. I'm not hurrying somewhere, but fleeing the suspicions of the love-stricken James.

Holy mackerel! And I thought my paranoia runs rampant.

I hadn't seen Hailey during the days leading up to her death, but James had and his impression of Hailey's mood—that clamming up by a reporter on a hot lead, but dying to share—is exactly how I act and exactly how I would expect Hailey to have conducted herself.

Face it, I tell myself. *You just don't think Hailey killed herself. And James inflamed your suspicions.*

What if Hailey's excitement wasn't about a scoop? What if her excitement was about the fact that she had found out she was pregnant? And the man she believed loved her lied and told her he would marry her? And killed her instead?

Nonsense? But I don't know. My paranoia gone wild? Maybe. But James had added not just his own impressions and feelings about Hailey, but a couple of curious facts: Hailey had not been around the office for two days before she killed herself. And the last time he saw her she had been in an elated mood.

I chew on the information because it is so inconsistent with the way I, like James, imagine the character of a suicidal person to be. While it is a given that her mood could have changed radically over a period of forty-eight hours, the state of her office adds another puzzling dimension: The office had been cleaned out. That is the only way I can characterize it in my own thoughts. Cleaned out as if someone was not planning to return to it.

While some people might be tidy about their possessions even when their head is full of killing themselves, James told me that Hailey had been in a very high mood the last time he saw her, two days before she died.

If that were the case, then Hailey would have cleaned out the office at a time when she appeared to a coworker as having a pleasant—even elated—disposition.

I shake my head. The contradictions are rattling my brain. If it isn't likely she would have cleaned out the office when she was in a good mood, then someone else came afterward and did it. My prime candidate for the mysterious someone would be the lover fearing scandal.

As far as getting access to the building without James noting him, that could have been accomplished any number of ways. In fact, I should have asked him if any strangers had been inside the building or if anyone else had obtained access to Hailey's office besides myself.

The brown study I'm in about Hailey almost makes me miss the trolley James told me to take. It's crowded and I'm pushed into a woman next to me as the rail car sets off with a jerk. She pushes back and then nudges me.

"Look at that foolish man."

A man with a bowler hat is running frantically to catch the trolley. He grabs a handrail at the rear corner of the car and nearly slips under as he loses his footing but hangs on and pulls himself up to get footing on the step.

"He's going to get himself killed one day. I saw it once with my own eyes. A man tried to do the same thing, running after the trolley and jumping on while it's moving. Only he wasn't as lucky. Raining like today; the poles were slippery. He lost hold and he went under. It was awful. He was crushed to death by the wheels." She shakes her head. "Mark my words, one day *he'll* end up with the same fate."

She's right; he had been foolish. I just hope that whatever his hurry is, it's worth risking his life for.

11

Four other passengers get off at my stop, including the man in the bowler hat who had defied death to get aboard. He had ignored the verbal jabs of other passengers about his feat and seems a surly type.

Even though the rain has basically stopped, the air still feels wet, as if it has soaked into my clothing. With Hailey's boardinghouse a long block up the street, I'm glad I took the umbrella.

The neighborhood of row houses reminds me of the large brownstones in Manhattan, except these are older and were more presentable decades past. A bit drab and blackened by the coal soot that is the bane of modern living, most of the houses need tender loving care. Many have been turned into boarding homes.

I'm puzzling over what to say to Hailey's landlady and mentally kick myself for not getting a note from the inspector giving me permission to examine her room and dispose of her effects.

I was so distraught over Hailey's suicide note it slipped my mind. Saying I'm a coworker probably wouldn't be the best approach.

I'm still wondering what to say when the door is answered by a young maid.

"I'm Hailey McGuire's sister from America," I tell her. The lie flows naturally off my tongue. I did think of her as a sister. "I've come to collect some of her belongings. Would you kindly take me to her room?"

This is not a complete lie, I do need to select clothing for Hailey's funeral, but I also want to go through her things and see if I can unravel the puzzle of her last days.

She appears hesitant and I fear my bluff isn't going to work.

"Mrs. Franklin isn't here right now."

"I promised the funeral director I would get clothes for him today."

"Oh. I'm sorry. She'll be back shortly."

"I'll wait for her." As soon as I am in the foyer, I add, "In Hailey's room, if you don't mind."

I find the foyer a surprise. It is a little more pleasant than I imagined; nothing fancy, just well kept, though still boardinghouse impersonal. A large grandfather clock is to the left of the stairway to the second floor. A parlor is off to the right and the dining room to the far left. It's much the same as the boardinghouses I'd lived in before I could afford an apartment; all were a little drab and lacking in the warmth a personal touch brings. A simple vase of flowers and brighter furnishings would give the place a more cheerful and homey look.

As we go up the stairs I ask the maid, "Did you and Hailey chat much?"

"We're not allowed to mingle with the residents." She gives me a look. "Your sister was a very nice person. She always said hello to me and would ask me how my day was. She didn't treat me as a servant."

"Yes, that's Hailey."

"I will need to stay with you," she says as she fumbles with a skeleton key as she opens Hailey's door. "Mrs. Franklin has very strict rules."

"Please . . . I need a few moments alone." I hate putting her in a spot, but I can't have her watching as I make a thorough search of the room. "Tell Mrs. Franklin that I insisted. I'll leave the door open."

"I suppose it's all right, you being her sister and all. I'll be just down the hallway cleaning."

Hailey's room is small. She has a window that looks out onto a garden area that has suffered the blistering of winterkill, but I can see how it must be pretty in the spring and summer months. Hailey was lucky to have a window. It makes the room feel more open.

She would have been able to look out when she was relaxing on her bed because the bed is on the wall opposite the window. Under the window is a small desk with a round, forest green cloth stool to sit on; to the left of the bed is an armoire that holds clothes and other personal belongings. To the right of the bed and across from the armoire is a washstand with a mirror and a little vanity table that has a lipstick, blush, comb—all laid out as if she is coming back.

The washstand has a small, white porcelain basin. On the floor underneath are two bowls: one has cat food and the other, water. No cat is around. I hope they found a good home for it.

I sit on her bed and look through her nightstand. In the drawer is a little notepad that has a rubber band around it holding a pencil tight. A quick peek tells me it's her expense accounting for rent, food, and the like. There are no notations for several days before her death, but I want to examine it more at length, so I shove it in my purse and continue going through her dresser. There is nothing out of the ordinary. Whatever stories she had been working on, she apparently hadn't brought them home. Yet she would have been working on a number of them at any one time.

Why can't I find any notes and clippings she was working on? She cabled articles every day to New York, most often not original stories she wrote, but just a rehash of news she found in London papers that she felt would interest New York readers. Yet nothing is at her office or in her room. Which begs a question: Why would she—or someone else—get rid of them?

Either Hailey was being overly tidy before she killed herself—and she was not a slave to being orderly with her work materials—or someone had cleaned out everything, to ensure that nothing would be found.

I do find a pretty brooch that I know she liked and stick it in my pocket as a memento.

"Where, Hailey?" I look around the room talking; maybe Hailey's ghost is lingering about. "Where did you hide the name of the man you were involved with?"

It has to be someplace very secretive, but where? I peek under her mattress, under the bed . . . nothing. I rummage through her armoire . . . nothing. I shove a bunch of hangers over to one side and one drops. When it hits the bottom of the armoire, it makes a dull *thud* sound.

Kneeling down I take out shoes and a hatbox, and tap the wood. It sounds hollow. In the far left inside corner is a tiny hole, barely enough to put my finger in. I lift off the false bottom and inside the recessed area is a book—*a diary.*

"Jackpot!" I go straight to the very last entry. She has a cryptic note: "I'm going on a journey further in spirit than my feet will carry me."

"Oh no . . ." barely comes from me as I sink to the floor. Anyone reading this would interpret it as an admission to suicide. There is *nothing* about bad love or being pregnant . . . nothing. Maybe in her previous entries . . .

"She told me she's her sister . . ."

I jump up, almost losing my balance. The maid's voice is pleading with someone.

"You know the rules!"

That has to be the landlady; her voice reeks with authority.

I slip the diary into the pocket of my coat.

When the Queen of Hearts walks in, I'm hanging up a blouse, not looking happy that she's out of the rabbit hole.

"*What are you doing in here?*"

Without waiting for an answer she grabs the blouse from my hand as if I had snatched the crown jewels.

"You might fool my foolish maid, but I will tell you the same thing I said when her so-called *brother* came, nothing goes out 'til I confirm it with the police."

"Her brother?" I'm baffled by her proclamation about a brother, but it doesn't last long. The nasty woman reminds me of Nurse Grupe, who I encountered during my ten days in a madhouse on Blackwell's Island and I hated that woman. If she thinks she's going to bully me, she's got another thing coming. "She—we don't have a brother."

"I know she didn't have *any* family."

"I'm her adopted sister and her supervisor at the newspaper we work for. I'm Nellie Bly."

"I don't care if you're the Queen of Sheba, nothing is leaving this room. I'm owed rent and this stuff will be sold to cover it as soon as the police are finished with their investigation. And it won't be enough to cover it, let me tell you."

Ah . . . I see, her heart is beating with that eternal rhythm that has driven human beings since the dawn of time—greed.

"How much is owed? My publisher will make good the full amount of rent." I glance around. "And, of course, other than the clothes I will need to have sent over to the funeral home, you can dispose of the rest of the items as you wish."

The woman's face softens to the texture of paving stones. "Well, there's many a charity in need, I always say."

I am sure that in her case, charity begins and stays at home.

"Tell me about this man who claimed to be her brother."

"He was British. He told me that they were estranged and I told him all the more reason he couldn't look through her stuff. Estranged in my books means you are no longer family."

"What did he look like?"

"I don't know. I wasn't planning to draw his picture. He was medium built, long dark hair. Blue eyes. Don't really remember anything else, nor care. As I told you, makes no difference who comes and who says what, nothing goes out until I get me rent. I'm tired of people coming in here like it was a public place, first that Abberline copper, then the one yesterday that made a fine mess going through everything, now you doing only the lord knows what. Nothing leaves here 'til I get me money."

"Very good policy. I only left the officer in charge of the investigation, Inspector Abberline, a short time ago. I have one other question. What was Hailey's mood in those last few days before she died?"

"How would I know? I leave my boarders to themselves. As long as they pay their rent on time, have no shenanigans in their rooms, and be here before I lock the doors at night, I don't care what their moods are or what they do. I keep my nose out of their lives."

She's lying, of course. The woman probably spies on her boarders.

"Did she talk to you or any of the other boarders about a particular story she was working on?"

"*No*, now—"

"Miss . . ." The voice comes from the maid.

"Maggie, go attend to your chores."

The maid quickly disappears down the hallway.

Mrs. Franklin turns back to me and points at the open door. "And until I see payment, you can leave, too."

"I'll arrange payment and be back to select the clothing."

What a witch—to put it politely—but I know I have gone as far as I can get with her, so I leave. Besides, the diary is burning a hole in my thoughts and I need to get somewhere to read it. What a find—if a young woman is going to confess her life and loves anywhere, it will be in her secret journal.

As I step out the front door of the house and start down the stairs, I hear, "Miss, Miss—"

The maid comes out the front door behind me and hurries down, looking nervously back at it.

"You wanted to know about Hailey's mood. She was happy, not depressed. And excited. We did talk sometimes. She told me she'd met the perfect man, that's why I was so surprised when the police came and found her note."

"Did she tell you who the man was?"

"No. She couldn't."

"Why not?"

"She said she couldn't because he was very important and well known with the rich and powerful. She said him and her needed time to figure things out before making their romance public."

"When did she tell you this?"

"Three days before she took her life. She came home late and I sneaked her in. I couldn't help notice she was wearing a beautiful ring. I asked who gave it to her and she told me it was a gift from the man she loved and that I mustn't tell anyone about it. It was a secret. She also said she was going to be moving out, that this man was going to take care of everything. She was so happy."

"What did the ring look like?"

"It was a ruby surrounded by diamonds . . . very expensive."

She didn't have a ring like that at the morgue. If she had it on when her body was recovered, the morgue attendant or someone earlier took it. "Did she talk to you about any of the stories she was working on?"

"Yes, yes . . ." She looks back at the front door.

"It's okay; she's probably still in Hailey's room adding up how much she can sell everything for."

Maggie puts her hand to her mouth to smother a laugh. "You know Mrs. Franklin for sure, you do. About a week before she done herself in, Miss McGuire said she was working on a story that would give her . . . oh, what was the word . . . recognition. She was so excited, but I have no idea what it was about. I'm sorry I can't be more help. She was always so secretive about the news stories she worked on. But I think I know something." Maggie uses a confidential tone and glances back again to see if the boogey woman has reared her ugly head.

"Three or four days before she died, I was cleaning her room and I happened upon an article on her bed stand that she had scribbled on. Of course, I never looked closely at it, knowing how she was about keeping things a secret."

"Of course not. What was the article about?"

"A doctor."

"Do you remember the doctor's name?"

"No."

"What about the doctor?"

"Some woman, Lady Somebody, had died."

"He killed her?"

"No . . . I don't know. I have to go back in."

"Wait. Please think. Do you remember *anything* about the doctor?"

She bit her lip. "He's . . . he's a health doctor. He makes people healthier. He was treating the woman with something that wasn't real medicine and she died. I've gotta go."

"Here."

I take her hand and put the brooch in it. Her jaw drops.

"This is expensive . . . I can't . . ."

"Yes, now go run before Mrs. Franklin catches you."

I, too, hurry away, taking a good deep breath, relieved to have gotten away from that terrible woman. I would not have been so kind and gentle to her if I didn't know that she would have taken my tongue lashing out on her poor servant girl.

I take the diary out of my pocket and stick it in my purse. Once I find a café, I will stop and read the diary over tea and biscuits.

My heart pounds . . . I have Hailey's diary, now I will be able to get answers.

The restraint of not plopping myself down and reading her diary is driving me nuts, but I can't chance the evil Queen of Hearts watching me from an upper floor window to see if I had stolen anything.

Which I had, of course.

12

Archer watches from a hundred feet away as Nellie Bly comes out of the boardinghouse. He picks up his step to stay close enough behind her to make a quick move if he has to. He doesn't want to bring attention to himself or risk getting his legs chopped off again if she boards a trolley.

He gets a jolt as the Bly woman pulls a red book out of her pocket and slips it into her purse without looking at it.

The diary.

It had to be the diary. It had that look and color. But the furtive way she slipped it into her purse was the tip-off that makes him certain she hadn't gotten the book with the landlady's permission.

How did she get her hands on it?

He had bluffed his way into the McGuire woman's room yesterday by showing his old police badge. Once inside, he did a thorough search of the room. He knew from over a dozen years as a copper that women are much more clever than men when it comes to hiding evidence. But leave it up to a woman to find another woman's hiding place.

He should have torn the place completely apart. Even without the police badge, the old bitch that runs the boardinghouse would have sold him anything he had wanted from the room for a quid.

The Bly woman turns the opposite direction from the trolley stop as she comes up to the corner.

She's anxious to take a peek in the book. *Going for hot tea and a warm place to read it.* Good. That means she hadn't had time to read it. And she wouldn't get her nose between the pages, either. Not on his watch. He has to get it before she reads it. That was made very clear to him if he wants to get paid very well.

Getting this job had been a fluke, saving him from the final slip into the gutter that he'd been sliding toward since he had been dismissed from the force for taking bribes from a bookmaker to supplement that lousy salary they pay junior detectives.

It wasn't his fault. He had had a wife who liked luxuries. That's how he kept getting in deeper, first for what *she* wanted to wear and eat and then she even demanded *he* wore expensive suits. "I ain't being seen with a man dressed like a street cop," is what she told him. So, he did the only thing he could, he went on the take, looked the other way for a tidy sum from the bookmaker who handled bets on the races and sports. As his wife's demands got bigger and his tastes got more refined, he started shaking down some of the criminals he'd collared. When one of them tried to turn the tables by blackmailing, he had beaten the man half to death. His only regret was that he hadn't completed the other half of the beating because the bastard was able to tell a doctor who he'd been smacked by and why.

If only he had kept his temper down and dumped his wife long ago, but he fell hard for her beauty and that she was an actress. He never understood why she married him, nor did anyone else. He was big and burly, with a face that had been bashed into too many times over fights he started; while she was delicate, like a china doll. She had manners, he had none.

He knew the other coppers were jealous of his gorgeous wife and expensive habits. They constantly were asking him how he did it—with every one of the bastards knowing and not a few of them also on the take.

The money he always had jangling in his pockets aside, he knew he had also made enemies on the force because of his temper. His way of solving anything, right or wrong, was to punch hard. Talking didn't get you anywhere, at least that's what he learned from his dad, who used his fists more than once on Archer until Archer got big enough to give tit-for-tat.

In his mind, no one on the force cared that he was taking bribes because others were on the take, too. They just remembered how many times he pushed his way in to get what he wanted. Ratting him out was their way of getting even.

Now he's answering to a wealthy aristocrat who's a lot more corrupt than him. No one made millions of quid in business without doing things under the table that would make a bank robber look like a saint.

He had come into contact with the rich man when he was still on the force. Soon after he was promoted to junior detective, the man's teenage son was being investigated for beating another boy severely over a girl. The father slipped Archer some money and the case got dumped.

Now the man has another problem, a problem the police couldn't handle. "You'll be my consulting detective," is what he told Archer.

Archer didn't care about his title; all he cared about was the money. He was sick and tired of being poor. And he wanted revenge, the kind he'd get when he looked up his ex-wife and made her green with envy with his pockets full of money. He'll shove money in her face. Then to really make her mad, he'll lavish it on another actress she knows. He's not worried about who he'll get, all actresses are sluts and will do anything for money. She did.

This book the American woman found in the dead girl's room will be his ticket back to the good life. He knows something valuable is in it, information that will make him a wealthy man. And if that aristocratic pig who hired him thinks he is just going to simply turn it over to him for a few lousy quid—he's in for a big surprise.

But first he has to get it from the woman.

Being the man he is, asking her for it politely isn't in the cards.

13

Blue-eyed brother? I mulled over what Hailey's landlady told me. With a British accent, no less. Now who in the devil is he? The elusive lover? Why he would want access to Hailey's room is the one thing about him I'm certain about. He wants the diary because there is something in it that will expose him as her lover. And I have the damning evidence.

"*Wha—!*" pops out of my mouth as a man comes up from behind me, grabs my purse, and takes off like a bat out of hell.

"*Help! Help! He has my purse!*" I yell at the top of my lungs as I give chase. There is no one else in sight on this gray wet day.

I only get a glance of him, but I'm positive it's the man who made the mad dash to get on the trolley near Hailey's office and got off with me at her boardinghouse.

His head goes down and I get the impression he's opening my purse. I try to increase my speed but my long dress, ridiculous petticoats, and bulky high-topped heeled shoes that encase a woman work against me sprinting.

A woman comes out of a food store and the man, concentrating on the contents of my purse, runs right into her. Her grocery bag flies out of her hand, exploding as it hits the ground. The man stumbles to stay on his feet.

My purse flies into the air as he throws it over his head back at me as the woman he nearly bowled over yells a curse at him.

Quickly grabbing my purse off the ground, I determine that my coin purse with my gold coins and folded money are inside, but something even more important is missing: Hailey's diary.

"What's happened?" the woman asks me. "That thief get your money?"

"No, not my money."

"Thank God. You all right?"

"Yes, and you?"

"Oh I'm fine, can't say the same for me groceries."

As we gather up her food, the grocer comes out of the store and they chatter about how unsafe the streets are for honest people. "And the police do nothing," the grocer says.

Even though I am hearing everything they say, none of it penetrates the fog in my brain. My God—the diary was stolen, taken from me in broad daylight by a man who must have been following me from Hailey's office.

"You sure you're all right?" the woman asks me again. "You look like you've seen the devil."

"Yes . . . I'm okay, I'm just amazed at how devious people are. And what terrible things rational human beings are capable of."

"Did you hit your head, dear?"

The murky stuff in my head is still there as I am carried away in a hansom cab to my hotel.

Shocked down to my socks, I admit. And angry. Is the lover so desperate about being exposed that he is resorting to criminal acts? It's obvious to me that this is the case. And I can't help wondering if there is more to it than just the man's identity. Is he also trying to cover up some complicity in Hailey's death? Did she get that bump on her head before she went into the water?

I don't know whether it's a lover trying to avoid scandal or one covering up murder, but I realize that I have been looking for a reason to find Hailey hadn't killed herself almost from the time I got the news in New York. Now that I know something is amiss, I am confronted with both a dilemma and a challenge: What can I do about it?

I'm alone, in a foreign country, thousands of miles from the resources and contacts that I can employ whenever I do an investigation. And I'm under a time pressure. The paper expects me to stay only a few days to lay Hailey to rest and "clear up her desk" as Mr. Cockerill instructed me. After that they expected me back, beating the bushes for stories.

Which is another quandary I'm in: do I want to return to *The World*?

Their cavalier treatment of me since my return from my trip around the world has me questioning if I want to continue working for the newspaper. Mr. Pulitzer and the editor-in-chief never even said so much as "*thank you*" or offered a salary increase or any other reasonable compensation a man would have received for a similar accomplishment. Bottom line, I did not receive one cent and my salary has been a very low one.

After my insane asylum exposé, which I know did not garner a fraction of the publicity and increase in ratings that my trip around the world did, I received a generous bonus check. I have yet to receive one.

And, not to sound petty, but the only "*thank you*" I received from Mr. Pulitzer was a *cabled* congratulation with a note begging me to accept a gift from India, another item I have yet to receive. Such treatment would never have been given to a man.

If I hadn't written *Around the World in 72 Days*,* I would be in horrible financial straights, for I am not just taking care of myself, I am taking care of my mother, brothers, and sister.

To make matters worse, shortly after I returned my favorite bother, Charles, died—inflammation of the bowel. He was only twenty-eight, five years older than me,† and that worries me. I've been having health issues myself and the doctor keeps telling me I need a vacation. I thought my trip around the world would be one, but instead it was very stressful.‡ But I mustn't think of that for now I have more pressing issues at hand. I must help provide for his widow, Sarah, and their two small children, Charles and Gertrude. After our father died, Charles and I made a pact always to take care of each other. I will not let him down.

So when a book publisher, N.L. Munro, offered me an incredible three-year contract to write dime-novel fiction§ in a series of installments for his weekly *New York Family Story Paper*—ten thousand dollars for the first year and fifteen thousand for each of the next two years¶—I couldn't refuse. While this is more than what Mr. Pulitzer will ever offer me, reporting the news is oxygen to my soul and I don't know if I'm ready to

---

* By August 1890, *Around the World in 72 Days*, first edition of 10,000 copies, had sold out and it went into a second printing.—The Editors

† Nellie constantly lied about her age. She was twenty-six when she went to the UK, not twenty-three.—The Editors

‡ The dangers Nellie encountered during her trip around the world are the basis for the novel *The Illusion of Murder.*—The Editors

§ Dime-novel fiction was mystery, adventure, and melodrama in a paperback form. Nellie was hired to write a series of mystery dime novels with a heroine protagonist. She never completed them. A friend told her, she had "no plot, characters, or ability to write dialogue."—The Editors

¶ Ten thousand dollars then is about two hundred thousand dollars today. Mr. Cockerill earned a similar amount from Pulitzer as one of the nation's highest paid editors.—The Editors

give it up, but I do know that health-wise, I can't write the books and remain a reporter.

My poor head wants to explode but I must focus back on the issue at hand—my attacker.

The first question is who was the man that attacked me in broad daylight on a public street? Hired help, I am sure. Nor did he appear to me to be someone that Hailey would have become romantically entangled with.

He looked street tough, the sort of man you'd find in a lower-class bar and hire to do dirty work, the kind that the police investigate.

I hadn't paid much attention to him when he came aboard the trolley, but reflecting now, my impression of him is that while he wore a business suit, it needed cleaning and some attention from a hot iron, indicating to me that he probably isn't married and that he might be down on the heels from a higher position in life than the one he now held.

He is hardly the important personage that Hailey had boasted about to both the maid and James the gatekeeper. Definitely just hired help, paid to get the diary and whatever else the lover wanted the covers pulled over. But what is in the diary that would make Hailey's lover take the risk of having his thug commit a street crime that could send both him and the street tough to prison?

The lover's identity? Or a more serious crime—the murder of Hailey?

That diary speaks from the grave. Words that might not be direct evidence of murder, but might point to the man who made her pregnant and raise questions that would make the police reconsider a simple verdict of suicide.

Then there is the other question eating away at my mind: How does the big story Hailey was working on fit in? She mentioned doing a major story to both James and the maid. Yet I found nothing about it in her room and found at her office only the red file with just filler stories. More important than the stories I didn't find were the ashes left behind. The only explanation for the burning that my head will accept is that someone, possibly the mugger who attacked me, went into her office and burned all evidence of the story.

There has to be a connection between the story and the man Hailey had become infatuated with. That all references to the story were destroyed because they led back to the man who wanted his identity kept secret seems a reasonable conclusion to me. But could the two situations be completely alien to each other? A coincidence? No way will I accept that. The diary and the news story Hailey was working on are linked to Hailey's lover and her lover obviously has no scruples when it comes to relying on violence to get what he wants. I might not have fared as well today if I'd met that thug in a dark alley.

But for the life of me, I can't imagine how the lover and the news story could be linked. Hailey imitated me in carving out a career in reporting. And that meant that inevitably, any story that Hailey would go overboard about would involve crime, political dirty dealing, or other scandalous matters. *The World* is not a scandal sheet by any means, but it did not become the circulation champ by being anything but a bare-knuckle street fighter when it comes to the news.

My gut tells me I can't go to Abberline until I have more evidence. He has the suicide note and I can't tell him what is in the diary. As for the mugger, he'll point out that purse snatchings are common instincts in any city anywhere—and it so happens that London is the most populous city in the entire world. I can almost hear him telling me exactly how many purse snatchings occur every day in the city—and my retort being, of course, how many of them discarded the money in a purse and ran off with a young woman's diary?

His rebuttal will be that the thief got confused and simply starting throwing things. And he'd want to know if I continued after the thief to see if he had soon discarded the diary. I didn't and my failure to do so would be the inspector's coup de grace in the discussion.

No, a simple purse snatching isn't going to impress him or win him over to my side, not without something solid. Nor will the feelings of a maid and an office clerk that Hailey wasn't suicidal, since neither was an intimate of Hailey's.

Until I have an explanation for the suicide note, I can't go to the inspector. At the moment, the only explanation that sits well with me is that she was coerced into writing it under duress. Unfortunately, I have no proof except the hairs standing up on the back of my neck and someone mugging me.

Where to start is not a difficult question for me. Like Hailey, I am a reporter and know the beat: She was working on a story about a medical scandal involving a health doctor and a high-society woman, so I will start there and see where it leads me.

Hopefully the news story and the man in her life who betrayed and probably murdered her will intersect.

I could drop by a newspaper office and ask reporters about recent stories featuring a health doctor and a dead noblewoman, but I already have an inside source for London high society and its rumors, innuendos, and scandals—basically an artery to all that goes on in London society.

"Drop me at the nearest telegraph office," I tell the cabbie, through the hansom cab's roof door.

It is time to contact an old friend, one who once fought killers with me, and who is not only a world-champion purveyor of gossip, but perhaps also the most common subject of gossip in the city, and a shameless instigator of the most outrageous, titillating, and racy scandals on the planet.

You will find me at the Langham under the name of Count Von Kramm.

—The king of Bohemia
from "A Scandal in Bohemia"
by Sir Arthur Conan Doyle

14

I'm meeting Mr. Ernest," I tell the maître d' at the dining room in the Langham Hotel, the grande dame of hotels in the world and the epitome of elite chic.

I'm escorted to a table to bide my time while I wait for "Mr. Ernest," who is my friend and sometime partner in crime—detection, of course—Oscar Wilde.

Oscar's reply to my telegraph had advised me cryptically that he would present himself "incognito" at the restaurant, thus the Mr. Ernest bit, and would offer explanations that must be kept "under the rose." It took me a moment to realize that "under the rose" was an idiom for secrecy dating back to ancient times.

As the wit and scandalous rascal of London society, both because of his sharp tongue and refusal to limit his sexual activities to those dictated by "respectable" people and straitlaced religious organizations, Oscar's need to hide out could have arisen from any number of things he said—or did.

The fact we were meeting in the most fashionable and exquisite hotel dining room in London at a time when Oscar is "incognito" is merely part of the charm of a man who upon his arrival in America to begin his speaking tour advised a customs officer that he had nothing to declare but his genius.

I admit I had been taken in by Oscar's secrecy-laden message, but when my cab dropped me off where the entrance to the hotel is completely lit with electric lights and the doorman, who is waiting to help me down and escort me in, is dressed as modestly as the admiral of the Royal Fleet, I decided Oscar may be more melodramatic than in danger.

My poor stomach grumbles and I mutter, "Where are you, Oscar?" as I await his presence. His response instructed me to meet him at ten-thirty, a fashionable time for dinner after plays are over. I check my father's pocket watch. He's five minutes late. And there is nothing fashionable about my healthy appetite.

I've never gotten used to chic late-night eating, not even after several years in New York, and I'm hungry enough to nibble on the wood table. In my hometown of Cochran Mills, Pennsylvania, population exactly 534, I grew up having dinner at six sharp, not hours after the sun has gone down.

I almost feel like getting up and going back to roam again in the encased garden atrium. It's really lovely and so unexpected in downtown gray foggy London. They took the inner courtyard and covered it with an iron and glass roof so it can be enjoyed year-round. Scattered among the flowers and trees are wrought-iron tables and cushioned chairs and benches so one can sit and gaze at the stars as they sip wine. I imagine it must be beautiful to sit and watch snowflakes fall. It would be like being in one of those glass balls my mother has that you shake and watch the snow fall on the animals in a forest.

I've traveled the world and seen many gorgeous hotels, but never have I experienced a place as elegant as the Langham. Throughout the public areas they have intricately laid mosaic flooring decorated in white, gold, and scarlet. Selectively hanging on walls covered with hand-printed wallpaper are Moorish murals and silk hangings—each having a story of their own to tell. White marble pillars that give one the feeling of pure wealth are standing guard all about.

Coming through the grand entrance, hanging on the hallway wall leading into the dining area is a Persian tapestry carpet that must have cost a king's ransom.

The dining room is enormous and simply dazzling. Their wallpaper is a light creamy beige adorned with little golden angels, each holding a black bow and arrow—some shooting arrows and some sitting on fluffy white clouds. And something I've rarely seen, electric chandeliers—thousands of crystals of all shapes and sizes lit with lightbulbs. There are over a dozen of these brilliant lighting fixtures hanging from the fourteen-foot ceiling which is a highly polished pinkish Italian Veneziano plaster—or as the Italians say, "the Women's Stucco" because it burnishes to an even gloss with very little effort. White marble pillars are scattered among the tables. One wall is floor-to-ceiling glass that overlooks the encased garden. All this creates a sumptuous atmosphere, perfect for eating . . . which I'm dying to do.

When the maître d' took me to my table, I paused for a moment and stared at a large stone fireplace with roaring flames on the opposite wall from the glass wall—the wood is not being burned. "A gas fireplace," he tells me, "with ceramic logs."

Amazing. What will they think of next?

Our table sits right in the center of the room. If Oscar wants anonymity, this is definitely not going to please him; however, if I take into consideration a pillar which is right by our table, Oscar might have a little privacy from the curious if he is truly planning to appear in some sort of disguise.

Each table is set with floral china sitting on top of silver charger plates, sterling silverware, crystal water and wine glasses, a small vase of flowers, and a candle in a decorative etched glass candleholder in the center of the table; some settings, like mine, have a crystal wine holder that looks like a duck.

After seeing what other diners are wearing, I'm not happy being in the center of the room and find myself leaning toward the pillar to hide. The couture is formal, men are in white tie, the women in evening gowns, some sleeveless with long gloves, most with feathered hats and almost every woman has either a pearl necklace, dazzling diamonds—or both.

Not many months ago I completed a seventy-two-day trip around the world with only one change of clothes that I carried in a small valise, yet managed to attend shipboard dinner parties without shame. I came to London with the same valise and the same one change of clothes and the same lack of embarrassment. I work hard and travel fast and light and refuse to load myself down with trunks in order to look fashionable.

If the other women in the world believe they are seeing an ugly duckling crossing the room, they are probably right, but I'd like to tell each of them that I earn my own duck food.

I hear a stir and murmuring among the diners and look toward the door.

There he is, in all his glory, pausing as he enters. I shake my head and sigh. *Incognito?*

Oscar is wearing a green velvet suit with wide lapels, a white silk shirt with a Lord Byron collar, and an oversized red tie that is loosely tied and as wide as a scarf. His cape is purple and reaches nearly down to the heels of his brilliantly polished black patent leather shoes. His hat is black and would have gone nicely on the head of one of the Three Musketeers.

Besides the clothing that would have raised eyebrows at a showing of *Alice's Adventures in Wonderland*, much less at a posh restaurant-hotel in the heart of London's West End, everything about Oscar is big—six-foot-three, soft and flabby with a low mezzo voice that people concentrated to hear yet reaches across a room. His mind is big, too, encyclopedic; his tongue a guillotine that cuts through hypocrisy and affronts with a razor-edged blade.

He excitedly waves his hand as he weaves around a sea of tables, coming toward me with as much subtlety as Sherman's march on Atlanta—no, make that Moses crossing the Red Sea: Oscar is carrying a white pooch dressed much the same way he is.

OSCAR WILDE

I think that God in creating Man somewhat overestimated his ability.

—OSCAR WILDE

15

N ellie!"
The pooch barks. It's a small white poodle wearing a duplicate hat and a purple cape that matches Oscar's. If Oscar's flamboyant entrance had not already captured every eye in the room, the barking of the provocatively dressed dog for sure brought stares from everyone.

I should have known that it's simply not in Oscar's makeup to isolate himself from the world. Lost on a desert island, he'd recruit the monkeys and the fish as a social circle.

There is no "rose" big enough for him to hide himself or his secrets under. Obviously, everyone's eyes are upon him, which is understandable since this man is like no other on the entire planet. Oscar Wilde is one of a kind—and God broke the mold after He created the man.

And I wouldn't change a hair on his head.

I get up to hug him. "Oh, Oscar! I've missed you!"

He gives me this huge smile and then immediately puts his hands to his mouth to cover his bad teeth as he giggles, "I've so missed you, too, Nellie-girl."

As we hug one more time before sitting down, the doggie he's carrying gets squished between us, again.

"Oh, you poor thing . . . what's your name?" As I pet the little fellow, he paws me and licks my fingers. "Oscar, he isn't wearing purple nail polish?"

"Of course! It must match his cape. Nellie, meet Lord Dudley."

"Lord Dudley . . . okay, I suppose that fits."

"Isn't this place magnificent? Look at all its beauty!" Oscar surveys the place as if he's admiring his kingdom. He's always been attracted to beauty. "This place is a tour de force. There is no other like it in the world."

"I know. It's the first to have hydraulically powered lifts, air-conditioning, and its own steam-pumped artesian well. The hotel bored three hundred and sixty-five feet below the basement floor into the chalk-basin and with the help of two fourteen-horsepower pumps they are able to pump twenty-five thousand gallons of water into iron tanks in the cu-pola tower that distributes hot and cold running water to every bedroom. *That,* my dear Oscar, is truly amazing."

"Yes it is. How did you . . ."

I love surprising Oscar with my knowledge since he believes us poor Americans are so ignorant, so I continue. "You must know that Sir James Langham built a mansion on this site in 1820, subsequently named Lang-ham Place, because it's ninety-five feet above the Thames high water mark on fine gravel soil, making it healthier than the peat bogs in Belgravia nearer the Thames. In fact, this area is not only regarded as the healthiest in London, but has a much lower death rate than any other of the city's districts."

Poor Oscar just sits looking at me confounded. I almost break down and tell him when I was waiting for him I overheard a gentleman explain-ing in detail, to his dinner companions from Italy, about the place.

"Nellie, you never cease to amaze me."

"Why thank you. What also impresses me is they have telephones, a real rarity anywhere, a post office, two libraries that have up-to-date news-papers and journals from around the world, public lavatories, a railway ticketing and shipping office, all under one roof. And their employees are qualified to converse in every language, from pure Yankee to High Dutch. I wonder if this is the way all hotels will be one day."

"Maybe, but they will never have the beauty like this place." Once again Oscar pauses, sweeping the room with his eyes, soaking in all its exquisiteness. "Art, which comes in all forms—paintings, sculptures, people, décor—has one purpose, to display beauty, and this place does it magnificently. I believe we are nothing but God's canvas. And it's amaz-ing what some of us do with it. Look at the elderly ladies here . . ." He pauses for a moment and nods at one and then another.

"They all have gigantic tiaras and parrot noses."

"Oscar!" But I couldn't help laughing. He's right.

"Thank God I won't end up looking like that truculent and red-faced old gentleman covered all over with orders and ribbons. Did you know that the romantic novelist Marie Louise de la Ramée or Ouida, as she liked to call herself, lived here for four years before she died? What a marvelous eccentric! One day she invited me to her room. She was lying on her bed wearing only a sheer, green silk, sinister nightgown, surrounded with masses of purple flowers and candles. She refused to have the black velvet curtains drawn; claimed the obtrusive daylight made it hard for her to think. Couldn't help but love a lady who said she did all her best work in bed!"

Oscar laughs with such delight I can't help but laugh myself.

"Your first American to be a guest here was Henry Wadsworth Longfellow. Samuel Langhorne Clemens, or better known to the public as Mark Twain, stays here whenever he comes to London. In fact, my own novel, *The Picture of Dorian Gray*, that will soon be out was negotiated with the publisher at this very table. Also present at that dinner was Arthur Conan Doyle, the writer of the Sherlock Holmes stories.* Have you read his mystery stories?"

"No, not yet."

"Well, you must. It will sharpen your detecting skills."

"Congratulations on your book. What is it about?"

"The philosophy of beauty. It's about what one can choose to do with his life and how he can either destroy it . . ." Oscar pauses for a moment, as if his life is passing him by.

As much as I hate silence, especially awkward ones like these, I keep quiet for his sake. He is a dear soul who has to endure a lot of cruelty and criticism from society, yet somehow he manages to keep his humor and love for life or, more appropriately, beauty. I wish I was as strong as him.

". . . or try to make it worthy. I think it is a masterpiece. One might say it's as lovely as a Persian carpet, and as unreal. I must say, the publisher was a bit disappointed that he didn't get all the words he wanted. It's true we had agreed on a manuscript of a hundred thousand words, but after I completed it I informed him that there were not a hundred thousand beautiful words in the English language."

"And I imagine that you used all the beautiful ones in your book. I shall

---

*The Sherlock Holmes book commissioned at the dinner by the American publisher who met with Oscar and Arthur Conan Doyle was *The Sign of the Four*.—The Editors

rush and buy it the moment I see it out. However, Oscar, I must say, you have me a bit confused."

"How so, my dear?"

"Well, with your story being published, something you've always wanted, which would make, I believe, life good; in your telegram you said that you are incognito, ducking trouble, that sort of thing. What's up?"

"I'm hiding in plain sight."

16

A h, yes, I should have thought of that. *Why* are you hiding in plain sight?"

"That thing called love that the immortal Dante said moved the sun and other stars. Unfortunately, that which can move heavenly bodies can sometimes cause utter ruin and devastation among us mere mortals."

"Which translates to . . . ?"

"As my miner friends in Leadville would say, I got caught with my pants down."

I am afraid to ask if it had anything to do with buggery . . . because I am absolutely certain that it does. I called poor Oscar a "sodomite" the first time I met him, that's before I got to know him and realized that his choice of lovers is a private matter about which no one has the right to throw the first rock. Regardless of Oscar's distaste for the hypocrisy of our legal system that is heavily influenced by religion—the law still has severe penalties for men who mate with other men.

"I met a young ang—no, not an angel, an Adonis whose appearance on even a bright day is as if a more brilliant sun had suddenly risen in the sky. And his looks . . . they are as if the gods had molded him from ivory and rose leaves. When I met him I had a strange feeling that Fate had in store for me exquisite joys and deep sorrows. I was not let down. Unfortunately, Nellie, as our first ancestors learned in Eden and I have discovered in this matter, behind every wondrous thing that exists there is something tragic. I like to think of it as there always being a snake in paradise."

"He loves someone else," I say, barely above a whisper, hoping to bring down his own volume.

"*Oh no!*" he booms. "It's his damn father. Even in that raw colony across the pond, you've heard of the Marquis of Queensbury."

"I believe we adopted the Queensbury rules of boxing as a matter of fact . . . gloves, no punches in the clinch, that sort of thing."*

"Yes, yes. What a vulgar creature he is—the marquis. He has a son who is the glorification of all that is beautiful and pure and the creature embraces a sport in which men sweat and bleed and punch each other and there is a ten-second count for a knockout."

This goes on for ten minutes while Oscar moans about the damage to his soul, how when one is in love, one always begins by deceiving one's self, and one always ends by deceiving others. His lamenting is what the world calls romance. Now, because of all this tangled web his lover wove, he is in hiding because the Queensbury marquis is out to practice some of his pugilistic talents on Oscar for "corrupting" his son.

Somewhere between Oscar's breaths for air, I manage to direct the conversation to Hailey and he is an attentive audience as I start with news of Hailey's suicide and end with being mugged for her diary. I tell him that I suspect Hailey was killed by a wealthy man to hide their affair.

"It's karma," he says, when I am finished.

"Karma?"

"Your consistent ability to stumble onto murder wherever you go. There is no other explanation for why people come to a violent end around you."

"You think my karma killed Hailey?" My features pucker, ready for tears.

"Oh my . . . no, no, no. Of course I didn't mean that." He reaches over and pats my hand. "That was a bad choice of words on my part. Your karma couldn't hurt a flea. You care too much for people. It's not your fault that they die."

"You're saying I somehow had a hand in them being murdered." My emotional state breaks.

Oscar quickly hands me his pink handkerchief before I flood dinner with my tears. "Nellie, you are taking this all the wrong way. Lord knows you try to prevent it and you do end up saving lives. You saved mine."

---

*John Sholto Douglas, The 9th Marquess of Queensberry, lent his name and patronage to what became known as the "Marquess of Queensberry rules" a set of twelve rules for conducting boxing matches which are basically in effect even today.—The Editors

That stops my tears and I remember why I love this gentle giant. "No, Oscar . . . you saved *my* life and that's why I need your help again."

"You're in danger?"

"No, I don't think so, but I can't let Hailey's killer get away with murder or allow the people who knew her to think she took her own life when she didn't. That would be horrible."

With my emotions back in control, I tell Oscar the news story about a health doctor and a society woman.

"Ah, yes, the Lady Winsworth matter," he says. "It was front page news until the next juicy story showed its head. You've heard of Dr. Lacroix, Anthony Lacroix? No, of course you haven't, you're a parochial colonist and only interested in what happens on your side of the pond. Where should I start?"

"At the beginning—with the doctor."

Our waiter sets down a crystal bowl of water on the floor for Lord Dudley. Oscar waits 'til he leaves and puts in on the table. "I can't let him out of my hands. He'll go socializing with the people."

"I believe you. Now, back to the matter at hand."

"Ah, yes, Dr. Lacroix. He has a mineral spa in Bath near the ancient Roman ruins. He sells a substance that my miner friends in Leadville, Colorado, with whom I bellied up to the bar during my American tour, would call 'snake oil'."

"We have quite a few salesmen of that type, and not all in western mining camps."

"Aqua Vitae." Oscar smacks his lips as if he can taste the name. "The Waters of Life is a mixture made from the waters the doctor gets from the mineral springs and his 'secret' ingredients."

"What's his snake oil?"

"I've heard it's animal organs."

"What?"

"Most animals are much faster and more powerful than humans. Rejuvenation researchers seek the essence of animal organs that will revitalize humans."

"Yuck. Sounds disgusting. People drink that stuff?"

"They do if they want to stay young and beautiful or in the case of men, still virile in old age. And can afford it. Youth is not cheap or pretty on the dark side of middle age."

"You're telling me this doctor mixes up a batch of animal organs and people pay to swig it down? Is this poison what killed the society lady?"

"What killed the society lady is still an open question at the coroner's office, but the newspapers tried the doctor already and found him guilty. Something I'm quite familiar with. Anyway, Lady Winsworth was an actress over forty, maybe older, she never told, at least truthfully, not only because she married Lord Winsworth, first baronet of Barberry, who, if I'm correct, is a few years younger than her, though she looks much younger. She was also very vain. It was imperative to her that she keep her youthful beauty. Being willing to try anything, the Fountain of Youth rejuvenation that Dr. Lacroix sold fit the bill. What she died of still puzzles the medical examiner. From your experiences as a crime reporter, you would know the coroners' doctors have very limited scientific resources."

"So, who or what do you think killed her?"

"I don't know. But I'm sure that she was having an affair with Dr. Lacroix."

"That's a perfect motive for the husband to kill her. But how do you know she was having an affair with the doctor?"

He grins. "My study of human nature tells me. A woman desperate to reassure herself that she wasn't growing old, a younger man who may hold the secret to her maintaining her beauty and who himself is considered attractive by women in general."

"And is there a jealous husband in this scenario?"

"Yes, the police are considering that angle, especially since he had a lover, who is quite a bit younger than Lady Winsworth. But I understand that he was quite devoted to his wife despite his wanderings because she was popular in social circles, an area in which he fared badly. He got lucky and made his pile in a South African gold mine, but his father had been a Liverpool dockworker. It was the gold strike that got him the baronet title after he spread around some of his ample abundance to the Queen's favorite causes. But, it was Lady Winsworth's popularity that got him in with the cream of society. He doesn't have the best of personalities. He's not just a bull in a china cabinet, but a mean bull.

"Now, while there's been no charges against Dr. Lacroix officially filed, and the case is still open, I can tell you that Lacroix has more to fear from Lord Winsworth than a police investigation. Winsworth is a rough and tumble guy, the kind who knows you can't make an omelet without cracking eggs. From what I've heard of the man, Dr. Lacroix would end up floating facedown in the river if Winsworth gets his hands on him."

I winced at the image of a body facedown in the water. "This Lacroix sounds like a charlatan."

"I'm not sure. I've heard things from both sides of the aisle about him. He believes in rejuvenation, taking years off of people, turning back the clock a bit. And he knows that most people will sell their soul for continual youth. It's people like Lady Winsworth and the rest of the men and women that gave me the inspiration for creating Dorian Gray."

Oscar continues in his musical voice and with that graceful wave of the hand that is always so characteristic of him. "I've been expounding on my beliefs about beauty for years. *The Picture of Dorian Gray* is just a . . . oh, how would one say it . . . a culmination of my spoken thoughts put down in the written word. My book discloses how our desire to keep young and beautiful leads us to do things we never dreamed we'd do and how in the end it destroys us. Well, it makes no difference, doctors—and witch doctors—have been practicing the art for thousands of years. The Ebers Papyrus, a three-thousand-year-old Egyptian medical book talks about using the organs of animals to give humans the power and strength of beasts. They used the organs of bulls, for example, to improve human vitality."

"That's a lot of bull." The pun is shameless on my part, but I can't help it.

"Don't be so certain. There's a very prominent French-American doctor in Paris named Brown-Séquard. He's renowned worldwide for his work with the human nervous system, yet, like Lacroix, he believes that rejuvenation can be accomplished with human beings."

Oscar leans across the table for his next pronouncement and I know it will be a bombshell.

"To revitalize his sex life, he personally takes an extract he prepares from the testes of a bull."

"Oh God." I can't hold back a giggle.

"He claims it enhances his virility. And there's a Liverpool fighter named Billy the Bull who claims he takes a teaspoon of bull semen before every fight and says it's made him a champion. I, myself, have no problems in the area of male sexuality, but I've been considering—"

"Oscar, spare me the details! Please, just tell me more about this Dr. Lacroix."

"That's about all I know. He's a doctor who has tuned in on a need aching to be filled—eternal youth. Let me tell you something about youth. There is absolutely nothing in the world but youth! Women want to return to the blush of youth and beauty, men want back those halcyon days when they bedded the headmaster's daughter and then went on to row for Oxford. And they will pay anything to get it. Naturally, rejuvenation is restricted to only the rich because the poor are too busy finding food and shelter to worry about what they look like. Nowadays, people know the price of everything, and the value of nothing."

"You're cynical, Oscar."

"Nellie, my dear, society runs on looks. I know, now, that when one loses one's good looks, whatever they may be, one loses everything. Shocking, but true. One day you will discover I am merely honest in a world in which people hide their motives deeper than their money." He reaches across and pats my hand. "Nellie, dearest, you have fled my tirades."

"No, I'm just confused, which isn't an uncommon state of mind for me. I find a connection between the doctor in Bath and Hailey hard to swallow. Bath is what, over a hundred miles from here, two or three hours by train? And while the story about the doctor and the society woman may titillate London society where the names of the people are known, it's not the sort of story that would interest readers on the other side of the Atlantic for long."

"Nellie, as I so adequately put it in my book, the search for beauty is the real secret of life. That said, my dear, this is not just a story about a doctor in Bath and a London society woman, but a story about a doctor who is trying to sell eternal youth, something even you barbaric Americans would find interesting."

Before I can object, he holds up his hand. "As you get older you will understand. In the meantime, if you change your mind I have a friend in Bath, Lady Callista Chilcott, who I'll refer you to if you want to follow up on gossip about the doctor. I know she has been treated for that terrible disease called ugly old age by the doctor."

I shake my head. "I don't think I will be pursuing the story."

"I just rained on your murder theory."

"No, not at all, you merely narrowed down my theories. I don't see a connection between Hailey and the Bath doctor. If Bath and the Fountain of Youth are out, there is still the wealthy man who would kill to hide an affair with an American woman that produces an illegitimate child."

I meet Oscar's eye. "He's out there and I'm going to find him."

I like hearing myself talk. It is one of my greatest pleasures. I often have long conversations all by myself, and I am so clever that sometimes I don't understand a single word of what I am saying.

—Oscar Wilde

17

By the time I leave Oscar I have a headache. Despite his many funny stories and perfectly outrageous observations of people and society in general, the pain in my head comes from my confused state of mind.

After I kiss Oscar good-bye in the French cheek-and-cheek fashion—he spends a great deal of time in Paris—and board a hansom back to my hotel, my thoughts are muddled. I'm basically at a loss as what to do next.

If it wasn't the dead of night I could let the sights of the city occupy my mind, but there is nothing to see after my cab leaves the glittering West End. Everything is dark and shut down, with an occasional gaslight glowing in the mist. The wet city streets are rolled up for the night, so I lean back, shut my eyes, and listen to the *clip-clop* of the hooves on cobblestones and the heavy breathing of the hansom cab driver from his elevated seat above me.

What a day. What a life! I am exhausted, fatigued, ready to drop.

I have hardly stopped running since I broke the madhouse story three years ago. A doctor told me I am suffering from fatigue, "pure exhaustion" is what he labeled it, and said I should slow down, but I never seem to have the time nor the opportunity.

If I let sleeping dogs lie and give up my chase for Hailey's killer—and I have not a clue about her rich man except that he might have blue eyes—I can go home, take some time off, and get the much-needed rest my body craves before deciding what I want to do with my career.

But then I would be deserting Hailey. And everyone would continue believing she killed herself. How can I do this when I'm not convinced that she did? And even if I had absolute proof that she had taken her own life because she was betrayed by her lover, my attitude toward those who harm others is definitely Old Testament—an eye for an eye. The biblical phrase has been called the law of retaliation and even though it is unladylike and lacking in Christian charity, as far as I'm concerned the lover can burn in the hell of public ridicule with his reputation sullied.

Or am I just fooling myself because I desperately want to believe she didn't commit suicide, as Inspector Abberline so adequately told me not once but twice?

Even dear Oscar who loves a good chase said, "Give up the ghost and go home, Nellie."

My cab stops and I open my eyes. Somehow I must have dozed off for it seems like I just left the Langham and now I'm in front of my hotel.

I give the doorman a grave smile as he helps me out. All I want to do is get in bed and forget everything. Maybe sleep will bring answers.

"Rats!" I'm just about to enter the lobby when I realize I didn't tip the doorman. I reach into the pocket of my coat where I keep a small hoard of coins for taxis and pull one out, along with a small scrap of paper.

As I walk across the lobby, I glance down at the piece of paper.

My feet come to a screeching halt.

It's a ticket stub for a train to Bath.

18

*B*ath. *The Waters of Life. Dr. Lacroix and the wealthy noblewoman seeking eternal youth.*

I sit in my room, on my bed, examining the train ticket stub for the umpteenth time. No matter how I look at it, how I read the words and numbers, it is obvious that the ticket is one to Bath—issued the day before Hailey killed herself.

It must have been in the diary and slipped out when I stuck the book in my pocket or as I pulled the book out to put in my purse.

So many stunning pieces to the puzzle have fallen into place that I am quietly contemplative, rather than wildly excited.

No longer do I have the slightest doubt that Hailey, her lover, and the news story are intertwined. I don't know how they relate, but shortly before her death, Hailey had set off for Bath. It may have been just one trip of several to research a story about the death of the baronet's wife.

Now, not by choice, but by necessity I am going to Bath.

It makes no difference that it's after midnight, I make my plans right away and prepare a telegraph for both Oscar and Inspector Abberline, informing them I am going to Bath and requesting their assistance.

Wasting no time, I go down to the telegraph kiosk in the hotel lobby and prepare wires.

In my telegram to Oscar I ask for an introduction to the society matron, Lady Callista Chilcott, who he said has had treatments at the Aqua Vitea spa. I also tell Oscar to tell the woman that I am doing a story about the spa and not to mention Hailey. If she is a patron of the spa, I doubt she would not be cooperative about intentionally revealing a scandal.

From the police inspector I request the name and an introduction to, if he would be so kind, the police official in Bath who is in charge of the death of Lady Winsworth at the spa, wording the request as if I were simply researching a story as opposed to sticking my nose in a police investigation.

The police inspector would not appreciate a knock on his door this late, and I'm sure Oscar will not be in for hours, so my instructions are that the two missives be delivered first thing in the morning with a request that the messenger boy take an immediate reply.

I don't know how people communicated before the telegraph wire revolutionized communications. I can hardly function without it. Getting mail delivered to the office three times a day in New York is simply inadequate, especially since it took days or even weeks to get there! Sending a telegraph across town or around the world, then having a boy rush it by foot or bike to the recipient, the feat often accomplished in less than an hour from almost anywhere, has brought the entire civilized portion of the world into contact.

As I leave the cable kiosk in the hotel lobby I can't help notice, only because of the lateness of night, a man sitting in one of the lobby chairs, with his head buried in a newspaper. Poor fellow, I hope he hasn't been stood up, for he appears to be waiting for someone—dressed in a raincoat, hat, with an umbrella, all ready to leave.

On my way up the elevator back to my room, a chilling thought follows me: What if Hailey was killed because of the story?

Maybe her married lover killed her to stop a scandal that would ruin his reputation. I'm unsure whether he has anything to do with the news story she was working on. Perhaps that was how they met.

Another angle is that Hailey had been killed because of what she found out about the story and her lover had nothing to do with her death.

My head is pounding, so before I leave the lobby I request a glass of hot milk, a cookie, and headache powder be sent to my room. I hate milk, but my mother always insists that it helps put me to sleep. She's right, but I'll still have to force it down as bitter medicine.

As soon as Nellie left the lobby the man with his face in the newspaper gets up and goes to the telegraph kiosk. Taking the pad he had watched Nellie Bly write two telegrams on, he tears off the top sheet.

"Wish to send a wire?" the attendant asks.

"Need to think out what I want to say."

He puts the blank sheet in his pocket to keep it dry and leaves the hotel. Ignoring a waiting taxi, he heads down the street to a pub.

After ordering a pint, he removes the blank sheet and begins to lightly run a lead pencil over the imprints Nellie's messages had left on the paper.

Holding it up to the light, he says to himself, "Let's see what you're up to."

The bartender sets down the pint in front of him.

"Got a problem with your lady?" he asks.

"Pardon?"

The bartender nods at the telegram message the blue-eyed man is trying to read.

"Pal of mine did that once, caught his missus sending off a wire to her lover."

"Ah, yes, yes, quite, very perceptive of you. Yes, I'm checking out where my, uh, friend is off to."

"See anything on the paper?"

"Yes, she's going to Bath."

19

The next morning a discreet tap on my door by a bellman brought replies to my wires.

Nellie dear, I have notified Lady Callista Chilcott of your wish for an audience and she has consented. I told her you are a dear friend of mine and I would appreciate her assisting you in any way possible. If I wasn't in hiding, I would join you. Please keep me posted. I'll be incognito at the hotel that is 95 ft above the Thames. I wish you the best and take caution.

Your loving, devoted friend, Mr. Earnest

An "audience." No doubt the dowager loves Oscar treating her as royalty. But then again, I'd do more than curtsy for information.

I dread opening the inspector's response. I know he's already not happy with my reluctance to accept that Hailey committed suicide. He believes I'm not willing to face the "sad truth" as he calls it and therefore looking to find a reason for murder. I also know he's doesn't like the idea of me interfering with police business.

Chief Inspector John Bradley will be available to answer questions and help you in any way in regards to your research.

Your Faithful Servant, Inspector Abberline

PS: Do I smell something more than a story with your quest?

All right! My soldiers are lined up. It is time to cross the Rubicon.

As I WAIT to board the train to Bath, I can't help staring up at the glazed roof and massive wrought-iron arches of Paddington Station.

"Absolutely amazing . . ." I say to myself.

"Yes, it truly is."

An elderly British gentleman wearing a top hat, a thick, black, wool winter coat, with a white, silk scarf wrapped around his neck, approaches me.

"Please, excuse me." He tips his hat. "I normally don't eavesdrop . . ."

"Oh . . . no . . . it's just that I'm from America and we don't have anything like this."

"Nobody does. It is the first underground railway system in the world and the original western terminus of the Metropolitan Railway."

"Really . . ."

"The roof that you've been admiring is six hundred and ninety-nine feet long and the gigantic arches supporting it span sixty-eight feet."

He looks up at it and I can feel his pride. Can't blame him; it's definitely an incredible feat. He tips his hat and is off to catch a train.

Finally, my train comes. It is midday and the train ride will take about two hours or so to reach Bath.

As soon as we are rolling, I leave my valise on my seat and make my way to the dining car. I had rushed out of the hotel too late to grab a bite.

The dining facilities are pleasant; tables have linen tablecloths, china, polished silverware, and there's even a vase in the center of each table holding a pink carnation.

At the end of the train car is a table for one—perfect for me.

As I make my way toward my table I notice a young gentleman looking down at a newspaper on the table across from the one I am heading for. He sports a mustache that isn't overpowering and light brown hair. I would venture to guess he is in his midtwenties, close to my age.

Something about him is vaguely familiar to me, but I can't place it.

He lifts his head and I inadvertently meet his eyes and get a jolt—*his eyes are blue.*

His countenance is rather grave and stoic but his striking blue eyes almost cause me to miss a step.

I focus straight ahead and take my seat. Quickly grabbing a menu,

I pretend to be absorbed by the sparse offerings while thoughts whip through my brain.

The man with his head buried in a newspaper was in the hotel lobby last night. I couldn't be certain it is the same man, I didn't see his face at the hotel, but the general form of his body . . .

I am dying to take another peek at him and force myself to pretend to just be casually looking around as I turn—*damnit I meet his eye again.*

Embarrassed at being caught, I do what comes natural to me. I attack.

"You were in the hotel lobby last night."

He smiles and shakes his head. *"Ich bin, Fraulein, traurig, aber ich spreche nicht Englisch."* He smiles. "No Ang-lish."

Oh, lord, how embarrassing. I don't speak German but caught the fact he doesn't speak English. Now I am even more embarrassed.

"Sorry." I turn away from him and try to bury my head in the small menu. I'm mortified. He must think that I'm some sort of hussy, approaching him in public. Oh no, did he understand the word "hotel"? Could I have left him with the impression that I—I—

I turn back around to try and get across to him what I meant by speaking about a hotel but he rises and leaves and I close my trap rather than sticking my foot in it again.

How asinine of me. Even if he had been the man I saw at the hotel last night, bumping into him on the train the next morning would be perfectly natural.

I order tea and a roast beef sandwich and sit back with a sigh, a little weary, a little lonely. He had been a reasonably attractive man and appeared intelligent. It would have been nice to wile away the time it took to get to Bath just talking to him about everyday things that didn't include murder and suicide.

However, there had been no romantic interest in his look, not that there should be, but I find it strange and get the feeling in that brief encounter that he was analyzing me, more like a scientist observing something of professional interest rather than as a man looking at a woman he might find attractive. Not a cool dispassionate look, but a probing one.

Maybe he's a scientist. The Germans are so clever about that sort of thing.

My cheeks burn again at the embarrassing notion I might have left him. One thing for certain—I will be happy *never* to see the likes of him again! Not only because of my slip, but thinking about it, I wonder why he didn't at least try to start up a conversation even with the language problem. In other words, what's so wrong with me that the man only looked at me like I am a bug under a microscope?

I know thoughts like that are my inadequacies acting up. I don't think I'm attractive and react poorly when I believe a man doesn't find me attractive. Sort of a lose-lose attitude. Even if a man finds me interesting, as a lady, I am forbidden by convention to show that I am attracted to him. Whoever made up that rule forgot that women have a need for intimacy just as a man does and perhaps, in a less frantic manner, even a greater need.

Am I lonely? Yes. And when women commonly are married by eighteen, I am bordering on being an old maid. It's not that I dislike men—to the contrary, I just haven't found the man I want to share my life with.

And I must say, the rule that women are supposed to marry early and whether or not they want to annoys me. I will marry when I please and if I am old and ugly—uglier than I already am—then I will just have to find a man who loves me for who I am. Of course, shallow as I am, if there really is something that would keep me young, I'd buy that, too.

"*MY VALISE IS GONE!*" blurts out of my mouth when I return to my seat after lunch.

"It's all right, dear, I have it."

A middle-aged woman doing needlework across the aisle nods at the seat beside her feet. She sets down her needlework and hands the valise to me.

"I'm afraid I may have stuck my nose in your business. I saw a man eyeing it a while ago and I took the precaution of safeguarding it. I'm sure I was just being silly, but I hoped you wouldn't be offended."

"No, not at all. I really do appreciate it."

"It's my pleasure, Miss . . ."

"Cochran, Elizabeth Cochran." I decide to use my real name.*

"Nice to meet you Elizabeth, I'm Mrs. Lambert."

*Elizabeth Jane Cochran was Nellie's real name. Because newspaper reporting was not considered a respectable job for a woman, her editor chose "Nellie Bly" from a Stephen Foster song, "Nelly Bly." Nellie's grammar and spelling were "rocky" and she spelled it "Nellie."—The Editors

Mrs. Lambert is a frumpish forty, wearing widow's black from head to toe. Rather stout with wide shoulders, she looks capable of thrashing a thief, especially with those crochet needles, they look lethal.

"Nice to meet you. And thank you for aiding me. Could you tell me what he looked like?"

"Not like a mugger, for certain. Rather a pleasant chap with striking blue eyes, looked like a clerk or a teacher, perhaps, but you never know, do you, my dear? Trouble can come from the most unexpected directions."

"If that isn't the truth." Blue eyes, huh. "Did he by chance have a German accent?"

"An accent? Why, I don't know, he never spoke. Are you expecting someone with a German accent?"

"No, just a shot in the dark." On that I hit the bull's-eye, I'm sure.

"So, my dear, what brings you across the ocean? You are American, right?"

"Yes . . ." I hesitate for a moment. For once, my liquid tongue is dry.

"Is everything all right?"

"Yes. Just, uh, tired."

"You do look worried. I'm a great listener, what's bothering you, my dear?"

I don't know if it's her kind voice or just that she reminds me of my mother, only younger, but I start talking. I tell her how I'm a reporter, which she can't get over and says more than once, "I'm so impressed. What an accomplishment for such a young lady!" and about Hailey—not everything, just tidbits here and there. She's very sympathetic. I must admit it feels good to speak to another woman.

"So, why are you going to Bath?"

"I'm just tracing Hailey's steps, and, I believe, she was investigating the Aqua Vitae spa and a Dr. Lacroix—something to do with the death of a Lady Winsworth."

"Oh my!" Mrs. Lambert puts her hand to her chest.

"Are you okay?"

"Oh yes, yes, I'm sorry. I didn't mean to startle you, but it's just that my sister, bless her heart, insisted I get out of the house. My dear husband of twenty-one years, bless his soul, passed away ten months ago and well . . . I've kind of become a recluse. She has been dying to go to *that* fancy spa, so I'm her reason to go. Are we going to be okay, because now that you mention it I remember reading something about that poor lady and how the police are investigating it, but they aren't certain if the spa has anything to do with her death. Silly me, I just didn't put two and two together."

"I don't know that the spa actually has a connection to her death." I lean over and pat her hand. "You and your sister will be fine."

"Well, according to my sister it is the most desirable spa in Europe. Very wealthy and notable people from all over the world come to it, so that has to count for something, wouldn't you think?"

"Of course."

She laughs and shakes her head. "My dear sister says this place will do miracles for me, I just hope it doesn't do me under."

So do I.

"So tell me more about this mysterious venture you're on," she says with such delight.

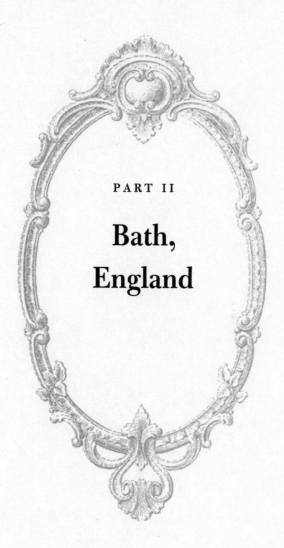

PART II

Bath,
England

But whoever drinks the water I give him will never thirst. Indeed, the water I give him will become in him a spring of water welling up to eternal life.

—JOHN 4:14

20

Bath, England

The Aqua Vitae spa sits on a slope at a higher level than the Roman ruins.

The ruins are what is left of a spa built nearly two thousand years ago when the town was called Aquae Sulis and the region was the Roman province of Britannia. Mrs. Lambert told me on the train that the baths are still in use, but the moneyed crowd naturally frequented luxurious private spas like that of Dr. Lacroix's.

I have the cabbie drop me off at the ancient ruins and I walk slowly up to the spa, gathering my thoughts. I can't barge in and ask the first person I meet if the doctor in charge is involved in the death of Hailey McGuire.

Not able to think of a clever approach to getting information, I do what I always do when I am in doubt: force myself to put one foot in front of the other and go forward and play it by ear.

The spa has the appearance of a Greek or Roman temple with Doric columns. The entire structure, or at least the façade, for sure, is marble, a building material that always translates as very expensive.

As I am nearing the building, an enclosed black town coach, fit for a queen, with a driver and footman, drawn by two black stallions, pulls up and stops. Deep, velvet burgundy window curtains hide whoever is inside, which obviously piques my always nosey interest.

The footman leaps down from his perch at the rear of the coach and opens the carriage door as the spa doorman comes forward with a parasol to shade the woman from the not very bright sun. The carriage door bears a coat of arms but even at a distance I can see that it has been discreetly covered over.

The woman who emerges from the carriage is dressed all in black—elegant black silk dress, black hat and veil, black gloves, and a small, black beaded chatelaine purse.

I wonder what she has in the purse attached to a waist belt. Chatelaines were originally a chain with necessary household items attached. Women hooked them on their belts and put keys, scissors, or other handy items on them.

According to *The Queen's* magazine, chatelaine purses have become a ladies' fashion item in which women carry not just a handkerchief, lipstick, or a card case, but secret things—like love letters they don't want out of their possession.

The doorman, whom I'm glad to see is dressed in a uniform rather than a Roman toga, escorts her inside.

From what Oscar told me about the spa, the woman could be visiting for medicinal reasons or rejuvenation. Whatever they are, she definitely doesn't want anyone to know who she is. Everything about her spells immense wealth and nobility, perhaps even royalty. And drama. To really be successful at maintaining a low profile, riding in a luxurious coach with its coat of arms would not be the best way. Oscar's comment about hiding in plain sight probably would protect the woman more from the eyes of the curious than a funeral getup.

The carriage has drawn away as I approach and the doorman gives me a once-over. He is obviously not used to women arriving on foot. I resist the temptation to tell him that my only mode of transportation is by shank's mare and merely give him a small smile.

He ushers me in and I quickly glance around to see if the mystery lady is about. Nope. She probably was immediately whisked off to some very private room.

My first impression of the Aqua Vitae spa is grace and serenity.

The entryway opens into a large, glass domed area. The walls are covered with murals. Scattered against the walls between the wall paintings are large-leaf green plants—tropical palms and ferns. Intermeshed in the greenery are exotically colored flowering plants in elegant Chinese ceramic pots. The atmosphere evokes a feeling of beauty mixed with earthiness.

All the murals have the same theme: young, healthy men and women, naked but portrayed with some modesty, in a Garden of Eden setting. Appropriate, since that is where it all began . . . or so the Bible says.

A string quartet dressed in white are on an elevated dais at the far end of the room, filling the place with a soft, dreamy melody.

In the center of the room is a marble fountain with Aphrodite and Michelangelo's *David* getting wet from water gurgling out of jugs held by stone cupids. The water is not crystal clear, but appropriately has the look and warm, salty smell of mineral spring water, no doubt from the spring the spa sits upon. The message the room gives is clear enough: The spa's waters make people look beautiful and stay young.

A vibrant blond woman in a glowing white uniform, with her hair pulled tightly back into a bun, approaches me. The impression is that of an elegant but energetic nurse.

"Good afternoon. I am Miss Carter, a therapeutic consultant. Have you treated with our doctors before?"

"No, this is my first visit. Your facility was recommended by a friend in London."

"Excellent. May we have the friend's name so we can thank her?"

She wants the friend's name to rate my finances, of course. "It's a he, actually. Oscar Wilde."

"Mr. Wilde hasn't treated with us, but many of the people in his social circles are our patients. You're American. Miss . . ."

"Elizabeth Cochran."

"Welcome, Miss Cochran. Many Americans come for our treatments." She rattles off family names that read like a list of who's who in big bank accounts—Vanderbilt, Rockefeller, Gould, all of whom she says have come to Aqua Vitae to "take the water cure."

I've heard people many times refer to visiting mineral springs to "take the water cure" but when you ask what they were "curing," the only responses I ever found credible were arthritic complaints.

Knowing from the lack of a wedding ring on my finger that I am not married, she inquires about the "health" of my parents in a clever way to find out what my father does for a living. Heaven forbid I actually make enough money working to pay for this myself. Once I'm done with solving Hailey's murder, I'm going to do an article about independent women who can stand on their own two feet without the assistance of their father's wealth or the need of a husband. I know we are far and few between, but things will change, mark my words.

To appease her, I casually refer to "mining and railroads" since those are the basis for most of the great wealth in America.

"Are you suffering from a particular ailment for which you seek treatment?" she asks.

Too young to claim I need to shed years, I resort to the truth. "I'm rather worn out, fatigued. My mother describes my condition as tired blood."

"Your mother is quite correct. Tired blood is a serious epidemic among young women as they try to please both their parents and the man in their life. And very important, it affects your ability to keep a youthful appearance. Let me introduce you to our medical facility that is administered by doctors."

Doctors, medical facility, therapeutic, ailment, treatment, epidemic . . . she has been dropping loaded references to the legitimate medical profession since the moment I entered. I guess she really wants to get across that they are not just selling any kind of snake oil, but curatives with real medical science behind them. Uh huh.

I give them credit for one thing: The place is so antiseptic, Dr. Pasteur, the great microbe hunter, would have a hard time finding germs here.

"This is our reception area in which you may relax until you are called for a treatment." She shows me an area with dark blue couches. A maid is serving fruit drinks and offering hors d'oeuvres to women. "We alternate times for women and men for the sake of modesty, though there are spas in Europe which permit bathing by both sexes at the same time."

"As I was arriving, I saw a woman enter dressed all in black. I wondered if she was a woman I met recently in London."

"I can't tell you. It's our policy to respect the privacy of our guests."

I'm tempted to remind her that she had no problem tossing out the names of prominent people from America, but I keep my mouth shut.

We enter a sterile white padded room that has a wicker chaise longue in the center and one metal chair to its far right. Across from them, in a corner, is a table with some medical looking items on it and on the floor is a large water hose.

"This room is exclusive, just for women. It's called our fainting room."

"Fainting room?"

"Yes. For centuries women have been suffering from a very common ailment called Female Hysteria. Our spa is the first to offer a full line of treatment for this painful medical condition."*

---

*Galen, a prominent physician from the second century, wrote that the hysteria was a disease caused by sexual deprivation, particularly affecting passionate women: Hysteria was

"What are the symptoms?"

"They vary, but the most common are nervous anxiety, a tendency to feel faint, irritation, a feeling of loneliness and rejection, and a tendency to be argumentative." She pauses and gives me a dark look. "There is often also incidences of self-abuse."

I nod my head. "Ah." Self-abuse is masturbation, a habit that many in the medical profession believe can lead to insanity or other dire consequences.

There didn't seem to be much medical apparatus in the room, the two most distinguishable items being a long tube about as round as a fire hose and the wicker chaise longue.

"How do you treat the condition?"

"Our most common treatment is having a woman recline on the chaise longue while the doctor or a midwife hand massages her pelvic area until she experiences hysterical paroxysm, which is usually a sudden outburst that can be very loud and sometimes violent. That's why we have the walls padded. We strive for privacy."

"Privacy . . . yes, that would be important." Holy mackerel. Hysterical paroxysm is what naughty girls in school used to whisper is a female orgasm.

"We also have the hydrotherapy treatment for women who prefer that method. A woman sits naked in that chair and her pelvic area is sprayed with that hose."

"*What!*"

The woman's eyebrows fly up. "It's quite safe. We use only our warm mineral water. For many it is very effective in bringing about the paroxysm."

"I bet it is."

She points to a large machine against the wall. "We also have the newest medical apparatus for treating the condition. This is an electric vibrator which shortens the treatment from hours to minutes. And that," she indicates a narrow metal rod with a rounded head, "is a speculum that is inserted into a woman's vagina to stimulate the paroxysm."

She smiles, rather dreamily. "Our goal is to give the patients different choices to aid them in finding a release of their symptom by experiencing hysterical paroxysm."

---

noted quite often in virgins, nuns, widows, and occasionally, married women. The prescription in medieval and renaissance medicine was intercourse if married, marriage if single, or vaginal massage (pelvic massage) by a midwife as a last recourse.—The Editors

I just nod my head.

For once in my life, I honestly have nothing to say. I don't know whether I should break out laughing or cry because so many women get so little of the passionate affection God created them to receive that they have to enlist huge vibrating machines, or a fire hose, or manual manipulation for relief.

INSIDE THE ROMAN BATH

21

We leave the feminine chamber of horrors.

"Now I'm going to take you into a room called, the Garden of Eden, because that is where it all began—life, love, eternal youth. However, I must insist on no talking. You'll see why."

We enter a room that has a round, stone fountain in the center of it. It's medieval looking with crudely carved stone images of the Garden of Eden—a naked man and woman wearing fig leaves and a snake hanging from an apple tree. In the center of the pool of water is one spout with milky water coming out of it.

Scattered around the fountain are lounge chairs, like the one in the "fainting room," only they are made of wrought iron and the people appear to be sleeping—no hanky-panky is going on in here. Beside each chair is a small round, stone pedestal table. On each one is a golden goblet. Filled, I'm sure, with water from the fountain. The floor is made of stones and on the walls are trestles filled with vines that have mingled with purple bell-like flowers.

Two barefooted women dressed in white silk tunics walk around holding a stone pitcher. They check the goblets and fill the ones that need the milky water.

The whole ambience is to make you feel like you have walked into a serene atmosphere where you can completely relax. And I'd have to say they did a very good job.

We quietly exit another door that is across the room from the one we entered.

"What you just saw is our fountain that dispenses the elixir of life, the waters of eternal life and rejuvenation. Ponce de Leon looked for the

Fountain of Youth and didn't realize it could be created. Our doctors have developed a very unique drink that is pure yet filled with ingredients that have rejuvenating powers."

"So, you've found the philosopher's stone . . . the legendary drink that grants eternal life."

"No, our drink won't permit you to live forever, but it will certainly help you live longer and better. And it does aid in getting back youthful vigor. With that renewed energy, our patients rediscover some of the blush of youth they once had."

Splitting hairs, is what my mother would call it. Not to mention that with vague generalities about "vigor" they are really not committing to anything. I decide to try and pin her down.

"Basically, your doctors are chemists who claim to have developed a potion for helping to achieve youth."

"They are not chemists, they are medical doctors, and they are *not claiming*." She almost spits her words at me. "Miss Cochran, you have a *very* closed mind. Have you considered that you might be suffering from female hysteria instead of tired blood?"

"*What?*"

"I noticed the symptoms as soon as I saw you. You are tense and holding back your emotions. That, of course, inevitably leads to outbursts of hysteria that are relieved by paroxysm."

I button my lips because I am about to have a paroxysm that will land her on the floor and me out the door. But keeping a volcanic outburst from exploding leaves me trembling with rage in my shoes. "What a bitch," my friend Sarah Bernhardt would have said about this woman or probably to her face.

"Don't worry, Miss Cochran, we have everything that is needed to make you well and a whole woman again. We have a facility that is perfect for you at this moment. It's a place to relax in a pool of our mineral water, to wash away some of the tensions of life, something you desperately need."

That, I couldn't agree with her more. If I don't release some tension soon, I will lose control of my hands and they will find their way to her neck and throttle her.

She proceeds to take me to a pump room, where the spring waters gurgle into a marble pool.

"Here the waters are divided, with some diverted for internal use and the rest for our bathing treatments."

She gives me a sample of the mineral water, which tastes like it smells. I wrinkle my nose. "Why does medicine always have to taste awful to be good for you?"

"The water comes from the deep bowels of the earth, bringing forth the healing powers of Mother Nature herself. These are ancient waters—Celtic priests experienced the curative effects of the springs long before the Romans."

She then takes me into a small room that is hot and wet and just plain stinks.

"Unlike most spas that crowd people into a single pool, we have a bath and pool for every guest."

The "bath" is a pit of mud about the size of a bathtub and the "pool" is spring water in a basin about twice that big.

"Not mud," she corrects me when I comment on how bad the bath smells, "this is peat moss from bogs in Dartmoor that are older than recorded history. It is one of the trade secrets that make Aqua Vitae the premier curative spa in the world."

"The peat moss I've seen in bogs, marshes, and swamps don't look very healthy to me. Or smell that way. What does peat moss do for you?"

"The substance we use is not what you see on the surface, but the decayed, organic sphagnum materials beneath. I'm sure you know that animals and humans who fell into peat bogs thousands of years ago have been recovered with flesh and bone perfectly preserved. Can you imagine that? Buried in a bog for thousands of years and their features unaltered!"

"Haraldskaer Woman," I say, recalling a story a fellow reporter had done on the subject. "People believe she was a queen of the Danes who was killed over two thousand years ago. Murdered, buried naked, her clothes laid atop her."

The "therapeutic consultant" appears a bit taken back at my connecting murder with curative waters.

I give her a smile. "And you're right. She was well preserved."

"Quite. Well, as I was saying, the fact that peat moss preserves flesh and bone in a natural state is one of the secrets discovered by our medical staff."

"Was it Dr. Lacroix who made the discovery?"

"Oh, no, although Dr. Lacroix has greatly improved the process, he now takes a different approach. The curative and rejuvenation powers of peat moss were first discovered by Dr. Radic, the managing director of Aqua Vitae, when he was a physician in Romania."

"What is Dr. Lacroix's approach?"

"I'm afraid I'm not at liberty to discuss that with you. Dr. Radic will examine you and set out a course of treatment to restore your damaged health before it is too late and your condition becomes irreversible."

"My friend referred me to Dr. Lacroix. I'd prefer to see him."

"As I said, Dr. Lacroix is not available."

"When will he be available?"

"He—I don't know, he's vacationing—researching—on the continent. It's time for you to see Dr. Radic."

I hoped I hadn't pushed her too far this time. She is really flustered and annoyed. Her pretense at friendliness has gone and her guard is up. I keep my mouth shut as I follow her into a sitting room.

"Please have a seat. Dr. Radic will be with you shortly," she says curtly.

I take a seat next to the door she disappears through with my back to the wall. Antsy, I get up and pace the room back and forth. To my surprise I see, out the window, the lady in black getting into her carriage. I wonder what type of treatment she was in for, it couldn't have been much of one. I also notice she is no longer carrying her chatelaine purse with her.

"That's odd . . ."

"What's odd?" Miss Carter startles me from behind.

"Ah . . . nothing."

"The doctor will be with you shortly," she politely tells me, but with a rigid body, then leaves for the main area.

The door into the doctor's office has not quite clicked shut behind her. I hear voices and give a quick look around to make sure I am not being watched and then give the door a nudge so it opens a foot wider and bend my ear in the direction of the voices.

A woman is sobbing and speaks in a drunken slur. "I want to see my little Emma."

"You know your child died from brain fever," comes from a male voice, spoken in English with a heavy Balkan accent. Dr. Radic, I presume; the discoverer of the miracle peat moss treatment in Romania.

"But she was a healthy child," the woman slurs.

"On the surface, but brain fever strikes fast."

I have never understood what "brain fever" is. One hears it frequently as a cause of illness and death and I abide by my wise mother's definition

A VIEW OF BATH, ENGLAND

of the ailment, "It's what people die of when the doctor can't find the real reason."

"Here, get some nourishment," I hear the doctor say. I don't know what he gave her, but from her mumbled thanks and the fact the woman sounds drunk, I suspect he's giving her money that will be spent in a gin mill rather than at a grocer.

"Take her out the back way," the Balkan voice says.

I lean back and freeze in place as the door opens and a tearful woman comes out with a man behind her.

"This way, Sarah." The man grabs the woman by the elbow and diverts her to a door to my left, as he glances back at me.

Two things are obvious: Sarah is a gin hag and most likely a prostitute on her last days earning a living on her back before she gives up the ghost facedown in a gutter.

The man with her is a ruffian; the kind found hanging around saloons acting as bouncers when they're not mugging drunks in an alley. He has an unusual item of dress for a Brit—pointed-toe cowboy boots.

Neither the woman nor the ruffian are the types one would expect to find at a health spa servicing the rich.

A tall, thin man with narrow, hawklike features and black, piercing eyes enters from the room I had been eavesdropping upon.

I stand up and offer him my hand to shake, an unexpected movement that almost always throws men off their guard.

"Elizabeth Cochran."

"I'm going to have you arrested for trespassing," he says.

22

You have entered my premises under a fake name and false pretenses," the man with the Balkan accent says, who I assume is Dr. Radic. "You will find to your regret that our premises are held in high regard by the local police."

The saloon ruffian pops back in. "Need some help here, Dr. Radic?"

"Hold this woman for the police," Dr. Radic says. He turns back to me. "You can explain your actions to the police."

"I shall be happy to talk to the police, Dr. Radic. In fact, Inspector Abberline of Scotland Yard knows I am here and I'm meeting with Chief Inspector Bradley when I leave here."

I look him squarely in the face. "As soon as I am through reporting the sexual activities taking place here to the police, I shall get out the story to every newspaper in Bath and London."

"There are no sexual activities on the premises. What you observed are standard medical procedures."

"What I observed was revolting sexual stimulation and tortures that when exposed will not only make you a laughingstock but prompt police action." I lock eyes with him. "If you know my name, Doctor, you must know my success at exposing the dirty laundry of medical practitioners."

I go around him, heading for the door when the thug starts toward me.

"*Stop!*" I snap.

He freezes.

"Come one step closer to me and I will give out the most horrendous bloodcurdling screams that you have ever heard. Would you like that, Dr. Radic? Perhaps some cries of rape and murder?"

Radic waves the man back. "It's okay, Burke, I'll take care of this."

The man gives me a dirty look as he backs off and goes through the door that he had entered from.

Radic faces me. I can see from his expression that he isn't intimidated by my threats. Rather, my impression is that of a man of expediency—battling me on his public premises just isn't advantageous.

"Get out of my sight and don't come back. Stick your nose in my business and I won't be able to guarantee your safety."

"Obviously, I wouldn't be the first woman who came to a sudden end dealing with this place. Did Lady Winsworth cross you, too?"

I flee, taking my big mouth with me, running as fast as my short legs and small feet will take me. I had expected I might be caught and it wouldn't be the first time I'd had a run-in with a charlatan like Dr. Radic, if he is in fact a doctor, but it isn't often I find myself having to verbally fight my way out of an upper-class establishment with a threat from a saloon lout—after encountering a poor, bedeviled, street gin hag.

The Waters of Life have some strange bedfellows, that is for sure.

My feet are moving quickly, not only because I want to get far away before I end up preserved in peat moss, but because I want to have a talk with Sarah.

What in heaven's name could the gin hag, her daughter, and Dr. Radic have to do with each other? The woman obviously couldn't have hired Radic to treat her child, nor did Radic strike me as a charitable soul who would take in mudlarks and let them freely partake in the curative waters that the rich pay so dearly to quaff down.

My gut is screaming that something stinks in Denmark and it's not just the smell of bog mud.

The art of ignoring is one of the accomplishments of every well-bred girl, so carefully instilled that at last she can even ignore her own thoughts and her own knowledge.

—H. G. WELLS, *Ann Veronica*

23

Herbert George Wells, Bertie to his family, H. G. to others, stands in the sheltered doorway of a closed shop and watches as the American newspaper reporter comes out of the spa. He finds it curious that she seems to be rushing out, instead of just walking at a normal pace.

He knows who she is, knew who she was when he stared at her on the train trying to dissect her and understand her with his probing blue eyes, almost succumbing to the temptation of stealing her valise. He would have stolen the valise if the nosey woman on the train had not scared him off.

She continues to walk fast, as if she is hurrying somewhere—no, he changes his mind as he watches her glance around: She's looking for someone.

She goes up the street to the corner and disappears around it. He doesn't know where she is heading, but he had already looked over that area and knows that there is a dead end alley there, a fact she will soon discover. He stays where he is because he doesn't want her bumping into him when she is retreating.

Wells is impressed with many things about her, especially her vibrancy. He senses that like himself, Nellie Bly is not a particularly happy person. He finds that puzzling since the young woman has climbed to career heights in such a short time. There are not many men, and few if any women, who have succeeded like she has.

He himself viewed life as a challenge and attacked it as a mountain climber would a high peak. But the concentration, the battle to succeed, was a trying one for someone from the lower classes in a class-conscious society.

He knows that people close to him often call him an angry young man and they are right. Much of his distemper comes from the fact that he is not satisfied with the way his life has gone or is going, which is a terrible quality he acquired from his mother, Sarah. She has never been satisfied with her life and constantly says, "I dread my time so much . . ."

He knows his mother will die unhappy and fears he will, too. She has always desired desperately to rise above being a domestic servant. She despises that she is of the lower classes and calls it a curse. The last time he talked to her she told him she wishes God would soon release her.

The memories of much of his childhood are not of the wondrous things most children experience, but of discord. They were a poor family and often went hungry. "A miserable half living," is what his mother called it. He was born in a house off High Street of Bromley, in Kent which is outside of London, and lived there with his three brothers until he was a teenager. Even though the home, which was also his parents' shop, was called the "Atlas House," it was an unpromising place to make a start in life, according to his mother. It had two tiny rooms, a front room and back room on each of its three floors. The only source of heat in the house was the kitchen stove located in the ill-lit basement.

His mother believes unconditionally in an all-powerful God, a simple God, which she continually tried to push upon her children when they were growing up. Religion has always been the dominant force in her life, rather than his father, Joseph. Religion was one of the wedges he believes tore them apart, besides his father's lack of ambition.

She constantly told Wells and his brothers that they must strive to be "Upstairs persons" instead of "Downstairs persons," which she labels herself. "It is my awful fate in life to be in the servitude position of life, both in work and marriage."

Today, she is still a lady's maid at Uppark, in a country house in Sussex.

His father, who is an "outdoor person" in domestic parlance and a freethinker, remains a gardener and sometimes amateur cricket player who never fit in well in anywhere except in front of a pint of ale at the local pub. His mother will never forgive him for losing the small crockery shop they acquired after receiving a small inheritance. And now they are no longer one, but two people living apart separated by anger, frustration, disappointment, and lost dreams.

Where is her simple God now? Wells wonders. As far as he is concerned, her God cannot be trusted. He's "the old sneak."

Wells has to think hard to remember happy moments in his childhood. He believes the sadness that would come to affect him began two years before he was born. His parents lost their only daughter, Frances; she was nine years old and the pride of Sarah.

From birth, his mother believed "little Bertie"—he hates that she calls him that even to this day—was born into "everlasting perdition" on account of their sins—the sins that took away their daughter.

In time, his parents were no longer able to support the family financially and Sarah, the logical, staunch Protestant, sought to place her boys as apprentices, while his father continued floating through life.

Being his mother's wish, Wells was apprenticed to a drapery maker when he was thirteen—and again at fifteen—failing both times. The draper said he was a daydreamer, and he still is. The last time he arrived at Uppark, he announced to his mother that "the bad shilling's back again!" She fears he will never amount to anything and be like his father, a failure and a freethinker.

He finally got a scholarship to the Normal School—a place where teachers are trained—and he studied to be a teaching assistant, not a very prestigious or well-paying profession, but at least he didn't spend his waking hours measuring, cutting, and sewing drapery materials; something his mother was very proud that her older sons accomplished.

"They now have a place in life," Sarah continually reminds him.

Wells realizes that his calling to education and science resulted from a broken leg as a child that made him bed bound for a long period during which he read books that his father obtained from the library.

Reading became his only solace. He'd read every book he could get his hands on so he could escape into a world of endless possibilities. The books had not just been an escape to magic lands for him—not seeing around him anyone he would want to emulate in life, he had found that the characters in books were people he could relate to and aspire to be like.

Books shaped his aspirations to do something other than working with his hands, and his ideals about love and the pursuit of happiness. He dared to dream and it was his freethinking father who lugged the books back and forth from the library for him. His mother might have good reason to have lost love with his father, but for Wells, he will always remember him fondly for bringing the books.

It is because of his ideals about "love" that Wells is now on the street in Bath following an American reporter, as she attempts to make sense out of the death of a friend.

The woman comes out of the dead end alley and he follows behind as she keeps up a fast pace.

He's impressed. She has energy and determination, qualities he likes and admires in a woman. When she stared fearlessly back at him on the train, challenging him, he realized that she is not your everyday lady—things could get interesting.

She pauses in front of a less than respectable pub, stares at the door for a moment, and then completely surprises him—she goes inside!

This woman is bold or just plain stupid.

A few minutes pass and he's wondering if he shouldn't go in and rescue her when she comes back outside steering a woman alongside her who is obviously a prostitute, to a bench.

Wells is surprised, but not because he's a moralist. To the contrary, he sees nothing wrong with prostitution. In fact, the profession should be regulated and controlled for the sake of both the prostitutes and the men they service, not to mention the poor wives who suffer medically from their indiscretions.

But the unfortunate prostitute with the American reporter is not far from her last swig of the gin she drinks to kill the pain, and she's probably no more than thirty, but looks like a badly used woman twice that age.

They sit down and start talking.

What in God's name does a poor saturated gin creature have to tell Nellie Bly?

24

The woman comes out of the pub with me only because I showed her a quid, told her I needed to talk to her about little Emma, took her by the arm, and steered her out the door and into the sunlight.

We face each other and I am saddened by what I see as I look into her eyes. The wrinkles on her young-old face are scars of life, her hair is dirty and straggly, her clothes appear not just slept in but *lived in,* but it's her glassy eyes that seem to come in and out of focus that tear at my heart. One moment her eyes clear to expose her damaged soul, the next they cloud over with gin. There is no fire in her, little remnant of the animal cunning that has kept her alive on the streets. Her life is quickly burning down, like a fire no longer fueled or stroked.

"What do you want?"

"I'm from the Women's Children's Charity," rolls off my liquid tongue. "We want to talk to you about Emma."

"Emma isn't here right now."

She starts to tear up. I suspect that whatever terrible life this poor woman has had got worse when she lost her daughter. As horrible as a life on the streets would have been for the child, she probably was the one thing that kept her mother functioning. She appears completely lost now and hopefully will find eternal peace before she suffers too much more. She is so far gone, nothing can be done for her—even the money I am going to give her will only help lessen the pain while hastening the end. Giving more will most likely make her a victim of a robbery and a beating—or worse.

"Emma passed away," I whisper, as gently as I can.

"Emma's gone . . . she's gone."

"What happened to Emma?"

"Brain fever."

"Yes, Dr. Radic told me that. Emma was sick when you took her to him to be treated."

"Oh, no, Emma was never sick. She was amazing, even Dr. Radic said so. Other children got sick but not Emma. He said she was the healthiest child he'd ever seen."

"Then why was Dr. Radic treating her for brain fever?"

"I don't know, I just don't know. She went to stay at the spa for a day and they paid me again and told me they were keeping her overnight. I came to pick her up the next day and they said she had to stay 'cause she had a fever."

"She had no fever before you took her over?"

"Emma was never sick."

"How long did they keep her before she, uh, passed—"

"They told me that the brain fever had taken her the previous night when I came to pick her up. She was dead, my sweet baby was pale like a ghost, sleeping and I couldn't wake her up."

"Did they tell you what caused her condition?"

"They said children die all the time from fevers."

That is true, but they usually don't have an illness that goes from perfectly healthy to terminal overnight.

"If Emma wasn't sick," I ask, "when you took her to the spa, what was the reason for her being treated there?"

"My baby wasn't being treated, she was helping others."

"Come again?"

"The doctor said she was so young and healthy, that she could help sick old people get well."

"How did she help sick people get well?"

"She was a good girl."

"But what exactly did she do to help the sick?"

"She was healthy. The doctor said she was young and healthy and could help."

"Was it Dr. Lacroix or Dr. Radic who told you Emma could help others?"

"The younger one. Dr. Lacroix."

Her eyes are clouding over. She appears not to have any notion of what went on at the spa. And neither do I. A child goes in . . . for what? And is dead the next morning.

Could something macabre or satanic have occurred? Or is it a medical treatment that went radically wrong? Just as another one did.

"Have you ever heard of Lady Winsworth?" I ask Sarah.

She shakes her head.

"Did Lacroix say anything about little Emma helping a particular person?"

Another shake.

She looks as if she is having difficulty focusing and I am feeling a bit queasy myself. Talking to a street woman about the mysterious fate of a small child is getting me nauseated. I need to get away from her and try to make some sense of what she told me.

I pay her and flee as fast as my feet can take me, my head once again swirling with facts that don't add up and information that I can't digest.

What in God's name could Dr. Lacroix and Dr. Radic and their snake oil salespeople have been doing at the fashionable spa with a small child? Did they have her sit next to old people in hopes that the sight of her would make them younger—a macabre thought no doubt generated in my head by Oscar's tale of a painting that grew old while its subject stayed young?

Did they have her bathe in the spring waters so some youthful essence washed off her and into the waters others bathed in—or drank?

All the scenarios I could think of sound bizarre, but I remind myself that the health claims of the spa are pretty fantastic.

I wish Oscar was here to help me. He has an incredible mind and in matters of beauty and what people would do, well, he might have some ideas. Maybe I'll telegram him my findings.

First I need to eat to help settle my stomach.

I find a pub that serves pasties, a favorite of mine—they're meat and potato pies used by Cornish miners as a compact, handheld meal. The miners brought them to American mining towns. The pasty and hot tea work perfectly. The food not only settles my stomach, but the baked smell of the meat, potatoes, and dough brings nice memories that help wash away the pain in Sarah's face.

Something my mother always says when she sees someone who has suffered the bad life of this world comes to mind: There, but for the grace of God, go any of us.

Checking back at my hotel, there are telegrams from both Chief Inspector Bradley and Lady Chilcott—both will see me.

Good. As Oscar's friend Arthur Conan Doyle would say, "The game's afoot."

25

Chief Inspector Bradley is about forty, younger than Inspector Abberline; also thinner and taller, with bushy prematurely gray hair retreating from the front of his head. He has a solid, almost stern cast to his features while Abberline has a little room for humor in his.

Stiff upper lip type, that very British exercise of self-restraint in the expression of emotion, is how I peg him.

His office is small, not a cubbyhole because he is a chief inspector, but it shows few personal effects. His desk is a library table heaped high with stacks of papers with chairs drawn up to it.

I imagine his officers gather around his desk to discuss cases. There are ashtrays the size of plates scattered about and I would bet I'd spot a spittoon or two if I took a peek under the table.

"Have a good trip across the pond?" he asks as he leans back in his swivel chair and prepares a pipe.

From the look he is giving me I suspect that preparing a pipe helps him kill time as he sizes me up.

"Atlantic storm put me at the rail a good bit of the way. I love the sea but hate the way it bounces great ships around with me on them like they were toys."

He chuckles and eyes me as he sends up a cloud of aromatic pipe tobacco smoke that has a hint of blackberry.

I know this will not be as comfortable as dealing with Inspector Abberline. The look I am getting from the chief inspector is one of caution. Bath is a small community compared to London and has an overabundance of the wealthy and titled, drawn here because of the spas. That no doubt draws considerably more attention on the police than in a large metropolitan area.

"Never cared for the sea myself." Another cloud of smoke and then he moves his first piece in the game of policeman versus reporter. "Doing a story on the death of Lady Winsworth?" he asks.

"Actually, I'm doing a story on the spa and the marvelous cures they claim, but yes, it would be hard to do a story about the facility and not mention that someone died from the treatment."

"Now, there's no evidence of that. The coroner's investigation is still open as to the cause of death. We still have other avenues to investigate before a verdict will be rendered."

"I guess I was misinformed. My understanding is that her ladyship died after receiving treatment at the spa."

"There's no question she drank some of those concoctions they charge an arm and a leg for at the place, but so have hundreds of other people. And still do. First thing the medical examiner did was look for poison and he found none."

"What did she die of?"

"Now, that's a question that falls in the bailiwick of the medical examiner and his boss, the coroner. But I can tell you this—they just don't know yet. Could be something she ate or drank, but as I said, she consumed what others did."

"What does Dr. Lacroix say happened?"

"Now, Miss, you do know the questions to ask that I don't have answers for. The doctor left for the continent soon after Lady Winsworth died and we haven't been able to talk to him."

"Rather convenient?"

He shrugs. "To some it plays that way, but we were shown proof that the trip was planned well before her ladyship passed. We have questioned Lacroix's partner, Dr. Radic, and he gave a list of what she had ingested. Basically the same as everyone else." He eyed me some more through the smoke. "You understand that this matter is being given very special attention, not ignored."

I nod. "Lord Winsworth is a very important man."

"Quite so, but there are also plenty of other high-muckety-mucks who swear by the spa and believe what they drink and bathe in there relieves their aching old bones or will turn them young and beautiful again."

"Which means from the standpoint of the coroner's office, it's a hot

potato and no decision will be made until the medical examiner is absolutely certain."

More blank stares through the smoke screen tell me that I have gotten
all I am going to get from him about the death of the woman, so I change
tacks.

I ask, "Is it possible to see the coroner's report on the death of a child
at the spa, a little girl named Emma? I don't know the last name."

"Another customer died at the spa?"

"She wasn't a customer. She had apparently been used at the spa for
some reason, her youthfulness rubbing off on people, maybe, I'm not exactly certain. Her mother is an, uh, underprivileged woman."

"Meaning a prostitute, I take it. How did the child's youthfulness rub
off on people?"

"It's a puzzle to me, but that's what I was told by the mother. Dr.
Radic told her that the child died of brain fever while at the spa."

"She received medical attention before she passed?"

"Yes, I suppose—"

"Then there wouldn't be a coroner's inquiry or any reason for the
medical examiner to make an examination because there is a known
cause of death certified by a medical doctor."

"I found it rather strange, a child at the spa, brain fever—"

"Miss Bly, you are a newspaper reporter looking for a story, the more
sensational the better. I have to deal with not just the sensational but
the mundane. Look around you. All of these papers deal with crimes,
some with murder most foul. If I investigated even one tenth of the deaths
of the mudlarks on the streets, I would spend my entire time at it. Now, if
you'll excuse me . . ."

"One more question, please. Did Hailey McGuire, one of our reporters, contact you about the Winsworth matter?"

"No."

The answer is snapped at me and I snap back. "Are spas like Aqua
Vitae so important to the economy of Bath that the local officials look the
other way rather than probing too deeply into their operations?"

"Madam, you have overstayed your welcome."

26

I leave the chief inspector knowing little more than when I arrived except for one important fact: Hailey had not contacted him.

I find that strange and mull it over as I slowly make my way back to my hotel.

Contacting the police to get as much information as possible is usually the beginning and end of a reporter's duties in researching a crime story. Since Hailey considered this story to be very big, interviewing others concerned would be also be in order, but again, the police would most often be the starting point to gather as many facts as possible before approaching others.

Hailey was an experienced crime reporter. In fact, almost all of her experience was hanging around the courthouse, talking to police, prosecutors, and witnesses.

So why didn't she contact the police immediately upon arriving in Bath? That she didn't was so out of character, it left me puzzled.

The only other significant information I got from the chief inspector was that he isn't convinced that Lady Winsworth's death is suspicious. It is out of the realm of possibilities that he would look the other way if the death is suspicious—besides ethics, and I'm certain the man has high standards, while spas may be an important source of revenue for the city, Lord Winsworth is rich and powerful. For sure, he is exercising pressure on the police and coroner to solve his wife's death.

I arrive back at my hotel to freshen up and check for messages before I go for my "audience" with Lady Chilcott.

The stuffy clerk at the front desk gives me a stiff frown as I approach.

"A *person* inquired about you earlier."

He left out the word "undesirable" but his tone implied it.

"What *person* inquired about me?"

"A woman of the streets."

Ah, Sarah, Emma's mother. Terrific. "Did she leave a message?"

"She was asked to leave by the manager. The presence of that sort of woman in our establishment would create the wrong impression."

"Did she say anything before she was ushered out?"

"She said she would be at the Albert Bridge trolley stop tonight at eight."

"Is that all?"

"We do not permit—"

"Yes, I got that. Thank you."

LADY CHILCOTT'S BATH ESTATE is a redbrick Georgian manor house with white window trim and black shutters. I have the cabbie stop at a florist on the way to purchase a bouquet of flowers as a "thank you" for seeing me and inviting me to tea. It's the sort of expenditure that the Draconian cashier at *The World* will refuse to reimburse me for when I submit my expenses.

My appointment with her is for two o'clock which I know from my travels around the world on British ships means we will have low tea rather than high tea. The names arose from the difference between the height of the tables and food served: Low tea, also called afternoon tea, is often served on a low table, like a coffee table in a living room, and is accompanied by cake and the cookies and flat bread the British call biscuits, while high tea, or "meat tea," is served later, in the dining room around five to seven with heartier foods such as cold cuts, boiled eggs, or sandwiches.

I am escorted by the butler to the garden where her ladyship is clipping roses while she waits for me.

I have never really comprehended the British designation of what the title "Lady" means, even though Oscar has explained it in great detail to me. All that seems to stick in my mind is that the woman's husband or father is most likely a knight or nobleman.

We sit in comfortably padded wrought-iron lawn chairs as tea and cookies are served on a low glass-topped table.

The butler supervises a maid who serves us tea in an exquisite pink porcelain tea set that has delicate flowers hand-painted on it. The cups are almost as small as a doll tea set—so petite are the cups, I will have to be very careful picking mine up, out of fear of breaking something that probably cost more than my month's salary.

Lady Chilcott is about forty years old, a bit on the sagging side, with treated blond hair. She wears jewelry and brightly colored clothing that convey to me a woman who is trying to subtract years from her chronological age by directing attention to things other than her own features. All in all, definitely a "patient" for the spa.

I thank her for seeing me and comment about the nice weather the afternoon has brought before we chat a moment about Oscar.

"Such a wonderfully irreverent gentleman," Lady Chilcott says. "He keeps us all amused by his wit and scandals—unless one is the target of his sharp tongue, of course."

I dodge the bullet as she tries to pump me about Oscar's current dilemma on the grounds I'm not familiar with the people involved and ask her about the spa.

"Marvelous place and Anthony—Dr. Lacroix is a genius. I understand that Dr. Radic is as competent, but I find his foreign manners less appealing than Anthony's."

"What does Dr. Lacroix look like?"

"Tall, a fine figure of a man, well-spoken, midthirties. Some women find him charming. Of course, the only thing of importance about him is his medical knowledge."

Uh huh.

"Frankly," she says, "when it comes to one's health and preserving one's vitality, Dr. Lacroix's treatments are considered the Fountain of Youth."

"So I've been told."

"You've been to the spa?"

"Yes."

"Then you're familiar with the peat bog preservation treatment that Dr. Lacroix developed."

"I was under the impression that Dr. Radic had developed the treatment."

"Dr. Radic had done work with peat moss at a spa on the continent before partnering with Dr. Lacroix here in Bath, but it's peat moss from a bog source Dr. Lacroix obtains in Dartmoor that is considered the most effective in the world. I suppose if the foul stuff can preserve a dinosaur for a million years, it can help keep us women from prematurely aging, wouldn't you say?"

I join her in a small laugh.

"You see the painting over there?"

She indicates a framed oil painting on an easel.

"That's a painting Dr. Lacroix commissioned the famous Dartmoor artist Isaac Weekes to do of the bog in the moors where he obtains the peat moss for the treatments at the spa. The location of the bog is a secret, but he had the painting done for me in appreciation."

She explains that she had the frame repainted because she didn't care for the color and had it placed on the easel to dry in the sun. She doesn't say what "appreciation" meant but I'm sure it means she gave him money for his "medical" research.

"Is Dr. Lacroix from Dartmoor?"

"Actually, my dear, I don't think anyone that matters is from that wild, isolated place. I've been told all of Dartmoor is of volcanic origin, and on many tors one can see the awful stabs which are inflicted on the still unhardened rock by the swords of subterranean fires. They say one almost feels like they have stepped onto the moon. Scattered throughout are nothing but gorse and blackthorns."

"Gorse?"

"Oh, it's a spiny, yellow-flowered shrub. Quite ugly, as are the black-thorns. Nothing like my roses."

"They are beautiful." And I mean it. Her rose garden is gorgeous—reds, pinks, whites, yellows. And the scent they give is heavenly.

"Thank you," she says, obviously pleased by my admiration of her roses. "I've won awards. Anyway, where were we . . . oh yes, Dr. Lacroix. He is of French descent on his father's side, but his mother was English and he was raised here."

"I've always wanted to visit the moors and see the bogs and tors and such."

"Why? They are gloomy, silent, desolate—nothing pretty about them and nothing to do."

"Oh, I've heard the moors can be quite beautiful—in a mysterious, unique way. Do you know what area his bog is in?"

"No, my dear, I haven't the foggiest. But Oscar said you are doing a story about the spa. I would hope it isn't a scandal piece about the Lady Winsworth incident."

I give her a smile that is meant to reassure her that I wasn't a scandal monger.

"I'm doing a piece on the rejuvenation effects of spa treatments, but frankly it's not possible to do without mentioning the incident."

"Your American readers must love tittle-tattle. Another young woman asked about the incident."

That gives me a jolt. "Hailey . . . Hailey McGuire."

"Yes, that might have been the name. Appeared rather young to be a newspaper reporter—as you do, my dear, although I've been told you're an accomplished one. Though I won't ask *why* a woman of any age would wish to do a man's job."

Because I like to eat and have a roof over my head, would have been my caustic reply if I didn't want information from her.

"Hailey spoke to you about the Winsworth incident?"

"Not to me in particular. Some other ladies and I were taking a stroll in the park across the street from the spa early in the evening after our treatments and the young woman approached us. I'm afraid her approach was not as professional as I find yours, nor did she come with the recommendation that you have. She was rather an excited type, much too anxious for information than any of us wanted to deal with after our relaxing therapy, so we politely dismissed her. That's about all I can tell you."

"Did she actually ask about the death of Lady Winsworth?"

"As a matter of fact, she did. We advised her that any questions should be posed to Lord Winsworth's solicitor."

The fact that I now knew Hailey came to Bath to investigate the Winsworth death made my heart beat like a drum. I also realize why Hailey approached the women first rather than the police—"early in the evening" meant that the chief inspector would have most likely left for the day.

I sipped tea to calm myself and get my mind on the right path again. "So, uh, none of the ladies at the spa are worried about the mineral waters or peat treatment despite whatever effect they might have had on Lady Winsworth?"

"You are obviously not well informed. Lady Winsworth wasn't receiving those treatments. Dr. Lacroix was giving her his new therapy."

"Which is?"

"I really can't say, because it's very hush-hush. Dr. Lacroix has developed a new course of treatment that is said to be revolutionary in terms of revitalizing people."

"Also rejuvenating?" I ask, because I'm certain Lady Chilcott and her lady friends are much more interested in taking off years than boosting their energy.

"Naturally, there are those interested in looking younger. But we're told the treatment is in the experimental stage and those who have been permitted to partake are sworn to secrecy."

"I see," the blind man says. I see nothing except that the spa has something new that Lady Chilcott and her friends are all dying to try—perhaps literally. Shades of Dorian Gray! Oscar hit the nail of middle-aged angst right on the head.

"Does the new treatment in any way involve children?"

"Children? What an absurd notion. Wherever did you get such an idea?"

I don't tell her it came from a prostitute. "I learnt through a source that a child, a street child, had died of brain fever after being at the spa."

"Miss Bly—I certainly hope that you are not insinuating that the staff of the most respectable spa in Europe, or the ladies and gentlemen who receive treatment at the spa, some of whom include the most prominent names in the British Empire, would harm a child."

Her lips take a firm set and I realize once again I am up against a wall of resistance and that I have worn out my welcome in asking questions about the charming Dr. Lacroix.

"I'll show you out."

She gives me a stiff "good-bye" that sounds more like "good riddance" and slams the front door behind me.

Back in the hansom cab I have waiting, I find it strange and fascinating the lengths women will go to look younger; the money they are willing to spend, the lies they are willing to tell, the pain they are willing to endure, all in the name of looking more beautiful, as if beauty is a monopoly of youth.

It is a sad state of affairs for women because other than those with inherited wealth, there is little for most women to offer the world outside the home except beauty and sex appeal, because the doors to achievements have always been closed—which brings up a question about myself.

When I mark up as many years as women who drink evil-tasting water and bathe in mud, will I join them in the pursuit for a more youthful appearance.

I don't know. I'm sure no one wants to grow old, but some obviously do it more gracefully than others. I just hope I will do it with grace. In the meantime, I won't throw the first stone at Lady Chilcott and her friends.

Too anxious to wait until evening, I have the cab take me down streets where I will most likely find Emma's mother. Explaining that I'm looking for a prostitute gets me a look from the driver.

"I'm with the Women's Temperance League," I tell him.

I have no luck locating Sarah and return to the hotel empty-handed, hungry, and tired.

27

A light mist is falling on this dark, moonless night as I leave the hotel for a rendezvous on a bridge with a prostitute.

While boarding a trolley I remind myself to keep alert—I had been attacked in broad daylight in London and now I am venturing out in the dark. Sometimes I wonder if Oscar isn't right and I invite trouble because of the situations I put myself in. Perhaps I create the "wrong place" at the wrong time myself. My only justification is someone has to find the truth and this is the only way I know how.

Meeting with a prostitute on a public street day or night is not something I relish although I did worse on the seedy streets of New York when I went undercover as a prostitute. It invites unwanted attention, jeers from passing men, and an invitation for rude, vulgar men to sling insults and dirty language. It was the most humiliating and aggravating undercover assignment I ever undertook.*

As the trolley car nears the stop, I see clusters of three or four people hanging together watching police activity on the far end of the bridge from the trolley stop. Police officers have lowered a rope on a pulley down to the riverbank.

Getting off the trolley, I keep my movements slow, dreading the worst.

A single gaslight streetlamp takes the edge off the darkness as a body wrapped in tarp with rope tied around it is hoisted up to the bridge from the rocky area next to the river. It has the eerie appearance of a ghost rising from the water.

---

*From Nellie's experience of going undercover as a prostitute, she wrote her first mystery novel, *Murder in Central Park.*—The Editors

I can't tell if it is a man or woman in the tarp, but my guts knot out of fear that it is Sarah.

"What happened?" I ask three men standing together as they watch the police activity.

"A woman fell off the bridge," one said.

"Killed 'erself," offered another.

I quickened my step over the bridge and spot Chief Inspector Bradley near the morgue wagon the body is being loaded into.

"Is the dead woman a prostitute?" I ask him.

He does a double take and looks me up and down as if he's puzzled as to how I suddenly materialized.

"Yes. Why do you ask?"

"May I see her face? I'd like to know if she's the mother of the girl I told you died of brain fever at the spa."

"This is police business."

"I understand that, Chief Inspector. I'm offering to help you identify the woman."

"We've had one identification. By a man who used her services in the past." He hesitates, then takes a deep breath. "Do you know her name?"

"Her name is Sarah. Her daughter was Emma."

Once again he eyes me with displeasure. In his mind, I am a nuisance who turns simple things complicated whether they need it or not.

"Let her see the woman's face," he instructs an officer.

I take a quick glance. She's had a head injury and it bled profusely. I've seen blood before, but it's never uglier than when it comes with violence.

"It's her. Sarah."

"Take it away," he commands the attendants.

"Well," I ask, after he ignores me and appears to be leaving, "are you going to investigate the daughter's death now?"

He stops and gives me a long stare as if he's deciding on what tack to take with me. I suspect I am getting what he considers to be velvet glove treatment because I am a woman and Inspector Abberline of Scotland Yard asked him to accommodate me.

"See that man over there?"

The man he indicates has the disreputable appearance of a saloon thug.

"That's the woman's pimp. He says she talked of killing herself all day. Seems *someone* gave her a quid and that bought her enough liquid courage to do the job proper."

I take the blow without flinching and walk away, but my knees are shaking. How dare he! I didn't kill the woman or assist her in killing herself. Life had taken everything from her worth living for when she lost her daughter. If it hadn't been my money, it would have been someone else's or she would have done herself in without liquid courage.

I'm just about to board the trolley when I spot Sarah's pimp talking to another man under the single gaslight streetlamp.

The man he is huddled in conversation with is Burke, the ruffian with a taste for cowboy boots.

A coincidence? Or had Burke arranged the death of Sarah because she had become too loud with her agony?

I return to my hotel, cold to the bone, climb into bed, and pull the blankets over my head.

28

G o away!"
    I yell at the poor maid when she enters to clean my room. I am definitely going to have to leave her an extra gratuity for my rudeness. The problem is that I just don't want to get out of bed and face the world. I want to stay with my head buried under the blankets and ignore the hazards and pitfalls of life.

I have never been a morning person, probably because I have a hard time getting to sleep at night. I believe it's because my mind won't let me go to sleep—I keep thinking of all the things I must do and how I might solve any problems at hand.

Last night the death of Sarah and loss of her daughter affected me. In such a short time, I have listened to a mother's tragic tale of the loss of her child and seen two corpses that shouldn't have happened.

Twice in a very short time I have been accused of contributing to the suicide of another person, one of whom was dear to me, the other a poor unfortunate for whom I had great empathy and compassion.

Another thing that kept me tossing and turning was seeing Sarah's pimp, or perhaps more likely the man who simply identified himself as her pimp, chatting like old pals with Dr. Radic's thug, Burke. Did Radic have Burke speak to the pimp about keeping Sarah quiet about the child? Was her death the way they silenced her?

The plot thickens . . . but where does it lead?

Hailey came to Bath. Didn't go to the police but she had arrived too late to contact the officer in charge of the investigation. She went to the spa and tried unsuccessfully to get information from Lady Chilcott and her snooty friends.

What would she have done then? Gone inside to the spa? Yes, just as I had.

What happened after that? Days passed because she returned to London. And then back to Bath?

By midmorning my mind is frustrated with all the whos, whys, and whats to a puzzle I cannot get a handle on, that I willingly get out of bed, but it's not enough to make me want to face the world and I mope around the room, slowly getting my clothes and my toilet together. "Putzing around" is what my mother calls it.

I bathe slowly and dally until the maid timidly taps on my door, slowly sticking her head in. Poor dear is fearful I'll chop it off—again.

When I smile and convey my apologies, along with the extra tip, she opens up and starts chattering away—how relieved she is that I'm not mad at her because she's had other guests blow up at her for no reason and then complain to her boss who would take it out of her pay; how guests have thrown things at her, yelling away and then leaving behind a horrible mess. If I had stayed I think I would have learnt all the dirty scuttlebutt about the guests and more about her rotten boss. Too bad I couldn't interview her. I know the hotel maids in America would love to hear how things aren't any different in England.

That's when it hit me—a likely source for information about Hailey's visit to Bath would be the hotel.

It makes sense. I chose this hotel for its location near to the train and because it's modestly priced. Reporters travel on what we call "beans" and not steaks. Mr. Pulitzer and his ilk are not overly generous with expense money and I'm positive Hailey would have sought out accommodations that would get by the paper's cashier without a lecture or a trip to Mr. Cockerill's office. Even when the choice is between a trolley and a taxi, the trolley will almost always win out.

Now I just need to figure out how to approach the front desk clerk for I'm pretty certain he won't give me information about another guest unless I provide him with a good reason.

Bless the gods for my cunning mind! I ingeniously think of one that I'm positive will make him eager to assist me.

"A reporter from my newspaper stayed here recently. Can you check her stay and let me know how much you are owed?" I give him Hailey's name and the date I believe she was in Bath.

He eagerly disappears into the adjoining room and comes back with an accounting sheet.

"There is no balance. She paid for the night she stayed."

"She stayed only one night?" That's interesting.

"Quite right. One night. But you should check at the Fontaine. She had her luggage transferred to there."

"Is that the hotel near the Aqua Vitae spa?"

"Yes it is. And a bit more pricey than we are."

"How much more?"

"Twice as much for a single."

"Really . . . did she say why she was leaving?"

"No, madam. And we offer excellent service for the price."

I leave for the Fontaine, stretching my legs to get my mind going. I recall seeing the hotel. It looked small and quaint—and pricey. And that puzzles me. Why Hailey would change from a suitable hotel to one that would raise Cain with the paper's cashier when she returned to New York makes no sense.

Her trip to Bath, with the necessity for train fare, hotel, and meals would have been questioned unless she had a major story to support the expenses. Even I will have to argue to get approval for beans for this excursion to Bath.

Pulitzer judges how good a story is by the amount of papers it sells and I'm still not convinced that the death of a British socialite while being treated by a health doctor would generate enough appeal for New York readers to support extraordinary efforts and expenses.

The Fontaine clerk is also eager to check the accounting register to see if Hailey left owing any money.

"She didn't pay the bill herself, but her two-night stay was paid," the clerk tells me.

"Really? My editor was under the impression it hadn't been paid."

"Well . . ." he looks at his books, "it's understandable he would be under the impression she didn't, because it was fully satisfied by the spa when it arranged for the room."

"The spa . . . yes, I see, Aqua Vitae arranged for the room."

"Yes, madam. They do that quite frequently for their spa patients."

"We were also wondering about her luggage."

I'm actually wondering where she went from the hotel—obviously back to London, but I want to make sure because it strikes me that it's possible Hailey checked out of the hotel the very day she died. Inspector Abberline told me that the exact day of death couldn't be determined because of the state of the body, so there is a range of several days rather than pinpointing one.

"You'll have to speak to the porter."

He taps the bell on the counter and an elderly man in a blue porter's uniform comes forward.

I explain to him that I am tracing luggage that left the hotel for the train station and give him the date and a description of Hailey.

"Yes, I remember her. We don't get many Americans, and almost never a young woman traveling alone. She requested her luggage be sent to the station. But we're not responsible for the luggage after it reaches the train station."

"Did she happen to mention which train she was taking?"

"No, madam, I never spoke to her. I was just told to take the luggage to the station. Westbound."

"Which city?"

"Could be Bristol, madam, or all the way down to Exeter in Devonshire."

"Devonshire . . ." I glance at a railroad map on the wall behind the front counter. "Is that where the moors are?"

"Yes, madam. Exeter is in the Dartmoor area."

"Did you, uh, happen to speak to Miss McGuire at the station?"

"No, madam, I merely delivered the luggage to the baggage room. As I said, the hotel is not responsible for lost luggage. You should speak to the head porter at the station if you wish to file a claim."

"One last thing," I give him a crown coin, "did you see Miss McGuire when she checked in?"

"Yes."

"What was her mood?"

"Her mood?"

"How did she appear to you? Sad? Happy?"

"She was a very nice woman, very polite, perhaps a bit more lively than the young women I usually encounter."

"What do mean by lively?"

"Bubbly, madam, smiling, laughed easily, full of life."

An apt description of Hailey. My head is buzzing when I leave the hotel, trying to make sense of what I have learnt.

Hailey probably spent most of her last day here, in Bath. Then she would have returned to London depressed and killed herself. But if she returned to London, which is east of Bath, why would she instruct her luggage be sent to the westbound platform?

The bellman also confirmed what both the boardinghouse maid and James the gatekeeper had said—she wasn't sad or depressed.

I realize I don't know which direction Hailey went because no one I've spoken to actually saw her at the train station. No one took the order directly from her as to where her luggage was to be sent.

So where did she go? Back to London without her luggage? Or west with her luggage?

Logically my next move should be to return to London and advise Inspector Abberline of my findings and ask him to check further into the matter. I would then board a ship for the return trip across the pond.

Logically . . . of course, but I have no intention of doing that. Instead, I return to my hotel.

"May I have a porter get me a ticket to Exeter while I get together my things to check out?" I ask the concierge.

"Of course, madam. Is there anything else we can do for you?"

"No, that shall do. Oh, are there any telegrams for me?"

He looks in the slot for my room. "Here you are."

It's a telegram from Oscar: "My dear Nellie, it's getting quite warm if not hot in dear old London. I'm thinking of leaving. How's your quest going?"

I immediately respond back: "Off to find the Fountain of Youth in a mud hole in Dartmoor. Next stop Exeter. Why don't you join me? We can be partners in crime, just like the old days."

That done, I go to my room, pack my valise, and freshen up for my trip westbound. I haven't the foggiest idea what direction Hailey went when she left the Fontaine Hotel, but I am fairly certain that for some reason, her luggage went west—perhaps as far southwest as the gateway to the moors.

The same moors where Dr. Lacroix gets his magic mud.

29

I love a journey and am usually up early and head out with vigor. Today my feet are dragging because I am unsure of whether I am doing the right thing. Hailey's body was found in London, yet I am setting out in the opposite direction without any good reason other than I suspect her luggage went in that direction.

Why would anyone want her luggage? For the same reason her office was cleaned out, papers burned, and her room at the boardinghouse searched. She had come into possession of something, probably information she had written down, that someone wanted destroyed.

Up to now I have been concentrating on her lover as the culprit but Dr. Radic and his cutthroat enforcer are crowding the field of suspects. Radic is a high-class, polished crook, but of the most dangerous variety— the fact he employs a man like Burke shows that he is not above cracking heads to get what he wants.

And the elusive Dr. Lacroix—where does he fit into the puzzle? Partnered with Radic and linked to the death of the little girl Emma and the high-society woman makes him a likely candidate for any number of high crimes in my mind.

At the station I speak to a porter who is assisting westbound passengers with their luggage. He wasn't on duty that day, but suggests I talk to the baggage master in the baggage room. Since the train will be departing shortly, I leave my valise with him and go to inquire at the baggage room.

"I don't recall a young American woman," the baggage master tells me, "but unless she spoke to me, how would I know she had a colonial accent?"

Good point. He smirks at referring to Americans as colonials. I've heard it before.

As I swing back around to return to the train before it leaves without me, I spot a familiar figure—the blue-eyed young man on the London to Bath train who had stared at me so rudely and took an unhealthy interest in my luggage. And only spoke German.

He hands a coin to the porter and heads to board the train. He must have considerable luggage because he is carrying a valise larger than mine and doesn't leave it with the porter. I assume the gratuity is presented for luggage handling.

I retrieve my bag and am about to board when I see someone else I know and exclaim, "It's old homes week!"

"Well, I hope whatever that means, it's an indication you are pleased to see me." Mrs. Lambert, the widow who protected my valise on the London-Bath train beams at me.

"Very pleased, but surprised. Can you imagine—I just saw the man that had been eyeing my luggage on the train from London board this one."

"You don't say! What a coincidence. But you know, my dear, they say that the steam engine has shrunk the world."

"Having raced around the world in seventy-two days on steam-driven ships and locomotives, that's an observation I wouldn't contest. But as you say—what a coincidence."

She explains that she finished her visit with her sister in Bath and is onto Exeter to see another sister.

"Unfortunately, we might find the train a bit crowded 'til Bristol, where most people will get off," Mrs. Lambert says. "After Bristol, the route south all the way to Exeter is a slow milk run because there are many small places and no big towns along the way."

Once aboard we discover she's correct. The only seats available are in the open day coach and only a few are left. I insist she take the first one we spot to ensure she won't end up standing.

"But what about you?" Mrs. Lambert proclaims. "I so wanted us to sit together, I'm dying to find out how your investigating is going."

I see another empty seat down the aisle and tell her I'll take it. "Well, I guess we'll have to wait 'til after Bristol to chat."

In some ways I'm glad we won't be sitting together. As much as I enjoy talking with her, I need time alone to get my thoughts organized and plan what I am going to do next formulated in my head. I find a seat quite a few rows farther down next to an older gentleman, who is completely engrossed in his newspaper.

As I lift my valise to place it in the overhead luggage net, I notice a folded sheet of paper that has been slipped into a side pocket I rarely use because my bag is usually packed so tight I can't get anything thicker than a hairpin into it.

I pull it out and after I'm settled into my seat I unfold it.

It's a pencil drawing—a humorous sketch of a man sitting at a table with pencil and paper watching a woman with a valise walking away from him. She appears to be hurrying away.

The woman is me. The man is the individual who had an unhealthy interest in my luggage.

Scribbled below the caricatures is *I've learned Ang-lish*.

30

Now I know why the man tipped the train porter—he had the porter slip his caricature in my valise. Obviously, he has given up whatever pretense he has been operating under and wants to meet with me. Why? Because there is no way I would consider his presence on the train as a coincidence after he showed an interest in my luggage. And he must know that the woman who chased him away reported his attempt to me.

He has blue eyes. So did the man who tried to get into Hailey's room and who I assumed was her lover.

"Well, we will see about this," I tell the older gentleman next to me as I set out to find the man who has been playing games with me.

The caricature and his pretense at speaking only German also show he has a sense of humor. But I'm not amused.

As I pass by Mrs. Lambert it occurs to me that I might invite her along for my confrontation with the mystery man, but decide against it. Instead, I give her a pleasant smile at her inquiring look. I don't feel the need to share any more information and already regret that I shared a few tidbits about my quest with her because I usually find it bad luck to talk about a story I'm investigating, especially to strangers, no matter how kind they are—you can't trust anyone. I'm ashamed to admit that I was drawn in by her being so in awe about me being a female reporter and she was just plain kind, so I let my guard down.

Normally I keep matters close to my chest—that is how I have survived years in a dog-eat-dog atmosphere of reporting. I will never forget the best piece of advice I received from my first boss, Mr. Madden, at *The Pittsburg Dispatch,* "If you believe you have a lead to a headline story, keep it under wraps like a treasure map—don't show nor tell any-one."

Well, Mrs. Lambert is just a sweet widowed lady, so no harm has been done.

I should have little to fear from the man physically because the train is crowded. Besides, this man didn't appear, on the surface at least, to be the type to resort to physical action. Unlike the thug who mugged me in broad daylight on a London street or Burke at the spa, the drawer of the comic picture is smaller built and as Mrs. Lambert put it, appeared pretty much like a counter jumper—a clerk in a retail store. However, I sensed a scholarly air about him.

He strikes me more as the type who would slice one to ribbons with pen and paper than with a knife. Then again, I once interviewed a quiet scrivener, a copyist, for an accountant who killed three people with an ax.

Whoever this man is, why he is following me, and why he has now made contact with me are matters I can't fathom, except that he has an interest in this matter and very well could be Hailey's lover.

Also puzzling is why he has chosen such a circumspect way of con-tacting me. Simply walking up to me and introducing himself would have done the trick. But instead, he started out sneaky and even tried to get a peek at my valise—probably for the diary he didn't manage to find in Hai-ley's room. For certain, he wants me to contact him and has chosen a rather unusual way to communicate his desire.

Miffed and puzzled at the same time, I must admit I'm excited for our meeting. One way or another I am certain that somehow, in some way, he has a connection to Hailey. There can't be any other explanation for him contacting me.

I have to wonder—did his tip also allow him a peek into my valise back at the Bath station? Not that it would matter, unless he had an un-healthy interest in female garments.

The notion that he is the man Hailey was romantically involved with gets cemented into my thoughts as I go through the train to find him. He's not unpleasant to look upon and has an air about him that conveys a cer-tain intelligence—a quality in a man that is appealing, at least for me. I have no idea what are the qualities in a man that attracted Hailey.

Two cars down is where I find him. He's at a writing table engrossed in making entries in a journal and has an unlit pipe clenched in his teeth.

He looks up, not completely surprised to see me.

"I'm not amused by you or your antics," I tell him.

"I don't blame you. Sometimes I don't like me much myself, but I'm saddled with me."

"Self-immolation is not an excuse for rudeness or spying on me. You have some explaining to do before I call the conductor and have him take charge of you so you can be turned over to the police at the next stop."

He takes the pipe out of his mouth and gives me a long, appraising look. "I can see why you are a success in your career. You give no quarter." He gestures at the seat across from him. "Please join me. Perhaps I can offer some extenuating circumstances before you have me arrested for whatever crimes you believe I've committed."

"Someplace where people can breathe." The smoking car is my least favorite place on a train and I refuse to sit here with him and talk.

He puts his writing materials in his carrying case and follows me. We stop in the gangway between the cars. The window on the door is open, allowing in breathable air, along with the sound of wheel over rails.

"Explain yourself," I snap.

"We need to start with a change of attitude on your part. I don't take well to bullying, even if it comes from an attractive young woman."

An unexpected answer, but one I can deal with. "Fine. If you'd rather not talk to me, you'll be doing your talking to the police."

"For what? Drawing a picture? Is that a crime in your country?"

"In my country, this country, and all civilized countries I have been in, the police frown on strange men stalking a woman. We'll see how the Bristol police deal with a man who has been giving uninvited attention to a woman."

I turn to leave and whip back around when he says, "Wait."

"You have exactly one minute to convince me not to have the conductor take you into custody and turn you over to the police at the next stop."

"You are a humdinger, Miss Bly. But don't push it. You're not going to say anything to the police."

"I'm not? Is that what your crystal ball tells you? Perhaps you'd like to share with me your vast knowledge of my thought processes."

"Because it would delay you. You are trying to find Dr. Lacroix before time, money, or the demands of your job cut off the search." He pauses and locks eyes with me. "I am also looking for him. Maybe we can join forces."

H. G. Wells

I have come to believe in certain other things, in the coherency and purpose in the world and in the greatness of human destiny. Worlds may freeze and suns may perish, but I believe there stirs something within us now that can never die again.

—H. G. WELLS

31

He sticks out his hand to shake, an unusual gesture by a man to a woman, but one that sets well with me. I shake hands, giving him a tight grip. My instinct is that I can trust this man. And I'll feel better about my gut reaction if he comes clean and tells me truthfully what he has to do with Hailey.

"H. G. Wells. My friends call me H. G."

"Sounds like the chairman of the board. What do your non friends call you?"

We agree on "Wells." I tell him he can call me Bly, but we agree upon Nellie when he says that sounds too formal.

So much fencing just to come up with names to call each other. I sense this sort of verbal dueling is a foreshadowing of our future discussions.

"I'm a teacher," he says.

"Fine. You're a book learner who teaches others how to learn from books. Now tell me what your relationship was with Hailey."

"I had no relationship with Miss McGuire. Never had the pleasure of meeting her, though I heard she was a very fine young woman."

I stare at him with exasperation. It is clear that information doesn't pour from him. "If you didn't know Hailey, why did you try to get access to her things? Why are you following me across England and trying to snoop in my luggage? Why are we having this conversation?"

He shakes his head with wonder. "Was your mother a Gatling gun?" He quickly holds up his hands to warn off my attack. "I apologize. This is hard on me. Actually, that is a dumb statement. It's obviously much harder on you because you lost your friend. I was trying to get information about Dr. Lacroix."

"Why?"

"He owes me money for research I conducted for him."

I am not comfortable with his answer, though I'm not certain if it's an outright lie or an embellishment of the truth. Running to different towns and getting on and off trains are hardly the way a debt is collected.

"Wouldn't it be easier to lay a claim in court with his spa? It looks like a place where mud is turned into gold."

"It's—it's not just the money, he took something else from me, valuable information from my research. It's personal and I'd really rather not go into it. But he owes me and I expect to collect."

"Why have you been following me?"

"I read up about you." He grins and shrugs. "You are known for finding and uncovering things people want hidden. Dr. Lacroix is hiding. I'm certain he is, and not on the continent."

"Why are you sure he hasn't left the country?"

"Because I'm certain he set up a laboratory in the Devonshire area. He's been quite secretive about it, but I became aware that he was shipping equipment and supplies to Exeter. Very complex items, not the sort of thing you duplicate at two places or in some cases, duplicate at all." He shakes his head. "No, I'm certain that he is somewhere around Exeter. Which is one of the reasons I continue to follow you. You must have found a lead to Exeter. What is it?"

I ignore the question for the moment. "How did you know I have been trying to locate Dr. Lacroix?" My statement isn't exactly true—I have been trying to unravel Hailey's last days and the trail has simply set me upon Lacroix's own path.

"James Anderson."

"Who is . . . ?"

"The front desk attendant at the International News Building. He was a classmate of mine."

That little rat. James had been holding back on me. "Okay . . . but I never told James anything about Dr. Lacroix."

"I know, you spoke to him about the reporter that killed herself. That's originally why James contacted me. She was going to do a story about the spa. James said she was fascinated by the subject of rejuvenation. She believed women back in New York would be excited about the research."

My heart skips a beat. "You spoke to Hailey?"

"No, we never were able to get together. James conveyed her wish to meet and talk about the subject, but I'd had complications from an injury and was indisposed at the time."

He did appear to be a bit pale.

"By the time I felt better, she . . ."

"Yes. Why did you pretend to be her brother? What did you expect to find in her room?"

"Ah, you know about that. I'm embarrassed to admit I was playing detective. I knew she had made trips to Bath and I hoped she might have a lead that I'd find in her notes. As you know, the ruse didn't work. That Mrs. Franklin is one mean-spirited woman."

"Is that why you searched Hailey's office and burned papers?" A shot in the dark, but I'm certain it's a good one. And I know I've hit the mark by his attempt to suppress a grin.

"Guilty of going through her office, not of burning any papers. I sent a telegram to Miss McGuire after I felt better and got back a reply that she'd contact me upon her return from Bath. After James told me she had taken her own life, I got him to let me take a peek in her office."

"What did you find?"

"Nothing about Bath. I took nothing out with me and certainly never burned anything."

"Did you see burned materials in the wastebasket?"

"They could have been there, but I didn't notice them if they were. What I saw appeared to be years of accumulation of news stories. I assumed that there was no current notes because she kept them with her. What do you think was burned?"

What I think is that I'm not going to give information to him until I have more answers.

"So why didn't you simply approach me if you thought I was seeking the same information that you are?"

"I've heard that you're a lone wolf. You work completely alone and are not in the habit of sharing information."

"That analysis of my methods is from my friend Hailey to James to you?"

"Yes, though I did do a bit of reading about you. What would you have done if I had contacted you in London? From what I've learned, you would have picked me clean of what I know and gave me nothing, like you are doing right now."

It's my turn to smother a grin. He's right. I'm wringing him dry of information and have told him nothing.

"How did you find out I was going to Bath? I never told James."

"I was waiting in your hotel lobby, arguing with myself as to whether I should approach you, when you went into the telegram kiosk and sent off two."

"That was you with your head buried in a newspaper?"

"Once again guilty. Anyway, I used an old schoolboy trick to read one of your messages—pretending to write out a message myself, I took the blank pad of sheets you used and rubbed my lead over the imprint your pencil left on the top sheet."

"Good lord, and you accuse me of being a secret operator? You could go to work for your government as a spy."

"Why, thank you." He smiles broadly. "I have taken quite a fancy to this detective work. I must say the procedures are not unlike chemical experiments. You keep trying different things until something works."

I don't bother asking him how he traced me to the westbound train. The clerk and porter at my hotel knew I was taking this train.

I turn and look at the passing scenery to get my thoughts organized. He is an intelligent man, but in terms of what it takes to deal with violence and criminals, he is a babe in the woods. He's a book learner and dealing with the likes of Radic and Burke takes skills that are learned on the street—where I learned them. That's where my guts got honed to deal with undesirables—sometimes by having my face rubbed in the dirt.

Bottom line: We see the world in two radically different lights and would be at odds at almost everything if I let him come along with me.

"Are you an artist?" I ask in reference to his comic doodling.

"Not at all, though I write a bit. Articles on science."

It is easy to see from his clothes that neither his teaching nor his writing has brought him much financial reward. He dresses respectfully, but modestly—not unlike a counter jumper.

It is time to brush him off. "Well . . . I must say, I am very impressed with your efforts at getting information, very much so."

"But not enough to share information with—or team up with me."

He doesn't pose the remark as a question. He has already decided upon an answer.

I smile demurely. "I'll give some thought to that."

He chortles at my vague and evasive response. "Well, I suppose I deserve that for permitting you to cross-examine me, turning me upside down, and shaking all of the thoughts out of my brain. However, I'll respect your decision. But do watch yourself with that other reporter."

"What other reporter?"

"Why, *your* Mrs. Lambert, of course." Like the Cheshire cat in Lewis Carroll's *Alice's Adventures in Wonderland*, he gives me a triumphant grin. "You are aware, I'm sure, that she works for the most contemptuous newspaper in the entire empire, a gossipmonger that prints anything but the truth."

A chuckle starts deep in his belly and rumbles like distant thunder as he delivers yet another blow. "But, of course, a smart woman like you knew you were being had—didn't you?"

32

I make a quick check with the conductor about train schedules out of Bristol before returning to the car that holds Mrs. Lambert and my valise.

"Mrs. Lambert . . ."

"Yes, dear . . ." She looks up from her crocheting. "Is everything all right?"

"Well . . . not quite. Could you join me at the back of the train car? We should take our belongings with us."

"Why, of course, my dear."

The train is just pulling into Bristol as she packs up her stuff and I grab my valise.

"I'm afraid I won't be going on with you to Exeter," I tell her in a confidential tone. "I'll be leaving the train here in Bristol."

"Really? That man you spoke with, the one I kept from getting into your luggage must have told you something. I hope he's not tricking you. I know you can't confide in me, but I've come to think of you as a sister. As a woman, I am proud of you and your accomplishments. Why what little you've told me, simply thrills me."

"Well . . ." I glance around to give the affect that I'm making sure no one is listening and tell her in a confidential tone, "I must have your word of honor that you won't speak a word to anyone."

"Of course, my dear. My lips are sealed."

"I've learned something from an absolutely reliable source. But remember, you must keep this a secret."

"Yes, yes . . ."

"That doctor I told you I'm investigating—I've learnt that he isn't in Exeter, but is staying at a manor house outside of Worcester."

"*No!* Are you certain?"

"Absolutely. The man I spoke to was there and he spoke to him. The problem is the moment this train stops in Bristol, I have to make a mad dash for the northbound Worcester train. It'll be leaving almost at the same time we arrive. I'll have to buy a ticket on board. No time to waste."

We hug and I promise to write her, already having exchanged addresses during our previous trip together.

"I shall not forget this little journey we've had together," she says, as we are pulling to a halt and I get ready to disembark and run for the train on the opposite set of tracks. "You don't know what you have done for me—adding excitement into my drab little life. Thank you, my dear."

"I won't forget you," I say as I dash off. *And I doubt you'll be thanking me later.* What a con artist. I could kick myself for falling for her words. Never again.

"You'll be hearing from me," she yells.

I seriously doubt that.

As I go up the steps and onto the northbound train—and down the steps out the other side—I move quickly to get out of sight.

Once both the northbound and southbound trains clear the station, I come out of hiding and make my way to the ticket office.

"Excuse me, sir."

Behind an open wooden booth, a ticket officer looks up from a mess of paperwork. He takes off his glasses and rubs his eyes. "Yes, Miss, what can I do for you?"

I hand him my ticket. "Is this still valid to Exeter?"

He puts his glasses back on. "Yes, it is."

"When will the next train be arriving?"

"In an hour."

"Thank you. Can you recommend a café for lunch?"

"There's one across from the station. Food's good; tell Mary I sent you."

As I enter, a waitress approaches me. "Your gentleman is waiting over there."

"Excuse me?"

She points to H. G. Wells who grins and waves from where he's sitting.

I take a deep breath and stand perfectly still for a moment.

He obviously is not as gullible as the scandal press reporter. I still need information about Dr. Lacroix from him, so I might as well give up the ghost in terms of getting rid of him and join him for tea and clotted Devonshire cream with scones.

With my best smile, I approach him.

"Wells, I have to admit that you are as hard to get rid of as poison ivy. And just about as welcome."

"Nellie, you will not regret your gracious invitation to have me join you in this quest. I will always be there for you."

"That's what I'm afraid of."

33

On the train en route to Exeter, I am in an aisle seat facing Wells. Next to him is a man engrossed in a newspaper. The seat next to me is empty.

I remind myself to make the best of the situation. Wells outsmarted me, but the game is not over yet. And I do find his comments about the situation keen.

Earlier over lunch, after I told him about my growing suspicion that Hailey had discovered something about the death of Lady Winsworth and had been killed to keep her silent, he made a salient point: Dr. Lacroix is very much a ladies' man.

"That's the main reason Radic wanted him as a partner. Radic is a shady businessman with all the charm of a viper, but Lacroix attracts society women. There are rumors that he was having an affair with Lady Winsworth."

"I had already presumed that he was romancing rich women for their money."

"That might be true, but if it is, it wouldn't be for personal gain. The man is a true fanatic when it comes to his research. I understand he puts every dollar into it and I don't doubt that some of the money comes from older women who are captivated by his attention. Lacroix had a society medical practice before he went into partnership with Radic and created the spa. But don't confuse the knowledge of the two. Radic claims to be a licensed doctor in Romania, but he's not one here, which makes me doubt his claim. Few people doubt that Lacroix is a brilliant doctor and scientist, but almost everyone in the medical profession and scientific community rejects his hypothesis."

"Which is?"

"Lacroix is trying to find a way for the human body to rejuvenate."

"To get younger?"

"A universal dream of man since Eve grew old and Adam started looking around for someone younger and prettier."

"But found his male virility had gone the same place as Eve's lovely skin," I counter. "I'm certain that every search for the Fountain of Youth has been based upon fraud and humbug."

"Your comments are the same as almost any medical man in London, but few people understand—or even care to understand—what Lacroix means by rejuvenation. It was even a standing joke at the college where he taught; students and faculty called him Dr. Ponce and referred to his class as Bimini, which was the mythical island where Ponce de Leon thought he'd find the Fountain of Youth.

"But Dr. Lacroix isn't advocating some hokum about turning back the clock, making a forty-year-old twenty again—reversing the biological clock that takes us from infants with perfect skin and organs to ripe old age with wrinkles and worn-out hearts and lungs. Instead, he is selective, focusing on skin. Just as a woman's jar of cold cream can delay or even get rid of wrinkles, he is seeking a natural substance that will revitalize the skin."

"Sounds more like alchemy than science. Don't alchemists search for some sort of universal remedy called a Philosopher's Stone?"

"In matter of speaking. Some alchemists seek a substance capable of transmuting common metals into gold, others an elixir of life that can reverse or stop aging. But you have to appreciate that their fruitless quests for things today we call magic, created a great deal of scientific knowledge and the scientific method used by modern researchers."

"You did research on this rejuvenation theory?" I'm curious. Wells doesn't strike me as someone who would be involved in fraud or hogwash, so I am very interested as to what he actually did for "Dr. Ponce."

"I did research on salamanders."

"Salamanders? Those lizards that live in water?"

"They're not actually lizards, even though they look like them. A salamander has some rather interesting characteristics. It can lose a leg or other body parts and regenerate them, but it's not the only creature that can do it. Some worms, shellfish, and insects also have this ability. We humans can do it in a very limited way—when our bodies form scar tissue over wounds, it's regenerating flesh."

"Have you found out why salamanders can regrow an arm and a leg?"

"No. Lady Winsworth's death put a halt to the research."

"The scandal and all."

"Not just the scandal—she was financing the research."

"Oh, I see, by putting up the money she got first claim on a new arm or leg or face or—" I shut up because the look on his face is not pleasant. I know, I'm being catty, but it really sounds like a lot of bunk to me.

He leaves without a word and I glance over at the man wondering what he thought of the conversation. He is crunched up in the corner next to the window, asleep behind his newspaper, his hat pulled down over his eyes.

I wait patiently for Wells to return . . . well, I'm not sure if that's true. Even though I have always considered myself a patient person, no one else I know would agree with me. When I am forced to sit still, I have a habit of shaking one of my legs, sometimes tapping it against something that causes others to ask why I'm kicking the object. And I have been accused many times of being afraid of silence, because when a conversation dies down I tend to pick it up again.

My other fault, one my dear mother says I have, is my dire need to make amends; that is I react badly to any sort of rejection. So, instead of sitting with my foot nervously shaking, I get up to find Mr. Wells and soothe over whatever feelings I have inadvertently ruffled.

This is why I don't care to work with a partner—I don't want to deal with the baggage that comes with working closely with someone else. I frequently find myself having to tiptoe around the other person because they are not keeping up or want to go in a different direction than me or I have in some way offended them and have to soothe the waters. And in the newspaper business, a partner almost always means a man. And they say women are moody.

I find Wells in the gangway between cars, leaning on the wall next to the door. The top half of the door is open and he is letting the wind soothe him.

"I'm sorry," I tell him, "I didn't mean to belittle your work." With that statement, I am being honest.

"You are a very intelligent woman, Nellie. More importantly, you know how to think. I admire that."

The compliment catches me by surprise and I don't know how to respond.

"Most women," he continues, "even those with intelligence, spend their lives in a dark, intellectual closet, trained from infancy to let the man in their life, first their father, then their husband, do their thinking for them."

"I suppose because my father died when I was a child and my mother never recovered from the loss of him, I didn't have anyone else to do my thinking."

"That may be. But even though you have a quick mind and are intelligent, you also rely almost entirely upon your instincts and evaluations of people rather than information derived from research or analysis."

The man certainly knows how to turn a compliment into a lecture and personality assassination.

"May I ask how you derived at this brilliant assessment?"

"Listening to you. You have learned everything you know by talking to people. You talked to your friend Oscar in London, a prostitute, eavesdropped at the spa—"

"That's how you get information when doing a criminal investigation. Criminals don't write their actions down in a book for us to peruse. Talking with people is the only recourse I have and that puts me miles ahead of you and your book learning. Reporters are not teachers and bookworms. We work in the real world."

I leave steaming. The gall of him.

Once again I find myself in the same quandary about Mr. Herbert George Wells as I did when I first caught him surreptitiously observing me. I am attracted to him, but I don't appreciate him dissecting me like I am one of those lizards he cuts legs off of to see if the limb grows back.

I end up in the dining car and order tea to soothe my irritation. I know why it hit me so hard—because it's true. I don't have as much education as other newspaper people and rely upon my instincts—very successfully, thank you.

Wells is suddenly standing next to me.

"My apologies."

He sits down across from me. I give him a blank stare. His comments have no meaning to me, I decide. I'm not going to let him affect me anymore. I hate emotions that drain precious energy from me.

"I was being analytical to a ridiculous extent. Your method of relying on your gut and going straight for the jugular has made you renowned in your profession."

"Fair enough." I set down my tea. "And I will admit that a little book learning never hurts anyone—until it gets in the way of real life. I don't know anything about salamanders, but I did notice a little while ago you took offense when I made a remark about Lady Winsworth. Is that because she supported the research you and Dr. Lacroix conducted?" My suspicion is that it goes beyond financial support for Wells, but I start with a bit of circumspection to throw him off guard—then I'll go for the jugular.

"Lady Winsworth wasn't just a benefactor of Lacroix's, she was extremely kind to me. I didn't know the man before she began supporting his research. She introduced us and encouraged him to permit me to conduct the research despite the fact I don't have the advanced degree in chemistry that he desired in a researcher. My degree is in teaching rather than pure science, but her sponsorship was satisfactory enough to get me the work, especially at a time when I was in desperate need of it."

In other words, Lady Winsworth controlled the purse strings and would have pulled them tight if Lacroix had not accepted her candidate. For sure, Lacroix wasn't going to bite the hand that fed him. I still get the hint of deeper currents, ones Wells keeps concealed. Recognizing a NO TRESPASSING sign, I keep smothering my natural intention to hit him with the big question.

"Your gratitude toward her is the reason you are searching for Lacroix?"

His eyes meet mine and I see smoldering anger. "I want to know what he gave her."

"So you do believe that some potion he gave her killed her?"

"I don't know what else to believe. She was a healthy woman of forty-five. Her one fault, if I can call it that, was that she didn't want to lose her beauty. She didn't realize that the more mature she became, the more beautiful she truly was. She would have taken any treatment he gave her."

"Even an unproved or untested one?"

"That is what I'm thinking—that he gave her a potion before thoroughly testing it. Lacroix is a risk taker. He's a mountain climber and has ascended the deadly Matterhorn." Wells gives an appraising look. "How much do you know about him?"

"He's a society doctor, attractive to women and uses unorthodox treatments, and somewhat sounds like what we'd call a snake oil salesman back home. Oh—and his partner is a jerk." I lean across the table and lock eyes with him. "And I don't need a textbook to tell me that."

"I haven't met Radic, but will take your word for it. However, you should know that Lacroix is a hematologist."

I smother a groan. I'm sure I've heard the word, but I can't remember exactly what it means. "Which is?"

"A blood disease specialist. It's a small but respectable medical specialty. It's not a popular area of practice for most doctors because so little is known about diseases of the blood. Lacroix was originally more of a medical researcher than a practicing physician. Extremely bright, he obtained a university teaching position despite his French-sounding name and middle-class background.

"He was not a popular teacher because he was exceptionally demanding. I've been told that he expected his students not only to be tireless in repeating experiments, but to reach further with their research goals than others had gone."

"He sounds a bit like Dr. Pasteur who also was completely engrossed in his work."

"You met Dr. Pasteur?"

From the tone of his voice, I can see that puts me up a notch in his evaluation of me.

"Yes, I met him in Paris." I can't brag any more than that, because then it would bring up the questions why and how, and I've been sworn to secrecy.* "And from what I've learned, Pasteur's feet and mind are on much firmer ground than Lacroix's."

"I'm sure you're right, but Lacroix's academic downfall wasn't from his teaching methods or his unorthodox research methods, but from his need for blood. You can't examine blood diseases, most of which are still undefined as to cause, without blood. Doctors proved reluctant to permit him to get out his lancet and cupping glass to draw blood from their sick patients in order to do his research. A bit shortsighted by the doctors since cures will never be found if research isn't conducted, but certainly not on the patients to whom the loss of blood might prove fatal."

"Many people use leeches to draw what they believe is bad blood," I interject.

---

*The aid Louis Pasteur gave Nellie in Paris is related in *The Alchemy of Murder.*—The Editors

"Yes, but leeches drink little and only the bad blood. Also the leeches don't cause the infections and sometimes death occurs when doctors go from patient to patient slicing veins and using cupping to suck out blood."

"Hmm . . . It's just like the controversy between Dr. Pasteur and the medical profession. He claims that doctors are killing their patients by not washing their hands and instruments as they go from patient to patient. They won't listen to him because they claim since he is just a chemist and not a doctor, he doesn't really know what he is talking about. Did you know they won't even let him administer a rabies shot to a patient, even though he discovered it, because he's not a doctor?"

"No, I didn't. But in regards to doctors killing patients, I tend to agree with him."

"So how did Dr. Lacroix solve his need for blood?"

"Grave robbing, for a while. At least a mild variety of it. He hired morgue and mortuary attendants to drain blood from corpses for him. Unfortunately, a church deacon found out he'd had his dead wife drained and brought the police and the church down on his head—hard. Taking blood from bodies wasn't a good scientific approach, anyway, because except in a few cases he couldn't tell what the person died of. Had he been better connected socially or at least less arrogant and single-minded about his work, he might have survived the crisis with a reprimand."

I have fleeting sympathy for Anthony Lacroix. Having been told that my aggressive reporting has made me more enemies than friends, I believe that some people will show up at my funeral not to pay respects, but to reassure themselves that I am really dead.

"What happened to him?"

"He was ordered by the medical board not to conduct any more research using human blood. Disobeying the order will result in the loss of his medical license. When he left the university, he really wasn't fit for the quiet life of a blood doctor—operating in the dark when handling patients because no one really knows the cause and cure of most diseases, then prescribing remedies that often seem to cause more harm than good. This is where Radic came into the picture."

"He recognized Dr. Lacroix's work with rejuvenation as a moneymaker rather than a scientific breakthrough," I offer.

"Quite. And I suspect that Lacroix teamed up with Radic more to get money to carry on his research than just to make money."

"How do you figure into the equation?"

"After he teamed up with Radic and offered his peat moss rejuvenation process at the spa, a remedy he has been experimenting with while at university, he went back into research with rejuvenation, this time financed by Lady Winsworth."

"Does he do any experiments with children?" I ask.

"Not that I know of. Why?"

"Did you ever come into contact with a woman named Sarah in Bath? She was a prostitute and mother of a child named Emma."

He shakes his head, and I tell him about the woman and her child.

"That makes no sense, but I've never even been in the spa." He appears genuinely puzzled. "Let me assure you I experiment on salamanders, not children."

He stands up and in a gentleman's way, takes my arm. "Let's return to our seats and I'll tell you about the black beast."

"What black beast?"

"The one we have to be on the lookout for if we are going into the moors."

The Black Beast of the Moors

Standing over Hugo, and plucking at his throat, there stood a foul thing, a great, black beast, shaped like a hound, yet larger than any hound that ever mortal eye has rested upon. And even as they looked the thing tore the throat out of Hugo Baskerville, on which, as it turned its blazing eyes and dripping jaws upon them, the three shrieked with fear and rode for dear life, still screaming, across the moor.

—Sir Arthur Conan Doyle,
The Hound of the Baskervilles

34

We return to our seats, with me eager to hear about the legendary creature of the moors. "Tell me about the black beast."

"You shouldn't be so eager. Not everyone who encountered it lived to tell the tale."

"My being ripped to pieces by a savage beast would sell newspapers back home, pleasing my publisher to no end."

"A worthy tribute to you. I'm afraid my death would only burden my family with brief mourning and unpleasant funeral expenses. As for the story, there are places in the world where so many unusual things have happened that they achieved a reputation for the strange and unexplained. The moors of Dartmoor is one of those places. Perhaps it's because the landscape itself is so alien to most places on earth—it's part of England yet one gets the feeling that they've left civilization behind when they enter.

"Most of the time it's wet, misty, black, silent, and desolate. The hills are topped with rocky outcrops and bogs lurk as concealed death traps. The tors are raging chaos, materialized and petrified. To people who don't live there, the moors are considered a savage beast."

"Why are the bogs so dangerous? Can't you just walk around them?"

"You may not know they're underfoot, especially in dim light or at night. The bogs commonly have a thin green coating on top that looks rather like the rest of the terrain. The scientific term is sphagnum moss. You'll be walking on wet ground that seems spongy and quakes a bit under your feet and not realize you're on a bog until it swallows you up. That's probably why they call them featherbeds or quakers."

"It sounds like quicksand. You wouldn't recognize it until you start sinking because it looks like sandy ground. Objects like leaves and small branches can lay on it because they're light and won't sink, and that gives you a false notion it's solid."

"Quite. But most people have a misconception of quicksand. Because of the density of quicksand, it's unlikely an animal or person will be completely devoured by it as long as they don't fight it. The key is to remain calm and slowly work your way out of the muck. But with a bog, once you sink into it, unless someone is around to help pull you out, you may not be able to escape. It's really quite scary and deadly."

"This happen often?"

"It's not an uncommon fate for the sheep and small Dartmoor horses that make up most of the living creatures in the moors. England is densely populated, yet Dartmoor is a wilderness, so the human footprint is small. It's fitting that in this strange, twisted landscape of the moors, there are legends of the mysterious and even the macabre. They are known for having more unexplained deaths than any place in England. I've heard people call it the moorland tragedies. Besides the bogs, there is also the mist."

"The mist? How can mist be dangerous?"

"Because it is thicker than the London fog. These mists are so thick that everything around them is concealed from view and a person can be in danger of losing themselves entirely. The mists will suddenly arise and put every object in so impenetrable a shroud that unless one is well acquainted with the area, it's impossible to find a way out. Even the locals get misled by the strange appearance that even familiar objects take on when they are distorted by the mist."

"Probably walked into a bog."

"Don't joke, it happens."

"Why don't they use a compass or a map?"

"Dartmoor is a trackless waste. A compass might help, but you need to know where you're going. I read about a woman who went out to milk the cow at six in the evening, as she does every night, when a mist quickly enveloped her. She was a short distance from her house, just a mile or two, but wandered in the moors until four o'clock in the morning when she reached home, drenched and soaked to the skin. Now, one last tale about the marshes. Do you believe in ghosts?"

"I'm not closed to the idea of spirits. But I'll fully embrace the notion when I see one."

"Well, you might encounter one or more in Dartmoor. It's said they have more ghosts than people. However, I fear the people mistake a natural phenomenon that occasionally appears over the marshes for ghosts. It's called a 'will-o'-the wisp' or *ignis fatuus*—Latin for foolish fire."

"In America we call them jack-o'-lanterns. They are seen at night or twilight over swamps and marshes, but I guess in your Dartmoor it would be over the bogs. It looks like a flickering lamp suspended just over the water and seems to recede if you move toward it or follows you if you move away from it. Very eerie. No one knows what causes it. But as kids we always said it was a ghost trying to lure you."

"When I was a kid, we called the flashes of fire corpse candles. What causes it are gases rising from the decaying vegetation in marshes and bogs. When phosphine and methane, produced by organic decay, come in contact with the oxygen in the air, it ignites. But it's just one of the many amazing aspects about the region that you will find challenging."

I don't feel daunted by what Wells is describing. Modesty keeps me from mentioning that Dartmoor is postage-stamp size, as is England itself, compared to the vast American west, much of which is trackless desert or impassible mountains. Not only have I crossed the west by train and stagecoach and spent six months traveling in rough and wild Mexico,* I have traveled around the world and seen many things that are strange and dangerous. But the chance of being sucked into the earth by a bog does sound ominous—what am I getting myself into?

"What about the black beast?" I have a feeling that there is something more to Wells's ghost stories than idle chatter and want to get to the bottom line.

Wells smiles. "Patience, Nellie, I am getting there. The most famous tale about the moors is that a doglike creature comes out at night to kill; dragging the bodies to a bog where they sink after it ravages them. This huge beast is said to be the ghost of a powerful landowner, a squire, who lost his soul in a deal with the devil. At night people have claimed to hear the wistful cry of the beast. They say its howling sweeps over the moors like a thousands wolves wailing to a full moon. Most importantly, Lacroix believes in the black beast."

"What! You *are* joking?"

"It isn't a theory he goes around uttering in public. We worked very hard for several long days and in a rare moment of companionship we ate

---

*Nellie wrote about her adventures in Mexico in a book called *Six Months in Mexico*. —The Editors

shepherd's pie and downed a few pints at a pub. He told me that he was pleased with my work—despite my lack of education in the field."

"He made a point of that, I take it."

"Quite. Typical of him. His lack of diplomacy aside, he said after I'm finished with the salamander study, he wanted me to do some experiments with his peat moss treatment, attempting to isolate exactly what is in the moss that acts as a preservative for human flesh. During the conversation, he brought up the tale of the black beast of the moors. He believes that most stories like this have to have some basis in fact to them because they've hung around over centuries. Dragons are an example. For thousands of years people believed that the bones of giant creatures occasionally dug up were dragons. It turns out they are dinosaur bones but that doesn't change the fact that giant animals, some winged like dragons, existed."

"Dragons are what the fairy tales might call them, but there were flying dinosaurs—pterodactyls."

"I'm impressed."

I just smile and nod my head. It gives me great pleasure to show women have knowledge in other fields like science and not just cleaning, cooking, and sewing. It's knowledge I picked up helping a fellow reporter with a story, but that still counts.

"But technically," Wells says, "pterodactyls are flying reptiles. They did exist during the dinosaur age, and that's why most laymen think they're dinosaurs, but they aren't."

"Touché, please continue." But if he thinks I'll forget he called me a layman, he'll be surprised.

"Lacroix believes that the black beast did exist, and perhaps may still be around. His theory is that a primordial beast was so well preserved by a peat moss bog that it even retained the spark of life."

"And occasionally waddles out of the muck to eat someone? Wells, I am having a difficult time connecting Lacroix's bog bogyman with our investigation."

"It's quite simple. Lacroix doesn't take peat moss from just any bog in the moors—"

I got it! "Oh, my God! He claims he's getting it from the same bog that has preserved the beast over the millenniums. So if we find the bog where he gets his magic mud, we'll find Lacroix."

"Vampires."

The word drops like a sack of cement between us. It doesn't come from Wells, but from the man who has been crunched up next to the window sleeping—or so I thought.

The man gets up from his seat and addresses us. "Forget the black beasts, mates. Look for the blood and you'll find the vampires."

He gets his luggage out of the net above and steps by us. The train is coming to a halt in Exeter.

Wells leans toward me after the man walks off.

"Don't be upset, he's just a rude buffoon."

"I'm not upset by his little joke or whatever prompted that remark. It's something else."

Wells raises his eyebrows. "What? You look like you've seen a ghost."

"I have . . . or a version of one. The suit's new, the collar fresh, the shoes shiny, and I didn't get a good look at him, but I'd swear that that man is the same mugger who grabbed my purse and stole Hailey's diary from it in London."

35

Aren't you taking this a bit too far?" Wells addresses me as I move my feet as fast as I can to get us from the train to a cab. "We have a perfect hotel to stay in right here by the rail station."

"No. This town, Eseter—"

"Exeter."

"That, too, is too convenient for that man from London to keep an eye on me. If you'd like to stay, please be my guest. I'm going to an inn, any inn, far out on the outskirts."

"My lady, where you go, I go." He tips his hat and gives me a sarcastic grin.

I ignore him as we board a cab. The air is nippy as night falls and dark clouds flow in off the cold waters of the English Channel. I wish we could have stayed. Exeter looks like an interesting town. The River Exe winding through gives it a Shakespearian feel, but I can't take any chances.

"You're going to miss seeing some of the most beautiful cathedrals in the world."

"Excuse me? I'm sorry, my mind is on that man."

"Understandable. You're sure it's the same man?"

"Yes. He might change his clothes, but he can't change that face. Excuse me!" I yell up to our driver. "Can you pull over to your right?"

He stops on a quiet street.

"We aren't being followed," Wells whispers dryly, with a deadpan face. "Not unless we're being spied upon by an aeronaut in a balloon hidden in the clouds above."

Satisfied we are not being followed I tap the roof. "You can proceed."

The cab moves forward, taking us away from Exeter and hopefully to an isolated inn on the outskirts of town.

"Is this how you spend your time?" Wells asks. "Dashing here and there, spying and being spied upon?"

"It's a living."

"Are there any more openings?"

"HERE WE ARE," the driver announces as he brings the cab to a stop. "Bog Rider's inn and pub, the farthest one out of town, as the lady requested." He jumps down and helps me out.

"Welcome!" The innkeeper is tall and sinewy, with coarse swarthy features. His hair is very black and curly, tied carelessly behind his neck with a narrow black ribbon. He has a dimple on his chin that is very prominent when he smiles. My mother claims dimples are a sign of intelligence.

"One room or two?"

"Two . . ." comes from Wells and me.

I'm pleased, but I have to admit a bit of silly woman feelings emerge— does he not find me attractive? Inwardly I scold myself for being so foolish.

"First time here?" he asks us as he turns the register over for us to sign.

"Yes." This time it only comes from me.

"Word of advice, don't go walking out by yourself and especially at night. We have bogs that are treacherous, if not deadly. That's how we got our name: A man walking across the moors one night didn't realize he was on the firm-appearing top layer of a bog. He saw a hat on the ground and gave it a kick. A voice from below asked him why he'd kicked his hat off. The puzzled man asked if someone was in the bog and the man below replied just me and the horse that I'm sitting on."

The innkeeper howls with laughter over his tale and Wells joins him. I take it the story is a local favorite to tell visitors.

"Watch where you put your feet appears to be the message," I tell Wells after we settle into a table in a corner of the room.

The place is crowded with locals, mostly men. We both order toad in the hole, which is sausages in a Yorkshire pudding, served with mashed potatoes and onion gravy. Wells orders a pint of ale.

"I guess there's no chance of them having champagne?" I imbibe very little, but when I do I enjoy champagne. Tonight I could use its nerve-calming effect.

"Here? No. Now, if we had stayed in town at that hotel I recommended . . ."

"Do I sense someone's a little miffed?"

"Quite the contrary; I'm fine staying here in this small, quaint pub on the edge of the wilderness of tors and bogs and crags. It's you who is wanting champagne and I was just pointing out . . ."

"Yes, yes, I get the message, but it's better safe than happy."

"Nellie, it's better safe than *sorry*."

"That, too. But right now I would be *happy* having a glass of champagne. I've been unsettled ever since I saw that man. And it's not because I'm in fear of the man himself—though I have to admit after already experiencing his handiwork as a mugger, I do appreciate the fact that he is a man who can be dangerous, but right now it's more because of his cryptic remark."

"Yes, that was quite odd, making a remark about vampires. But I believe he was just being obnoxious and facetious."

"That's interesting coming from someone who talks about dark beasts."

He starts to object, but I continue. "And it was 'look for the blood and you'll find the vampires.' Anyway, I don't believe it was a coincidence that he was on that train—I'm certain he is following me. Not that it's that difficult—I left a clear trail for an army to follow. One thing I've learned as a reporter—what looks like a coincidence usually has crafty hands behind it."

"Even vampires?"

"You think he was joking, being obnoxious, but I don't take it that way. I don't believe he was giving a warning, either. I'm sure he wouldn't care if I was eaten by a moor beast or had my blood drained by a vampire."

"So what does your gut tell you about his motives?"

"My gut, thank you, tells me that the man has a big ego and he was boasting. He knows something we don't and couldn't resist taunting us. And for the life of me, I can't figure out what he was alluding to."

"Understandable because there is nothing behind it. He was joking, pulling your leg as my father would say. And he has succeeded."

"I don't believe it. He was being facetious, for sure, but I still believe his choice of words has meaning."

Wells gives his head a shake and shrugs. "Perhaps he said his remark because Lacroix is a blood doctor who once paid for blood? I told you about the Ponce de Leon jokes."

"What if Dr. Lacroix has gone back to experimenting with blood? Could that be the reason the man made the crack?"

"Maybe. But he'd lose his license if he obtained blood illegally."

"No risk is too great for a person obsessed with seeking power, wealth, and fame. But I suppose the most important question is not the significance of what he said, but who is he? More importantly, my *gut* tells me he's a hired hand, not a principal. Someone has hired him to follow me and I'd like to know why."

"I'm afraid I didn't pay much attention to him. Seemed like a pretty ordinary chap, don't you think? Maybe a traveling salesman?"

"Or a copper."

"You think he's a police officer?" Wells looks surprised. "Why would you think that?"

"Had much dealing with the police?"

"Frankly . . . none at all that was of any consequence."

"I've had a lot, almost always very good . . . though once in a while I've had to deal with a rotten one. And when a cop's bad, watch out, he's got a gun and a nightstick and likes using both."

"So you think he's a police officer?"

"An *ex*-copper, I'd say. He's cut out of the same rawboned mold that most of the coppers I know are. Long arms to throw a punch, big knuckles when it connects, long feet for a kick. And his shoes. They are the heavy shoes good for walking on sidewalks that help the aching feet of flatfoots."

He raises his eyebrows. "I didn't realize bobbies were so uniform."

"It's attitude, too. In a small town, you always knew who was going to grow up to be a police officer. It was the toughest boy who liked ordering people around."

"And why do you think he's an ex-copper?"

"When I saw him in London, his suit and shoes were worn, the kind of wear you get from not having a wife to take care of them and no money for the laundry. No police captain would permit an officer to show up for duty looking grubby. No, I think he's been a police officer and ran afoul of the law himself. He fell from grace and into the gutter. He was paid to get that diary from me and from the looks of him, it's obviously increased his fortunes."

"Amazing. I don't know what to say. What else do you have up your sleeve about this fellow?"

"Mr. Wells, I sense a bit of sarcasm in your voice."

"Perhaps jealousy would be a better description of my attitude. I apologize. It's just that it's rare to hear a woman be so analytical. Or a man, for that matter. I'm quite impressed. Please, continue."

Another notion about the man has been brewing in my head and I share it. "It is possible that he didn't follow me to Bath. What if something in the diary sent him to Bath?" I tell him about finding the Bath ticket in the diary.

"But if he didn't follow you to Bath, how did he happen to end up in Exeter?"

"He could have easily learned my destination. I made no secret about it at the hotel. Or there could have been something in the diary that directed him to Bath and Exeter. Hailey might have been jotting thoughts in the diary about her investigation of the spa."

"Does your analysis hint at *who* hired him?"

"That is the question, isn't it?"

We sit on the question for a moment while Wells downs the rest of his pint and orders another.

"I would venture a guess," he says, "that it was Radic and Lacroix who hired him to get the diary."

"Perhaps."

"Ah, Nellie, that perhaps was very vague."

"My instant reaction would be a yes as to the spa snake oil doctors, but his comment about vampires throws me off. It has to have something to do with Lacroix and I don't see the man flaunting the connection of the man who pays him."

We silently mull over the puzzle for a moment before I share another thought with him.

"I'm bothered by the notion that Hailey would have put information about the story she was doing on the spa in her diary. A diary is kept for personal matters. Knowing Hailey, that diary would bare her innermost feelings. It doesn't add up any more than Hailey spending several days in Bath, much of it at an expensive hotel at the expense of the spa."

"I've told you Dr. Lacroix is quite a ladies' man. Faced with a threat from a female reporter, his reaction would have been to charm her." Wells pours a small glass of ale from his pint and pushes it across to me. "It's not champagne, but it does wet the whistle."

I'm not crazy about beer, because of my stepfather, but I don't want to be rude, so I take it.

"Thank you." Ale must be an acquired taste because I find it rather bitter. "Hailey was extremely impressionable and immature when it came to dealing with men. Mostly, no doubt, caused by her lack of experience and lack of training from parents because she was orphaned. I've seen her get giddy around men who flatter and flirt with her."

Wells strokes his chin and nods. "So she may well have put things in her diary about Dr. Lacroix after he turned his charm on her. And in doing that, she could have included information about the spa, what she saw, heard. Even, perhaps, information about a laboratory in the moors?"

"Quite," I say with a smile, being British for a moment.

"Which means Lacroix and company would have a very good reason to want to get their hands on the diary."

"I agree. But we are leaving out another fine candidate."

"Which is?"

"Lord Winsworth. I understand he's a tough, two-fisted, rags-to-riches type. Owns mines. One of the other things I've learned about coppers is that the man who mugged me also matches the modus operandi of the type of man hired by mine owners as strike breakers. If Winsworth is that tough, it's hard to imagine him letting a society doctor get away with killing his wife without exacting a bit of revenge."

"You should have been a lawyer." Wells smiles. "Of course, you're the wrong sex." He leans forward and meets my eye. "That is both a compliment for you and an observation about the unfair way women are treated in society."

Vain as always, I blush with pleasure down to my toes.

"Let's get back to vampires," I tell him.

36

"The Vampyre,'" Wells says, "and *Frankenstein* were written by a pair of friends at the same haunted time and place. The two books of horror came about in 1816, due to a cool, wet summer in what historians now call the year without a summer."

"Yes, I remember that . . . well, my mother told me stories that were passed down from her own mother. The weather turned very strange. Sheep froze in meadows, flocks of small birds were found dead in the fields. Pennsylvania got snow in June. Crops were ruined and prices went way up, not to mention so many deaths, especially with the elderly and very young.

"What my mother thought was interesting were people's interpretations on why it happened. Priests were supposedly saying it was God's way of punishing them for their sins and the sins of others. Another theory for it was Benjamin Franklin's lightning rod experiments—some people believe he affected something in the air that changed the weather."

"Yes, stories like that were passed around, all because of ignorance, a lack of knowledge. My father's favorite was a merchant ship was found under full sail with nobody aboard. Scientifically, the cold, damp summer happened because of a series of severe climate abnormalities caused by enormous volcanic eruptions. Unfortunately, as you said, a great number of people starved that year including many in northern Europe. But out of every catastrophe something good arises from it.

"In this case a group of very talented young people, including the poets Shelley and Lord Byron, were staying together at a manor house in Switzerland. Stuck indoors because of the awful weather, they began reading ghost stories and then challenged each other to write their own.

Shelley's eighteen-year-old girlfriend and future wife, Mary, created the Frankenstein monster and their friend, John Polidori, a doctor, produced the famous vampire book in three days."

"Amazing."

"Quite. I must confess I am fascinated with this type of fantastic writing and the stories are among my favorites. As it happens, in 'The Vampyre,' spelled with a Y, Lord Ruthven, a mysterious stranger, appears in London, where he seduces society women. A young man becomes intrigued by him and travels on the continent with him. The young man eventually discovers that every woman Lord Ruthven seduces ends tragically. He investigates Lord Ruthven, but his own life is lost after his love is killed and he fails to save his sister from the vampire."

"Good lord, what a horrible story."

Wells laughs. "It depends upon your tastes. Certainly not a good choice for someone who likes a happy ending. I love a good tale of gothic horror. What's your preference?"

"A good mystery. My favorite right now is the new Sherlock Holmes mysteries."

"Why does that not surprise me?" Wells smiles. "Maybe you should try your hand at one."

"I did. I wrote, *The Mystery of Central Park*, which was published last year in October. After I went undercover as a prostitute, I decided to write a mystery. It just seemed fitting and the whole setting of Central Park is perfect for such a tale."

"Miss Nellie Bly! You are full of surprises. A reporter and writer. I'm deeply impressed. You went undercover as a prostitute?" His eyes twinkle.

"Yes, but I remained a lady."

"Never doubted it."

Our food comes and we eat in a silence, a quiet moment I'm enjoying despite the fact that I most often feel the need to chatter away to fill the void.

Once our plates are cleared, Wells leans forward and whispers with a glint in his eye, "So what do you think, Nellie, is Dr. Lacroix a vampire?"

"Why not? Perhaps the ex-copper or whatever he is was speaking metaphorically. He's a blood doctor who seduces wealthy women either physically or with promises of eternal youth."

"I don't think that quite fits the definition."

"He is also a stealer of blood, at least in the past. That certainly places him in the vampire category, as far as I'm concerned."

He gives a smile that is almost quizzical.

"What?" I ask.

"I was just thinking that I am hiding out from a copper turned bad, while sitting in a pub talking to a mysterious foreign woman about murder and monsters. There are two amazing things about that. The first is that I have a tremendous imagination which leads me not infrequently to storming castles and rescuing fair princesses, all without leaving my teacher's podium, and the second is that I am talking to a *woman* about these incredible subjects."

"I can assure you, Wells, that if Mary Shelley or my friend Sarah Bernhardt were here, they would conjure up more fantastic ideas than I ever could." I put my elbows on the table and lean forward. It is decision time.

"So, Mr. H. G. Wells, you do agree with me that Dr. Lacroix is a modern vampire type?"

He sits up straight, adjusts his tie, and noisily clears his throat. "In a word, Miss Bly . . . no."

I suck in a deep breath. "Please tell me why?"

"I rather suspect that Dr. Lacroix is a victim of mad science. Or perhaps science gone mad, is a more accurate assessment."

"What are you talking about?"

"Nellie, think about the age of scientific discovery the world is in. For thousands of years, literally since the beginning of recorded time, the world had changed little in terms of technology, then during a few decades of our own time, we got the telephone, the telegraph, electric lights, the steam engine, and a thousand other innovations.

"Dr. Pasteur in Paris is finding whole new worlds under a microscope, a man named Bentz in Germany is building a carriage driven by a gasoline engine, aeronauts are soaring in the heavens with dirigibles and hot-air balloons; they even say we will have flying machines during our lifetimes."

"What are you saying? That Dr. Lacroix is just another scientific trailblazer like Pasteur and Edison?"

"No, dear Nellie, the fact is that there is another side to science, a dark side. You know about *Frankenstein,* are you also familiar with *The Strange Case of Dr. Jekyll and Mr. Hyde* by Robert Louis Stevenson?"

"Yes. A little. A doctor makes a potion, drinks it, then goes around killing people."

"Quite. Do you see the similarites between Victor Frankenstein and Jekyll and Dr. Lacroix?"

"I'm in a fog."

"Let me explain. What Jekyll and Frankenstein did was venture beyond the realms of rational science in their experiments. Unlike Pasteur who is moving slowly, taking one step at a time, building on one small finding and then another until there's a mountain, Frankenstein, Jekyll, and Lacroix all have the same method—to attempt in one giant leap to create in a test tube matters that are in the hands of the gods.

"Do you see the logic and even simplicity of their methods? Victor Frankenstein believed he could inject electricity into the body of a dead person and ignite life back into the body. Jekyll thought he could control human nature with a concoction because substances like opium can affect behavior, and Lacroix believes he can reverse the aging process with what you call his magic mud because preserved bodies have been found in peat moss."

"Wells, they are madmen—Dr. Jekyll, Victor Frankenstein. Besides, aren't you forgetting something . . . they are fictional characters."

"No, I haven't, but what you have obviously forgotten is that what many authors have written about have come true or inspired inventions. Case in point: Jules Verne and his many literary inventions that have come about. They completely accepted science as their god and set out to create miracles. Instead, what they created turned against them, and when it did, it first broke their spirit and then their minds."

"You think science has driven Dr. Lacroix crazy?"

"I wouldn't doubt it. Remember, this was a successful university professor who instead of conducting himself in the way customary of men in his profession, threw all caution aside, crossed moral lines, and broke the law to get the blood he needed for his experiments."

I mull over that for a moment. "You believe that's what happened to Lady Winsworth. That Lacroix once again was the risk taker, a man willing to cross the line and try something radical regardless of the consequences."

"Yes, that is my take on him. Working with him, experiencing his fanatical nature, his obsession with results when conducting experiments, I felt I was dealing with a man possessed."

"Stop," I tell him. "My head is swirling. All this mad science is driving me crazy. I've dealt with more insanity in the last hour than I did spending ten days in a madhouse."

He reaches over and takes my hand in his.

"My apologies, darling Nellie. But I have one more question to raise."

"My head's splitting, but go ahead, though I may run screaming out of this pub."

He leans forward and speaks in a confidential tone. "Lovely Nellie, will you make love with me tonight?"

I was never a great amorist, though I have loved several people very deeply.

—H. G. WELLS

37

I almost knock over my chair as I leave him at the table and march to my room. He is lucky that I didn't slap him in the face right there and have the innkeeper evict him. What nerve! What a cad! And I believed the man to be a gentleman.

"*Nellie!*—I must explain."

I swing around to find him running down the corridor toward me.

"You have said quite enough." I turn back to the door to my room. I'm so angry I fumble trying to get the key into the lock.

"Please let me explain."

I take a deep breath and face him. "I suggest you retire to your room and sleep off whatever disgusting thoughts the alcohol has created in your mind. We will discuss in the morning our arrangements."

"Please, you must understand, I fell under your spell."

Oh boy, that was a showstopper with me. But it's only a brief moment before my insecurities step in. "Under my spell as a woman of beauty and charm? Do give me some credit for intelligence. I look in the mirror each morning and I'm well aware that I am not a Helen whose beauty launched a thousand ships."

"I was referring to your mind, your spirit, your wonderfully rational attitude."

"Oh." Oh damn—only my mind is beautiful.

"You are a complete woman. I've met only a few of them in my life. It is much more attractive than the external beauty society gives such importance to. I misunderstood, I thought because you had freed yourself of so many of the straightjackets the world puts on women, on all of us, that you had a broader, more worldly attitude about lovemaking."

I stare at him, befuddled.

He appears to be completely remorseful. I don't know what to say or think. I'm not a prude, I have been in a man's arms before, held a man in my own. I am well aware that the best reason not to be promiscuous is pregnancy—like Hailey, I have no one to turn to if I become pregnant. I support and love my dear mother, as she does me, but she would be devastated if I was with child without a husband, especially when I am her sole means of support.

I know there are ways, none of them surefire, to avoid pregnancy, but I am definitely a conventional woman when it comes to a relationship with a man—which is why I found Wells's comment offensive.

"I hesitate to ask, Wells, but what exactly is your, uh, worldly attitude toward lovemaking?"

He takes a deep breath and relaxes just a little. Pulling his kerchief out of his breast pocket, he pats his forehead.

"I must confess that I was caught up both by the moment and the ale, the moment being my admiration and amazement at meeting a woman with a free spirit."

"Yes, you've mentioned that. Now tell me about your moral attitude."

"My moral attitude . . . well, I guess you could say that my way of thinking is that men and women are free to do what they care to do as long as they don't hurt others. It strikes me that most of the laws and customs in regard to whom, when, and where sex is to be conducted come from church people who either don't have sex, don't enjoy sex, or don't know how to enjoy sex, and hate to see others enjoying it."

"Are you married?"

"No, but let me assure you that when I am married, my attitude will not change. If a man and a woman are attracted to each other, a tiny wedding band shouldn't be enough of a barrier to keep them from enjoying each other's bodies, to keep them from touching and kissing and caressing and—"

"*Go to bed.*"

He stares at me.

"Go to your room and get some sleep. And don't ever speak to me again with such lewdness or I will have you arrested. And this is not a minister speaking, it's me. A lady."

SLEEP IS IMPOSSIBLE. I lay in bed, angry at myself.

I am not angry at my behavior with Wells. He had been impertinent.

And it is not what I said that makes me angry.

It is my weakness that has me tossing and turning, my mind swirling with sinful thoughts.

H. G. Wells is a brilliant man; that I have come to realize. And there is another side to him, a side of passion and sensuality. He is a man hungry for love. And I am a lonely woman who at times like this, could use the arms of a man.

I am too young to be a spinster, but sometimes that's how I feel. Most women my age are married and have children. I have stuck to work, my nose to the grindstone, my love and attention have been directed solely on the wrongs I have investigated, the stories I wrote. My desire in life is to help change the world—only unlike the Red Virgin, the fiery French feminist and revolutionary who presses her demands for social change in the streets, my pen is my sword.

I am a *working woman* in a man's world.

That means sacrifices, lots of sacrifices. I've had to put everything aside except my dedication to my job. I have to be faster and smarter than the men around me to survive because few of them believe a woman should be doing *their* job.

It irks me no end that I can't vote, I can't sit on a jury, and that many states curtail the property rights of women, that women are barred from most jobs and paid less than what a man receives even if they do the same job, and forget about being promoted—that never happens. But I try not to think about those injustices because if I did, I would never get anything done. And as silly as this sounds, I hate that men can wear pants and women can't. I'd like to see men ride a horse sidesaddle wearing a dress.

I don't know about the afterlife. I have not a clue as to what I will find in heaven or hell or whether I'll get sent anywhere after I've given up the ghost, but I do know that I have *one* chance to go around, one chance to do exciting things, one chance to accomplish the impossible and to climb mountains only men have been permitted to scale.

And I am not going to pass it up because I am, by society's terms, "a woman."

I can already see the writing on my tombstone: HERE LIES NELLIE BLY, WHO WAS HUNGRY FOR LOVE BUT TOO AFRAID TO EXPERIENCE IT BECAUSE IT WOULD HAVE KEPT HER FROM CLIMBING MOUNTAINS.

38

The next day we had an unspoken truce between us and we went along as if nothing had happened. We had to return to Exeter in an attempt to locate the artist. While there, I sent off a telegram to Oscar asking him if he had ever heard of any connection between Dr. Lacroix and the hounds of the moors.

"I am certain that most of the gossip in London society passes by Oscar Wilde at some point," I tell Wells.

"I've never heard of the gentleman."

"Oscar would be mortified if he heard that. He wrote a book you might find interesting, *The Picture of Dorian Gray.* As a matter of fact Oscar believes Dr. Lacroix got some of his ideas about eternal youth from his book."

"Interesting . . . I must take a peek at it when I return to London."

We have no luck at the post office locating the artist and go into a shop that sells painting and art supplies.

I inquire of the proprietor whether he knows a painter named Isaac Weekes and get a positive response.

"Yes, yes, Weekes is noted for his Dartmoor scenes. I have several. Here, let me show you."

He takes us to three paintings, each of which is a broad, picturesque view of the moorlands, its rolling hills and tors topped with exploding granite crags.

"I'm looking for a particular painting . . . it's of a bog," I tell the man.

"I'm sorry, I don't have one. I can query Weekes about preparing one. It would take a few months to obtain, knowing Weekes. Does what he wants, when he wants." The store owner laughs and throws up his hands.

"Are you familiar with a Weekes painting of a bog? It was commissioned by a friend of ours, a Dr. Lacroix."

"No, I'm sorry. I have no knowledge of such a piece or your friend. Weekes doesn't display all of his artwork here. He has the majority of his paintings displayed in London. More money there."

"Do you know where Mr. Weekes lives?" This time the question comes from Wells.

"Yes, in a small Dartmoor village called Linleigh-on-the-moors, about ten miles west of here. You'd have to rent a pony cart to get there."

"Perhaps a taxi," I suggest.

"Won't find one to take you out there. Road is too rough for a regular carriage. I wouldn't even call it a road, most of the way. It's more for sheep and goats. The stable will rent you a cart that can do it. Better get an early start in the mornin' though to return before dark. I don't recall the village having comfortable accommodations though the pub might have a room or two."

"Poor, quiet, and remote," Wells says later, after consulting a map at the rail station. "The sort of small village where people raise sheep, grow their own food, and there probably hasn't been a new house built since the Norman conquest. The only daunting thing is there is only a dirt road to the village, a common trait to most of the small villages scattered around Dartmoor. By dirt road I am of course referring to what the art gallery proprietor called a goat path."

At the telegraph office we find a reply from my missive to Oscar.

"He says that the expert on hell hounds is the author, Arthur Conan Doyle, the man who writes about the detective called Sherlock Holmes. He says that Doyle is in Dartmoor at present."

"I read *The Sign of the Four* excerpts in *The Strand*," Wells says. "An excellent mystery tale. From what you've said about your friend Oscar Wilde, detective stories would not exactly be his cup of tea."

"They've met because they have the same publisher. Anyway, he says Doyle is in a place called Buckfastleigh researching a book."

"Buckfastleigh is about twenty-five miles or so from here." Wells looks at his pocket watch. "I believe we can get there by train by noon, if we go now, so we better get to the station if that's your plan."

"Any chance the train can drop us near the village artist?"

"No, it's in a different direction. And it's already too late to get out and be certain we can make it back to Exeter before dark."

"We'll just have to chance it. If we meet up with a black beast of a hound, I shall simply tell it that it's not permitted to eat an American."

At the stable, I soon discover the difference between a carriage cab and a pony cart is *comfort.* The buggy has two tall, thin wheels, but no springs, so we will feel every rock and rut on the road. The seat is an un-padded board and backboard, which means after a few miles I will be very sore. And the pony is a runt, much smaller than what we would call a pony back home, though I wouldn't call him that because he's very cute and looks sensitive. The buggy wheels are taller than the little critter.

I pull Wells out of the pony's hearing. "We can't have the poor little guy pull us. That would be cruel."

"Don't let his size fool you. It's a Dartmoor pony. They are strong and have stamina. And this one is lucky to be pulling a cart under sun and stars. Cruel is what happens to his fellow ponies. These small ponies have been used in tin mining and at the granite quarries here in Dartmoor since before the Romans. Unfortunately, because of their small size, they're also used in underground mines to haul ore carts. Once they're down there, they never see the sun again and are even buried in the mine to avoid the expense of bringing them out."

"That's horrible! They should have the mine owners pulling the carts and leaving them down there."

"The cart has to be back tonight," the stableman tells us. "Needed for milk delivery at five in the morning." He removes two big tin milk pails from the storage rack behind the seat and then gives us a narrow look. "You're not going to make it out and back before dark. I'm going to need an extra deposit to cover a broken wheel or pony leg."

"I'd pull the cart myself before I'd let the pony break a leg," I tell him.

Off we go, but not at a speed that would impress the owners of Kentucky Derby runners. And true to my previous experiences with buggies that lack springs, I feel every bump on the road.

"After hearing so many stories about the eerie moors, bogs that swallow people, and black beasts that run them to the ground and rip out their throats," I confess to Wells between bumps that, "I do wish we'll be able to get to the village in decent time, talk to the artist, and return to Exeter before dark."

"Might not be a problem with this guy taking us," he assures me,

DARTMOOR PONIES

pointing out how effortlessly the pony appears to be pulling the buggy on the cobblestone street. He grins. "But we'll have to see how bad the goat path is."

"Have you visited Dartmoor often?"

"This will be the first time. But I have studied the geology of the area as part of my teacher's training."

Uh huh. Book learning.

39

The road changes from cobblestone paved, to just paved, then packed dirt, and finally to "paved" with boulders and ruts.

As we trudge along at a slow but steady pace, the hours pass and we leave behind all the remnants of mankind's footprint except for the narrow path. The landscape transforms from city, to rural, and finally to wilderness.

Now I can understand why moorlands are not just described simply as "wilderness" as the mountains, forests, and deserts of my own country are, but seem to have their own category. With the moors there are also shapes and images that are strange to my eye—mysterious and preternatural, even fear evoking.

Craggy, wild-shaped tors, with winding, tumbling rivulets, and green fields that Wells, from his book knowledge, assures me are not the moss-covered bogs, the quaking-earth variety that suck you down, never to be found again.

No wonder this scarcely populated land off the beaten track has generated so many tales of ghosts and ghouls that are stranger than fiction.

My imagination starts to go wild and I can imagine a dinosaur peeking its head out from one of the granite mounds or Druid priests conducting a sacrifice on a moonless night within the confines of a stone circle.

Despite his estimate that we might be able to conduct our business at the village and return to the city before nightfall, it is obvious to me that we will be lucky to reach the village while the sun still shines.

"Anything out there dangerous? Other than the bogs and ghosts you've read about in a textbook?" Petty, but I can't resist the jab.

He gives the landscape a look, as if he's scanning it. "I don't know . . . might be a viper or two."

"Poisonous?"

"Yes, but the snakes tend to mind their own business unless someone provokes them."

"Wonderful. My experience with snakes is that they tend to feel provoked when you accidentally step on them."

A light mist is falling and haze is gathering in the distance, blurring the landscape, making it even eerier.

"We should have waited and set out at the crack of dawn," I complain.

"Quite. My fault. For not relying upon my instincts and letting you make the decision."

"I made the decision because I have more experience than you have."

"Been to Dartmoor often?" he asks.

"Don't be snide. I've been to the Wild West, Mr. Wells—and I'm sure your black beast offers little danger compared to dealing with boozed-up cowboys and miners shooting up a town and each other. Our snakes would make vipers run so fast, they'd shed their skins."

This time I get a long, appraising look from him.

"Why are you staring at me?" I ask.

"I was thinking how different—pleasantly different—it is being in the hands of a woman instead of just in her arms."

"Let me assure you that if a great black hound comes galloping at us, you will have to run very fast to be anywhere near my hands." Ah, but again, vain as I am, I waddle in the compliment but don't ignore the fact that he has made a reference to romance. "Do you spend much time in the arms of women?"

"Not as much as I'd like. Not having a title, money, or a handsome mug, I must reply upon a woman's charitable disposition."

We share a laugh at his self-debasement that is interrupted by one of our wheels rolling in and out of a large rut. I am so sore, I feel as if I'd been paddled on my seat.

Linleigh-on-the-moors is set in a flat area where a narrow river comes out of a rocky gorge and spreads out. Barns and small granary towers are visible outside the village as we top a hill and come down to the rural community. It is still daylight, but less than an hour of it is left.

Grazing sheep, a few ponies, and a few lonely farmhouses are the only signs of life we've seen much of the way, but as we come into town we see a large number of carts in the center of the town square and even a full-sized horse, almost all clustered around the alehouse.

"Probably market day," Wells says. "Since the roads are rough or nonexistent and the terrain unruly, I'm sure the village gets visitors only when it's absolutely necessary. Some of the Dartmoor villages are so isolated, they've developed dialects that are different than the king's speech and almost impossible to understand even for Brits like me."

Wonderful. If I had difficulty understanding the people in Exeter and he's saying he's going to have a hard time understanding the people in this rather isolated town, I'm in a pickle—as my mother would say.

The houses are built of stones gathered from the moors, with the cracks closed with mortar. They are gray, darkened by time, but appear strong enough to withstand any storm that Mother Nature sends roaring in from the sea. Most have a porch facing south and granite mullioned windows. A general store, an alehouse, and a small church—probably just a chapel because I see no residence for a minister—comprise the most prominent buildings in the village square.

"I think the general store will be our best place to find where Isaac Weekes lives." Wells says.

"Fine. You can do all the talking."

"Finally," he says.

"In Linleigh," I add.

I just smile and gladly get out of our cart.

"You'll find him at the alehouse or he'll be there soon," the proprietor tells us.

"Steady customer," Wells asks.

"Every day but Sunday and he'd be there on the Sabbath if the place was open. Old Isaac goes out with his painter's kit and stays out in the fields the whole day, rain or shine, painting and doesn't come back into town until the last bit of light is leaving and the alehouse has opened its door for business. He enjoys a pint or two before going home to face the dickens."

"The dickens?" comes from me.

"That's Isaac's wife, a woman with a sharp tongue and a broom. She's generous at using the hard end of that broom against man or beast or whoever else gets in her way. Old Isaac is just the opposite, living up to his biblical name as a man of laughter."

"Is something special happening today?" I ask; so much for Wells doing the talking.

"Market day, but I do say it's unusual to get so many strangers in town. Got a man on a full-size horse. Don't see many of those around here. Next thing you know we'll be getting the horse with the iron hoof."

"The horse with the iron hoof is—"

"A steam locomotive." I finish Wells's attempt to explain to me as we leave the store. "That's similar to the same name Indians use to describe a train out west. But small chance they'll be seeing an Iron Horse in these parts during our lifetimes, unless they discover gold."

The alehouse is dark with a black-beamed ceiling low enough for a man to reach up and touch, crowded with small tables and large people, noisy and smoky. The small amount of breathable air is saturated by the heavy perfume of stale malted beer.

Wells asks the barmaid about Isaac Weekes.

"Bellied up there." She jerks her head in the direction of the short bar.

"Would you tell Weekes we'd like to buy him a drink?" I hand her a coin.

There is no room at the bar and no empty tables, but at the sight of hard money from out of towners, she quickly orders three men up from their table and has us take it. I tell her we are buying the men their next drink and I get grins of approval from them. A moment later, she's back with the artist.

Weekes is a rather diminutive gentleman, pint-sized I'd say, probably not much taller than his wife's broom. Slender and small boned, he has a thick mop of black hair, thick black eyebrows, gray eyes, and black eyelashes that any woman would envy. The wrinkles around his eyes form a delicate network, woven from gazing great distances for his paintings; ruddy cheeks hold the deeper laugh lines, while on brow and neck are the deep imprints of sun, snow, rain, frost, wind—nature's markings.

He could use some of Dr. Lacroix's magic mud; his age is hard for me to guess because I can't tell if he is an old man with young features or a young man that appears older than his chronological age. My impression is between forty to sixty, but I could be off decades, especially since the storekeeper called him Old Isaac.

We introduce ourselves as lovers of the moorlands and interested in a painting; "Of one of the famous Dartmoor bogs," I tell him, mentioning that our friend Dr. Lacroix referred us.

"Ah, good Dr. Lacroix, a gentleman, he is, and a fine one at that."

He offers a toast to Lacroix, he and Wells with ale, me with apple cider. The artist does appear to be jolly, but I suspect some of it comes from what he drank before we got there.

The place is so crowded, we have to lean over the table to be heard and we are brushed by others standing close by as they move about.

After he gets another pint he salutes us with the mug, then takes a long swig and smacks his lips. "Yes, Dr. Lacroix is a fine gentleman. In fact, another friend referred by him been askin' about his bog painting."

I try to act nonchalant at the startling statement but I'm sure my face registered surprise. "Who asked? I mean, it may be a mutual friend."

"Never got his name. Big man, from London, I'd say, though I never asked and he never offered to tell where he's from."

"New suit? New bowler hat?" I question.

"Might, yes, I'd say his clothes looked new, but then again, I don't know much about the clothes worn in London. This gent a friend of yours?"

"Actually, no, he's not. More of what you'd call a competitor. I have a confession to make. We're newspaper reporters doing a story about Dr. Lacroix and the miracles he's creating with his peat moss treatments."

"He told me you'd be coming."

"Who told you we were coming?" I glance at Wells, puzzled. He shrugs his shoulders.

"Dr. Lacroix. When he had me do the painting, he said I'd get visitors someday who would want to know where the bog is that fills his need. Said people would want to know in order to steal his secret. That's why he came to me and didn't hire a local artist to do the painting. He paid me well to keep my mouth shut. And I'm good at that, even after I've had a few."

I always find it interesting to find out how far into his cups a man has to get before the "demon rum" loosens his tongue just enough for me to get any information I need from him.

"Have another, Mr. Weekes," I say.

"Don't mind if I do."

Neither do I. I signal for another pint for him.

"You mention that there was a local artist. That was at . . . ?"

The question remains hanging as the man reflects on something.

"He paid me well, Dr. Lacroix," Weekes says. "But it almost cost me my life. I've seen plenty of strange things out in moors, but it was the first time I saw the ghost of Lady Howard, with her coach of bones, pulled by a black beast of a hound." He gives us a glassy-eyed stare. "Near scared the life from me."

He coughs out spittle and stares at me. I don't know what to say. His eyes turn glassy and his face goes beet red. My impression is that he's suddenly holding his breath.

"Are you all right?" Wells asks.

Weekes stares ahead and then coughs again; blood dribbles down the corner of his mouth.

"My God, I think he's having a stroke." I look to Wells. "What do we do?"

Weekes gives out a gasp that sounds like a nervous rattle from his lungs and then seems to simply relax in his chair. *Dead.*

I can't breathe.

I stare at him then look at Wells who stares back at me. His mouth is open and so is mine.

Weekes slumps forward.

The handle of an ice pick is sticking out of his back.

There's a scream.

Mine.

A DARTMOOR ROAD

40

Everything stopped. The talk, the laugher, the slap of ale pints onto tabletops, the loud, sucking noise some men made as they slurped down the beer. For me, time itself stopped in a frozen moment during which I gape at Weekes. *The last remains of Weekes.*

Then all hell broke loose as the realization dawns that there is death—*that there is murder*—before their eyes.

My entire world is a small, crowded, smoky little pub in a wilderness village that is probably too small to be on most maps. First there is more confusion than questions—My God! It can't be! What happened? How? Why? Who did such a thing?

When the last question makes its way around the room like a juicy rumor whispered at a party, the room grows silent and two dozen pairs of eyes stare at the two strangers in the room.

Wells and I look at each other. We don't need a Ouija board to realize that we are the only candidates for murderers in the room.

"You killed him," a grizzled man with the body of a blacksmith says to us.

"The strangers killed Old Isaac," another man yells.

"Murderers!" the barmaid screams.

A growl goes around the room and panic moves my feet and mouth.

I step up to the barmaid. "*Stop it!*" I spin around to the tightly packed crowd surrounding us. "*Look at us!* We're not killers. We were talking to Isaac about a painting. Someone killed him, but not us. We hardly know the man."

"No man in Linleigh-on-the-moors would have touched Old Isaac. Only a stranger could have done it. If not you, lady, then him!"

More growls of concord go around the room. Poor Wells is wide-eyed. He tries to say something and it comes out as a stammer.

"*Wait!*" I shout. "We were facing Mr. Weekes. He's been stabbed from behind!"

Another frozen moment as the men digest what I told them. I hear mumblings of assent and others of doubt.

"Where's the other stranger?" I ask.

There's confused mumbling and the man who accused Wells says, "There are no other strangers."

"There has to be, the man at the general store said there was." I pounce at the barmaid. "You served another stranger in here tonight, didn't you!"

"Yes, by the lord, yes, I did." She looks around. "He was here a moment ago. Where'd he go?"

"There was a man standing behind Isaac earlier," Wells says.

"Yes, I gave him a pint," the barmaid says.

"That's your murderer," I tell the men. "Find him!"

Wells and I pour out of the alehouse with the others.

"The horse is gone!" someone yells.

The statement is about the full-sized horse we'd seen earlier. As the men gather to talk, I pull Wells away and to our buggy.

As we leave town, I tell Wells, "Keep the speed down."

"Why? They may think about it and come after us."

I look back. There is no pursuit.

"I don't think so. These people think the moors are haunted. They'll wait for morning, I'm certain." If I was them, I wouldn't go out on the moors at night.

"Why do you want me to keep a slow pace? There's a full moon, we can see the road pretty well."

"There's a murderer ahead of us. Let's keep a good distance from him." I don't say I am also concerned that our little horse could step into a rut. I don't think he would appreciate my concern for a horse at this time.

Wells is silent for a moment. "We should go back to the village. They'll have the police out there tomorrow. They'll want to question us."

I sigh. "Wells, you have too much book learning to be a good investigator. My *experience* with coppers tells me that if they get ahold of us, we won't be going anywhere for days. If we're not lynched by those farmers back there after they get boozed up. The delay would mean I'd have to return to New York without answers. For me, that means the horseshoe and the kingdom's lost or whatever happened at the battle."

" 'For want of a nail, the shoe was lost. For want of a shoe, the horse was lost. For want of a horse, the rider was lost. For want of a rider, the battle was lost. For want of a battle, the kingdom was lost. And all for the want of a horseshoe nail.' "

"That, too. Who uses an ice pick?" It's a rhetorical question, not one for which I expected an answer.

"An ice pick," he repeats.

"Knives, guns, poison, clubs, hands and cords for strangling, all common weapons. But an ice pick is a singular weapon."

He is silent for a moment and then says, "The Rustlers."

"Come again?"

"A London gang from the Whitechapel district. They wear American cowboy boots and call themselves rustlers."

"Cowboy boots," I repeat.

"They're known to kill with ice picks."

"Clean wounds, easier to use than a knife, placed right in spine, heart, or brain, brings instant results without making noise."

"But it doesn't make any sense." Wells shakes his head. "There wouldn't be a Whitechapel thug out here."

Whitechapel was the violent, poverty-stricken area in London made notorious for having been the scene for the killings by the fiend known as Jack the Ripper.

"It's just as likely," I tell him, "to find someone from Whitechapel out here as it would be finding a female newspaper reporter from New York or a teacher from London. The person was hired and sent here."

"Why? Who in God's name would kill that old painter?"

"This time it's easy. There's only one candidate, actually two acting together. Lacroix and Radic. They are the ones who have a motive to keep Isaac silent. And I'm at fault, too."

"What? That's nonsense. Why would you say such a thing?"

"I've left an open trail for a horde to follow. The interest I showed in the bog painting must have been conveyed to Radic by Lady Callista Chilcott."

"And you believe they acted that quickly? What? Took a train to London and picked up a Rustler off the street in Whitechapel?"

"No, there must have been a prior connection. When I was in Dr. Radic's office, he had a thug there." I meet Wells's eye. "He was wearing cowboy boots."

41

We arrive back at the stable after midnight—avoiding being murdered by a Whitechapel cowboy or ripped to pieces by a moors beast, but we have a sleepy, angry stableman to deal with. Meeting his demand to be paid double soothes his ruffled feathers, but it doesn't get us a ride into the heart of town where we can find lodging.

"Taxis stopped hours ago and don't come down here unless they have a fare, anyway."

"We need lodging."

He points to the faded word GUESTS on a shingle hanging from the gatepost to his house next door. "Me wife takes in a traveler now and again."

"How many rooms do you have?" I ask.

"Just the one." He eyes us. "You're married, aren't ya?"

"Of course," Wells says.

I give the stableman an extra shilling. "For a good meal of fruit and your best grain for our tireless pony."

The pony accepts my big hug. "I'm going to miss you," I whisper in his ear. He nods his head. I like to think it's his way of telling me he'll miss me, too.

The wife greets us at the door, sleepy-eyed, wrapped in a robe with her hair up in curlers. Fortunately, she is less evil tempered about our late arrival than her husband, but no less mercenary.

"The room's a quid."

Wells starts to object and I interject, "We'll take it."

A quid is five dollars,* which is several times more than what I'm sure

---

* About one hundred dollars today.—The Editors

her going rate is, but I pay it. I am too tired to haggle or pack my sore body and valise to go to another inn.

"Beggars can't be choosers," I whisper to Wells as we follow the woman up a dark and narrow stairway. The bedroom is tiny with a frumpy brass-railed bed topped with a heavy quilt, a small dresser with a washbasin and mirror above it on the wall, and a single stuffed chair.

"The water closet is down the hall."

The landlady pauses at the door and turns and smiles at us as we stand together, worn and ready to drop.

"It's so nice to have a good Christian couple as our guests."

The moment the door closes I fall backward onto the bed. "Oh God, I am so sore and tired I could sleep a week."

Wells collapses in the stuffed chair. "I confess that had we not gotten this room, I would have laid down on the ground and slept 'til the sun came up."

I close my eyes and the grim image of Isaac Weekes's eyes popping, blood dribbling from his mouth, came to me. So does another horrible thought—I am sure I caused him to be targeted for death.

"Don't think about it, Nellie."

"What?"

"I could tell from the expression on your face you're agonizing over Weekes. Unfortunately for him, Weekes signed his own death warrant when he did the painting for Lacroix. If it wasn't you seeking him out, it would have been an investigator for Lord Winsworth, the police, or another reporter and the result would have been the same. It's a little too much to imagine that we were being followed so quickly that an assassin got to Linleigh before we even decided to go there."

"Thank you." I close my eyes again, too worn out to get up and take off my shoes and freshen up in the washroom down the hall.

I am dozing when I hear Wells say, "I'm sorry."

Slowly pulling myself into a sitting position, I ask, "What are you sorry about?"

He is slumped in the chair with his eyes closed. His lids open and our eyes meet.

"For not being the man I would like to be."

"I see . . . and what is the reason for this profound observation of your presumed failings?"

"You have been paying our way because I don't have money. You had the courage and determination to stand up to that mob in the village, while I stood by shocked and speechless. I was frightened to set out in the night through the moors because I felt that if we were attacked by the murderer, I would not be strong enough to protect you."

Men and their egos! Even Wells, who insists he wants women to be strong and equal, is slighted if I'm too assertive.

"And who made you master of the world, Mr. Wells? You're not responsible for me. As for what happened in the pub—"

He throws up his hands. "You're going to tell me that you reacted because you had experience dealing with a mob before and I, poor devil that I am, have only read about mobs."

"As a matter of fact, I was going to say exactly that. And while you're castigating yourself, let me tell you something. It's a rare man of courage and determination, indeed, who would have left town with a potential posse chasing us and a killer on the road. I don't know what would have happened had we ran into the murderer, but I do know that the man I was with had guts to face the dark night and I'm confident he would have fought valiantly for me had it come to a fight."

He stares at me for a long moment.

"Do you really believe that?"

"Have you heard me ever say anything I didn't believe?"

"Nellie . . . you do lie a bit."

"White lies . . . they don't count."

I bend down and kiss him on the forehead. "Thanks for taking care of me tonight."

He pulls my head down and my lips meet his, warm and soft and smooth. I can feel the kiss down to my toes. I pull back and he stands up and pulls me to him. We kiss again.

"Let me make love to you," he says.

I shove him back into the stuffed chair. "Make yourself comfortable. You can use the floor if the chair doesn't work out." I bend down and give him a peck on the forehead. "It's a true knight in shining armor who lets a woman have the only bed in the place."

42

Bright and early the next morning, Wells and I go to the train station to-gether and obviously buy two tickets to London, letting the ticket seller know that I am an American and that Wells and I are traveling together.

Short of waving an American flag, or mentioning to the ticket seller that the police might be inquiring about us, I can't think of anything to make the two of us more conspicuous.

When Wells slips over to tell a baggage handler that we will be sending over several pieces of luggage for our London trip, I spot a familiar-looking black coach waiting on the street. As with the carriage of the woman in black in Bath, it is an expensive town coach and has much the same lines, only this time the coat of arms on the door is visible though I can't read it from the distance. I don't see a passenger as the carriage pulls away.

"I just saw a black coach like the one I saw in Bath." I tell Wells when he comes back from seeing the baggage man.

"Really . . ."

We next go to the telegraph office, where I send a cable to Mr. Cock-erill, my editor in New York, advising him that I am catching the eight o'clock train from Exeter to London.

The message should puzzle my ever-suffering editor who constantly complains that I never keep him advised of anything. In this case, since he has no idea that I am in Exeter, or probably not even where Exeter is located, he will be more surprised than pleased that I advised him. I picture him rubbing his bald head as he tries to figure out what the heck I'm up to.

While at the telegraph office, I send a messenger lad to the train station to purchase a ticket for me south to Plymouth. Our destination is actually Buckfastleigh, a town about halfway to Plymouth, but since everything

I am doing is to confuse and throw off a pursuit, I have only one ticket purchased in advance and for a destination twice as far as we will be going.

Wells and I will be going to the station to catch the Plymouth train, but separately, arriving from two different directions. Staying strictly away from me, he will purchase his ticket just before boarding the train.

Assuming that someone set out from Linleigh-on-the-moor at dawn's early light to notify the police in Exeter of the artist's death, Wells assures me that a small-town policeman would not immediately launch a search for us. "Things move very slowly outside of London and Liverpool. And also because we're both a small country and an island, it isn't as easy for criminals to hide. We're safe for a while."

"You're sure?"

"Yes. Besides I'm sure the Exeter police will want to investigate the matter first before making arrests based upon what a farmer or shop-keeper from Linleigh says. Based on that, I calculate that at the very minimum, it'll be midday before the police get up to steam and wonder what has happened to us. And if I'm completely wrong, we'll have a great deal of explaining to do." Wells gives me a sheepish grin.

In other words, based upon his lack of practical experience with police and murder, he has absolutely no idea of how and when the police will react.

"Wonderful," I tell him, "I just hope your calculations are correct."

I remind him that while we have a backup plan to tell the police in case we are apprehended and questioned, we need to do it in a manner in which we won't find ourselves unable to continue the pursuit.

"Oh what tangled webs we weave, when we plan to deceive." Wells wearily smiles.

"I'm sure Shakespeare would approve of our continuing the pursuit at all costs."

"Sir Walter Scott wrote the phrase."

"Whatever, they are both dead, anyway."

"I just hope," Wells says as he opens a café door for me, "that we have a very imaginative police officer to listen to our story if we have to explain why we salted our train ride out of town with false information for the police to follow."

I don't point out to him that police consider flight in the face of a crime to be an admission of guilt.

"Well, I personally am quite pleased at our cleverness." I smile at Wells after we order breakfast before going to the station.

"Me, too. Do you know that this is the first time I've been wanted by the police? How about you, Nellie?"

"Uh, basically . . ." I mumble with burnt toast stuck to the top of my mouth, hoping it muffles my response. I wonder what he would think of me being arrested by the Paris police and having to go into hiding for days from them, not to mention I started my New York reporting career by getting arrested as a madwoman and committed to an asylum.

WALKING BY MYSELF to the train station as we planned, my thoughts go to last night—we both slept deeply from physical and nervous exhaustion, but I could have used more rest and I'm sure Wells could have, too. He was unable to find a comfortable position to relax on the stuffed chair and ended up curled like a cat on the floor, wrapped in a blanket.

While I had slept hard, I had a difficult time initially getting to sleep. Having a man I am attractive to romantically sleeping a few feet from me not only got my thoughts gurgling, but those urges women keep a firm rein on were heavy on my mind as I wondered what it would be like to make love to him.

I find myself drawn to him, perhaps more than any young man I have ever met. I tend to be attracted to older men, rather than young men like Wells. My mother claims it's because I was so close emotionally to my father, who was over sixty-years-old when I was born and lost to our family when I was six.

Wells, I believe, is about my own age and in truth, as he implies himself, he is not the average woman's idea of a heartthrob. He's neither tall, athletically built, nor particularly handsome, though there is both personal warmth and intellectual intensity about him that I find attractive.

I sense a deep current of sensual sexuality within him, more passion than any other man in a casual relationship with me has conveyed. I feel he has caresses ready to be shared, passions on the verge of exploding.

Even though I was shocked at him saying that he believes a man and a woman have a right to sexually explore others outside the relationship, even if they are married, what he calls "free love," it's not my cup of tea. But I respect his openness and honesty about his own feelings—it's refreshing. Most men lie or skirt around it.

I also am attracted to his analytical approach to so many things, especially how he thinks of women—as equals, a rare thought in our society. I know I poke fun about his book smarts, but I realize long term it has greater use and meaning than what my editor has described as my "street smarts."

Inviting him into my bed crossed my mind not once but quite a few times, but I'm not prepared for the risk. As a modern young woman, I am aware of the facts of life, and that includes the various methods of contraception, besides the surest method of all—abstinence.

Being a woman, an unwanted pregnancy is the most dominant thought when it comes to sex. I am certain that Wells ranks the satisfaction of his passions as of primary importance rather than a woman's pregnancy since it is almost impossible to prove who the father of a child is.

There is a rather awkward but reasonably safe method of contraception—Mr. Goodyear's rubbers. These are tubes made of rubber that a man can buy and are usually only purchased by married men. Kept in a small box, the rubbers are washed after use, coated with a petroleum jelly, and then stored away for the next time coitus is had. From what I've overheard from the boys in the newsroom, one of these vulcanized rubber objects can last a number of years.

Suffrage leaders have spoken out against the use of rubbers and have lobbied lawmakers to make their purchase difficult because they believe the use of the contraceptive gives married men free rein to cheat on their wives without fear of consequences.

Single men rarely use them, except a smart few to avoid syphilis when having sex with a prostitute.

The other methods available—withdrawal by the male, calculating one's fertile period to avoid it, douching, and vaginal sponges soaked in vinegar, are all risky, with most of their "success" based upon wishful thinking by women. I've also been told by some women that they've successfully used "womb veils"—a penny inserted inside a woman's private part.

While doing a story on prostitution, I was told by a prostitute that she clamps the man's penis between her thighs, leaving him with the impression that he is having vaginal intercourse. She claimed that men she had sex with rarely realized they were not actually entering her.

However you cut it, the techniques are highly risky and most of them would take the pleasure out of lovemaking.

With the train station in sight, and the possibility of policemen waiting for us, I put away my girlish thoughts about sex and worry about being arrested for murder.

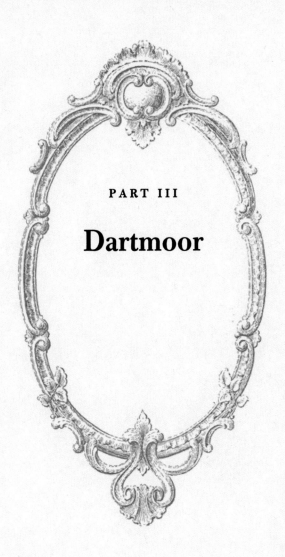

PART III

Dartmoor

There's the scarlet thread of murder running through the colorless skein of life, and our duty is to unravel it, and isolate it, and expose every inch of it.

—SIR ARTHUR CONAN DOYLE, *A Study in Scarlet*

43

Buckfastleigh, Devonshire

Conan Doyle mulled over the telegram he received from Oscar Wilde. An American reporter famous for her stunt reporting, including a race around the world to beat a record that existed only on paper, and a young science teacher were on their way to consult him.

The Scottish author was a medical doctor, but from the context of the telegram he already knew the visit was not to be about their health but a mystery that featured black beasts and the death of the woman's friend.

Rereading the telegram, he chuckled over Oscar's description of the situation in which Oscar described the purpose of the visit as work on a novel. Clever of him to make it a work of fiction, Conan Doyle thought, since telegrams pass through a number of hands as they make their way from sender to receiver.

Oscar had an amazing mind, a clever wit, and a tongue that could lay bare the worst hypocrisies; the thing he lacked most besides respectability was modesty. An incredible persona that could leave people awed, he often spoke in hyperboles. Understatements were not his strong point, that was for sure. Nor was keeping a low profile, a fact which made him a target for gossip and personality assassination.

Doyle hoped that the two visitors had simply come for information about the legend of the black beast, the great hound that is said to be the evil reincarnation of an evil man who lost his soul to the devil.

The other possibility was that they had come seeking help solving a mystery. That was a problem he faced since his fictional detective caught the interest of a reading audience.

When he is asked to step into the shoes of his fictional detective, and such requests have ranged from a police inspector investigating a crime to a businessman plagued by theft, he explains that while Sherlock Holmes may sound like he is unraveling a complex problem, Holmes in fact knows all the facts and the solution from the very beginning. "Because I don't scribble out the story until I have all the puzzling facts and clever answers already jotted down," he tells them, deflating the notion that he could stand in the shoes of his detective and solve a mystery.

People were generally disappointed, Doyle thought, when they found out that he was himself neither a master detective nor was his protagonist as spontaneous as they imagined. Some people even believed that there was an actual detective that he based the stories upon and he had, in fact, borrowed the traits of a living person when he constructed his fictional detective.

Dissatisfied with his medical practice, which proved a constant struggle to make a living at and which over a few short years moved him from one city to another in a quest to build a profitable practice, he finally set out to write.

Storytelling was in his blood. His father had been a great teller of tales to him as a child, and Doyle had gone from listening to tales to becoming a voracious reader of them. Reading tales of honor and adventure had filled the gaps in his own life, permitting him to experience at least vicariously what few men had experienced in real life.

Finding his historical writing attracted neither publishers nor readers, he had turned to writing a mystery novel featuring a detective. Stories featuring a detective had been done before and he particularly admired one created by Edgar Allan Poe in what was considered the first story featuring a private detective, or as Doyle preferred to think of him, a consulting detective.

Poe's tale, *The Murders in the Rue Morgue*, featured C. Auguste Dupin as a detective smarter than the police in solving a crime that seemed completely impossible to have been committed. But solve it Dupin did, even though the solution was rather bizarre, because as Conan Doyle has his own detective observe, "Once you eliminate the impossible, whatever remains, no matter how improbable, must be the truth."

Conan Doyle also admired the thought processes of a French police officer, Monsieur Lecoq, created by author Émile Gaboriau, and the way Lecoq didn't just collect information about a crime but used reasoning and what little "forensic science" was available to solve offenses.

He paid homage to the American and French writers who he drew upon to create his own detective by having Sherlock Holmes claim he was a better detective than either of them.

After several not very successful ventures in storytelling, he knew that to succeed, to catch the eye of a publisher and the loyalty of readers he had to come up with something different. As a person trained in the art of medical science, he knew that doctors approached diagnosing an illness not unlike an investigator's approach to solving a crime. His professor at the university, Joseph Bell, had drilled into his students that a successful diagnosis was the recognition in the symptoms of the minor differences—those differences leading the doctor to eliminate causes in order to arrive at the one that most fits the symptoms.

It occurred to Doyle that that was exactly how a detective should analyze a crime—looking for the minor, perhaps almost imperceptible differences in the evidence that lead from one suspect to another until the actual cause and perpetrator is found through a series of deductions, observations, and arriving at conclusions.

Viewing crime solving as a *science,* not just an art, was to be the formula he would use to create his detective.

He created a character named Sherrinford Holmes, then simplified the name to Sherlock and gave him a sidekick, Dr. Watson, to act as both a foil and a sparring partner for Holmes.

His first Sherlock Holmes book, *A Study in Scarlet,* was to be a major disappointment to him in many ways. First, presenting a manuscript to a publisher is a trying task for any writer. Manuscripts are handwritten, can run into hundreds of pages, and he had to laboriously copy by hand the entire manuscript for each publisher to which he submitted.

The reaction from publishers was also not elating. To find publishers rejecting his story after all the work and enthusiasm he put into writing it and the grim task of hand copying, was deflating to his ego and his aspirations.

Though he had been insulted by an offer of twenty-five pounds* from a publisher to purchase all rights to the story, with no further payment of royalties, he accepted the offer.

Publication was followed by such a lukewarm reception from readers, that he cast aside the Sherlock Holmes character, intending never to write

* Twenty-five British pounds in 1890 was one hundred twenty-five U.S. dollars and the approximant equivalent of twenty-five thousand dollars today.—The Editors

another book about the detective who solved cases with scientific deductive reasoning.

For four years he floundered, trying to get his medical practice in good order while he wrote other stories that publishers and readers found even less gripping than the Holmes book.

His writing career had undergone a dramatic change the previous year during a dinner at London's Langham Hotel. That night he and Oscar Wilde, a poet and social wit who Doyle had never met before, and who himself had never had a novel previously published, were both offered surprisingly respectable publishing arrangements by an American publisher of magazines who desired to publish the novels in weekly installments.

The reason he received an offer from an American publisher was that his Holmes novel had proved more popular in the United States than in Britain. And the offer, while modest for the amount of work it would take to create the story, was much fairer than the previous one.*

Even better, the short novel he produced, *The Sign of the Four,* was a significant hit in both Europe and America, leading to publishing agreements for more Sherlock Holmes stories.

CONAN DOYLE

*Doyle was paid one hundred pounds, which was five hundred U.S. dollars, the equivalent of about ten thousand dollars today. He also retained many future rights for the work.
—The Editors

At thirty-one years and just beginning to have the success for which he had strived for years, he felt old. And still dissatisfied with his medical practice.

It was probably the slow, passive nature of his family-oriented practice that kept him from fully loving the profession he had studied so hard to obtain.

Thinking about the cryptic message he had received, he decided the visitors would provide an intriguing interlude for what had been a rather dull afternoon. While he was on holiday from his medical practice, he did have an occasional request for his medical services in Buckfastleigh from acquaintances.

Death and the black beast had to enliven a day in which the most exciting moment had been an elderly patient telling him that he had finally unplugged this morning after eating a large number of prunes.

44

No police are waiting for us at Buckfastleigh. Neither is a taxi.

We are told a taxi only comes to the station when it has been requested in advance. Buckfastleigh is a small town, a market town larger than Linleigh-on-the-moors, but still too small to host many city amenities.

We get instructions for Old Bridge House where Conan Doyle is staying. Since it is only a half mile walk, not terribly far since neither of us has a large piece of luggage, though Wells's is more than twice the size of my valise, we set out on foot instead of by taxi.

"Wells, I hate to admit it, but my limited knowledge about Conan Doyle is from what Oscar told me—that his first name is Arthur, but he prefers to be called Conan. And I have a confession to make."

"Really . . . this should be interesting."

"I haven't read any of Mr. Doyle's books."

"But you said—"

"A little white lie. I, uh, glanced at it in a bookstore. I meant to read it someday."

"What is the purpose of this confession?"

"I was just thinking that, since you've read his detective stories, you'd be so kind as to tell me the plots so I could be courteous and pretend I had read them."

To my surprise he refuses. "That's not polite. It's a fraud. Besides, it's very easy to get tripped up."

"I've done it many times and never had a problem."

"Why don't you just read the books?"

"Because, *Mr.* Wells," I say tartly, "I am *quite* too busy climbing mountains, crossing rivers, and storming castles to have my head constantly stuck in a book. As I have pointed out to help you improve your opportunities in life, you spend too much time reading instead of doing."

"You are absolutely right, *Miss* Bly. In fact, I have been counting my blessings since you brought action rather than just words into my life. To date, I am wanted by the police, stalked by a killer, and in the hands of a woman who was committed to a madhouse after being examined by three psychiatrists. One has to wonder how you managed to pull off being hopelessly insane so well. I'm sure you've heard that expression—where there's smoke, there's fire."*

So he knows about my insanity caper. I shut my mouth and grit my teeth. Sometimes the man is insufferable.

On occasion I have also found Wells mulish with his attitudes and I drop the subject knowing we will just end up in petty squabbling. While I admire his fine mind, cold logic and reason can be the enemy of invention.

OLD BRIDGE HOUSE sits next to a narrow stone bridge that looks ancient enough to have been used by Celtic farmers to herd sheep across and then by Roman legions marching to conquest. In the distance upriver there is a modern railroad span of steel girders that time and man will turn into a pile of rusty dust while the stone edifice built by hand will still be feeling the foot and wheels of mankind.

I would feel quite at home in the house next to the bridge. If houses have a spirit, I would say this one was a tranquil old soul.

"What a charming house," I tell Wells. It's another moor-stone granite, but larger than any we saw in Linleigh-on-the-moors, with four chimneys, and a large stone archway over the entrance to the property big enough for a carriage to pass through. Thatch, moss, and clinging vines cover the roof and top of the arch.

The bell at the front door reminds me of the one we had at the house my dad built for my mother—smooth gray metal that appears almost liquid and a little handle that looks like a fish tail to ring the bell with.

---

* In order to get a job with Pulitzer's New York newspaper, Nellie went undercover to investigate conditions at the notorious women's insane asylum on Blackwell's Island. She had to convince police, a judge, and three psychiatrists that she was hopelessly insane. She wrote about the experience in *Ten Days in a Madhouse*. The madhouse escapade was also featured in *The Alchemy of Murder*.—The Editors

"Miss Bly and Mr. Wells . . . welcome." Conan Doyle greets us after I clang the bell. "Please, come in."

My instant impression of the author is that he appears to be in the medical professional he is—or even a counterjumper, I think, because Dr. Doyle looks a bit like H. G. Wells, with a similar thick, dark mustache, though he is a larger man.

The house and its furnishings are old and venerable, as seems Conan Doyle. Though Wells told me earlier that the man is only in his early thirties and while his features are that of a young man, he impresses me as an old soul as he observes me with a grave expression and large, gray eyes that radiate intelligent curiosity.

"I read about your exploits when you passed through London on your race," Dr. Doyle says to me. "I was less amazed at your accomplishment in timing transportation than the raw courage it took to travel around the world when there is danger everywhere. Oscar told me that you even refused to carry the pistol that a friend offered."

"The problem with relying upon guns is that it encourages others to get bigger ones or more of them to fight you with. Thank you for the compliment, but I must say the honor of our meeting is all mine, Dr. Doyle. I so love your Sherlock Holmes stories."

"Thank you. Which one did you find most entertaining?"

"Oh . . ." I chirp and gesture to Wells as I am sinking beyond despair. *Why didn't I read the books?* "All of them."

"She enjoyed both *A Study in Scarlet* and *The Sign of the Four*," Wells says, "as did I. I've written a few modest scientific articles, but hope someday to break into writing fiction."

"A word of advice: Write because you desire to, not for the money or fame—that may take longer than you think or never come. Now shall we go into the parlor?"

Wells gives me an "I told you so" glare as Dr. Doyle leads us to the parlor.

We settle into some charming overstuffed chairs and partake of tea and cake while we chat.

"I don't want to discourage you from writing fiction," Dr. Doyle tells Wells, "that isn't my intent. But it can be, as it was for me, a bumpy, depressing road before even modest success. Taking up the pen can be like taking a wolf by the ear.

"Miss Bly . . ." Mr. Doyle looks me.

"Yes?" I silently cross my fingers hoping he won't ask me something specific about his books.

"Please, tell me what pitfalls you must encounter reporting crime stories, especially being a woman, which I'm very impressed by. Oscar is right when he said you are one of a kind."

"Thank you." For a moment I look down at my napkin. I'm really not used to compliments, especially from men. "The biggest difficulty is getting the newspaper to believe a woman is capable of such a task. They believe a woman's place is in the home." I give him a brief rundown of wrongs I have exposed, from the miserable conditions at a madhouse to the treatment of domestics and the terrible life prostitutes endure.

I get chuckles when I share with them Jules Verne's agitation over the refusal of the French Academy to make him a member because they prefer what he calls "comedies of manners" over his bestselling adventure stories.

Very quickly the small talk and "war stories" are over and we face the task of explaining why I have journeyed several thousand miles and teamed up with Wells. I'm not sure how Wells feels about me giving the writer a rather whitewashed version of events, but from the way he is looking down at the floor a jury would easily peg him as guilt stricken.

The most significant details I omitted are the interest that New York police have in Hailey's handling of the New York murder case, because I didn't want to take away any sympathy Dr. Doyle would have for her, and that Wells and I are presently sought for questioning by the British police.

The fact we are probably on a wanted list would most likely get us escorted to the nearest constable by the respectable doctor-writer.

Dr. Doyle shows keen interest in the conversation I overheard regarding the child, Emma, at the spa. He stops me from going further with my tale and asks me to repeat everything I know about Emma and her prostitute mother, scoffing when I say the child died suddenly of "brain fever."

"The deuce you say!" Dr. Doyle rubs his jaw. "Brain fever. What bunk! The use of a child at the spa for any purpose is completely outrageous. The authorities in Bath are obviously overlooking the situation because the spa attracts a wealthy and influential clientele. And you, H. G., in dealing with Dr. Lacroix you've never heard of children being used in his experiments?"

"No, children were not experimented upon, as far as I know, nor did

I hear anything about children in regard to his university difficulties. But I only did research for him for a short time, so he may have had children involved at some point and I just wasn't privy to the experiments."

"I'm not familiar with Dr. Lacroix," Dr. Doyle says, "though I've heard of the spa. Does he strike you as even capable of doing experiments that could harm a child?" His question is directed to Wells.

Wells chews on it for a moment. "I don't find Lacroix to be an evil person in the sense that anyone would look upon him as capable of doing deliberate harm or acts of a criminal nature. I find it difficult to believe that he would *intentionally* harm a child. However, there is no question he becomes quite fanatical in terms of his medical research. I have no direct evidence to support this, just my impression from observing him, but I strongly suspect that he could consider experiments on a child that he believes are being done for the greater good of mankind, no different than experimenting on an adult or even an animal."

"Ah, yes, like Jenner and the smallpox researchers." Dr. Doyle taps tobacco down in his pipe and lights it before he continues. "As you both may recall, during the closing years of the past century Jenner was a small-town doctor in Gloucestershire. He was an inquisitive sort, enjoyed experimenting with medical remedies. Smallpox epidemics were frequent in those days, killing tens of millions around the world and leaving many more millions scarred and blind. But he had observed that one group of workers never seemed to come down with the disease—milkmaids who had gotten cowpox, a disease similar to but much less lethal and damaging than smallpox.

"Jenner ultimately came up with a procedure that he called vaccination, from the Latin word for cow, *vacca*, where he injects people with a small amount of cowpox. As you know, it does protect most people from coming down with smallpox, so the benefit to mankind is enormous.

"However, during that era when Jenner and other physicians were trying to discover the cure, it was not an uncommon practice to conduct dangerous experiments on people, especially prisoners and small children. Some of those experimented upon naturally died or otherwise suffered the horrible consequences of smallpox or other foul diseases before the ultimate cure was reached. Medical science was crude, cruel, and ignorant at the time and some of these ghastly experiments really fell more under the auspices of alchemy than true scientific research."

"I can see why they would use prisoners," I interject. "Prisoners have less to lose and can be rewarded with money and their freedom, but what was the attraction of the experimenters to use children?"

"Availability and lack of resistance to whatever is done to them. I should have qualified that statement to say *poor* children. The children were obtainable for a price, as was the prostitute's daughter."

"If you dug up the researchers from their graves," Wells says, "and ask them if buying poor children for their experiments was cruel, no doubt they would point out that most of the children would never have lived to reach adulthood anyway."

"Regretfully, that was true then and still is," I point out.

Doyle leans back with his pipe, blowing smoke up. "As I was saying, there were experiments conducted with children, and that included infecting them with pus from smallpox sores. The end result of this era's experiments was a vaccine for smallpox and a great benefit for mankind, but that provided small comfort for the many children who suffered horrible deaths to pave the way. And from what you have told me about Dr. Lacroix, his experiments are for the benefit of mankind at any cost. And it seems he also has a bit of the alchemist in him. No doubt his aims are for the better good of all, but his vision is twisted. I shall write a letter to the Royal Coroner in Bath pointing out that a review should be made of the child's death."

Another puff of smoke and Dr. Doyle invites me to continue my tale.

I stall with a sip of tea to get my thoughts in order. We are now on dangerous ground and I need to use various shades of white lies to avoid telling Doyle about the murder of the artist. Wells and I had argued over this point on the walk from the train station because he wants to relate the entire matter to Dr. Doyle, insisting that the man would hold us in utter contempt later when the inevitable happens and he discovers we lied to him. While I would enjoy the respect of Dr. Doyle, if lying is the best way to handle the situation, then I shall not falter in doing so.

"We witnessed a murder yesterday."

That came from Wells.

So much for being clever.

The startled expression on Arthur Conan Doyle's features makes me wonder if we are about to wear out our welcome at Old Bridge House.

I give a little sigh, set down my teacup, fold my hands in my lap, and give Wells a small, gentle smile despite my inclination to poke out one of his eyes for having uttered the naked truth.

45

I take center stage from Wells in the hope of salvaging some of the cooperation I was anticipating the writer-doctor would give us.

"We were innocent bystanders, of course," I offer Dr. Doyle.

"That goes without saying. But," he smiles, "after meeting the two of you, I have to wonder which of the two of you, or the three of us for that matter, is the most innocent in the ways of the world."

Wells and Doyle enjoy a male chuckle at my expense and Wells raises his hand as if he had been asked a question in school.

"I confess, Dr. Doyle, our world traveler is much more versed on the world than I, who has stayed warm before the hearth, with my feet in slippers and my head in a book."

"If you gentlemen are finished poking fun at me, I shall go on."

"Please do," Dr. Doyle says, "and don't take our little slings and arrows too seriously. I am certain that Wells and I have the same opinion of you as has much of the world—you are a woman of great determination and talent."

"Thank you." Glowing, I go on. "We need to start a bit before the events of last night. What drew us to Dartmoor was a painting I saw when I visited Lady Chilcott, a wealthy middle-aged matron in Bath who takes the cure at the spa and who is a supporter and admirer of Dr. Lacroix. My impression is that her admiration may also be of a romantic nature."

"Not a surprising reaction," Dr. Doyle says, "to a doctor you describe as both attractive to women and who offers them eternal youth and beauty."

I relate how I saw the painting of the bog that is the source of the peat moss used at the spa and how I was told by Lady Chilcott that the painting had been commissioned by Dr. Lacroix and presented to her as a gift for assisting in financing his research.

"Research into what you call magic mud," Dr. Doyle says.

I shrug and shake my head. "I know peat moss preserves bodies but so does ice and formaldehyde. Perhaps they should have people at the spa also bathe in chilled embalming fluid."

"But you see, Nellie, to Lacroix a tiny glimmer of hope that a substance in peat moss can be isolated to rejuvenate skin bursts like an exploding star in his head. He sees a benefit to mankind and scientific immortality for himself as its discoverer."

I explain how we tracked the artist to Linleigh-on-the-moors, a village Doyle says he'd seen on maps but had not traveled to. After I told him about the ice pick and the cowboy boots on the Bath spa thug, Dr. Doyle also immediately made a connection with the Whitechapel gang in London. After I tell him about the death of Weekes and the "avoidance" of the police by Wells and myself in Exeter, he is red faced and I know we are in trouble.

"You must go to the police immediately! This spa and its villains must be put behind bars before they hurt others."

Even Wells realizes it is time to backpedal or we will shortly be in the hands of the police—literally. He resorts to the truth again, telling Dr. Doyle that going to the police would mean an abrupt stop in our investigation and a return to New York for me without finding out what had happened to Hailey.

"We're not withholding any evidence vital to a police pursuit of the Linleigh murderer," he tells Doyle. "We saw nothing of the killer while others at the pub did, including the barmaid who served him. As for the connection between the spa in Bath and the killing in the village, it's a real reach to connect a man with cowboy boots at the spa with an ice pick killer in Linleigh via a notorious gang in London—"

"You're right," Dr. Doyle cuts in. "The connection is obvious to us because you have experienced the incidents firsthand and three of us are people of imagination, but there isn't a policeman in Dartmoor or probably London for that matter who wouldn't find the connection far-fetched. That doesn't excuse you from evading the police, but," he rubs his jaw, "if you can't identify the killer, there's no harm done, is there? You can just proclaim your ignorance of police matters."

We could if Wells doesn't get an irresistible impulse to confess our charade at the Exeter train station. But I am much relieved by the doctor's analysis and the fact he doesn't appear ready to turn us over to the nearest constable.

"Another problem," I add, "of convincing the police of the connection between the crimes is that cowboy boots are not just worn by the Whitechapel gang. Oscar says they are a fashion item in London."

"Now that you mention it," Wells says, "I recall reading in the papers that Oscar and the crowd he hangs out with have taken to wearing them with evening wear. Seems Oscar still has a pair from the tour he made of the American west."

Doyle relights his pipe and blows out smoke. "Going a step further, if the chief inspector in Bath says that the prostitute's death was a suicide, that will be the finding of the coroner and that matter will close tight. Trying to connect the death of the unfortunate artist in the moors because he had once painted a landscape for the doctor, a pair of cowboy boots on a spa employee and a gang in London . . . as you say, quite a reach in imagination for a police officer whose duty is to view the evidence objectively and not make imaginative connections.

"With due respect to you, Nellie, and the battles in life you have fought and won, the average police officer hearing the tale you've told me would assume that your suspicions are a result of female hysterics."

"It wouldn't be the first time that conclusion was drawn."

"Oscar's telegram also said you wanted to speak to me about the black houndlike beast that is sometimes claimed to have been spotted in the moors. The story and claims of seeing the beast and victims of the creature go back centuries. It piqued my interest because that type of creature has been spotted in other parts of England and I am, in fact, researching the legend for possible use in a future book.* How does the story fit into this matter?"

"We're not certain that it does," Wells says. "However, it's an issue we feel necessary to pursue because Dr. Lacroix had an interest in the black beast. At a pub over some pints, he confided in me that he would someday scientifically investigate the black beast legend. His theory is that the beast was a primordial animal, perhaps a creature left over from the age of dinosaurs—"

* Conan Doyle's *The Hound of the Baskervilles,* published in 1901, is based upon the black beast legend.—The Editors

"And that creature was preserved over the ages in a peat moss bog," Dr. Doyle says, "and miraculously came alive one day. He is also a man of imagination."

"What we would like to know is whether there is a particular bog on the moors that the story of the beast has been identified with," I ask.

"No, there isn't. And I owe you an apology for rudely usurping the rest of the tale. But by now I have a little insight into what I perceive as Lacroix's thought processes and saw the conclusion. It smacks of great logic and scientific nonsense. But more particularly as to your question about the beast, there are two stories about the hound that Lacroix could have been referring to.

"One arises from a squire about three hundred years ago here in Buck-fastleigh, one Richard Cabell. He was the most important landowner in the area and not one who found favor in the eyes of those who worked for him or had to deal with him. It's claimed he sold his soul to the devil for eternal life, but the devil tricked him, making him a houndlike creature after he died. He has been sighted many times in the area and there have been many claims of deaths or near misses.

"The second tale of beastly hounds is that of the Yeth hound, a giant, coal black beast with flaming eyes that terrorizes people at night in a manner similar to the Buckfastleigh animal. However, other than the fact that both creatures appear in tales of the moors and there are bogs in the moors, I know of no connection between the stories and any particular bog."

My disappointment shows on my face and I give Dr. Doyle a smile in return for his raised eyebrows. "Yes, I'm disappointed. I really hoped that Lacroix's comment about the black beast is a clue to locating his bog of magic mud. I am convinced that if we find the bog, we will find him somewhere in the area."

"And what do you plan to do if you find him? Ask him as a gentleman and medical professional to kindly accompany you to the nearest police-man and turn himself in? After he confesses, of course." He winces. "I don't mean to be facetious, my dear, I just don't want the two of you going into harm's way against a man you believe has commissioned murder without a clear plan for your safety."

Wells chuckles. "Let me assure you, I'm neither as brave nor daring as Nellie. When I am certain that I know Lacroix's whereabouts, the matter shall be handed over to the nearest police officer."

I let out a sigh and apologize to the gentlemen. "Sorry. Now that we have hit a dead end, I feel deflated."

"Don't be, my dear, you are simply tired from all the hurdles you two have been vaulting. I suggest you take a day or two of rest before you bounce off in whatever direction your bloodhound instincts take you."

He gets up and we start walking toward the front door.

"We beg your forgiveness for having intruded upon you," Wells says, "but we hoped the black hound tale would point us in the right direction."

"No bother at all, in fact, a welcome break from the hard task of writing. Feel free to wire me if you have any more questions. And let me know if you come up with more tales of moor hounds. As I've said, I may use one in a book someday."

"There is the other hound, the Lady Howard one, that Weekes, the artist, claims he saw when he was painting the bog picture."

"Lady Howard's coach dog." Doyle isn't asking, but stating. He stops and unconsciously taps his pipe in his hand. "Are you saying that the artist claims to have seen Lady Howard when he was painting the bog portrait?"

"Yes."

"Well," he smiles as if he found something he'd been missing, "if that's the case, Isaac Weekes shot an arrow in that conversation that pointed toward your magic mud. You had better sit down."

We hurry back into the parlor, my heart in my throat because Conan Doyle is not a man to exaggerate.

"The Lady Howard legend is about a death coach. Like the Buckfastleigh hound, it's based upon a real person that lived several hundred years ago and has grown with its telling. It's also somewhat reminiscent of the Goddess of Death who travels through the night collecting human souls. As with the local squire here, Lady Howard was an unpleasant woman, quite as mean and miserly as one can accomplish while being very wealthy."

As he talks he picks up a folder and begins to leaf through what I assume are research notes.

"It's been said that she beat her children regularly without cause and even disinherited them, a not very kind gesture toward those who looked to her for guidance and support. The sightings of her are between the clock striking midnight and the cock's crow. Her ghoulish coach has been described as made from the blackened bones of the many husbands she murdered. It's pulled by a great beast of a hound, a black dog with sharp fangs and fire in its eyes. I confess that my favorite version of the tale claims that Lady Howard, like our curmudgeon squire, runs through the night herself in the form of a hell hound. Ah, here it is, Lady Howard's Devon ballad, passed down over the centuries."

He reads from the notebook:

> My ladye hath a sable coach,
> And horses two and four;
> My ladye hath a black blood-hound
> That runneth on before.
> My ladye's coach hath nodding plumes,
> The driver hath no head;
> My ladye is an ashen white,
> As one that long is dead.*

This is all very interesting, but I am still on the edge of my chair waiting to hear why Lady Howard was an arrow shot by the artist.

"Do you see how simple it should be for the two of you to find the bog?"

"No," Wells and I echo.

Doyle grins at us. "Why it's elementary, my dear Watsons. Lady Howard's ghost haunts the castle ruins of Okehampton! If the painter saw her ghost, he was most assuredly near the castle."

---

*The ballad can also be found in S. Baring-Gould's *A Book of the West,* 1899.—The Editors

46

"I have visited Okehampton Castle," Dr. Doyle tells us, "some years ago. I wasn't researching beasts of the moors stories at that time and now regret my stopover wasn't between midnight and the cock's crow. It would have gotten my creative juices flowing, not to mention my adrenaline, had I spotted the wicked old woman. Hopefully, my blood would not have flowed, too." He asks Wells, "You're not familiar with Okehampton?"

"Not at all, I'm afraid."

"It's a day's journey, perhaps two, depending on how you intend to get there. Okehampton is almost due north of Buckfastleigh, thirty miles or so as the crow flies. But that direct route from here to Okehampton is straight through part of the wildest and most sparsely populated part of the moors. The path has few villages and even less civilized accommodations. However, if you took the train back to Exeter or to Plymouth to make a connection to Okehampton, you would travel much farther but also quicker and in infinitely greater comfort."

Wells and I exchange glances and I can see that for once, we are in agreement. Neither of us wish to risk getting back on the train until we have something positive to report to the police to explain our strange behavior.

"I see," Doyle says. "Trains are out. Unfortunately."

He shows us a map of the region. No question, Okehampton is a straight shot, almost across the very center of Dartmoor. Doyle says the few markings of any sort between Buckfastleigh and Okehampton are mostly small villages, some of which are no more than a few houses clustered near crossroads.

"I dearly hope you understand the task you are undertaking if you attempt to cross the moors?"

"I've traveled in the Wild West and Mexico," I proudly state.

"Yes, Nellie, and I'm sure rattlesnakes and bandits are bad hombres, but crossing the moors is probably more like trekking the badlands of Mars, if you will forgive the otherworldly analogy."

"How so?"

"There is a reason the moors generate so many tales of the haunted and the horrid—it is a strange place. Strange as in eerie—as in haunted. Even in broad daylight the land is unusual, its vestiges twisted and grotesque. There are constant tales of ghosts. Here's one related to me by another doctor: A patient brought his wife in because she was in horrible fright. It seems she wouldn't believe the servants when they told her they wouldn't go for milk in the late afternoon because a woman in a gray cloak walked on the road at dusk. Fed up, she decided to investigate the matter herself.

"One evening she went out to milk the cows and there on the road was a woman in a gray cloak. She followed her and the woman disappeared over an impossibly steep place. The woman went for help, but no body was found by the rescuers. The next night she went out again and once again there was the woman in a gray clock walking and again she ended up going over the steep place."

He pauses and raises his eyebrows. "I know the woman and she is as sane as any of us. So a word of caution: Be very careful, you never know what you will find out there."

"What about the bogs?" I ask. "Are they as dangerous as I've heard tell?"

"You read and hear about the trembling earth," Dr. Doyle continues with his tale of horrors, "places where you suddenly find yourself walking on bogs without realizing that the greenery underfoot is not solid ground but is literally thin ice, ready to break with your footfall and send you sinking into a mire that feels as if it has grabbed hold of your feet and is pulling you under." He raises his eyebrows. "If you should fall into a bog, be sure to remember to treat it as you would quicksand—don't struggle because it's counterproductive. Fighting the suction will just pull you under faster. I am told that the correct posture is to spread yourself out and try to lie upon it, spreading out your weight rather than pushing your feet down into it."

"I hope it won't become necessary for us to perform bog survival," Wells says, "but we need to remember the advice."

Wells gives me a look that raises my dander. I know what he is implying—I will not bother learning the survival technique until I am confronted with the danger. He is right, of course, but if I tried to learn everything thrown at me in life, I would have no room in my head for investigating and writing news stories.

"We'll have to rent a carriage," I say.

"Would be difficult, though you'll only need a buggy, since I assume you won't desire to make a round trip. I have a pony buggy you can use. Shall we go out to the stable?"

We follow Doyle as he continues telling us about Okehampton.

"In Okehampton, you can hire a man at the stable to bring it back to me. The long way, of course; you would have difficulty finding someone eager to come through the wild area."

"It's a Dartmoor pony buggy?" I ask.

"Yes, but I use two ponies to pull my large frame. Even though there's an inn on your way, you'll need bedrolls and extra food. With poor roads and uncertain weather, you might find darkness falling quickly and be in need of shelter short of the inn."

"How long do you think it will take us?"

"The good part of two days, if it doesn't rain hard and your buggy wheels don't get too bogged down too often in mud. You'll find, by the way, that the ruins of Okehampton Castle are a pretty picture. It's atop a wooded spur above the River Okement. It was once the largest castle in Devonshire before its last owner ran afoul of Henry VIII and lost his head. His castle slowly dissolved into a ruin haunted by that rather nasty old woman I told you about."

He helps Wells harness the two ponies as I make a list of items to obtain from the general store.

When the buggy preparations are done, he stands by, and we have a long moment of quiet. I have found Dr. Doyle to be an interesting person with many facets. Like Wells, he is someone whose intellect not only challenges me, but inspires me to reach deeper into myself when faced with a problem.

Conan Doyle tells us rather sadly, "You are going on an adventure. I'd love to come with you, but I have my medical practice on my back and a Sherlock Holmes tale in my head."

He gives one pony a slap on the rump. "Go now, the game's afoot!"

47

We drive away from the writer of mystery stories in silence, both of us wishing he had been able to join us.

It is late in the afternoon and we want to get on our way. We take the road to Ashburton which Dr. Doyle told us is a small town, but will be the largest community we pass through after we leave the main road and enter the very heart of Dartmoor. It will be our last chance to purchase the supplies we will need.

Before we left the house, Dr. Doyle pulled out a map of Dartmoor and went over it with us.

"The route will take you through some very small villages with accommodations and a number of settlements which have a few houses clustered together and others spread out on farmlands and grazing fields. Most of the settlements have no shops or lodging. As you already know, the roads will be very narrow. Depending on how you go, some dirt roads will become mere paths, but you should try to avoid those. It will probably rain and that makes the roads even nastier.

"Now, from what you've told me, you plan to go as much as possible the way the crow flies. I appreciate your need for expediency, but getting off of what passes for the beaten path in the wilds of the moors is not a good idea. You'll need a compass and, of course, good waterproofs . . ."

So much has happened during the past few days, I feel a bit drained rather than chomping at the bit as I normally would, as we set off. Wells also appears to appreciate the solitude.

We are closing in on our goal, I am certain of that.

We are both convinced that we will find Lacroix at or near Okehampton

Castle. I've mulled over Isaac Weekes's remark about Lady Howard and I'm convinced that as a Dartmoor local, he would know that Lady Howard only appears at Okehampton Castle. If she had appeared somewhere else, I think he would have mentioned it.

Not that a ghost should be expected anywhere. And the skeptic in me has to wonder what he had imbibed that night before he saw the ghost.

A decision pressing on both of us is a realistic response to the question Dr. Doyle asked: What is our plan once we locate Dr. Lacroix?

I hardly plan to walk up to him with a list of people I believe he's murdered—or had murdered—and ask him for a confession. Not to mention that he might slice me to ribbons with one of his scalpels if I were so bold or he might have some Whitechapel Rustlers hanging around, pronging the lice on their cowboy boots with their ice picks while they wait for the next victim to show up.

We said we'd go to the police, but only when we have solid information to hand them. We could reveal to the police that Lacroix isn't on the continent, but that has doubtful consequences because he's not a wanted criminal even if the Bath police have questions for him. The fact they are not actively seeking him is a good indication that they have nothing incriminating to firmly link Lady Winsworth's death to the spa. And Dr. Lacroix doesn't sound like the type who would run off the mouth during police questioning and incriminate himself.

"Thinking can be dangerous when it comes to you," Wells says, interrupting my musing.

"I was thinking about Lacroix and Lady Winsworth. The police had the spa waters, the elixir concoction, the peat moss baths, all of them, tested and found nothing poisonous."

"Correct. People take those types of products every day, by the many thousands if you count the number of people drinking and bathing in similar waters all over Europe and I imagine America."

"So the only reason the spa is suspected is because she appears to have been in good health."

"No natural causes like a heart attack or stroke were found. And she had taken nothing out of the ordinary except from the spa."

We are moving along at a nice pace and Wells barely needs to hold onto the reins. The Dartmoor ponies seem to know where they are going and what speed they need. Wish I could take one back to America with me. Most children get a dog or cat for their first pet—mine was a pony from my dad. Because of that horses have always held a soft spot in my heart.* When my father died I rode my pony alongside his casket.

His voice breaks my thoughts. "No evidence of a known poison was found by the medical examiner, either, though as Dr. Lacroix or any hematologist would tell you, the scientific analysis of blood for anything other than recognized diseases and toxins is very inadequate."

"Then it wasn't anything at the spa."

"What? How do you conclude that?"

"Being around Conan Doyle has gotten my detective juices flowing. You told me that Sherlock Holmes says that if you eliminate the impossible, whatever remains, no matter how improbable, must be the truth. It's not possible that the spa's stinky water and magic mud baths are the cause because everyone else gets them and hasn't died or gotten sick enough to draw attention. What remains is the improbable conclusion that her death wasn't from something at the spa."

"All right. What's on your list of causes *not* at the spa?"

"My short list includes a child."

Wells nods. "Emma, the prostitute's daughter. But, we don't know what her role was there."

"No, that's not exactly true. I think that focusing on a connection between Emma and the spa misleads us. Her connection is more to Dr. Lacroix."

He gives me a sharp look. "How do you know that? You've been withholding things from me again."

"Not at all, I have simply looked at the evidence."

"Now you are sounding like Sherlock Holmes. I guess that makes me Watson."

We both laugh. It's a nice interlude to our problems.

"There is no question that the child has a spa connection," I tell him, "because she was solicited through the spa, but from what I determined from talking to Lady Chilcott, the child was never used as part of the cure routine at the spa."

"Perhaps not for her, but how about others?"

"She socializes with others at the spa and I'm sure a child being used in treatment would have been a subject of talk. Besides, she's not just a customer at the spa. Like your Lady Winsworth, she was a financial supporter of Lacroix and I suspect both the women were his lovers, too."

* Nellie was an accomplished equestrian as a young girl and even won ribbons. —The Editors

"Nonsense!" Wells suddenly snapped. "Lady Winsworth was never Lacroix's lover. She was interested in keeping her beauty, that's all."

Wells's reaction is a strong emotion. Obviously he's not just protecting the reputation of a woman who was his friend and benefactor.

"Let's go back to your theory about the child," he says flatly.

"Her mother, Sarah, told me that the little girl had been promised a nice trip from the spa people."

"A nice trip? That's what she said?"

"Those were her words. I regret that I didn't think about them at the time, but I didn't know then that I would be taking a trip to find Lacroix."

"You believe we'll find the child in Okehampton?"

"No, the child's dead, I'm certain of that."

"Why?"

"Because there's no reason for Radic to pretend otherwise. The prostitute was a serious embarrassment, coming to the spa, maybe talking to people she saw coming and going. If the child was still alive, he would have gotten rid of the annoyance by showing her the child or even taking Sarah to her, wherever she was. Bought another child, for that matter. It seems easy enough for doctors. But that doesn't mean the child died in Bath. Sarah also complained that there was no grave to visit."

"So, you believe what we find at Okehampton will be the concoction that killed Emma and Lady Winsworth. That means it probably won't be the magic mud, at least not in the form used at the spa."

"Exactly. How long ago was it that you caught on to the fact Lacroix was setting up a lab in this region?"

"A couple of months."

"So he could have had plenty of time to set up the lab and concoct whatever killed Lady Winsworth and the child. You've told me that he's a fanatic about his research. He'll still be there, cooking up whatever in his test tubes, looking for the secret to unlocking the disease of growing old and wrinkled."

"You're right." Wells sighs. "Lacroix is no longer in control of his research. I'm certain that by now the science has driven him quite mad. Crazy enough to kill people to accomplish his aims. Like Dr. Jekyll and Victor Frankenstein, there comes a point where a researcher becomes so blinded by his ambition to recreate in a test tube what only God has created, that the science devours the man."

Wells gives me a long look. "Like the fictional mad scientists, Lacroix has left a bloody trail of murder in his wake."

48

We pick up salted beef, bread, dry cheese that won't spoil in cool air, and fruit, at a general store. Also a compass, and more rugged waterproofs because we could spend hours sitting on a buggy in the rain.

Once again we sought out an inn away from the center of town, this one on the road that will lead us in the direction of Widecombe-on-the-moors where we expect to find civilized accommodations if we are unable to make it all the way across the moors because foul weather forces us to seek shelter.

"I suggest we pretend to be married and get one room again," Wells says.

I give him a stern look. "And what would be the purpose of that?"

"To keep you from speaking. We're just another couple among thousands until you say something and people know you are American."

He is right. There is also no question in my mind that he is as motivated by lust as he is to hide my accent.

"You get the floor again," I tell Wells.

"We'll flip a coin for the bed."

"Not if I'm paying."

"You get the bed."

I smile and make vague listening responses as Wells registers us as Mr. and Mrs. Prendick at the inn's front desk.

"Where did you get the name, Prendick?" I ask Wells on our way to the room.

"It was a friend of my father's who was lost in a shipwreck."

Great. It doesn't seem propitious to adopt the name of a dead man when tomorrow we'll be back in the haunted moors with bogs that swallow people. But I keep my peace rather than expose my superstitious nature.

Dining is a communal affair at the inn with several large tables that accommodate about ten people each. To ensure I won't have to hold a conversation and end up broadcasting that I am an American, we avoid the two tables that have diners even though there's room for us and find seats near the wall at the far end of the room.

"They'll assume we're honeymooners and desire privacy to coo over the caresses we'll be sharing tonight," Wells says.

I lean close to him, just a kiss away, and whisper, "I hope you have a nice pillow to share your love with tonight."

Food is brought to the table in communal bowls and platters, boiled lamb, potatoes, green beans, cabbage, and bread.

As we eat, we have the map of Dartmoor between us. It lists quite a number of places, but as Dr. Doyle had pointed out, most of them are what he called "settlements," little more than a small group of houses along the road in a thinly populated area. He told us we'd most likely find more sheep and ponies than two-legged creatures once we got past Ashburton.

I suck in a sharp gasp of air as a man suddenly sits down in the chair next to Wells and smirks, smug and arrogant—this is the man who attacked me in London.

"You know, my old boss at the Yard always said that life's a circle, and if you stand in one spot long enough, the criminal you want to apprehend will come strolling back to you."

"That's a surprise," I counter, "not the circle of life, but the fact that you have a connection to Scotland Yard besides your criminal activities. Obviously a past connection since you have crossed the line to the other side of the law."

"She's a sharp-tongued one, isn't she?" he says to Wells.

"Just a good judge of character," Wells replies.

"Do you have a name?" I ask. "One found on police ledgers and WANTED posters?"

He laughs—a rather unpleasant, grating sound on my nerves. Everything about this man gets my teeth clenching the way they did when I heard fingernails on blackboards in school.

"Looks to me like the pot's calling the kettle black, don't you think? Here you two are wanted all over the kingdom for murder and other high crimes—"

"And treason, I'm sure," I throw in.

"Especially that poor artist who got an ice pick in his back."

"Own an ice pick?" I ask.

He shakes his head and looks to Wells for help. "I can see the woman has mistaken me for a Whitechapel boy. My name's Archer, Detective Archer."

"I'd like to see your badge," I ask, knowing the answer.

Another coarse laugh erupts from him. "So would I. But you see, dolly bird, I gave up my official police position to enter the trade as a consulting detective, like the one that writer gent you went visiting scribbles about."

I exchange looks with Wells. It isn't necessary to push the issue. It is obvious that the man's change of careers wasn't voluntary. And that he has managed to keep good track of us.

"From what I've heard from my police friends, you two are a regular Jesse James and Belle Starr. Why, if I called over the innkeeper and told him to send for the constable, I'd have a fat reward and you two would find yourselves on the wrong side of bars."

He's lying about the reward, but he isn't bluffing about the constable. He will turn us over to the police if we don't give him what he wants.

"You obviously want something from us. Fine. Tell us what you're after and what Hailey wrote in her diary and we'll share our information with you. Why don't we start with who hired you?"

"My, isn't she a spirited lass," he says to Wells. "The kind a man likes to tame with the whip he carries that women love to get a beating from."

Wells springs from his chair. "Listen you disgusting lout—"

"Please." I put a restraining hand on Wells's arm. "People at another table have turned to look at us." I smile and tug at his arm. "Smile. We don't want to attract attention."

Wells sits down, but he's red in the face. He gives Archer a grin that looks more like a wolf sneering.

"He has the upper hand." I look at Wells. "He knows it, but he wants our help or he would have already turned us in." Turning back to the lout, I say, "I don't take offense at your vulgar manners, Mr. . . . what did you say your name was?"

"Archer, that's what I'm called."

"Mr. Archer, I am sure that inappropriate language is the least bit of foul behavior I can expect from a man I first encountered when he mugged me on a public street. As for the name of your employer, we know it's Lord Winsworth, which means we have a common goal."

Even as I speak the words it strikes me that this man isn't just working for Winsworth, but is grinding his own ax, too. The fact I'm sure he had previously betrayed his police employers enough to lose his badge is an indication that he has all the honor of a gnat in a garbage can.

"Let's get down to business," I tell him. "Tell us what Hailey wrote in her diary."

"No, love, we'll play the game my way. You tell me what you know and I won't call for the constable."

"We have a stalemate that can last forever and won't do either of us any good," is my reply. "We are willing to share information with you only up to a point because if we tell you everything you want to know, you'll turn us over to the constable as soon as we're finished."

"You have my word of honor."

Wells bursts out with a guffaw and I give him a warning look. We have the same opinion of Archer's capacity for honor, but I don't want to attract attention from the other diners or turn him completely against us.

I lock eyes with our uninvited dinner companion. "Mr. Archer, you don't have to ask the landlord to call the constable. I'm going to do it myself and have you arrested. A woman you nearly knocked down during your attack on me can easily confirm you are the attacker by providing the local police with a description of you."

"You are a tough one, aren't you?" He reaches into an inside pocket of his suit coat and brings out Hailey's diary and puts it on the table, but keeps his big paw on it. "Now tell me what I get for telling you what you want to know."

"You get to follow closely behind as we take each step."

Both men stare at me, a bit amazed, and I'm surprised myself because I don't know where the notion came from. It just slipped out. My tongue goes liquid sometimes when I'm in need of an escape route.

"Come again?" Archer says.

"It's elementary, my dear Archer. You have been following us because you have no leads yourself. You must realize that we are closing in, that we now know where Dr. Lacroix is. What I am offering is to tell you our next step in exchange for information from you. You can join us, or preferably since it's how we have been successfully operating up to now, you can follow closely behind. We can make use of your skills as a police officer," I add, deliberately omitting the "former" from his police status, "when we bring Dr. Lacroix to bay."

Archer looks to Wells and shakes his head in wonderment. "Did I just hear this woman, who is minutes away from being in police chains, tell me I could follow her around?"

Wells leans closer to Archer and speaks in a confidential tone. "I'll let you in on a secret. I've been following in her footsteps for days and if it wasn't for her bloodhound nose, I'd still be going in circles."

"We know where Lacroix is," I say, "and we will lead you there as long as you share information."

"I also know where the man is. Tell me where you think he is—just so I can see how much you're bluffing."

Archer is lying, of course. If he knew where Lacroix was, we wouldn't be having this conversation.

"Mr. Wells did research for Lacroix." I decide to humor him. "He knows the man set up a laboratory in Dartmoor, not the continent."

Archer smacks his lips. "Where in Dartmoor?"

Ignoring the question, I continue. "Lady Chilcott gave me the clue that led me to the artist. So did a prostitute in Bath, who died rather mysteriously soon afterward." I pause for a moment for effect, to see if there is any reaction in his face about the prostitute. Nothing. I continue. "Before he was murdered, the artist gave us another lead. Earlier today, all the pieces to the puzzle came together."

"You visited that detective-story writer. Dropped by to see him myself. Not a very friendly gent, considering how much me and him got in common."

Which translates as Dr. Doyle refused to discuss our visit with him. The only thing Archer and Dr. Doyle have in common is that they both breathe air, and I'm sure Archer's fouls the atmosphere when exhaled.

"You don't know where Lacroix is, we do," I repeat. "And we know what evidence to look for—not only for the death of Lady Winsworth, but that of a child."

"The prostitute's kid?"

"Murdered."

"Vampires!" Archer exclaims.

49

Archer laughs at the surprised look on our faces.

"Don't know everything, do you?"

I don't ask him to elaborate about the vampires because I know he won't. No doubt he had thrown out the word as both a boast and as bait to see what we would say to his statement.

He slaps his palm on the table. "Let's go back to the question that swings back and forth over us like a hanged man on a gallows—where is Lacroix?"

"A place where we will ultimately lead you to."

He gets up from his chair, sticking the diary back into the inside pocket of his coat. "I'm sending for the constable."

I turn to Wells. "We'll have the innkeeper also send for Dr. Doyle. As he said, he'd speak to the authorities if we have any difficulties. He can make sure the woman in London, Anne Carson, who saw you attack me is contacted." He hadn't exactly said that, but I'm certain he would. Anne Carson is the name of my favorite grammar school teacher. It slid off my tongue when I needed a name for the woman since I failed to ascertain hers.

Waving Archer away like a pest, I tell him, "I don't react well to people who bully me. I'll have plenty to talk about to the constable when he gets here. I'm certain he'll have a number of questions not just for you, but for your employer when I tell him about London. By the way, I hope your employer still plans to pay you even though he will be arrested as an accomplice for your crime."

Then with my sweetest smile I end with, "But I wonder what Lord Winsworth will say when he reads in the papers about how his hired thug brought criminal charges and scandal to his door. If he lives up to his reputation, he'll have your tongue cut out and fed to his parrot."

Archer bursts out with that nerve-grating laugh of his and sits back down, slamming his palm back on the table. "By God, I declare, if I didn't have my detecting career keeping me so busy, I'd take the time to show this saucy woman what she'd think about in her dreams tonight."

"You mean in her nightmares," Wells says, beating me to the line.

Archer pulls out a cigar, cuts off the tip, wets the end by popping it in and out of his mouth like a sucker, then lights it and leans back with a satisfied expression.

I glance at Wells, barely able to hold back a crack that Archer is about to tell us something, but not until he is puffed up and stage center so we'll appreciate how clever he is.

"Your reporter friend was infatuated with Dr. Lacroix. Fell madly in love with him at first sight. Wrote down her most passionate feelings, detailing what she experienced for the doctor from the moment she met him. Sort of the corny romantic trite you'd expect to hear from much younger girls in the throes of puppy love."

Even though I don't doubt that is what Hailey wrote, it breaks my heart to hear it. My fear has been that she had become overly impressed with Lacroix, not only because of whatever sales pitch he gave her about his visions for helping mankind, but his appeal to women, especially one who reaches out to help a woman look and feel more attractive.

Her immaturity and inexperience in dealing with men in a romantic vein would have made her easy prey for Lacroix.

Not being able to resist the temptation, I ask a question I know will only feed his ego when he refuses to answer.

"What did you mean when you spoke of vampires?"

"It'll shock you down to your pretty little toes, love, but that'll have to wait until you and I get to know each other better."

"She's not going to get to know you any better," Wells says, hotly. "She may trust you to travel with us, but I don't. I'm wiring Lord Winsworth and will warn him to call off his dog or he can join you in jail."

Archer lets out a ho-ho-ho laugh as he blows cigar smoke in Wells's face.

"I don't think your demand to Lord Winsworth will have much weight coming from one of his servants who's been bobbing his wife."

Wells turns a deep red and Archer leans forward to further impale him.

"His lordship found those love letters you sent off to his wife, thankin' her for the money and babbling like another lovesick puppy about how much you enjoyed those pleasurable moments with her. If his wife had been bedding down with a gentleman, it wouldn't have been so disgusting, but to know she laid with a domestic—"

"*Shut up!*" I snap at Archer. "One more word out of you and I will call the constable."

Wells is rigid and almost purple. I'm sure he's about to attack the much stronger man, not only getting a beating in return, but ruining our entire mission. "Please," I whisper to him, "please don't strike out at him, that's what he wants. He's baiting you. Please, for me and for Lady Winsworth and for that little girl, go up to the room."

He rises slowly, never taking his eyes off of Archer, his fists clenched. I am in awful suspense because I'm certain he is ready to leap on the man.

"Don't," I warn Archer as he takes the cigar out of his mouth to make another crack.

Wells slowly walks away, stiffly, but with dignity.

As soon as Wells disappears up the stairs, I turn to the thug. "Mr. Archer, I do hope that after this is all over, you will visit me in New York."

He gives me a smirking leer. "You like a man who handles himself, don't you?"

"Actually, I think what you did to my friend was disgusting. The reason I'd like to have you visit is because there's a bare-knuckles champ I want to have knock all your teeth out."

I get up and smooth my dress. "We'll leave here after breakfast in the morning. We're taking the ten o'clock train to Exeter. Once we reach Exeter, I'll tell you the next phase."

He eyes me with suspicion. "If you're planning to take a train, why'd you load up a carriage?"

"To haul to the station. I didn't want to take the time to buy supplies in Exeter where the police might be interested in us. We'll rent another carriage there for the next leg."

"We're going back to Linleigh-in-the-moor. That artist told you more than you're letting on."

"That artist told us more than I'm willing to tell you. And you know more than you're telling me. So we both have our secrets. When I feel that you've been fair with us, I will share more with you."

His features twist into a mean sneer. "You had better be careful. I don't mind a bit of wordplay back and forth, but I expect results. If I don't get them from you, you're not going back home as pretty as you came." He smirks. "You can let that boyfriend of yours know that the next time he faces me, I'll cut off his balls and have them fried for dinner."

Even though I am trembling with anger and disgust, I control my voice. "See you at nine in the morning? Or should we make our way to the station separately in case Lacroix's people are looking for us?"

He chews on that for a moment. "Separately." He jabs his cigar at me. "But don't think you can lose me. I've caught up with you before and if I have to do it again, I won't be my gentle self."

"I'm trembling with fear."

With a stiff back and head held high, I head for the steps, not giving him one ounce of satisfaction that he has frightened me, which he might have, just a little. What he has really done is anger me and I hope I've shown that.

My heart is heavy for Wells. He has been stripped of his dignity and his secret life. Even worse for a proud man, it was in front of a woman. How devastated he must be feeling right now. I wish I had someplace else to go. He needs time and privacy to sort his emotions. And he definitely doesn't need to see me.

Never have I seen a friend more defeated than when Archer maliciously slashed with what appears to be the awful truth. The domestic class? A servant? That is mind boggling, since he is both a teacher and a scientific researcher.

England has a very structured society, based upon money and blood. The more the money, or the bluer the blood, the more doors are opened. The same is true in America, but to a much lesser degree—there it's mostly just a question of the size of one's bank account.

Hopefully my news to Wells that we will not be seeing Archer's face again will cheer him up.

Despite what I said to Archer, I have no intention of being around in the morning to take the Exeter train.

50

Wells is standing at the window, staring out when I enter. He has taken off his coat, collar, and top shirt to prepare for bed. He doesn't turn to look at me and I know he is hiding his embarrassment about the revelations Archer spit out so viciously.

Quietly I close the door behind me and go to him, putting my hand on his arm and turning him to me. His features are grave, with a grim set. Like most men, he considers it a weakness to reveal his hurt.

I caress his cheek with my fingers and brush his lips with mine. His lips open as I press mine against him and we melt together in a long, warm kiss.

Embedded female instincts make me break away.

"I find you to be a strange man in wonderful ways, Herbert George Wells. You are the most intelligent man I have ever sparred with."

"Ah . . . so you will love me for my mind, but . . ."

"I do admire you for your fine mind . . . but if I am to love you, it will be because I sense that beneath the intellect is great passion, not just for life but for me."

I look away, trying to organize my thoughts, for what I am about to say is against all I've been taught. It's been a struggle, but I've come to realize I am a woman who has desires and needs and yet I don't want to get married, at least not right now. However, I am not always able to lock away my feelings or desires. Nor do I want to.

"I have to give you fair warning," I tell him. "I have fought long and hard to find a path in this world. I will never give up my freedom for a man—any man. The love I give today will still be in me tomorrow, but my body will be an ocean away."

"I expect nothing less from you, Miss Nellie Bly."

He turns to look out the window to give me privacy as I remove my jacket and my blouse. I don't sleep in my outer clothes because they would become horribly wrinkled, but my underclothes are significantly modest, the type a woman would not be embarrassed for her father and brothers to see her in. He speaks to the window as I undress.

"Society has such ridged rules and laws that inhibit people from advancing and being what they want to be. As a woman, you cannot vote, or be equal to a man in work and love. I, as a man, am enslaved into a position in life because I was born into it. An accident of birth, like a king, except the benefits are a bit less."

As he's talking I have my back to him as I hang my clothes and brush them out.

"What did you and Archer talk about after I left?"

"We played cat and mouse about what information he was to give for what I gave in return. It ended up a stalemate. I asked him about his vampire remark and got the expected evasiveness."

He turns back around. "We can hope that one of those vampires he keeps talking about will bite him."

"He obviously knows, but it makes no difference. He is so instinctively dishonest and deceitful, no matter what we can't rely upon anything he tells us."

"You realize that when we find Lacroix, the greatest danger will be a knife in our backs by Archer. He's not going to want to share the credit."

"From what I've seen of the man, before turning Lacroix over to his employer, Archer will have a bidding war to see who will pay him the most."

He leans back against the wall and stares at me. Not impolitely, or with lust, but with tenderness.

"I thought about Archer making a deal with Lacroix, too." I make busy with the clothes, fighting my feelings, resisting the fiery urge I feel in my entire body. "Dealing with him will be a lost cause no matter how we go about it."

Once again, I turn my back to him wondering how am I going to handle this.

"You are an incredible woman, Nellie Bly."

"Thank you . . ." is all I can barely say.

I feel his warm breath behind me on my neck and my will power vanishes.

"I am going to make love to you, Nellie."

"I know."

51

Archer ordered his third double shot of whiskey at the inn's bar. He was feeling good after the conversation with the reporter and her teacher companion. In the morning, he'd get off a wire to his employer and tell his lordship that he was making great progress and that he needed the pump primed with more money.

His nibs won't be satisfied with Archer's bare statement, of course. For some reason that delighted Archer and he chuckled to himself. No trust left in this world, and he could testify to that. He ceremonially saluted his whiskey to no one but himself and slugged it down. The booze was spreading good cheer in his mind and body.

He had needed something to tell Winsworth that would impress him enough to loosen the notoriously tight grip the baronet kept on his hoard of South African gold. Now he could claim he was closing in on Lacroix, but he knew Winsworth would wire back and want details—ones that Archer didn't have yet, but was sure were in the bag.

"Another?" the bartender asked Archer.

"Keep them coming."

Archer mulled over the conversation he had had with the two amateur detectives. That was how he thought of them, himself being a professional who once carried a badge. That American reporter is a dandy, to be sure. She trusted no one. Smart girl, but too smart for her own good. This gave him another chuckle. He had to admit, she was a good judge of his character.

She hadn't revealed much, but neither had he, though he had whetted her appetite for information with his remark about vampires. He was confident that they were onto where Lacroix was hiding out. The laboratory had been the key all along. Now he had to get the information out of her . . . better yet, wait until they have Lacroix cornered and then he can take care of business all around.

Lord Winsworth knew a lab existed in Dartmoor because his late missus had told him there was one. Fortunately for Archer's own pocket-book, she hadn't told her husband where in Dartmoor, making it necessary for him to hire Archer.

He jerked down the whiskey and tapped the glass on the bar to signal for another. He was feeling good. Too bad the inn didn't have any women for hire.

"Ah . . ." He got it. He knew what he would prime the pump with to get more quid out of his lordship. He'll tell Winsworth that a child had suffered the same fate as his wife.

He mulled over how he would code the wire to his employer to convey Lacroix killed a kid, too, without raising Cain at the telegraph office.

He wondered why a man with as much gold as the baronet was so stingy about spending it. One thing was for certain, once he uncovered Lacroix's secret place, Lord Winsworth would be giving him plenty more money, a fistful—before he revealed the location. That thought drew a deep sinister laugh from Archer.

He'd gotten no instructions from his employer as to exactly what the plan was once Lacroix had been located. Winsworth knew as well as he did that there was no real evidence to tie a crime around the doctor's neck. Maybe with time and money, Winsworth could pull it off, but the baronet didn't strike him as a patient man.

Finding a way to get an even bigger wad out of the situation had been brewing within Archer ever since he found the diary. That would require taking another step forward after finding Lacroix.

He had asked Winsworth what the game would be once he collared Lacroix and the man had stared at him for a moment and then said, "We'll deal with that at the right time and place."

The correct place and time for Archer was one in which he got paid even more than he had been promised.

If Lacroix suffered an "accident" rather than being dragged into a slow and uncertain justice from the courts, Archer had a feeling that his pot would become much, much bigger. Winsworth was the kind of mine owner who wasn't afraid to call in strike breakers to crack a few heads, and was willing to have a union leader pulled out of his home in the middle of the night and hanged.

Of course, the other side of the coin was to see what Lacroix had to offer in order to make a getaway.

Archer was about to tap for another whiskey when a man slipped up next to him and said, "Let me get this one."

The man tapped the counter twice with his own empty glass. He was about thirty, with a heavy build.

"My thanks." If this stranger wanted to get him a drink, fine with Archer. He bought many a drink for other pub patrons when he was in the chips.

"I could tell you are a fellow Londoner just by the way you're dressed," the man said. "Thought we might chat. Hard to pick up a conversation with these local yokels, don't ya think?"

The innkeeper walked by, pleased that the two men were drinking whiskey rather than cheap ale. He took them to be a couple of salesmen from the city, Bristol or London, probably.

Odd, though, he thought. The one who had just bellied up to the bar next to the other man was wearing a type of shoe he'd never seen before. Might even be boots, it was hard to tell because the upper part was hidden under the man's pant leg.

The pointed toes of the footwear is what threw him off. It made the boots look uncomfortable.

52

We lay together, Wells on his back, my head on his chest. I feel more relaxed, more focused, than I did when I arrived back in our room after verbally dueling with Archer.

I have been running, mentally and almost physically, basically from the second I learned of Hailey's death. Shortly before that I had been racing breathlessly around the world to beat a "record" that existed only in the imagination of Jules Verne. My body and mind have been in high gear for . . . well, since I got my job with Pulitzer at *The World*.

A thought comes to me—the woman at the spa in Bath showing me how they help women release their "female hysteria" and how important it is. So this is the end result. I can't help but smile.

"I'm sorry," Wells whispers.

"What are you talking about?"

"I'm sorry I didn't punch that ass in the jaw. He would have finished me off proper, but not before I got in one or two."

"And for certain the innkeeper would have called the constable and we would be in jail right now or out in the streets without a room. Either way, you were right in leaving. Besides, we needed to string him along and find out what he knows. He baited us again with that vampire thing. I am just sorry he tried to insult you."

"The worst part about his probes is that it was all true. My parents are domestics and they once worked at the Winsworth estate. Lady Winsworth took an interest in me. I—I came to be fond of her."

"You loved her?"

"I loved her for what she was, a kind, generous, and intelligent woman. She was beautiful in mind and soul. I was, am, infinitely grateful for her help and support. Her husband is a tyrant, who cares nothing for her except as a display piece in his collection of art and fine furnishings."

"Winsworth's extremely rich, which I imagine for her made up for a great many of his shortcomings."

"He was a mining engineer who struck it rich, as much from luck as skill, as those things usually are. He bought himself a title and now thinks of himself as the cock of the walk. He's insufferable to be around. He doesn't talk to people, he talks down to them. My parents didn't stay long in their service because he constantly yelled. The last straw was when he went into a fit of rage over a maid breaking a vase and threw a broken piece at her as she was trying to clean it up."

I have a hunch that part of Wells's feelings toward Lady Winsworth were in the vein of a knight in shining armor. I could tell he is being evasive about his relationship with the woman and being the person I am, I want to know.

"Were you lovers?"

"We—we found comfort in each other's arms. Just once. She had come to me after her husband slapped her for some transgression or another, so she said. I imagined he was just in a bad mood and took it out on her. He had a habit of doing that. I had suffered an injury and was emotionally distraught over life, over the struggle to be something more than the draper's apprentice that I was headed for. It was my dear mother's wish that I become one. 'A much better position in life than hers,' she constantly told my bothers and me. I saw it as a life of servitude."

He kisses me on the forehead. "I did write her some letters that gushed with passion and gratitude. I'm not a hopeless romantic, but I see nothing wrong in showing emotions. May I remind you that you are a bird that will fly off to your next story or your next adventure. Well, in a sense I'm no different. I do not believe I will ever give my love to a single woman for all time. I find that unhealthy and stressful. Just as I would imagine it would be for a woman. I am polygamous, like that religious sect in Utah Conan Doyle wrote about in his first Sherlock Holmes book. I believe in free love, not love that is smothering."

This is a conversation I don't want to partake in, at least not right now after I've just finished making love with the man. All I know is that I am a woman who has been raised in a very strict society—especially for women. It's hard for me to grasp his free love theory. But I do know that I am not polygamous. I don't believe in sharing. It's just not for me and I feel it's a disrespectful way to treat your mate. If Wells is fine with it, that's his choice, and I just hope he finds a woman who has similar feelings.

But now it is time for me to put aside love and what I want out of life, at least for the moment. There are more important things to concentrate on. I slip off the bed and start getting dressed.

"There. I've driven you away with my babbling. Forgive me. I truly do love—"

"Get dressed. It's time to go."

He stares at me and then looks to the window before stating the obvious.

"It's nighttime. Dark outside."

"Yes, it usually is about eleven o'clock in the evening, everywhere, I'm told, except those places that enjoy the midnight sun."

I grab his pants off the chair and toss them to him.

"We have to get out of here when Archer isn't looking."

"We're not teaming up with him?"

"Of course not! Whatever gave you that idea?"

He gets off the bed and starts hopping into his pants. "I suppose I should have known you were lying. You do it so well. But, pray tell, sweet Nellie, shouldn't we wait until the crack of dawn to sneak out?"

"Archer is not a stupid man." I think about that statement. "More sly like a fox than bright, I suppose. And the fox in him will tell him we'll make a getaway about the time the sun is rising. I told him we'd meet him after breakfast, but I'm sure he took that with a grain of salt."

We continue dressing as we chat.

"You don't believe that there is any advantage in teaming with him?" Wells asks. "Remember, there's a killer out there. Archer is an ex-policeman and I'm sure he can handle himself. He may even have a gun."

"If he has one, he'll probably end up using it on us. And yes, I'm sorely tempted to team up with him, but I also keep reminding myself that he smacks of criminality, starting with the mugging I got from him. People tend to stay consistent in life; criminals tend to commit more crimes. That means we can never trust him and will always have to be watching our backs. Worse, when he does betray us, we may be defenseless."

"What about the diary? It may have more information."

"I don't want to be clutching for the diary with my dying breath and I have a feeling it will end up that way if we let him lead us around with it like a donkey with a carrot. Besides, I don't believe he has much more to tell us from the diary. What he told me about Hailey's infatuation with Lacroix rang true. Hailey was immature in many ways and dealing with a man in a romantic situation is just one of them. But she apparently wrote nothing in the diary about how to find Lacroix or where his laboratory in the moors is. If she had, Archer wouldn't need us."

"Quite, but, as I'm sure you are aware of, we are only going to shake him temporarily. He'll find us again and he'll still have the diary. You'll still have an opportunity to find out if there is any more to grasp from it."

I give a bit of thought to the idea of running into Archer after we run out on him. He doesn't strike me as a particularly forgiving man.

"My dear Wells, I do believe that our next meeting with Mr. Archer will not be on a friendly basis."

"Point taken."

What I don't convey and he knows as well as I do, is that we shall be lucky just to get away and stay away from the man long enough to find Lacroix.

53

We had left our purchases for the trip with the buggy at the stable, so we didn't have to haul anything more from our room than our valises.

After we're dressed, we pack up our clothes for a quick escape.

As quietly as possible I open the door a crack and check the hallway to make sure the coast is clear. There are only eight rooms, four on each side of the hallway with a set of steps at each end. Since I don't know which room is Archer's or even if he has returned to his room, I hesitate, wondering which direction we should take.

For all I know he could still be in the bar below and if he is, he might see us going out the front because the exit passes by the double-door opening to the bar.

To my left the hallway leads to the stairs that would take us back downstairs and through the lobby, past the hotel's small front desk and the wide doors to the pub.

To the right is a set of stairs that I'm guessing leads to a rear door.

Our room is already paid for, so we don't have to stop at the front desk.

"We'll go out the back," I whisper to Wells.

As we hurry down the hallway I can't resist the temptation to glance back and see if Archer's head is poking out of a doorway. It isn't.

The hallway is dimly lit with gaslights at each end. The stairway is a dark pit and we have to watch our footing going down.

At the bottom of the stairs we get an unpleasant surprise—*the rear door is locked, bolted tight.* It takes a key to get out.

"Damn," Wells hits the door, "should have guessed. Keeps people from running out on their rent."

"I don't suppose you learned how to pick a lock from one of those books you read?"

Wells shakes his head. "Only cutting up salamanders."

"Then we have no choice, we'll have to risk going out the front."

"In that case, I think we should wait a couple of hours until after the bar closes. Archer struck me as the type that hangs around to the very end. We call them pub closers."

"We can't. The stable will be closed. The stableman's not going to be happy and if we wait any later he won't answer the bell, period. Besides, it's already dark and it's getting foggy. We need to make our way to another inn before it gets worse."

"And what is your plan if he catches us red-handed?"

"We'll pretend we're coming to see him."

"With our luggage?"

"We tell him we have to leave now because we're afraid the police are coming, but stopped by to tell him where we're headed."

"Amazing . . ."

"What?"

"How you do it." He walks down the dimly lit first floor hallway shaking his head.

"Do what?"

"Come up with these lies."

I don't volunteer that I doubt that Archer would fall for the lie, but it will at least give him pause.

Wells is ahead of me and he is going by the open door to the men's water closet when he comes to an abrupt halt.

"*Good lord!*"

"What? What's the matter?" I rush up beside him.

Archer is sitting on a toilet. Motionless. Dead.

"Oh . . . my . . . lord . . ."

The handle of an ice pick is sticking out his right ear. Blood is running down the side of his neck. He is staring straight ahead, blankly, dull eyed. The expression on his face is one of permanent surprise.

"We have to keep going." I give Wells a push.

We start to rush away when I stop. "*The diary!* We have to get the diary."

I turn back and go in. My whole body shaking, I slowly approach Archer's body. He appears to be staring directly at me and I almost lose my nerve. Giving out a slight yelp, I reach inside his coat where I'd seen him put the diary.

It's not there.

I pad his chest to find it. Nothing. His weight shifts and he starts to fall forward. This time I cry out and push him back.

Wells grabs my arm and pulls me out of the room. He closes the door and turns the sign on the outside from UNOCCUPIED to OCCUPIED.

"It's not there," I tell Wells as we move quickly down the hallway. The diary Archer stole and so blatantly boasted possession of had cost him dearly.

My knees are trembling and I'm afraid they will give out, but I force my feet ahead with sheer willpower.

Just before we come out of the hallway I stop.

"We need to compose ourselves."

Once we get our breathing in order we move forward at a speed I hope doesn't look like we are running from a fire—or a murder.

We pass through the dining room and as we go by the open doors to the bar I pause and look in. My eyes automatically go to the shoes of men, looking for cowboy boots. Thank God I don't see a pair because I don't know what I'd do.

As we head for the exit the innkeeper, who's behind the front desk, looks up from an accounting book and asks, "Are you leaving?"

"Mother's sick," Wells says. "Must rush to her bedside. We're taking the train."

"You won't be getting a refund on your room. Stay a minute, stay the whole night, it's same to me."

"Thank you," I respond inanely and then realize I'm not supposed to say anything because of my accent.

The stable is half a block away and it is everything I can do to keep from breaking into a run, but even running would not have gotten us there any quicker than the swift stride Wells sets out for us.

We get lucky—the stableman is working late to make repairs on a carriage wheel. Our buggy is still loaded and the ponies are quickly harnessed.

As we come out of the stable yard a man bursts out of the hotel and runs down the street away from us. It's the innkeeper.

"Going for the constable," Wells says. "Change of course."

He quickly steers the ponies in the opposite direction.

"Please tell me you have an idea of where we are going."

"No, but I'm sure that somewhere ahead will be a road that can take us north."

I know we will get lost, I just feel it, but there are no other options than to head out blindly.

We wander for a while, trying to find the road without finding the constable first. It's an hour before we reach a simple wood sign at a crossroad that says POUNDSGATE and has an arrow pointing left. We haven't passed an inn.

Wells and I exchange looks. No words are needed. The only certainty about turning left is that we will leave a small town for a long, poorly maintained road with few accommodations on it. But if we continue straight, we're certain we'd end up at the train station.

Taking a train back to London is tempting. We could leave all this chaos behind, Wells would return to teaching, and I could catch a ship back to New York.

"I don't think we will be able to make out what is ahead on the road." I stated the obvious.

My rational mind knows that probably little will change in terms of the scenery of the moors after we leave Ashburton, but the part of my brain that sometimes imagines the unimaginable tells me that the night has grown darker, the fog thicker, the road more deserted.

"Maybe we should pull over and wait 'til morning?" I'm still trying to put off the inevitable.

"And let the constable find us . . . I don't think so."

"When you and Dr. Doyle were perusing routes for us to take, did he tell you anything about Poundsgate?"

"A small but comfortable inn, good ale. And the devil."

"Why does that not surprise me? Is the Dark One the innkeeper?"

"Giving equal credit to each sex for evil, I'm not certain Satan is a 'he' as opposed to a 'she,' but we can refer to him as a 'he' to keep things simple."

"Just tell me about the devil. It's cold, it's dark, it's creepy and I'm sure there are things out here that would give pause to Satan himself."

"It's said that the devil stopped at the Poundsgate inn on his way to collect a soul in Widecombe, which is farther north."

"How did the innkeeper know it was the devil?"

"His cloven heels were a tip-off. He was dressed in black and rode a black horse. As he downed a mug of ale all in one long chug, the barmaid heard a hissing sound. He left money on the bar that appeared to be coins but turned out to be dried leaves when she picked them up. The mug he set on the bar left a scorch mark. After he left the bar, he found the man whose soul he'd come for at church services in Widecombe. He collected the man after causing damage and a death or two in the church."

"Other than the cloven hooves and his bad bar manners, is there anything to corroborate the visit of the Dark One or can we just attribute it as another old wives' tale?"

"There is the matter of the ball lightning."

"Which is?"

"Our image of lightning is of long, narrow flashes. There is a rare variety which appears as a fiery ball. The earliest know verification of ball lightning happened that day when a ball of fire went through a church window and wreaked havoc at Widecombe."

Cloven hooves, ball of fire, it was good enough for me.

"No rest for the wicked," Wells states flatly.

"I wish you hadn't put it that way."

We turn left, heading for the wild moors.

It occurs to me that left-handedness has always been associated with the devil.

54

The moors . . . the dark side of the moon as far as I'm concerned.

On this chilly, foggy, gloomy night with just the ghost of a full moon sailing through a sea of ashen clouds, our Dartmoor ponies somehow manage to maneuver down a dark, dirt road without breaking a leg, an axle.

Mr. Poe, genius of the horror and the macabre, could hardly have imagined a night with more unseen but felt terrors. The most frightening element of all is that we can see so little. We have no idea of what lies before us and I mean *right* before us. Everything is shrouded, distorted by dense fog. The effect is otherworldly, nothing which I have experienced before.

I look at Wells whose eyes are trying to focus on the dirt road ahead. "I feel like we have entered into the Dartmoor mist you were telling me about."

"Quit." Is all he says. His back is ridged and his hands grip the reins tightly as he leans forward trying to focus on what lies ahead.

What my eyes don't see, my mind imagines—which is nothing good. Nor does my imagination stop flaring up with the landscape—images of the black beast of a hound are conjured in my head every time I hear the howl of a farmer's dog, the ice pick killer on his horse whenever something appears to move in the dark. On occasion, there is the eerie howl of a hound that sends quivers up my spine and causes me to edge closer to Wells.

"We should have bought a gun," Wells says.

Should have, would have, could have. "But we bought a compass," I try to say in a cheerful voice.

"Wonderful, we can ward off demons and murderers by leading them in the wrong direction."

Wells's attempt at humor does nothing for either of us.

Instead, just the mention of demons and murderers brings horrible images to my mind. I keep seeing the ice pick in Weekes's back and the one in Archer's head. The ice picks are left as a boast and a trademark, Wells concluded earlier.

Which brings up a question—what direction has the ice pick killer taken?

If Lacroix is in Okehampton and the murderer is returning to his nest, he could be taking the direct route across the moors just as we have. Could he be on horseback? I regret not asking the stableman if another man had picked up his horse shortly before we arrived. He could have headed out in any direction—especially ours, since he has now twice appeared at the same location as we have.

"Is he following us?" I ask Wells. "Or are we on his heels?"

It takes him a moment to realize who I'm talking about.

"He . . . or . . . they?" he asks. "Why must we assume there is only one? If it is the Whitechapel gang, there may be more of them out there."

"Out there" of course included where we are.

"The ice pick and cowboy boots serve a number of purposes for the London gang," he continues. "It's a trademark and a boast, making it easier to intimidate people. But what if in our case it's also a red herring?"

"Something to throw us off?"

"Throw suspicion on the Whitechapel bunch and direct the police, and us, to look for the wrong person?"

"Thank you, Wells. A moment ago I was watching out for a killer with an ice pick and cowboy boots. Now I have to worry about everyone on the planet."

There's an edge of humor to my remark, but there is nothing funny about the situation. While I had not found Archer to be the most admirable or finest specimen of humanity, he didn't deserve to die, nor did the artist Weekes, who seemed like a pleasant fellow who just wanted to enjoy life and paint.

"Why not us, too?" I ask Wells. "He—they—wanted to keep the artist from revealing the location and wanted the diary from Archer. Is it just a coincidence that they were killed after talking to us or did we lead the killer to them?"

"Perhaps both." Wells readjusts his body on the wooden buggy seat. "If it is the Whitechapel gang, there's probably more than one involved. They could have been following both us and Archer."

"Wait, I just remembered, when we talked to the shopkeeper in Linleigh-on-the-moor, he said something about strangers in town. I was sure he was referring to us and only one other person because he talked about the stranger with the full-sized horse. I didn't think anything of it because I assumed that anyone we had to fear would be following us and no one had passed us on the way."

"You think the killer got there before us because Lady Chilcott spilled the beans."

"Yes, I'm sure of it now. But that still doesn't answer why they haven't tried to kill us yet."

"There's an answer as to why they haven't attacked you." Wells's voice seems to be relaxing a bit. Maybe it's because we're talking instead of sitting in silence, letting the ghostly thoughts and images feed our imaginations.

"A couple deaths in small Dartmoor towns are a tragedy," he continues, "but they will not be a national issue. The police could even consider them random killings by some sick bastard who kills whenever he gets the opportunity. But the murder of a famous American reporter would cause a sensation and an intense investigation, especially since you've made it obvious to the police in both London and Bath that you suspect Lacroix and the spa in the death of your friend."

He leans against me and gives me a kiss on the cheek. "But killing a teacher wouldn't even raise an eyebrow in London. Stay close to me. I'm safer when you're around."

An unpleasant thought strikes me. "You might not be completely right about being safe with me. We are on an isolated road where no one can hear our screams. And he can easily get rid of our bodies in a bog . . . never to be found again."

The unnerving thought that we have put ourselves at the mercy of the killer makes my heart jump up to my throat.

"I wonder what it would be like to slip down—way down—in peat." I look at Wells. "They say it's not cold beneath the surface, that it generates its own heat, sometimes smoldering for years and even starting forest fires. So, on the brighter side, if our bodies were thrown into a bog, we'd be down there for thousands of years until someone dug us out and put us in a museum. We'd be preserved forever."

"I think the mist-fog is affecting your brain." Wells pats my leg. "If you keep this up, I'm turning this buggy around and heading back for Ashburton."

I glance to our rear. "Don't. He may be following us. Or . . ."

"Nellie—"

"I have to say it. Or ahead of us. We could be trapped."

On that charming thought, we grow silent, drawing into our own thoughts.

The bumpy road makes for very slow going and unfortunately plenty of time to think, which right now I don't want to do. All my thoughts are negative.

"Are we lost?" I finally ask Wells.

"No."

"How can you be so sure in all this fog?"

He takes a deep breath. "The compass has us going in a generally north direction."

"But the way the road twists and turns I would think it would make the compass hard to set even for a generally northern course. One moment we're going north and the next east or west. It's too dark to see anything on the horizon to help steady out the course or decide which fork in the road to take."

"Good point."

"So . . ."

"I agree." Wells looks at me, tired. "We have no idea where we are."

"Terrific—wait, is that a farmhouse?"

A home materializes in front of us and we hear the howls of dogs and the telltale ratchet of a double-barrel shotgun being loaded.

"Wells . . . did you hear that?"

"Yes . . ."

"Who's out there?" comes the nervous voice of a man.

"Don't shoot!" I shout. "We're lost in the fog."

A moment of silence, then, "Your voice don't sound right to me."

"I'm an American!"

"And I'm British—Herbert George Wells, from London. We were making our way to Widecombe, but our compass has led us to a dead end."

We hear the crunch of footsteps and a man comes into view. He's carrying a shotgun and wearing a woolen cap and a full-length nightshirt.

55

Farmer Hayes raises sheep on the rugged land and maintains a garden that provides enough for himself and a little left over to sell at market day.

The small farmhouse he has invited us to stay the night is a stone cottage with a thick gray thatch roof. It is much smaller and more roughly hewed than the Old Bridge House, both inside and out. Just two rooms, a bedroom, and living room-kitchen.

The sink has a hand pump that brings in water from a tank outside. The few pieces of furniture—a small table, sideboard, two chairs, and a large rocking chair heavily padded with wool—are all of wood, only finished by time and smoke from the fireplace when a gust of wind reverses the draft.

He does, in fact, have two delightful companions—two big, friendly Old English sheepdogs, Hansel and Gretel. They have thick shaggy coats and long, straight hair that drops down over their faces and covers their blue eyes.

Farmer Hayes told us that not only do their shaggy fur coats keep the dogs warm, but their undercoats shed water. "Can get four or five pounds of hair from them every year. Women weave socks and sweaters from it."

The sleeping accommodations are basic—a padded woolen mat in front of the fireplace and a warm quilt with dog hair on it—but after being lost in the moors and chased by creatures of my imagination, I wouldn't have felt more snug at the Langham Hotel.

"I'm a bachelor," Hayes tells us as he puts a log on the fire. "Had a wife once, but she couldn't take the solitude. Said it's too lonely for her out here. Not too lonely for me. Any itch I get for people gets satisfied with a couple pints and a game of darts once a week. And that's more than enough."

Satisfied with the fire, he offered us a cup of home brew "to keep you warm" but we both politely declined.

"If my wife had been here when you two came along, she would have been properly frightened. She was superstitious and scared of things that went bump in the night."

"Get many strange sightings?" Wells asks.

"No more than anyone else. The black beast is out there, but if you leave it alone it'll just take a sheep or a horse now and again, though some say it likes the taste of human flesh even better."

"Ever seen it?" I ask.

"Never had it come up and eat out of me hand if that's what you mean, but you can't have spent your life on the moors without now and again seeing things that make the hair on the back of your neck stand up."

Amen to that.

"Mr. and Mrs. Wells" once again lay down together. Even though we are fully clothed, as soon as Farmer Hayes turns down the lamp and retreats to his bedroom there will be a bit of necking and petting with the newlyweds sharing his wool mat.

The moment I lay down I am smothered with hot, wet kisses and I start giggling. Wells, too, receives attention as both the big dogs flop down next to us.

When Hansel and Gretel are settled beside us, Wells leans over and kisses me and then puts a finger on my lips to hush me.

"I know what you're going to say. The dog kisses better."

56

Hansel and Gretel awaken me as they get up to leave the house with Farmer Hayes. Wells is still sound asleep, snoring very softly, as I lay for a moment hating that I have to get up and go outside to the privy. Indoor plumbing, which lacks the cold walk and icy seat of an outhouse, is perhaps the greatest boon to mankind.

The fire in the fireplace has died down and now just ashes linger, leaving the room slightly chilly and crisp. I see the farmer has left breakfast on the table, some bangers and bread and a jug of what people who have to work outside on cold mornings take a swig of to warm their insides.

It's a gray morning, quiet and hazy with the fog not burned off yet. After I endure the privy that blocks of ice could well have been stored in, I hear the dogs barking and decide to watch how the famous breed herds sheep.

The barking is coming from beyond a small ridge at the end of rows of cabbage. At the top of the ridge I see sheep being herded by one of the dogs over another hill and I can hear the other dog barking.

Rocks are placed nicely for me to use as stepping stones to cross a small stream. A large green patch of low-lying turf is beyond the creek and I hurry to cross it as the dog and the last sheep disappear over the hill.

I've gone no more than four or five steps when I realize the ground is quaking beneath my feet.

I stop and freeze in place.

The ground feels spongy. Standing perfectly still for a moment I can feel the surface trembling underfoot.

I'm on a bog.

I thought I was on a patch of grass but it's the deceptive green covering that hides the pond of decaying vegetation.

Oh God. I'm on thin ice. If I step in the wrong spot I will sink.

I begin to tremble. My heart is pounding and I can feel icy fear racing up the back of my legs and along my spine.

"Help . . ."

My heart has jumped into my throat blocking it and my cry is barely audible. I give a louder shout for aid, but I can hear from the barking that the dogs are now far away. I don't know how sheep are herded, so I'm not even sure the farmer is with them.

The bog is a flat area surrounded by slopes on all but one side. It strikes me that the ground where the slopes come down might have a grade beneath the surface that makes it slippery and would cause me to fall. I start taking cautious steps toward the flat area.

The surface beneath my feet is soft and wet, with an elastic feel as it presses down under my feet. My knees are weak and shaking, my breathing shallow as I move slowly, afraid that my next step will puncture this greenery that covers the bog like the skin of a primeval beast.

What did Dr. Doyle say? If a bog starts to draw you under, don't fight it with your feet. Lay on it, putting as much of the surface of your body on it as you can in order to spread your weight.

Like floating in water, I tell myself. If it starts to take me, I'll float.

But it's not water. It's more like quicksand. And lying flat may just make it easier to swallow me.

I realize I had been wrong to have continued across. I should have retraced my steps back to the creek, back the way I had come without sinking instead of venturing on to unknown footing.

Do I turn around and go back? That would require major movement which could bring on sinking.

Do I lay flat and pray someone will come before I'm swallowed under?

I see something above, on the ridge across from where the sheep had been herded. It's a movement. I can't make out any of the details, it's just a dark figure in a patch of fog, but I'm sure it's a man on horseback.

"Help! I'm down here. Help!"

Like the man, the horse is just a black shadow in the haze, but from its size, it appears to be a full-grown one, not a Dartmoor pony. I suddenly freeze, mortified even more with terror—the horse is moving quickly on the ridge, but I don't hear the sound of its hooves hitting the ground.

Fear drives me to move.

Since I have no good choices I take a deep breath. I'm going to make a mad dash to the hilly area.

My right foot goes down and slips into the muck.

I try to pull it out, but the bog hangs onto my foot as if I'd stuck it in the jaws of an animal.

A BOG IN DARTMOOR

57

A rider all in black, a horse that makes no sound." Wells casts me an appraising look as he hitches the ponies to our buggy. "I'm just glad Mr. Hayes realized he forgot to leave out a loaf of bread and a leg of mutton for our journey or . . ."

"Don't say it. I thought my life was over and it would have been if Mr. Hayes wasn't such a kind soul. Most people would have decided to just continue on with their work. He saw me before I realized he was there because I had my eyes closed, but can you imagine the look on his face when he came over that ridge and found me trying to be calm lying on a bog?" I'd laugh, but I'm still too shook up.

When I realized the bog wasn't going to let go of my foot, I gave in and lay flat, as Dr. Doyle recommended. It felt that with each breath I took the beast was pulling me down, just a little each time, to torture me. After what seemed like forever, I heard Farmer Hayes's voice. He came running toward me with a long pole and pulled me out. Never in my life was I more grateful. I didn't stop hugging him until he appeared to become embarrassed.

"The dear man saved my life." I didn't tell Hayes about the phantom and even hesitated about telling Wells. I had been so frightened on the bog and having heard so many tales of the stranger, I fear I might have conjured it up.

"You don't believe I saw a dark horseman, do you?"

"Of course I believe you." He tightens a hitch and then turns to me. "But I also believe in ghosts and creatures that are only supposed to belong in a child's nightmares, in dinosaurs still to be found in a land lost in time, and that the canals of Mars were built by an advanced civilization."

He gives me a peck on the cheek. "I'm just happy that the dark horseman you saw was His Satanic Majesty and not the ice pick killer. Do you realize you beat the widow maker?"

I nod my head. I'm just happy the devil isn't ready for me yet.

But, maybe it is a warning.

After going back into the farmhouse to say our last good-bye to Farmer Hayes and Hansel and Gretel, we make good time en route to Widecombe.

As our buggy rumbles along and goes over every bump and dip in the dirt road I want to scream out in pain as my body comes into contact with the wood seat, but I don't. I keep watching our valiant ponies pulling us along uncomplaining, avoiding falling into a bog.

"Doesn't the cold, damp morning air remind you of the sea?" I ask Wells, hoping a conversation will keep my mind off my aches and pains.

"Quit."

So much for conversation, but I can't blame him, he's focusing on the road ahead.

The sun is out and has burned off most of the fog, but there is a thin haze that gives the tors in the distance an unearthly feel. Since Dartmoor is part of England's West Country peninsula and lies between two great bodies of water, the English Channel and the Bristol Channel, they get a lot of fog, mist, and haze which lends to a very spooky atmosphere.

We pass through Widecombe and stop for a midday meal and repair a spoke on the buggy wheel, then continue on, determined to get beyond Chagford before we find an inn or a house that accommodates guests.

"Wells." I can't stand the silence anymore and need to talk, if just to kill time. "While you went to find out how the repairs on the buggy were coming along, I was told a story by the waitress in the pub. She said that on our way to Chagford we will pass the grave of an orphan girl. Her name is Mary Jay. Supposedly it was common at the time to give orphan girls the surname 'Jay'. Anyway, what's uncanny about Mary Jay's situation is it's so similar to Hailey's."

"How's that?"

"As a teenager, Mary was sent to a farm to work and became pregnant by a farmhand. Some say it was rape, others say she was simply so young and inexperienced she didn't know better. Whatever the cause, faced with an unmarried pregnancy and nowhere to turn, poor Mary Jay killed herself."

Wells looks at me. "I see what you mean, but unfortunately it is a common story. I can't tell you how many stories I've heard about young, single girls getting pregnant and then killing themselves."

"I know, but this one gets worse. Because suicide is considered by the church to be a great sin, her body was refused burial on consecrated ground and simply buried at a crossroad. The locals believed that the intersecting roads would keep her restless soul confused and unable to escape and harm them."

"So they can live in peace, her body lives in confused hell."

"Exactly. But it does have a happy ending. About the time I was born, good Samaritans had her body removed from the crossroad, properly casketed, and put in a simple mound at a pretty sight along the side of a road. Ever since she was reburied, fresh flowers appear rather miraculously at the grave and the locals claim it is the work of pixies. If you don't mind, I got specific instructions on how to find the grave. I want to leave flowers on it."

"Okay, but the pixies are already doing that."

"I know. I'd like to give them a break."

As night is falling and we are still on the road, I'm worried that we made a mistake in passing satisfactory accommodations to put more miles behind us, and complain to Wells that I shouldn't have listened to him, but I give him a peck on the cheek as we come to an inn.

"Wait here while I go see if they have a room." Wells hands me the reins as he gets down.

As he walks away I know this time there is no question we will register as man and wife. There is no pretense between us. We are lovers . . . what exactly does that mean? To me, it raises a question—am I in love with Herbert Wells?

I enjoy his company, I feel comfortable lying beside him at night, and I confess that he arouses my passions, the yearning I have to unite body and soul with a man, but is that love?

All in all, my emotions and mind are in a state of confusion. I have met other men who I felt a deep passion for, but my feelings for them were not powerful enough to alter my path in life, though in each case I left a piece of my heart behind and have warm memories.

Wells is different.

He has many of the same traits of two men I have loved—intelligence, ambition, moral and physical courage—both of whom were at least twice

Wells's age. Women were only a small part of their lives, their attention being directed to their careers.

Probably most significant about these men is that each of them is a man's man. The joy they get from life is in doing things that men enjoy doing with other men.

I am much the same as those men, but I have sensed that Wells loves women with a deep commitment. I know his intent is not to commit himself to any one woman. Quite the opposite, he loves women in general, and has the capacity to love—and love—and love.

While he is no less ambitious than successful men I've known, he does not isolate himself from the opposite sex. Rather, he celebrates companionship with women. He is more content to have a romantic dinner with a woman than playing a sporting event or solving the world's problems over brandy and cigars. He is a woman's man.

"All set." Wells hops back into the buggy. "Let's freshen up before going to the pub."

I nod my head. So engrossed with my thoughts I didn't see him return, I find myself blushing as if he was privy to my mental conversation about him.

"Did you say you came from Ashburton?" a local at the bar turns and asks us as we are eating.

"Yes," comes from both of us.

"Did you spot anything peculiar on the road through the moors?"

I smother an inclination to tell him I'd been chased by the devil as Wells tells him that everywhere we look on the moors, we see something peculiar.

That brings chuckles from the man and his companions.

"Isn't that the truth," another man says. "But we've heard sightings of the black beast and a sheep's been killed."

"Some say it's a wild dog," a third companion pipes in, "but others claim what they've seen is *too* big to be an ordinary dog."

"How close have they gotten to what they've seen?" Wells asks the men.

"Far enough away to still be alive," brings a laugh all around.

We are no more than a couple hours or so from the Okehampton area, so I ask, "Could it be Lady Howard that's being spotted?"

"No," comes from all of them along with shaking of their heads.

"Her ladyship, or at least her ghost, generally stays nearby the castle," one of the locals says. "Besides, Lady Howard is a collector of souls for the devil, she's no sheep killer."

"Can you tell us anything about the castle?" Wells asks them.

The men shake their heads as one and say, "It's too far away."

The answer doesn't surprise me. It is something we have run into all along—despite the closeness of these men to Okehampton, none of them have been to the castle. It's part of the narrow, provincial nature of rural England—in America a hundred miles is not a great distance and there are places where you'd find little in between. A hundred miles in England covers thousands of years of history and while the language is all called English, people not only speak differently than those dozens of miles away, but often think of themselves as different.

"Wells," I whisper in his ear, "I'm weary . . ."

"Do you mind going up by yourself? I'd like to go over the map with the men."

"Of course . . ." I get up. "Gentlemen, I shall say good night. It's been a pleasure talking with you."

I head for the cottage in back while Wells stays behind.

Next to a work shack I spot a woodpile. Perfect. I'm excited. My mother always said little things thrill me. What thrills me right now is the thought that I'll get enough extra wood to keep our fireplace going hopefully throughout the night. When I stoop down to grab some logs I hear footsteps.

Thinking it is Wells, I turn around to tell him what I'm doing.

Instead, a dark beastly figure is coming at me.

"*Aughhhhh!*" escapes my mouth and I grab a piece of wood, ready to strike the great furred monster.

58

Good lord, Nellie-girl, that scream will wake up *all* the ghosts for miles."

I don't swoon out, but I drop the wood and collapse against Oscar's black fur coat.

"We've come to storm the castle with you," Oscar proudly announces.

And he didn't just bring himself, but his friend, Dr. Conan Doyle.

Oscar's fur coat answers the rumors about a black beast that is roaming the moors—his coat is big enough to wrap around me, head to toe, at least twice.

Knowing Oscar loves being the center of attention, as we make our way to the pub, I tell him the rumor about a big beast roaming the countryside.

"Oh my!" Oscar unconsciously covers his teeth as he giggles. I can see the mischievous person in him coming out.

Not to my disappointment he insists on walking into the inn first with Doyle and I in tow.

Oscar creates the sort of sensation only Oscar's mere presence can ignite.

Surrounded by the locals, Wells, our two new arrivals, and I sit at a table with a big platter of beef, another of the ever-present mutton, plus bowls of potatoes, vegetables, and bread. Oscar is in heaven. The whole place is glued to his every word.

"As we were making our way through the moors I kept thinking about life and how it is a terrible thing for a man to suddenly realize that all his life he has been speaking nothing but the truth," he says in a melodious voice.

The whole place goes up in laughter and for the first time in a long while my spirits are up because as we close in on the enemy—I hope—we are now twice as many.

However, it does occur to me that the only weapons the four of us have against these cold-blooded killers are our words and our brains, but I'm certain empires have been conquered with no more—though I can't think of any at the moment.

"I became concerned after that boorish man showed up at my door," Dr. Doyle explains after we got Oscar to sit down and stop talking, which quickly dispersed the crowd. "I assumed you had already started across the moors before he showed up, but I went ahead and tried several of the inns in the area to find the two of you, but came up blank."

"We were at an inn near Ashburton," Wells says.

"I discovered that the next morning when my housekeeper arrived bursting with the singular news that a murder had been committed with an ice pick. A check with the police revealed that it was in fact that Archer fellow."

"Do they believe we did it?" I'm almost afraid to ask.

"They found out from the innkeeper that the two of you had left in quite a hurry just before the discovery of the body. And since they had already been on the lookout for an American woman and British gent who had left a previous location on the heels of a similar crime, yes, let me assure you that the police are most interested in talking to you. However, I have related to them much of what you told me and I believe their interest in you will be focused more on your failure to stay and inform them of what you know."

"My fault entirely," I confess, "because to delay is to fail and return to America without my friend's murder being solved."

"I'm certain that a good result in their investigation from information supplied by you will greatly temper their attitude toward you. Naturally, I told them about the cowboy boots and the probable connection to the Whitechapel gang. The innkeeper did in fact notice a man with very narrow-toed boots but unfortunately remembered more about the footwear than the man's face. The police are seeking patrons who were in the pub that night to see if anyone else saw the killer."

"A wire from Conan after you left his house that said you were knee-deep in some very serious difficulties was my cue to enter stage left," Oscar says, with all the modesty of a prince of the blood.

"As it happens," he goes on, "I found myself under some stress arising from a romantic issue in London as the Marquis of Queensbury, a rather socially inept and disagreeable chap, became rather incensed over the attention I was paying to one of his offspring."

Wells has a puzzled look. "I thought the marquis had three sons."

I notice Dr. Doyle doesn't bat an eye.

Oscar waves away the triviality. "Whatever. I immediately left London for Buckfastleigh to offer my sword in the battle to come."

"Did you by chance bring the sword?" Wells inquires. "For we could certainly use one."

"Guns and blades are for barbarians. My weapons are the righteousness of my cause and the power of my spirit."

If someone could be talked to death, Oscar would be a prime suspect. But I have doubts as to its effectiveness against an ice pick.

"We weren't completely certain that you knew about the killing near Ashburton," Dr. Doyle intercedes, "though your hasty departure had convinced the local constable that you were indeed involved. This second murder, however, threw out any possibility that the Linleigh-on-the-moor death was not connected to your investigation. With Oscar arriving on the heels of news of Archer's grisly death, we hired a buggy and set out immediately to find you."

"I must hope, my dear Nellie," Oscar says, "that the next time I set out to rescue you, it will be in a coach with a more comfortable seat than one of these carts they call a buggy in Dartmoor."

Amen to that.

The conversation shifts to the subject of how we can go about finding Lacroix's laboratory. Dr. Doyle had devised an investigatory approach as he and Oscar set out to find us.

"I don't believe Lacroix's laboratory is at Okehampton Castle itself," Dr. Doyle tells us. "I suspect it is in the vicinity, but I don't think we'll find it at the castle despite the fact that it's abandoned and generally avoided because of its reputation. However, it's only locals who shy away from the place. In the summer an occasional hiker would venture by, so the risk of exposure would be high."

"The castle, the magic mud bog, and the laboratory are all in the same vicinity," I inject, "but that could cover a lot of territory. Is there anything about Weekes that would give us a clue as to where the laboratory might be located? He had gone to the area solely to do the painting and probably wasn't that familiar with the terrain himself. Even though we were told he spent most of his time outside, he didn't strike me as someone who would hike far."

"I agree," Wells says. "He seemed like a man who limited his physical activities. I suspect he headed each day for one of those natural granite caves that form . . . or maybe he visited a farmer's widow, but whatever he did, he wouldn't spend the day on his feet."

"What would you say his excursion on foot to be?" Dr. Doyle asks. "An hour . . . two hours?"

"Two hours at the most," Wells answers.

"At the very most," I add. "I suspect more like an hour."

"Then let's split the difference and make it an hour and a half at best. Now a person normally walks perhaps three or four miles per hour on a flat surface. So let's assume that because of the roughness of the terrain, Weekes would have walked at best about two miles per hour. An hour and a half walk would take him three miles."

"So the bog is probably within three miles of the castle," I exclaim.

"But six miles to us," Wells says, and Dr. Doyle nods in agreement. "Weekes could have set out in any direction. To cover all of them, we'd have to draw a circle with a radius of three miles, which would leave us with a diameter of six miles to cover."

I get the idea even if I don't understand the terminology. "Once we find the castle, the bog would be three miles from it in any direction."

"Or the laboratory," Oscar states. "He might have started from either location."

It never occurred to me that Weekes could have been at the laboratory. But it is not out of the question. Lacroix may have been more tolerant of having a discreet visitor at his laboratory because the painting was done before Lady Winsworth died.

"This, of course, assumes our assumptions about Weekes's energy level are correct. And while covering a three-mile radius from the castle does not seem a daunting task, it won't be an easy one, either. The castle is in an area that has rough terrain and is heavily forested, not to mention the threat of bogs. It makes a search time consuming."

"We need a hot air balloon."

There is a stunned silence as the three men stare at me.

Finally, Oscar explodes with a great laugh. "Nellie-girl, the gods on Olympus could not have come up with a better idea."

"Unfortunately, I don't believe we'll find aeronauts and a fleet of balloons at Okehampton," Dr. Doyle states grimly.

"It's not impossible." Wells looks at us somewhat excited. "I have an interest in aeronautics because I believe that someday man will conquer the sky with more efficient airships than what we have constructed to date. I read recently that since there are no large cities in the region, it's attracted some balloon enthusiasts."

"Wait." Dr. Doyle sits up. "I have a friend in Okehampton who I attended medical studies with. If there is such activity there, he'll know about it."

Pleased with their revelation, Dr. Doyle leans back in his chair and lights his pipe while Oscar offers Wells one of his cigars.

"Gentlemen, if you'll excuse me, I shall leave you to your brandy and cigars. I am going to step out onto the porch for some fresh air."

Oscar and Dr. Doyle nod their heads in approval and Wells courteously rises to go with me.

I motion for him to sit back down. "I'll be fine. It's enclosed and others are about."

59

The porch has a chilly edge to it despite the windows, but the air is refreshing and the oxygen necessary for my brain to continue functioning.

A young couple are down at the other end of the deck. They are watching the stars and sneaking kisses and an occasional bit of petting comes from the young man's roaming hands.

They catch me watching and I quickly turn away. I don't want to spoil their fun. From the corner of my eye I see them coming toward me to leave and I turn around to address them.

"Please, don't leave, I'm going back in."

"It's no problem. We're going in anyway," the young man says. "It's too cold out here."

He seems embarrassed that I saw them necking, but the young girl is blushing and excited. "We're newlyweds," she giggles, then looks lovingly at him.

"Congratulations! I wish you the best."

"Thank you," is said in unison as they leave.

I'm a little sad as I watch them leave, not for them, but because I am feeling sorry for myself. Truth be told, I'm envious of their happiness. I can't help but wonder if I will ever find that blissful happiness they are sharing right now.

Right now I can't even find contentment with my job. I've tried, but I can't seem to get settled after my return from dashing around the world. My resentment of Pulitzer for not being fair with me is a thorn in my claw. He tried to keep me from going and wanted to send a man instead, but because of my determination he let me go and rang the cash register for his papers as I sent circulations soaring. Yet he still hasn't acknowledged it with a "thank you" in person.

Because of a contract to write mystery novels and endorse certain products I can risk leaving my reporting job, but I will miss it. It's in my blood. If only I could do everything I want to do.

I take a deep breath and leave the porch. I'm tired of thinking. Soon, I presume, Wells will be returning to our cottage and I'd like to freshen up beforehand.

I am certain Oscar will have a clever aside for me when he discovers that Wells and I have become lovers. Trying to deceive Oscar will be impossible—if there is any mortal who knows more about love than those gods of Olympus he cited earlier, it is he. Having been married, fathered children, carried on affairs with men, and associated with lesbians, I am certain there is little about love—or lovemaking—that Oscar couldn't write a book about.

I barely get into the cottage when there is a knock on the door.

It's the inn's maid. She seems a bit hurried. "Your friend sent me to tell you to come to the stable. There's a problem with one of your ponies."

"Oh no. Did he say what's wrong?"

"No, madam, just for you to come quickly."

I throw on a shawl and head for the stable which is only a hundred feet from the inn.

We named the ponies Adam and Eve and I dearly love them both. They belong together, they're a team. Wells laughs at me for worrying about what will happen to them if they were separated. The most common serious injury to a horse is to its legs and I hope that isn't the case. It is a given that a leg injury to a person can be healed, but for a horse it is almost certain death.

I confess, I love animals and unfortunately because I feel such a bond with them, I react emotionally to their injuries. They are like children, so helpless.

As I'm coming up to the stable I notice a black carriage parked off to the side of the building. It's the most luxurious rig I have ever seen.

To my surprise I find the stable doors shut and bolted. I stop. A thought flashes that petrifies me—*I've been set up.*

I didn't tell the others I was returning to the cottage or leave a note for Wells that I went to the stable. No one will know where I am.

I spin around to get the heck out of here, when I hear a familiar voice. "Fancy meetin' you here."

A man steps out of darkness not reached by the oil lamp above the wide stable doors.

Burke—the ruffian from the spa.

"Ugh" barely escapes my mouth as a hand comes around from behind me and smothers my mouth, as a sharp point is thrust against my neck.

"Open your flap, dolly, and I'll shove this all the way to your brain." *Ice pick.*

My heart stops. Horrible visions of Archer and Weekes flash before me.

Burke takes my arm and keeps the ice pick on me as the man behind releases me. "Now let's calmly walk to the carriage and get in."

With the ice pick to my throat, we make our way over to the carriage. A few times my knees feel like they are going to collapse, but I force them to move forward only because I know that if I fall I will be impaled with the pick.

A gold crest of nobility is on the side of the carriage.

I am shoved inside with the thug coming in behind me, still holding the ice pick.

The woman I had first seen getting out of the black coach at the spa entrance faces me. A small oil lamp takes the edge off the darkness in the carriage designed for the rich and noble.

She is elegantly dressed in black, the cloth being of fine lace. A veil most women wear for fashion alone is again hiding her features for reasons only she knows.

"What do you want from me?" My voice is controlled anger. If the ice pick wasn't next to me I'd slap her. How dare she.

The woman raises the veil.

She is old and wrinkled at first glance, but as I take in more of her features I realize that she has aged prematurely because there is a youthfulness that is almost completely hidden behind the mask of old age.

She smiles at me.

"I want your blood, my dear."

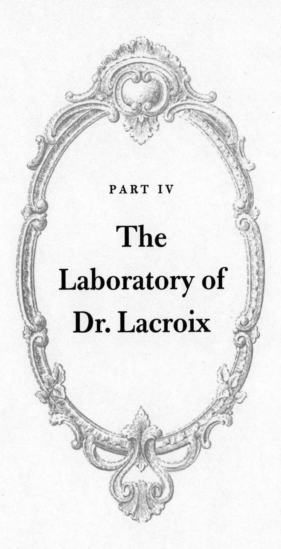

PART IV

The Laboratory of Dr. Lacroix

But first, on Earth as Vampyre sent,
Thy corpse shall from its tomb be rent;
Then ghastly haunt the native place,
And suck the blood of all thy race;
There from thy *daughter, sister, wife,*
  At midnight drain the stream of life.

> —From Lord Byron's "The Giaour," quoted by
> JOHN POLIDORI in "The Vampyre," 1819,
> written that haunted night during which
> Mary Shelley's *Frankenstein* was also born.

60

W hat *exactly* did you tell her?"

Wells's question to the inn maid, who delivered the message to Nellie, is asked in a grim, angry tone. The girl, cringing like a rabbit frozen in place as it stares at a predator, appears ready to bolt.

"Just what her friend asked me to tell her, sir."

"How do you know he's her friend?"

The woman is on the verge of tears and Oscar puts a restraining hand on Wells's arm.

"You've done nothing wrong," Oscar tells the girl in a soothing tone. "You did exactly as you were told. But, my dear, Nellie has disappeared and we need to find her."

"She probably went off with her friend."

"There is no doubt she left," Oscar says gently, "but the man wasn't her friend. He's a criminal and he has taken her."

The maid gasps and covers her face.

"It's all right, it was not your fault, but you want to help her, don't you?"

"You can be sure of that!"

"What did the man look like?"

"I don't know. He looked a little like my brother Jeremy. People say Jeremy is tough, you know what I mean, with his fists. But he didn't dress like Jeremy. His clothes are London fancy."

"How old is Jeremy?" Oscar continues.

"He's my older brother, I think he's 'bout thirty."

"Was anyone else with the man?"

"No sir, just him alone. Told me to go tell his friend one of the ponies is sick and she must come to help him. So, I did that. I didn't do anything wrong."

"No, of course not, my dear. We are just trying to find out what you saw." Oscar says in a sweet tone. The village girl had no knowledge of the murderous machinations.

"Was he wearing boots? Ones with pointed toes?" Wells asks, trying to control his frustration and anger at this maid for being so stupid as far as he's concerned.

"Boots with pointed toes? I've never seen boots like that. I didn't notice what he wears on his feet. I don't pay attention to people's feet."

Wells and Oscar turn their attention to Conan Doyle who is hurrying toward them.

"There was a carriage," he tells them, a little out of breath, "parked near the stable. An expensive rig with four horses. The innkeeper and stableman both say it doesn't belong to anyone in the area and that they've never seen it before. Had some kind of emblem . . . a gold crest, they think, on it, but they couldn't be sure in the dark and all."

"No one saw Nellie?" Wells asks, his tone gripped with tension.

"No one. The maid?" Doyle gestures.

Oscar and Wells turn to see the maid darting away.

"Let her go. She knows nothing of importance," Oscar says to Wells and then answers Doyle's question. "Apparently a man about thirty, tough looking like her brother, said to tell Nellie a pony was sick."

"It was a clever ploy," Wells states bitterly. "Nellie loves animals. She rushed right into the trap without even thinking."

"Boots?"

"She didn't notice," Wells answers Doyle's question. "They must have taken her north. I don't think they would have gone south, not in a big carriage, the road's too rough. I'm getting my buggy and going after them."

"Wait a moment, please." Doyle grabs his arm. "The innkeeper tells me that it's less than an hour to the main road to Okehampton. They probably made the road already. There's no way our pony buggies can overtake a four-horse rig, especially on a good road."

"I'll get a horse—" Wells stops as Doyle shakes his head.

"I've asked. There are no full-sized horses in the vicinity. And not even a local constable. Okehampton has the closest police station."

"No place to wire from here?" Oscar asks.

Doyle shakes his head again. "Okehampton is the closest. When we get there, we'll send out a wire to every police station in the region. We can be there in less than three hours, but it will be the middle of the night and everything will be shut down and locked tight."

"Then we shall awaken the entire town," Oscar says. "We'll organize search parties. Territory that would take us days to cover can be done by volunteers in Okehampton in hours."

"We don't even know where to begin," Wells says. His tone is as worried as his gloomy expression. "We really don't know if Lacroix's laboratory is within a six-mile range of the castle. That's an estimate based on the artist's endurance. He could have visited the castle in a buggy, for all we know."

Doyle turns to Wells. "The equipment for the type of experiments he conducts, does it involve any large or heavy apparatus?"

"No, I would think not. Nothing that can't be easily lifted by a man. Why do you ask?"

"From what you've said, Lacroix must have known for some time that he could ultimately be traced to Dartmoor. You suspected the laboratory is in Dartmoor from the shipments you learned about. We believe the artist Weekes knew where the laboratory was because of the bog he painted. That leads to the theory that the facility is in this region, but begs the question as to whether it is still where it was when Weekes painted the bog."

"You're wondering whether he could have broken down the laboratory and transported it elsewhere?" Oscar looks at Doyle.

"My God, *yes*." Wells throws his hands up. "It wouldn't be that difficult. For the type of research Lacroix does, his entire laboratory could be boxed up and transported in one large wagon. Once he became aware that we were searching for it and had some idea of the location, he probably moved it. It could be anywhere."

"Logically anywhere *in this region*," Doyle offers. "Weekes was killed to prevent him from pointing the way to Okehampton, although he did so with the Lady Howard story. That and the other death implies that even if the laboratory was moved, it's still in Dartmoor and most likely the northern part."

"Then, my friends," Oscar says, "if the lab is so easy to move and hide, it raises a most puzzling question."

He didn't have to put the question into words. All three men had analytical minds and extraordinarily fantastic imaginations. Not being a man of few words, Oscar spoke the question.

"If they can easily hide, why would they have exposed themselves to so much danger and police attention by kidnapping Nellie?"

Wells takes a turn at further stating the obvious. "They've had opportunities to kill her and haven't done so." He stares at the two men, his features a mask of dread.

"Vampires!"

"*What?*" Oscar and Doyle both exclaim at the same time.

"That's what Archer kept toying Nellie and me with. He kept saying look for vampires."

"And . . . ?" Oscar asks.

"They want Nellie's blood," says Conan Doyle.

61

The dark night reveals no clue where I'm going as the carriage rumbles along. The only sign of habitation I can see out the carriage window is the occasional dim lamplight from a farmhouse.

I sit facing the countess, with Burke beside me.

The only other person on the coach is the driver, whose name I heard is Hare, a chip off the same hard-edged block as Burke. Both of the men wear cowboy boots. I haven't gotten a good look at Hare, but I assume he is the man who killed Isaac Weekes.

An expensive coach pulled by a team of four moves surprisingly quick despite the narrowness and ruts on the road. I'm certain it's making better time than Wells and I did with the small buggy despite the roughness of the track. From the turns it makes, I know the carriage is taking me north on a route that will connect to a more traveled road that flows west from Exeter to Okehampton and beyond. The same route we were taking to get to Okehampton.

The fact we are heading for Okehampton offers, I hope, one small advantage to me—it's the route Wells and I were on and the natural one that he and the others will follow to affect a rescue, since we concluded that the laboratory was there.

I am frightened to death but won't satisfy them by showing fear.

No word has been spoken except when Burke, sitting next to me, starts to light a cigar and the woman in black says, "No." He immediately extinguishes the match.

The words she spoke to me when I was forced aboard are the cause of a knot in my stomach and a lump in my throat. From my conversations with Wells about the nature of Lacroix's research I am certain I know what she meant.

While I keep my features impassive, my innards are convulsing and I fight to keep panic from gripping and paralyzing me. I am completely helpless at the moment but if a chance to escape arises, I need to be ready to take it. Screaming is futile, there is no place to run or hide, no one to shout to for help.

I am still stunned by their simple ploy to take me, how utterly clueless I was about the situation and so foolish to mindlessly walk away from the inn without even telling my companions.

My eyes keep going back to the woman in black.

Burke calls her "Countess" and never uses anything but the title. Strange, but I don't think of her as having a name. I wonder if she is a widow or if the clothes are a reflection of her dark spirit.

An hour has passed and I am certain by now that my friends will have discovered I am missing. They are clever men, brave and resourceful. Fortunately, Dr. Doyle is also familiar with the area. I'm sure their immediate plan will be to get to the police and organize a search for the laboratory in the Okehampton Castle area that we have estimated its location to be.

Soon it becomes a much smoother road than the goat paths Wells and I seemed to have always been traversing in the heart of the moors. We now proceed at a quicker pace. I realize that we have reached the main road and a shock hits me—*we turned right onto the road.*

From the map Wells and I had pored over, Okehampton is a left turn when reaching the main road.

A barely audible chuckle comes from the woman. "Yes, the laboratory is no longer in Okehampton."

"It doesn't matter where you are taking me. My companions are extremely capable of finding me. You will be caught. You don't believe it because you are so desperately caught up with your desires, you are not thinking clearly. And you, sir," I tell Burke, "we know about your gang and the killing of the artist. If you want to avoid the hangman, you'll do no more crimes for this woman."

Burke grins. "You really have me scared. Is that what's gonna happen?" he asks the countess in a mocking tone. "This woman's gonna have me meet the hangman?"

"No, that won't happen—not that you haven't earned a trip to the gallows many times over." She directs her next comment to me. "We are going to a manor owned by a duke and loaned to me. No one would dare invade its grounds. And when we leave, there will be no sign we were ever there."

She has a continental accent, Italian, I think, but there is a British edge to her English.

"Do you believe in God?" I ask, curious about how she deals with the evil inside her.

"My personal beliefs are drawn more from the East."

"Really? Has it occurred to you that the punishment for the evil you have committed in this life is to be reborn as a worm in a cesspool?"

She leans across the carriage and slaps me, hard, across my face.

I freeze for a second and then start to move forward to swing at her when Burke blocks me with his arm and an ice pick comes up and pricks me on my neck under my ear.

"Settle down," he says.

"If you cooperate and do what you are told, you won't be harmed," the woman says.

Won't be harmed?

Does she really expect me to believe that? Murder has followed in the wake of this woman and Lacroix and she assures me that no harm will come to me if I play along? But I keep my mouth shut because the more I say, the more opportunities they will have to hurt me.

It seems we've traveled for more than an hour before we turn off the main road and follow a side path to tall iron gates.

The glow of a full moon breaks through the foggy haze, enough to reveal the manor house that commands the top of a hill in the distance.

The estate is almost castle looking, truly fit for a grand nobleman bearing the title of duke.

I don't see any lights in the house.

From the distance, the house appears dark and forbidding. As we draw closer it becomes evident that the house is also made of moors granite, but the stone has been finished.

The carriage follows the curve of the road up to the main building and we continue past it to a coach house. Two large mastiffs chase the carriage, barking.

"Don't bother trying to run," the countess warns me. "There are no neighbors and the dogs will treat you as game to kill."

The door to the carriage storage house that is used for foot traffic opens and a young woman comes out.

62

Hailey comes to me to give me a hug and I push her hands away.

I am not surprised a bit. The fact that she is still alive has been gnawing at me for some time, but I just didn't want to face it. Instead, I buried the revelation deep inside me.

"I'm sorry," Hailey says. "But everything will be all right, I know that for sure. They promised me you won't be harmed."

I smile sadly at her. My jaws are tight. I don't have the urge to strike at her like I did with the countess before she slapped me. Instead, I feel like hugging and crying with her—after I grab her and shake her and scream my lungs out about how she could be so stupid.

"Please, Nellie—"

I get right into her face. "People are dead and I'm going to be joining them. Do you think that sorry might be a little inadequate right now?"

"No, that's not going to happen, you won't be hurt."

"How can you say that? I've been kidnapped with an ice pick at my throat by murderers who have left bodies in their wake."

The mastiffs come sniffing up to me and I let the big male smell my hand.

How could I have so misjudged her? My editor at the paper had called her a loose cannon and told me I better learn how to duck because you never know in which direction she will go off.

She is ready to cry. "Please, come inside, you must meet Anthony."

"You make it sound like I've dropped in for a bit of tea. Did you happen to notice that I have been kidnapped by thugs who kill people with ice picks and a madwoman who wants my blood?"

"Get inside," Burke snaps.

"Come, please," Hailey begs me.

She reaches for me and I brush away her hand. With nowhere to run or hide, I reluctantly follow her into the coach house.

The main room, large enough to park two large coaches, has been made into a research laboratory. A long table in the center has microscopes, test tubes, Petri dishes, Bunsen burners, surgical instruments— the tools of the trade by researchers in the biological sciences. I suspect that Dr. Pasteur's laboratory in Paris isn't much different except for one thing: I see many glass containers filled with a deep red liquid that I'm certain is blood.

A chimpanzee is lying on its back, tied down to a table, with tubes to its throat.

"It's sedated," Hailey says.

"The whole bunch of you should be sedated. I'm sure the poor thing would rather be dead than live through the horrible things you're doing to it."

I wince when I see more chimps in cages. I wish I could free them.

"Anthony does research with chimpanzees because Darwin says we are descended from apes."

"Where is my cage?"

Tears run down her face and her features twist as she quietly sobs.

I'm not in a forgiving mood. "Those can't be real tears for me, the people your friends have killed, or these poor creatures. You know why they call your kind of crying crocodile tears? Crocodiles shed tears when they are eating their victims. I'm just another victim to be devoured."

"No, Nellie, you have to understand, Anthony is taking his research where no one else has ever gone before."

"Has it occurred to you what he's doing is criminal?"

"He's doing work that will go down in history."

"I'm sure he will. Right beside Jack the Ripper."

"Nellie, I thought if anyone would understand it would be you. You have such an imagination and are so daring. You've seen with your own eyes what Dr. Pasteur has accomplished with research."

"Pasteur saves lives. He doesn't take them away to give vain women beauty treatments."

"You're wrong on two counts."

The pronouncement comes from behind me and I spin around to face the man who spoke the words.

Anthony Lacroix.

He is slender, with thin blond hair combed straight back, narrow features, and emerald green eyes that focus on you, with an intense, fixed gaze that is almost an impolite stare.

His fervent features convey the impression of determination. But there is also the hint of a bad temper and a handsome fragility to him, the sort that would make him a mother's favorite and cause her to open her purse strings for him even when he misbehaves.

Exhaustion shows on his face, as if he has been operating at a super speed for a long period and is on the edge of collapse.

"Dr. Pasteur has saved lives by developing rabies and anthrax vaccines," he says, "but those discoveries came at the expense of others who were infected with the diseases by bad doses of the medicine before the process became a success. The same is true about smallpox and other maladies. The cures served the common good at the expense of a few."

"I don't recall murder being part of the scientific method for beauty treatments or anything else."

"I haven't murdered anyone."

"Splitting hairs," I interrupt him. "Maybe you didn't do the deed, but you condoned it."

"*You* have no notion at all of the nature of my research. You are wrong if you believe I am trying to make women look prettier. The spa is just a place to provide the money to finance serious research."

"You may fool Hailey, but I saw a poor woman in Bath crying for her child and a nice old gentleman in the moors—"

"Your small mind will never comprehend my work," he snaps. "Take her upstairs. And keep an eye on her. We don't want her wandering around. The dogs will attack strangers."

As I follow Hailey up the stairs to the second level, she tells me they are staying in the servants' quarters so Lacroix can be closer to his work. I am only half listening because my concentration is on one thing only—escape.

"He works day and night, barely taking time off to eat. He sleeps very little, a few hours here and there, never a full night."

"He's a murderer and you're an accomplice to his crimes."

She stops on the stairs and spins around to me. "*Stop it.*"

Her voice is quiet, but with desperation.

"He's not any of those things." She starts to say something else, but looks back down the stairs.

Hare, the other ice pick thug, is at the bottom of the steps, looking up at us.

We go up to the landing and move away from the stairway, into a sitting room with a hallway to the right were I assume bedrooms for servants are located. Closed French doors lead out onto a small balcony and I wander over to get a look through the windows. There's enough moonlight for me to identify a pasture behind the carriage house.

"Anthony isn't a murderer," she tells me in a low voice.

"Why don't you ask the artist in the moors who got an ice pick in his back or another man who got one in his brain?"

She shakes her head, frantic, and puts her hands over her ears. "They're not things Anthony would do."

"See no evil, hear no evil. Tell that to the police when they come for you and to the hangman when he puts the rope around your neck."

She stares at me, swaying, ready to collapse, and sits down on the couch. I take a seat on a chair facing her.

She really doesn't understand.

I find it incomprehensible.

She's a grown woman. Yet this is not the first time she did something bizarre. Because of Hailey's own traumatic background I found reasons to justify why she aided a woman in New York who killed her abusive husband. But I can't comprehend how she can close her eyes to these atrocious crimes against innocent people.

Is she completely devoid of reason and common sense?

"Hailey . . . tell me what you think is going on here." I gesture toward the stairway. "What is being done down there? Why have people been killed? And please, don't tell me they haven't. I witnessed the murder of two people and there's three more I know of, beginning with Lady Winsworth and a child." I actually hadn't seen Archer being killed, but looking at his still warm-blooded body was close enough.

For a moment we sit in silence.

Hailey finally meets my eye. "We're prisoners. Anthony is doing research on rejuvenation, on defeating the aging process of our bodies. You call it beauty treatments and it's true that women like the countess want to stay beautiful longer or get back their youthful appearances, but that is not the true purpose of his research. He does that work because wealthy women are willing to finance his research if they think they will get what they want."

"Who do the thugs downstairs with cowboy boots and ice picks work for?"

"They work for Dr. Radic and the countess. She put up most of the money that Radic used to build the spa in Bath. She controls everything."

"How many of these hired killers are here?"

"Only the two you've seen."

"That's two too many. So your Dr. Lacroix just shuts his eyes to what's going on around him and you shut yours, too. Why?"

She avoids my eyes.

"Because . . . because you love him."

We sit in silence for a moment.

"Hailey, listen to me. It's not adding up. You say you and he are being held prisoner. Those two brutes were away from here, kidnapping me. So was the countess. Why didn't you just leave?"

"We are not prisoners like that. Anthony's research can't continue unless the countess keeps financing it. And keeps the police from bothering him. She has powerful friends. He didn't hurt Lady Winsworth deliberately. When blood transfusions are done, sometimes people die."

Sometimes people die.

She said it as if she is speaking about nameless people in a textbook, not a woman and child of flesh and blood, real people with loved ones saddened by their loss. Good lord—she is so mesmerized by Lacroix, so infatuated, that she simply takes whatever he says as the gospel, no matter how strange it may be.

"Was she getting blood? From a child? A little girl?"

Hailey nods. "Yes. But the woman had a bad reaction."

"So did the child." I shake my head, trying to get the pieces rattling inside to fall into place. "What a . . . a horror story. You simply fell for this man and tolerate this insanity?"

"It's not just that." Her eyes are that of a wounded doe. "Anthony needs my blood."

63

Inspector Mulcher, the highest-ranking police officer in the Okehampton district, is not happy about getting the local manager of the telegraph office out of bed to open the wire station. Nor is he pleased about planning a widespread search for a *foreign* woman in the middle of the night, waking neighbors and sending them down the streets to wake others and have them gather into groups to spread out and hunt for the woman.

A police officer for thirty-two years, most of his police duties had centered around stolen livestock and an occasional domestic dispute. The only serious case he had ever investigated had been that of a woman who split her husband's head with an ax, and he had been a young officer when that occurred.

Like the telegraph office manager, he had been awakened by banging on his door and shouts from strangers outside. Then he listened with some astonishment about a woman being kidnapped—not *any* woman he was told, but a famous American newspaper reporter, Nellie Bly, and that the kidnappers drove the most expensive brand of carriage in the kingdom.

The amazing situation doesn't end with the victim and the kidnappers.

The men at his door, it turns out, include a well-known writer and a high-society wit from London.

He keeps his temper stowed because he has heard of the author's stories about a detective named Sherlock Holmes, and his wife has read in the newspaper about the rather large and unusually attired individual from London, whom the inspector's wife says is a London society nob.

However, he cares less about the social butterfly than the author who is also a respected medical man.

The third man, a teacher, also appears respectable, though not one he or his wife has heard of. And none have been imbibing, another point in their favor, though he himself could use a stiff shot right at the moment to settle his own nerves.

He's never handled a significant police investigation and has no idea as to what steps to take, although it did occur to him that kidnappers want ransom money.

Told that the motives of the people who seized the young woman were not monetary and were in fact not even known, left him with no clue as to how to proceed to get her back.

The inspector made it clear to the men from out of town from the moment he agreed to take action that he was fully in charge, but being prudent, he had listened carefully and took notes as the excited men tossed about ideas about rescuing the young American woman.

Now as he awaits news from a volunteer search party, he stands with the doctor and the socialite and watches the young teacher, Herbert Wells, who is pacing nervously, as if he is struggling with a demon.

Wells finally approaches him and his companions.

"Does anyone in the area have a black coach? Not an ordinary one, but an expensive rig, the finest, a town coach with four-in-hand."

"None that reside down here except in the summer. A handful of nobles and wealthy squires have good coaches, one or two may be black, though I don't recall for certain."

"There was a noble crest on the door," Wells says.

"You saw the carriage?" Dr. Doyle is surprised to hear this.

"No, I saw a similar one in Bath."

"A similar one in Bath?" howls the inspector. "What does that have to do with the price of tea in China?"

"I think there's a connection. Both Nellie and I saw the town coach in Bath, though she saw it from a different angle and watched a woman wearing widows' black get out of it. She also saw that the coat-of-arms crest on the door had been covered. When we arrived in Exeter at the train station, she saw a duplicate carriage, also with a coat of arms, but this time it was uncovered."

"Whose crest was it?" the inspector asks.

"She wasn't close enough to make it out."

"Was it the same woman in Bath and Exeter?" asks Dr. Doyle.

"We don't know who was picked up or dropped off, for that matter.

Not only was the coach an expensive one, it had unique markings that tells me it belongs to the same nobleman, though I can't explain why the crest would be covered in Bath and not in Exeter."

"It may be that the woman had her noble crest covered to hide her identity as she patronized the spa." Conan Doyle paces back and forth as he speaks.

"Or the coach is owned by a nobleman who doesn't want to make it obvious that the woman is using it," Oscar says. "If it doesn't belong to the woman in black, the man may not want to feed rumors about himself and the woman because it would become drawing room talk in London."

"Quite." Conan Doyle stops pacing and rubs his chin. "But he couldn't care less if the situation generated talk out in Exeter."

"I'm sure the coaches are duplicates," Wells says. "It's not uncommon for rich people to order the same custom-made coaches for their city and country places."

"But you didn't see the one she was carried away in," the inspector says, "so it may not be the same one."

"True, but it's worth checking out," Conan Doyle says. "Black coaches in Bath, Exeter, and in the moors; three are too much of a coincidence. And there is an obvious connection to Bath, it's where all this started."

"There can't be that many luxurious black town carriages in the area," Oscar says. "We should be able to find out with some inquiries."

"Let's wire the police in Exeter," Wells says.

The inspector started to object but an excited Conan Doyle cut him off.

"An excellent idea! It would also show them that our esteemed police inspector here is on top of the matter and is where credit should go. What do you think, inspector? Will you wire Exeter and other police facilities in the region specifically about black town coaches?"

"I was just about to do that very thing when the subject was raised."

"The chief inspector in Bath, too," Wells interjects. "Ask him about the coach and the woman in black. Nellie spoke to him. He might know something about the wealthy women at the spa."

64

"Anthony is a hemophiliac," Hailey quietly says.

The statement throws me for a loop. I have to think about what a hemophiliac is. "He bleeds more than other people? Is that what you mean?"

"Yes. He has to be very careful because he can bleed to death from a small cut. His blood doesn't clot like others, and he can also bleed inside without even knowing it."

I nod, chewing on the situation. Now I know why Archer joked about vampires. It isn't just the countess. "Anthony needs blood. And yours works for him?"

"Yes. You can't just go around taking blood from one person and giving it to another. No one knows why, but sometimes a person's blood is poisonous to another person.* People have died getting transfusions. Some doctors have even killed people giving them animal blood. Anthony developed a way to test a person's tolerance for another's blood by giving just a tiny bit of blood. If they tolerate that, he slowly increases the amount until the need is filled."

"Is that what happened to Lady Winsworth? Was she a bleeder?"

"No. As part of his blood work, he's developed a rejuvenating blood elixir for use at the spa, but he wasn't ready to give it to just anyone. Lady Winsworth insisted that he let her try it. It—it didn't work. Anthony thinks she took more than she was supposed to at one time."

"Ah, I see, it seems he can't resist rich women, can he?"

She pouts. "Anthony is a genius, a savior of mankind."

* Blood types were not discovered until eleven years later in 1901.—The Editors

"A regular saint. What about the countess? She told me she wanted my blood. Is she another bleeder? Or another aging woman looking for the Fountain of Youth?"

Hailey looks away, refusing again to meet my eye.

"It's her face, isn't it? She thinks his treatments can erase her age with . . . with my blood."

I get a lump in my throat. There is a reason they call it *life's blood*. I really don't think I have any to spare.

"I'm so sorry you were brought into this. You weren't surprised to see me. Did the countess tell you I was here?"

"The only thing the countess told me was that she needed my blood. I more or less knew you were alive when I found out about your luggage in Bath. I just didn't want to face it. I trusted you as if you were a sister." My voice breaks and I turn my head, struggling not to cry.

"What about the luggage?"

"The luggage had been directed to a train going toward the moors instead of back to London. I assumed something had happened to you and Lacroix was getting his hands on the luggage to search for evidence against him and get rid of it. But you were supposed to have gone back to London. It would have been stupid of Lacroix to send the luggage in the direction he was fleeing. And I'm sure he's not a stupid man.

"It also made no sense that you stayed over in Bath and permitted the spa to pay for your room. That was unprofessional. It just wasn't adding up."

She nods. "The luggage was my fault. Radic went into a rage when he found out I didn't have my luggage sent to the London train. Anthony didn't want me to go back to the hotel and pick up my things, but I needed my stuff, so I sent a message to have it delivered to the southbound track, not knowing they wanted to create a pretense it was sent to London."

"The young woman in the morgue in London—another blood donor with a bad reaction to the procedure?"

"No, Anthony bought the body from an undertaker. She was a prostitute who died and would have ended up in a pauper's grave. He told me he needed me to drop out of sight. Once I had established a connection with the spa, he didn't want anyone—like you—looking for me and finding him."

I suspect that is a lie from Lacroix, but I let it pass. There are more than enough dead bodies to go around. Then I had another revelation. "I was lured here from New York."

"No, Nellie—"

"*Don't lie to me.* You knew I would come if something happened to you. And that I would be suspicious of the body at the morgue because no matter what I was told, I would sense it wasn't you. But the real clue was the diary, wasn't it? The diary was left behind so I would find it. When I read it, I would suspect you were killed and follow the leads, but Archer stole it from me. It cost him his life."

"Anthony never hurt him."

"For someone who treats everyone with kid gloves, your Anthony leaves a lot of dead bodies in his wake."

"He is on the brink of history with a discovery that will change the world. Someday—"

"I'm not sure I have any days left." There is still a big question left unanswered and I almost hate to ask it. "Why was I lured here all the way from New York? What does your mad scientist and his 'change the world invention' need me for?"

"Listen up."

I nearly jump out of my shoes. Burke has come to the top of the stairs without us noticing.

He speaks to Hailey. "The doctor will need you in a few minutes. He said to bring her with you."

He turns and heads back down the stairs. I ask Hailey, "Time for his blood?"

"I guess so."

"And time for the countess to get her blood."

"Nellie, please, you have to understand—"

"What's to understand? I'm in the hands of murderers." I rub my head, this is all too bizarre. "Hailey, I have a terrible headache. Do you have powders?"

"They're in the bathroom. I'll get them."

She goes down the hallway. As soon as I see her disappear through another door I run to the balcony doors, pull them open, and slip out onto the small balcony.

The fenced pasture below that spreads out behind the carriage house is for the carriage horses. I am on the second floor, but it's not too far down. Directly below the balcony are the roofs of the horse stalls.

I lift my skirt and get one leg over the railing, then the other, and carefully get a footing between the rails. Trying to control my panic because

I'll probably break a leg, I drop down. It is about a ten-foot drop and I hit with both feet but fall backward, tumbling onto my backside, smacking the roof hard with my back, knocking the wind from me.

Rolling over, I get to my feet and scramble to the edge of the stall roof and drop again, this time into dirt softer than the stall roofing, only going down onto my backside.

I rush for a gate on the side opposite the direction of the manor house. As I run, the thought of getting on a carriage horse and riding bareback flashes through my mind, but without reins I wouldn't be able to stay on, even if I managed to get on in the first place.

The gate is not locked but has a rope looped to a post to hold it shut. I pull the rope off the post, swing open the gate, and dash out, running as fast as my adrenaline-driven feet will take me.

There is nothing right or left except long fields of grass. I head straight for a copse of oak trees a hundred yards away.

Behind me I can hear shouting and then a sound that curdles my blood.

The howl of the hounds.

65

Hounds snapping at my heels.

They're not ripping at my flesh yet, but I hear them and know they will soon be on my back.

What insanity has Hailey dragged me into?

Is she so damaged from her childhood trauma of murder and violence that she is immune to the violence happening around her?

As I run through the thickets, stumbling over bushes and rocks while tree branches grab at my clothes, I hear the hounds getting closer, their barking more excited. I know from my memories in rural Pennsylvania that when hunting dogs get excited chasing prey they become instinctually savage, ripping and tearing with their fangs at creatures they might normally just bark at.

My heart is pounding, my breathing labored. I can't outrun the dogs or hide from them and there is no one to hear my cries. It strikes me that there must be servants at the main house year round, but at the same time I saw no light at the house when we arrived. Lacroix must have had them sent away.

On big estates like this there would be gardener and gamekeeper cottages, but there are no houses visible in the moonlight. If they are out here, I have run the wrong way to find them.

I reach the thickets, half out of breath, but keep my weakening legs moving. The copse is dense, branches jab me, thorns cut my face and grab at my clothes as I dash into them, going around trees, not sure exactly where I am headed except uphill in the hopes there is rescue on the other side.

I gain a crest of granite and stumble down a slope toward what appears in the dark to be a small meadow.

The dogs come up, running behind me growling and snarling and I turn to face them as they bound right at me.

"*Heel!*"

It's not a command I know but a scream borne of pure panic and desperation. It is something from my childhood, recalling how my father yelled at his bird dogs when he wanted them to calm down and be next to him and not scattered about.

I lash out at them with the word and the reaction is startling—both of them *stop* running. For a moment they are confused. They're estate dogs, used to people and running free, not killer guard dogs.

"Heel," I repeat, in a softer tone.

They come up to me growling, anxious and excited, but still confused and unsure of how to act. Suddenly the male whines and I kneel down so I don't tower over him and carefully reach out and let him sniff my hand. The female snarls and he turns on her snapping, causing her to back off.

"Com' here, baby," I tell her.

She hesitates but reluctantly comes up to me and sniffs my hand.

I reach out to both of them and scratch them behind the ears.

I hear crashing in the bushes and I get back up and bolt down the hill. Running full speed down, the dogs gallop alongside me.

"*Bitch!*"

I don't turn around to look, I just keep running in pure panic. I know it's Burke, with his cowboy boots and ice pick.

I stumble and fall forward as I come onto the flat area, my momentum carrying me forward faster than my feet can keep up. The ground is soft and moist and I quickly get back up as I hear him closing in fast behind me.

I dash with a burst of panic and suddenly a shock runs through my entire body as if I'd been hit by lightning—*the ground is spongy*.

I slip on the wet surface and suddenly Burke is at my back, crashing into me, sending me sprawling. I scream as I hit the soft flora and feel suction against my whole body. The dogs are bounding about, excited, snarling.

The thug hovers over me, an ice pick in his hand. "She won't let me kill you yet, but I'm going to poke out both your eyes so you can't escape again."

The big male mastiff gets in between us and leaps up at Burke, snapping, sending the man lurching back.

"*Get away from me, you bastard!*" I yell.

He swings out at the dog with his ice pick, smacking the dog not with the sharp end but with the side of his fist holding the weapon.

Burke jerks backward and gasps as his right foot suddenly sinks beneath the surface with a *pop* sound. As he jerks his foot back up, his other foot goes down, halfway up to his knee, each time sinking him deeper and deeper in the muck.

He screeches, realizing what is happening to him as he frantically jiggles his feet, pulling them up and down in short bursts, but in seconds the muck is up to his knees and he is unable to pull his feet up more than a few inches.

His features are twisted with terror.

Sweat has broken out on his face and his breathing comes in frantic gasps.

I scoot back up, on my rear, feeling the softness of the bog moss covering, keeping as much of my body spread out on the surface as I can as I watch the man working his legs with a frenzy, but sinking deeper.

"*Don't fight it,*" I yell. I don't know why I bother, he's a murderer who seconds ago was going to blind me and take me back to be drained of my blood, but the advice came out.

The dogs are still excited and moving about and I call to them as I am squirming away, keeping my body flat. I don't want them to get sucked in and I yell to them, "Shoo, go over there, shoo, shoo."

When the man is up to his chest, still clutching the ice pick, he stares at me. His mouth gapes open. "Help," he pleads.

I can't. I'm still in danger of sinking myself and there's nothing for me to grab and hand to him.

"Stop struggling," I shout. "Try to lay sideways, flat."

It's no use, he doesn't understand and even if he did, it's too late to maneuver into a flat position because three-quarters of his body has been sucked in.

There are no sticks, nothing to throw him. If I can get onto solid ground and back up to the woods, I might be able to find a branch to hand him.

Still moving slowly off the surface that is trembling from Burke's frantic struggles, I see Hare, the other gang member running down the hill toward us.

He stops at the bottom of the slope where the ground becomes flat and stares down at his own feet. He takes a quick step back, as if he were jumping out of a fire.

"*Get a branch,*" I yell.

"*Hurry!*" Burke, now up to his shoulders, shouts. "*For the love of God!*"

Hare looks quickly around and then stares at his mate and shakes his head—there are no long branches about. Burke is too far from him and too deep into the mire to save him without risking his own life.

So much for honor among thieves.

I watch sick and paralyzed as Burke goes under, still screaming for mercy and rescues. I turn my head and close my eyes to the horror.

Turning over onto my knees as I feel the firmer ground beneath me, I crawl until the trembling beneath stops and get to my feet.

I take a few steps and a blow between my shoulder blades sends me dropping to the ground, the breath knocked out of me.

I'm flat on my stomach and unable to breathe as Hare grabs me by the shoulder and rolls me over, an ice pick in his hand.

"*Leave her alone!*"

Hailey comes up behind him and jumps on him, the force of her body pushes him off me.

Dr. Lacroix is suddenly with us.

"*Stop,*" he commands the man, then gestures at me. "Get her back to the house. We need her blood for the countess."

66

As I walk to the house I am beaten and defeated, exhausted physically and mentally. Stone cold, dead inside and out. I can't focus. My mind is racing wildly but my thoughts are not about escape, they're not even coherent. I only know one thing: There are too many of them to fight and no one is around to help me . . . there is no way out, no chance to reason, everything is too insane.

I know my friends are searching for me, but the countess is right—who would suspect a duke's manor house? What local police officer would even approach the place without hat in hand and mumbling apologies?

I can see from Hailey's troubled features that the sheer stupidity and naïveté of her actions are finally coming home to roost. Once again I have the urge to grab her and shake her and scream, *"What were you thinking?"* but I already know she wasn't thinking rationally.

Whatever spell Dr. Lacroix casts on women had worked twofold on Hailey. Fulfilling his need for blood because he is a bleeder gives her a chance not only to be a martyr, but in her naïve conception of the world it provides a genuine medical basis to justify the madness of his rejuvenation work.

Even though we have fallen behind a bit from the two men, I don't dare try to escape again. It will just give Hare an opportunity to stick an ice pick in my eye, which I'm sure he would be more than happy to do. Instead, I use the distance to ask Hailey a question she hadn't answered earlier.

"Why was I lured all the way from America? There has to be plenty of blood over here for that crazy woman to use. And they don't even know if she's compatible with my blood."

"You are healthy, have more energy than most people, you're intelligent, and you cut yourself once when we were together. You sucked the wound and told me that it was no bother, you heal very fast."

"You just described attributes for most of the people my age. It has to be more than that."

Hailey looks straight ahead. "Yes, you are always so perceptive. Your real name is Cochran. Your father's heritage was that of the Scottish Lowlands. Countess Lucrezia was born in Italy but her mother was also a Cochran, the daughter of a Lowlands earl. When I told Anthony that your mother was a Cochran, he said they had been tracing the countess's Scottish ancestors because he believes that the blood from a common ancestral pool has more chance of being compatible than that of someone randomly selected. He believes you and the countess share a common ancestor."

"God, I hope not. That woman was spawned by Satan. Couldn't he find people in the Lowlands?"

"He has, several times, but to no avail. As I was telling you, he has developed a method to take tiny amounts of blood and inject it into a person so they only feel slightly ill rather than violently ill or dying if the blood is not compatible. He thinks over time by using tiny amounts he can build up an immunity in people to whatever is bad in some blood. He started taking samples to use, but silly rumors started up about vampires and they began investigating and the process had to stop. They even seized his samples. He was nearly arrested."

"So when you told him that I would come over to take care of your funeral arrangements, he decided I would be a perfect guinea pig. But first you joined him in this crazy scheme."

"He tested my blood after asking me questions about my background and found out it is compatible with his own. He asked me to join him in his research and not just because of my blood, but because I immediately understood the high aims of his goals and what a benefit it would be to society if he succeeded. But since he was having so much trouble with the police, he decided it would be best if he disappeared so he could work in peace. And that I should disappear, too, be thought of as dead, so there wouldn't be talk that always erupts about his blood work."

That she would have to disappear, be considered dead, to keep down rumors didn't make sense to me.

"No, Hailey, I don't believe it. He didn't fake your death to avoid rumors. How are rumors going to spread out here, in the middle of no-where? He did it because people have a tendency to die around him. He desperately needs your blood, but he can't afford another police investigation if you die."

"He's not—"

"Stop telling me he's not a bad man. Look who he keeps company with. It's *his* blood research that's left a trail of death. He's a fanatic, so caught up in his research, in his drive to play God with people's lives that he's lost control. He lets Radic and the countess do his dirty work because it keeps him free to experiment. I don't believe that girl I saw in the morgue was a prostitute who killed herself. With his track record, I'll bet you she died when he experimented with her blood."

I grab her arm to get her to look at me. "He has been experimenting with children, hasn't he?"

"I—I don't know."

"Tell me the truth, Hailey."

"I told you before, he wouldn't hurt a child. There is some belief that the blood of children revitalizes older people."

"Well, I know for sure he's been experimenting with children, no matter how much you want to avoid admitting it. I'll tell you something else. I bet if I have the body in the morgue that's supposed to be you reexamined, they'd find a mark on it from the blood he took. No one bothered to look closely because they believe she was a suicide."

"Please . . ."

She sounds sick, but she has to face the horror that she has gotten herself involved in and the terror she has dragged me into.

She is my only hope and even at that, I have no idea what she can do to save me. Even though she doesn't have an ice pick at her throat, she is also a prisoner. She just doesn't know it.

I get another horrible thought.

"The woman in the morgue was pregnant. He stuck needles in her to draw out the blood from her unborn child."

Hailey stumbles, weak-kneed, and I hold her up with a grip on her elbow. I'm not going to let her avoid the horror with a swoon.

"He's like those priests back during the days of the Inquisition," I hiss, "the ones so obsessed with the demons in themselves, they tortured women into making false confessions of being witches." I lash out at Hailey.

"He's a zealot so driven by his mission he has become unbalanced, mad. The dream he's pursuing is a nightmare to the rest of the world."

"No, *please*—please stop, I love him."

I don't have the heart to keep pounding on her. It wouldn't do any good, anyway. There is nothing she can do for me. Finding a compatible blood supply from a willing supplier, Dr. Lacroix would do everything he can to keep her, even resorting to force if he needed.

As we neared the carriage house, my own knees get weak and I tell her, "I don't want to die."

"You were picked up in a boat, starving. The name on the boat was the *Lady Vain,* and there were spots of blood on the gunwale."

At the same time my eye caught my hand, so thin that it looked like a dirty skin-purse full of loose bones, and all the business of the boat came back to me.

"Have some of this," said he, and gave me a dose of some scarlet stuff, iced.

It tasted like blood, and made me feel stronger.

—H. G. WELLS, *The Island of Dr. Moreau*

67

I am to take the place of the chimp. As the poor creature is unstrapped and carried to its cage at the back wall, I look around desperately for something to use as a weapon. The hair on the back of my head is grabbed and my head jerked back. The sharp point of an ice pick goes against the side of my neck.

"Don't even think about escaping," Hare's rough voice whispers in my ear. "I'm not finished with you for killing my mate."

"He died because you're a coward."

"Stop it." The commands comes from the countess. "Tie her down. It's time for my treatment."

Hare forces me onto my back on the table. A strap is put across my chest and tightened until I can hardly breathe.

Hailey is suddenly beside me. "She needs to breathe." She loosens the belt so I get my breath. Wiping sweat on my brow, she leans down and whispers, "Forgive me, I've been so stupid."

Hailey moves away as Dr. Lacroix comes to my side. He talks as he unbuttons the dress cuff on my right arm and moves the sleeve up.

"Transfusions have been tried for centuries, but with bad results because the practitioners didn't know how to do them. They tried putting the blood of animals into humans to give people their traits, make them strong like a bear or a bull, make them calmer with the blood of a lamb, but it usually results in the death of the person."

He selects a lancet, a sharp-pointed knife used by surgeons to make small incisions.

"The first actually documented transfusion took place when Pope

Innocent VIII was dying several hundred years ago. When the sixty-year-old pope was on death's bed, the blood of three young boys was infused into him in an attempt to help him recover. He died and so did the boys."

I watch with a macabre fascination, as if I am not involved, as Lacroix heats a small, round glass container over an alcohol burner.

"I am going to draw blood from your vein, what we call breathing a vein," he says too calmly. "The blood is taken by cupping. I do it by cutting a small hole in your vein and then put this warm glass cup over the wound. The heated air in the cup creates a suction that draws blood. It is safer and causes less infections and internal bleeding than sticking a needle into the vein."

He feels my arm to locate a vein. "This will hurt very little."

I hear his words but they are meaningless to me. The only thing I comprehend is that he will take blood from me.

He leans down to me with the lancet and I give an involuntary cry as he slices into my arm deep enough to reach a vein. Removing the heated glass cup from the burner, he places it over the wound.

I feel both the heat of the glass rim and the suction as it pulls blood from my vein. My body is shaking uncontrollably and I bite down on my lip to keep myself from whimpering or crying more from terror than the pain.

He leaves me and Hailey is suddenly there.

She bandages my wound by wrapping a white cloth around my arm and pulling it snug. Then she undoes the strap holding me down and helps me sit up.

I am shaking so badly I can't hold the glass of water she offers. She holds it for me and I guide it to my lips. She sets down the glass after I have drank my fill and says, "I'll be back."

Sitting on the edge of the table, I am weak and faint, but watch with dark fascination as Dr. Lacroix speaks to the countess while he prepares an injection of my blood for her.

"The first injection I give you will be minute, just a tiny drop. If you feel no effects from it, I will slowly increase the dose over a period of hours, pausing between each injection to ensure that your body is not reacting negatively to the injection. No one knows why an injection of blood taken from one person can harm the person receiving it and the same amount taken from another person can be of benefit. But the technique I have developed should ensure that you have no serious reaction. If you feel ill at all, I will stop it immediately and we will know that she is not the proper donor for you."

His last words about the possibility of not being the right donor prompt another hair-raising question in me.

What if I am not the "proper donor"? Does that mean I am disposable?

My life hinges on the compatibility of my blood with hers?

As the time ticks away, I sit and watch the countess as she reclines on a couch with her eyes covered.

Hailey has disappeared somewhere.

The countess has no reaction to the first injection and he tries another and then a third. My eyes are getting lazy, trying to close, when I hear the countess suddenly screech. For a moment it sounded like a death rattle to me, but she sits up with a wide grin.

"*I feel rejuvenated!*" she shouts.

Dr. Lacroix welcomes the news, but the two briefly argue as the countess demands a full dose.

"It may just be your excited desires," he tells her. "We have to move cautiously."

He gives her another injection, but this time she is only down for a few minutes before she is on her feet again.

"I tell you it's working," she shouts at him. "*I want more.*" She stares at me, her eyes wild and crazy. "I want *all* of her blood. *Now!*"

Mother of God!

68

It's too dangerous, we can't just give you all the blood," Dr. Lacroix says, "we have to follow the protocol I've established."

"We have to rush, you fool. Don't you realize her friends will be here soon? In this sparsely populated area, the carriage has to have stood out. Someone will have seen something."

She gets up and faces Lacroix and he fades back just enough to make it obvious to me that he is not only under her control, but frightened of her.

"We've spent years trying to perfect your procedure and looking for a match." Her voice is controlling and demanding. "I am not going to lose this one. We can drain her blood, put it in airtight containers, and store them in the estate's icehouse."

She turns to Hare. "After we're finished with her, take her to the bog. She can join your comrade."

Drain my blood? Dump me in the bog?

I'm off the table with my feet on the run the moment the soles of my shoes hit the floor.

I hear the countess shout, *"Stop her!"*

Hare comes at me and connects his shoulder against mine, sending me staggering, hitting a lab table. I go down as the table flies over, sending scientific apparatus flying everywhere. Flames burst up from an alcohol burner.

He stands over me with his ice pick. "I told you I would put out your eyes."

"Leave her alone!"

Hailey has come down from upstairs and pauses at the bottom. She has a double-barreled shotgun, holding it with both hands, the butt against her side, just above her hip.

"I told you she was crazy," Hare yells to the countess as he charges Hailey.

"*Stop!*" Hailey screams.

Hare keeps charging and the shotgun goes off with a sound that is deafening. Hare spins around and falls backward onto the floor.

For a frozen moment everything in the room is still.

I've gotten up onto my knees and stare wide-eyed at the large blotch of red spreading across Hare's chest as his arms and legs shake compulsively as if some energy source is trying to escape his dead body.

I feel the heat of the fire caused by the broken alcohol burner—it's raging next to me.

"*Run!*" I scream at Hailey.

The countess has pulled a dagger and is going toward her.

Hailey backs up, her heel catching on the step behind her and she goes down, the shotgun going off. The blast appears to me to have hit the countess because she spins around and loses her footing, but goes down only for a second and then is back up.

The burst from the gun actually hit Lacroix—he's down on the floor, on his back, lying still.

The countess still has the dagger. Once on her feet she sways for a moment, then like a rabid dog that is mindless except for its rage, she goes for Hailey because that's who's in her sights.

I grab a microscope that is lying on the floor next to me and get up and run as fast as I can.

As the countess comes up to her, Hailey rises and pulls the trigger of the shotgun again, but nothing happens—she's used both barrels.

The countess raises the dagger and plunges down.

Hailey hand-deflects the strike, but the sharp blade catches the inside of her bare arm, slicing down it.

Grasping the microscope by the narrow lens end, I swing it as a club, the heavy iron footing hitting the countess on the side of her shoulder. It's enough to make her drop the dagger and send her sprawling.

Behind us there is an explosion as the fire below spreads to another alcohol lamp. The escape path out the front is swallowed by roaring flames and the room has become dense with smoke.

"Hurry," I tell Hailey as I start up the stairs. I don't realize she isn't with me until I've taken several steps. I turn around and she has gone to Lacroix's body. She sits down next to him and puts his head in her lap. She has the countess's dagger in her hand.

"*Hailey!*"

She looks up at me and shakes her head. Her face tells me she has made her choice. She would rather join the man she loves in death than face life without him.

I turn my head as she raises the dagger with both hands to plunge it into herself. I don't look but start racing up the stairs.

Reaching the top of the stairway, I stumble across the living space, my eyes and lungs burning from the fumes. I reach for the doors to the patio only because I know where they are.

Pulling open the doors, I am grabbed from behind by female hands that claw at my throat and start pulling me back into the smoke-choked room.

"*You're mine!*"

Crazy bitch!

I bring my arms up and bend my knees to break her grip. She leans down with me and I rise suddenly and push backward. As I force her back, I twist, loosening her grip on my throat and break free.

I step back and ball my fist to strike her.

With a screech that comes out of my mouth but sounds like it came from a wild beast, I throw what my bare-knuckle pal would call a power punch, straight at her face, my fist connecting with her nose, feeling the nose squish and squash as my fist makes impact.

A spray of her blood hits me—*her blood.*

She falls backward and I screech with glee as I race out onto the balcony. I want to get the hell out of here.

Suddenly the countess is coming at me again. I don't know how, but that insane rage of hers keeps her going. She comes flying wildly out of the door behind me, but her momentum keeps her going, over me and over the railing. She sweeps by me with just a quick gasp as she realizes at the last moment of life that she is soaring headfirst toward a hard surface.

I hear the thump of her hitting the roof below and leap over the railing as I did before, dropping down to the roof.

The countess is there, too, lying with the quiet of the dead, her head flopped almost beneath her, twisted in a grotesque angle.

My first thought as I drop to the ground is to get the pasture gate open to make sure the carriage horses won't be harmed by the fire consuming the building.

That's when I see my three friends come running, Wells's voice shouting my name as I swing open the gate for the horses.

"Where are you going?" Oscar shouts as I turn and race back to the burning house.

"To open the chimp cages," I shout back.

69

Nellie, a toast to you!" Oscar lifts his crystal glass of champagne. "One can live for years sometimes without living at all, and then you, daring Nellie Bly, come around and one suddenly is dangling precariously on the edge of a cliff."

"Amen to that!" Wells chimes in.

I curtsy the best I can sitting down. "Thank you, gentlemen. I must say, I will miss you all terribly."

My friends insisted we all get together for one last time at the Langham Hotel before my ship sails for New York.

After long conversations with the police, I was able to give Hailey's remains a proper burial. She might have had bad judgments in men, but she had a heart of gold and in the end saved my life.

Besides the Dartmoor police, we spent many hours explaining to Inspector Bradley in Bath and my dear Inspector Abberline in London as to what happened from London to Dartmoor.

"However," I add, "I believe many women in Bath and London will not be too sad to see me leave, considering I had a hand in getting their rejuvenation spa closed down."

A proper arrest was made with Dr. Radic, and Aqua Vitae was shut down.

"You probably are correct." Oscar addresses me as he pets his dog, Lord Dudley. "But one day people will realize that the tragedy of old age is not that one is old, but that one is young, and no spa in the world will help them."

We all laugh.

"Oscar," I say, reaching over and holding his hand, "I am so going to miss you and your wit."

"So, Nellie, tell me, am I going to have another competitor in writing mysteries?" Conan Doyle smiles.

"I doubt it."

"Ah, but you have a wealth of information and firsthand experience to write from."

"Yes, but I don't have Sherlock Holmes to help sort out the killer."

"Well, as far as I'm concerned, murder is always a mistake . . . one should never do anything that one cannot talk about after dinner," Oscar says.

"Ah, but murder and mysteries do bring entertainment," Doyle responds.

"That's because such dark deeds are so lucrative—to writers," Wells adds.

"Quite true, but look what we have found out in this adventure—"

I interrupt Doyle. "An adventure is what you call a harrowing experience—*after* you survive it."

"Yes, but we also found that the more bizarre Dr. Lacroix became, the less mysterious he proved to be. It's your commonplace, featureless crimes which are really puzzling, just as a commonplace face is the most difficult to identify."

"May I interject—" Oscar starts to say, but I stop him before he spurts out another one of his witticisms.

"Gentlemen, before you get into a long discussion of murder and mayhem, I must say good-bye. I have a long day ahead tomorrow and a girl needs her beauty rest."

"Quite," comes from all of them as they get up.

"Oscar, take care of yourself." I give him a big hug. "I truly hate saying good-bye to my partner in crime."

"You, too, Nellie-girl."

"Conan, it has been a great pleasure meeting you. I hope we meet again."

He gives me a hug. "The pleasure is all mine. You, young lady, have solved a great mystery for me."

"What's that?"

"My next story."

All I can do is blush. What a compliment . . . but I wonder what he means.

"Nellie," Wells comes over to me, "while Oscar and Conan solve the mysteries of the world, I shall walk you to your room."

Away from the others, Oscar grabs my arm and whispers softly in my ear, "I'm proud of you, my dear. I, too, advocate free love."

HISTORICAL NOTE

ARTHUR CONAN DOYLE WENT ON to write "A Scandal in Bohemia," a Sherlock Holmes short story published in *The Strand Magazine*, 1891, featuring Irene Adler, the only woman who outwitted Holmes. Thereafter, he continued to write the tales of the detective and his bumbling doctor friend until he tired of them and killed off Holmes—later bringing him back alive at the demand of his fans.

Following the success of *The Portrait of Dorian Gray,* Oscar Wilde went on to write numerous plays and poetry. In the 1890s he wrote and produced four society comedies, making him one of the most successful playwrights of late Victorian London. By the mid 1890s his lifestyle, in which he openly flaunted the mores of the day, came crashing down on him when his love affair with the Marquis of Queensberry's son became a catalyst that sent him to prison after he foolishly sued the marquis for libel. After prison, he moved to Paris and spent the last years of his life in the city that was considered the intellectual beacon of the world.

H. G. Wells went on to become one of the most highly regarded science-fiction writers in history. *The War of the Worlds, The Island of Dr. Moreau, The Invisible Man,* and *The Time Machine* are still selling over a hundred years later and each has been made into a movie—at least twice. *The Invisible Man* and *The Island of Dr. Moreau* were both premised upon mad science.

Wells also is noted for being one of the great intellectuals of his era, a socialist, pacifist, and . . . a free-love advocate, a belief he maintained in his personal life. After a brief marriage to a cousin that was unsuitable for both of them, Wells remarried. The marriage lasted thirty-two years, until the death of his wife, but true to his beliefs about love, he conducted a number of love affairs.

Nellie, too, went on to write mystery stories. Sadly, only one of them, *The Mystery of Central Park,* survived the ravages of time. The editors have not been able to find a copy of any of her other books. One has to wonder if any of these adventures she kept secret at the time were included in the lost books.